IMMORTAL KISS

"Answer me this, wife of Gaarius. What do you fear the most? What is it that fills your sleep with nightmares, that haunts your almost every waking moment, that threatens to drive you almost mad because you know it's out there, waiting, and there's nothing you can do about it."

"I'm not really sure. I've been afraid of so many things for so long."

"Perhaps it is death which fills you with the most dread. It was my greatest fear. That's why I fought it for so long. But I need fear it no longer. Look at me, wife of Gaarius. And let me show you what it means to live forever . . ."

Curious, I looked at him. And then I realized what had made me stare at him so often before. It was not his face; it was not his body or his manner of moving or his clothes. It was his eyes. It was his eyes that I had been so drawn to. It was his clear brown eyes that so fascinated me. No; they were not brown now. Agyar's eyes glowed a bright red that burned clean through my thoughts and went straight for the soul.

I remember that he began kissing me, and then I felt the slightest prick of pain that was just as quickly replaced by a gentle sucking, a soothing rush of warmth that felt as though warm water were being slowly poured over my shoulder. I shut my eyes and my head fell back as I felt a dizzying sensation of pleasure.

Books by Traci Briery

THE VAMPIRE MEMOIRS

THE VAMPIRE JOURNALS

THE WEREWOLF CHRONICLES

WOLFSONG

Published by Zebra and Pinnacle Books

THE
VAMPIRE
MEMOIRS

Mara McCuniff
& Traci Briery

Pinnacle Books
Kensington Publishing Corp.
http://www.pinnaclebooks.com

For Tom Holland, for making Fright Night; *J.M. DeMatteis, for writing* Greenberg; *Lou Stoumen, for his great enthusiasm; all the poor souls who had to hear this story over and over (and over!); and, of course, for my mother, without whom I would not have been possible.*

PINNACLE BOOKS are published by

Kensington Publishing Corp.
850 Third Avenue
New York, NY 10022

Pinnacle and the P logo Reg. U.S. Pat. & TM Off.

First Printing: March, 1991
First Pinnacle Printing: June, 2000
10 9 8 7 6 5 4 3 2

Printed in the United States of America

BOOK I

BOOK 1

Prologue

My friends and family advise me not to write this, or, if I do, not to publish it. I can understand their concern, as I realize what a book like this could do to all our lives, and especially mine. As I write, however, I am undecided about publishing my "memoirs." Hopefully I'll reach a decision by the time I finish, but I am certain the final decision will be mine alone.

My friends and family have good reason to worry about this little diary of mine. I am a vampire, you see, and so are most of my friends. But now that I've made my decision to write this, I don't think I can, or should, go back.

I hope you brought all of your preconceptions about vampires with you, because my intention is to confront many of those notions and to set them straight, if necessary. The most important misconception concerns the average vampire's temperament. Let's just say most of us are tired of being portrayed as despicably evil creatures of darkness—the vast, vast majority, mind you—though I'd be dishonest to say there aren't bad apples among any group.

And for myself, writing this has helped me to remember a lot of things, and to understand them. But bear in mind that it was some sixteen hundred years ago. A lot of things have certainly become embellished and exaggerated by now, but I honestly couldn't say what. Perhaps it's simply that the people I knew weren't really as wonderful or as awful as I make them out to be. I could not say; all I *can* say is that I hope you enjoy this book, not to mention, learn something from it. But until then, good reading and STAY HUMAN.

—Mara McCuniff, 1990

One

I was born in the year 362, give or take a few years, in a small village named Keston in the British Isles. Keston was near a small lake that ran into the North Sea; nearby were several fields where cattle could be raised. There was little farming, if any. Most of our food came from the lake and the cattle, as well as from the occasional raid on smaller and weaker villages.

My father was a warrior, a rather typical occupation for the men of Keston. I never knew my mother. She died at my birth, as there were complications that forced me to be cut from the womb. My father—I cannot say whether or not his wits were ever completely about him before my ill-fated birth. But the untimely death of his wife—my mother, that is—made him bitter beyond normal measures of bitterness.

As far as he was concerned, I was a double disappointment. I had killed my own mother, and I was not a boy. There have been very few times in history when girls were favored over boys, and this was definitely not one of those times. My father was obsessed with the idea of raising his son as a warrior, and my birth should have shattered that idea. Not so. My father rejected me. Not rejected me as his offspring, but rejected me as his daughter.

"I don't have a daughter," he often told me. "She killed her mother and she isn't here anymore." You can imagine how little I wanted to hear him say that. He often used the verbal reproach before resorting to physical punishment.

So I was raised as a warrior. I was forbidden to show any signs of weakness, that is, femininity, in his presence, but I was still expected to perform all "female" chores, such as cooking and looking after his cattle.

He was not very popular among the other villagers. They usually avoided him and his foul temper, and most of them tended to avoid me, as well. After all, I was the unfortunate daughter/son of the mad warrior, and many villagers were probably afraid that I would end up just like him. Sometimes I wondered that myself. I also wondered why he didn't just kill me at birth if I was such a curse to him.

The latter question I couldn't answer. Maybe underneath the insane exterior was some pity for me. Or, since he was so obsessed with raising a son, and the death of my mother took away that opportunity for "another try," then zap, I might as well be a son!

As the years passed, certain signs inevitably began appearing that threatened my father's illusion of having a son. When I turned twelve, besides granting me the day off from chores, which was my only gift from him on birthdays, my father took me aside and warned me about certain things that might happen to me. He muttered things about blood, and lumps, and other things that I didn't understand at all at the time. But he made me swear to come to him immediately and tell him the first time I ever bled without being cut. I was thoroughly confused but didn't dare refuse him, so I swore to it. Then he made me swear never to let a man touch me. I was a warrior, not some harlot, as he put it, and I swore to this command, as well.

I was about fourteen when I first bled "without being cut." I was milking my father's only cow when I was horrified to see blood dripping down both legs. I almost screamed but thought of what he might do if he found out I'd been behaving "like a girl." I stood up and pressed my legs together quickly and felt the milking stool for some splinter, or a nail, or anything that could have cut me like that and not have me feel it.

Leaving the milking undone, I lumbered back to our hut, still trying to keep my legs pressed together, and found my father. At first he was angry that I had returned without the milk, until he saw the blood. Immediately he tore up some cloth and made me lie on my back; then he spread my legs apart and bandaged me right up to the crotch. I asked if I was bleeding there, and he said yes, and that I was to wear a bandage there every day from now on. I didn't understand his reasoning at all, but he told me to keep silent and double swear that no man would ever touch me. I swore to it.

Life in Keston came to an end before I turned seventeen. A roaming tribe made its way to the village and decided to sack it. They swarmed in on horses with no warning whatsoever, and in broad daylight, no less. I was carrying wood to our hut when they struck, and I remember seeing my father's head poke out of the hut, duck back in; and then he came barreling out toward the attackers, sword in hand. I was right in his path, and he slammed into me, knocking me back several feet and strewing my wood everywhere. Picking me up roughly, he screamed at me to hide in the hut before shoving me away again. I ran, terrified more of him than of the attackers, and dove underneath piles of fur.

Several minutes passed before I dared to move, and I slowly lifted my head, hoping to see what was happening. My ears were flooded with sounds of horses, screams, clashes of steel, and fire, and I caught glimpses of villagers rushing by our hut, carrying food, animals, women, and children. I thought of what might be happening to my father in the chaos, and almost burst into tears again, but I clenched my teeth and fought them off. *I am a warrior,* I thought. *I AM A WARRIOR! Why does he make me lie here when I can help? He could be dead now and I won't have avenged him because I lie here like a coward! Does he think I'm afraid, like a woman? No, I'm not afraid. I'm not afraid. I'm a warrior; I'm not afraid!*

Such were the thoughts racing through my head, and I grasped for my sword and rose up from under the furs.

Outside was chaos. For each sound I had heard under the furs there was a sight that was much worse. Blood and fire were everywhere. Villagers and attackers, alike, lay dead or dying, but there were more villagers on the ground, by far. Then I found my father. He was not dead, but fighting some fifty feet from me, roaring with rage. He was not a terribly skilled fighter, but he was an exceedingly brutal one, and most of the attackers were giving him a wide berth.

Clenching my sword, I ran to his side through the smoke and blood and began swinging. One of the attackers thought to rush me, but his throat met my sword before his axe could come down on me. He stopped dead in his tracks and dropped his weapon. I stared wide-eyed at the blood gushing from his mouth and neck, and he made a gurgling sound before falling over dead. My sword froze in my hand. Bodies lay all about me, blood all over; until that single moment, I had never actually been the cause of any death. But that was what I had been trained for; this was the life my father intended for me.

My thoughts were halted by a rough hand whirling me around. I stared wide-eyed at the enraged face of my father. He was screaming something at me, but I heard none of it. My mind was locked on to the memory of the blood from the man that I had killed, and my father's ravings were only gibberish to me.

My last memory of that day was of myself, tumbling backward down a hill. My father had shoved me away again as several attackers started for him, and I was still in too much of a daze to keep my balance. Dirt and rocks scraped my face, arms, and knees as I flipped over and over toward the trees and bushes below.

That was the last I saw of Keston. Or at least, the last I saw of Keston as a village. A rock to the back of my head ended my plunge down the hill as well as my consciousness, for how long, I do not know.

It took me some time before a rational thought came into my mind, but I realized, soon enough, that things were not right. The disturbing silence didn't register until after I had crawled back up the hill and gazed at the remains of my village.

There weren't many remains left. The raiders had done a thorough job of burning and looting the place; not even a cow was left.

I searched dazedly among the bodies for my father. I recognized each villager who I found: the other warriors, their wives, their children, even the village tanner, who was one of the few who ever spoke to me, all lay dead. But my father was nowhere in sight. I had no idea if he was dead, captured, or otherwise. I tried to grieve for him, for all the villagers, but no tears came. I was too numb to feel anything at the time and still dizzy from the blow to my head.

One consequence of my father's failure at logic was the fact that, while he chose not to accept me as a female, the rest of mankind was not about to accept me as a male, either. For myself, I didn't know which I was supposed to be. I was raised as a warrior, and that's all I knew at the time. Still, finding employment as a mercenary was not the easiest of tasks; most of the time I was laughed at or told to "go home to my husband."

I had to make up for my lack of upper-body strength with ferocity and brutality in combat. Often when I was hired, then, it was for my berserker furies and boldness rather than my actual skill.

The shock I felt when I first killed became just a memory; I killed again and I killed often. The lives of others no longer mattered to me, as long as I was paid enough after the battle. I started to enjoy killing. I liked the smell of blood and the sound of dying men, especially if I was the cause of it.

My father would have been proud of me; I was just like him. People feared me now; men gave the "she-wolf" wide berth, and even other warriors avoided quarreling with me. And, yet, I was still a woman, much as I wished to deny it, and women were not warriors. Combat for me was rare, and so were the times I had money. Most of the time I was without funds, but only occasionally did I resort to thievery to get something to eat; otherwise, I simply went hungry.

My life continued like this for several years: kill, eat, sleep, and steal, if I had to. And no man would touch me. I remembered I had promised that.

Two

It was during my twenty-third year that my life changed forever. There were two reasons why I was passing through a forest one day rather than the usual, and safer, path: one, it seemed like a good short cut, and two, I didn't want to have to deal with other travelers along the way. I was not interested in people and I wanted to be alone.

I was a good distance into the forest when I had the unnerving feeling that I was being followed, even tracked. Several backward glances revealed nothing at first, until sometime later I heard the definite cracking of leaves and twigs behind. I whirled around, sword in hand, expecting some animal, but was face-to-face with a man, instead. He was still some fifty feet from me, but even from there I could see that he was a large man—perhaps even taller than I, which few men were.

I held my sword threateningly, and he stopped in his tracks. He made no threatening moves against me, but slowly started toward me again.

"That's far enough," I said. "Who are you? Why have you been following me?" He stopped and adopted a friendly countenance. His sword remained sheathed as he called to me.

"I am Gaarius Latticus," he said. "But 'Gaar' will do. And I was about to ask you a similar question."

"What do you mean?" I asked quickly.

"Do you live in this forest?" he asked.

"No. This is a short cut to the next town. And why do you follow me?"

"Am I following you? I thought I was taking a short cut, too. I assume you must know this place or you wouldn't be going this way?" During our conversation, Gaar had been taking cautious steps toward me. He was now about thirty feet away.

"I *don't* know this place. It just seems faster and quieter."

"Oh," he said. "Then we both could be lost. Perhaps I shouldn't have followed you—"

"Then you were!" I broke in quickly. "And you still won't answer me why."

"Very well," he said calmly. "The truth, then. I *was* following you. But not to do you harm. I saw you last night—"

"Where?"

"At the inn—last night. You were assaulted by that barbarian?"

I thought back to the night before. I'd been eating some ribs at the inn (meat—a very rare treat for me), when an overly amorous barbarian wanted me to join him at his table. I refused, of course, and when he grabbed my wrist in an attempt to drag me there, I twisted my hand to grab his and pulled him face-forward onto the table. Then I stood and clubbed him once on the head with a large rib. He slumped off the table and then lumbered back to his chums, confused more than hurt, no doubt. I hadn't noticed Gaar that night, but he had been there and apparently had seen all.

By now, he was about ten feet from me, and I held my sword out menacingly.

"That's far enough," I said. He stopped. "Yes, I remember last night," I continued. "But why follow me because of that?"

"I was intrigued," he answered. "That is, I like women who can take care of themselves. And you had no trouble with him last night. That, and—I cannot say that I've ever seen a female warrior before."

"Well, I am," I said, "much as I hate being that way."

"Then why be a warrior?"

"No, not that. Female."

"What?"

"I hate being a woman. It's weak. And I hate being weak."

"You don't look weak to me."

"I didn't say I'm weak! I'm strong; I'm a warrior, like my father. And I want you to leave me alone."

"What if I don't?" he asked.

"I'll just kill you, then."

"You will? You'll just kill me? I don't even have my sword out."

"That's your problem. Now just stop following me and leave me alone."

"I can't go back to the path. It's too far," he protested. "And I told you I come in peace. I only wanted to meet this female warrior who hates being a female, it seems."

"Well, you've met me. Now go."

"You could at least be kind enough to give me your name."

"Mara. Now go."

(By the way, that's pronounced MARE-a, not MARR-a. Just being picky, that's all. Mara).

"I think you should stop pointing that sword at me, instead. I don't want to go back—not after walking this far," Gaar said.

"Have it your way, then." I brought my sword back, making ready to slice him and rid myself of this pest. But before I could finish my stroke, Gaar whipped out his own blade in a blur and struck my sword straight from my hand. It landed some fifteen feet to my right, and I made to retrieve it, but Gaar stopped me with a feint to my throat. I stopped dead and could only stare at him. He continued holding the blade at me for some time, and then, suddenly and surprisingly, sheathed it. I stared at him for some seconds more before he gestured to my right with his head.

"Well?" he said. "Aren't you going to retrieve your sword?"

I wandered over cautiously, still keeping my eye on Gaar, and picked up the sword. I looked back at him again, and he smiled at me and continued walking!

My initial fear and surprise were soon replaced by anger and humiliation, and I set after Gaar again, hoping to avenge my honor. He stopped and whirled about before I reached him; his sword was redrawn and we stood face-to-face, each taking in the other's measure.

"I have no quarrel with you, girl, though you think me an enemy," he said calmly.

"You humiliated me," I growled. "How could you not be an enemy?"

"If you think that, then so be it. But you'd better think before you take up a quarrel with me. What if I win again?"

"You 'won' nothing," I said. "I just didn't expect that last time."

"So now you're ready for me. But I'm ready for you, too. And I want no blood on my sword today—but there will be, if you don't put that away."

He was so calm, so sure of himself. If he was afraid, I certainly couldn't tell. I was terrified, myself, but I was hardly going to let him see that. Nevertheless, my sword was slowly becoming heavier to me, and I found myself occasionally having to grip it tighter.

We faced each other for an uncomfortably long time. And for the first time in my life, I was the first to break off from an attack. I let my sword arm drop ever so slowly, and I stood up straighter. Gaar, meanwhile, kept his intense gaze on me and wouldn't relax a bit until after I had sheathed my sword somewhat defiantly.

Gaar nodded grimly and sheathed his own sword.

"I'm glad," he said. "I wished for no killing this day."

I said nothing, but passed him briskly into the forest and tried to stay ahead of him the rest of the way.

Our first meeting, then, was not exactly love at first sight. It never occurred to me at the time, but Gaar held an enormous amount of respect for me. In those days, a fight was not left unfinished, whether between men *or* women.

One morning in the forest, we were both awakened by a bear that was ripping through Gaar's pack, searching for the food within. Gaar was alert and up long before me, and, sword in hand, attempted to frighten the bear away. The bear was enraged, instead, and swiped at him several times. By this time, I had my own sword drawn and moved behind the beast and jabbed. The bear roared and turned toward me, where Gaar was then able to stab it several times. I managed to stab it once in the back, but as far as I was concerned, Gaar had done the most damage. We were both shaken by the encounter, but Gaar was also scratched in the arm. He was more concerned with my well-being, however, and only asked to be bandaged after he found I was unharmed.

He spent the rest of the day skinning the bear, which I thought was a waste of time, until he announced that bear-skins can be sold to rugmakers and such. We were fortunate enough to find a man who dealt with furs and skins in the next town, and Gaar was able to sell it only after a rather impressive display of haggling and dealing. The man gave him less than maximum price for a good skin, though, as it had been poked a few times.

The man dealt only with Gaar, however, and as soon as he handed Gaar the money, I became peeved and began scheming as to how to get some—or all—of it; I didn't trust him completely, you understand.

Gaar surprised me no end by giving me not some but *half* of the money and thanked me for helping him kill the bear. I was amazed at his actions, but I was still irked by his following me into the forest and humiliating me there, and I ran from him before he could pocket his own money. I quickly lost myself through a crowd and breathed a sigh of relief in having rid myself of this strange and frightening man.

But it seemed that I was never able to avoid him. In that town and every other town, I would catch glimpses of him through the crowds, watching me or pretending not to notice. He both infuriated and interested me. My thoughts were ever after constantly on him, although not always in civil terms. No one likes to be followed, but he also fascinated me in his persistence. And he was the most persistent human being I had known thus far.

One night, using the pay from the bearskin, I was treating myself to a hearty meal when a figure moved near me and sat right at my table. I looked up. It was Gaar, of course. I sighed in frustration and lowered my food. He flashed one of his usual friendly smiles, and my spine shivered.

"You're persistent, I'll give you that," he said.

"I'm persistent? Why don't you leave me be?" I demanded to know.

"Why do you still treat me as an enemy? What have I done to you?"

"What have you done? You've . . . you've—you won't leave me alone!"

"I only want to talk to you. Will you grant me that?"

"Why? What do you want from me? I just want to be alone."

"Alone? No one should be alone. Men need other men. And women."

"Stop taunting me with that. I'm a warrior, not a woman," I protested.

"You're a warrior *and* a woman, whether you want to be or not. Just as I'm a warrior, and a man. Listen," he said, and reached out and took my hand on impulse, "I wish to be a friend, not foe—"

"Let go of me," I warned, staring wild-eyed at my hand. Gaar responded by gently caressing my hand, and my spine began doing flip-flops again.

"Let go," I repeated in near-panic.

"I'm not . . ." he began, but I quickly twisted my hand the same as I'd done to the barbarian in the other inn. Unfortunately, Gaar knew that move already and twisted my arm right back into his grasp. He began to draw my hand toward him slowly, and in a panic, I yanked my arm free and stood up. My mind was awhirl with thoughts, but I managed to blurt out, "Leave me alone!" before storming from the inn.

I originally intended to run as far from the inn as I could, but I remained just outside the door. Possibly, I decided to "deal" with Gaar once and for all, or perhaps I actually enjoyed having my hand held and couldn't make myself leave. Whatever the reason, I was not at all rational when Gaar stepped out a few moments later. I thought of running again, but that thought disintegrated as Gaar caught sight of me and smiled. He held his arm out and was about to speak, when panic seized me again, and I struck him full in the face with my fist. He turned away quickly and held his face, while I babbled almost incoherently at him.

"I was— You didn't— Does— You shouldn't have—followed me!" I gasped. I expected Gaar to turn and throw his arms out and tell me how he didn't want a fight, but again, I was surprised.

With a roar, he whirled about and plunged himself into me, knocking me flat onto my backside, and the wind out of me. He hunched over me then, teeth gritted and nose dripping blood, while I scrambled to get away before he struck me again. He let me rise to my feet, though, or it seemed that way, before he came for me again. Both of us were hurt and angry now, and I attacked first by slamming my whole body into his and pushing with all my might until he tumbled backward. Unlike him, however, I kicked at him as he tried to rise, but he caught one of my legs and twisted, forcing me down with a painful thud.

Our battle continued for some time outside the inn, and to the several spectators that we attracted, our different techniques of combat became painfully obvious.

As a warrior, I was my father: all brutality, all brute strength, and little skill. Gaar, on the other hand, was stronger than I and had the skill to match. I honored no rules in combat and continually attacked when he was down, and only his endurance and skill allowed Gaar to escape my rage. My technique was usually to throw myself into him and knock him about, while Gaar often retaliated by using my very attacks against me. Nonetheless, both of us became more than knocked about and nearly exhausted from our brawl. But neither of us was about to give in; this was a fight to the end.

At last, we both stood facing each other, struggling to keep our arms up and the blood from our mouths and eyes. We were two wolves fighting for domination, and we both meant to be master. I took in Gaar's condition. His nose and mouth were covered with blood, his and mine. His arms shook ever so slightly as he held them up, and his legs looked as much in danger of giving out as mine felt. I probably looked just as bad or worse, but I didn't care.

Gathering up every last bit of strength I had, I held my fists as tightly as I could, raised my arms just an inch or so more, and took a step toward him.

There was no possible way I could have avoided Gaar's blow. His reserve of strength turned out to be much greater than mine, and he threw his fist into my jaw just as I began to move. My arms dropped, my head lurched to the side, and I swayed, but I did not fall. Gaar's face soon became little more than a blur to me, but I remember seeing a shape swing at me from the other side before everything went black.

I coughed and sputtered. My face was wet, and water, mixed with blood, had flowed into my nose and throat and threatened to choke me. I heard loud voices nearby but didn't recognize them, and I tried to rise, but the pain in my jaw and head kept me down.

I lay in the dirt, silently, struggling to sort out the sounds from the pain in my body. The loud voices became clearer, and I recognized one of them as Gaar's. The other I did not know.

He was arguing with someone, but I chose to ignore the words and concentrated on regaining consciousness so I could get away.

The arguing continued as I forced myself up from the dirt, and then more voices were added. I saw a man beside Gaar, and someone else, who pointed at me occasionally. I chose to ignore him, too, and began lurching down an alley away from Gaar and everyone who was staring at me. I was furious, and my anger helped me to regain strength and consciousness as I left the scene. *First, he humiliates me in a forest, and now he humiliates me in public!* But even as I limped away from him, I couldn't help wondering if it wasn't futile to even try to escape this man.

It *was* futile. Gaar was soon after me, telling me that I couldn't leave now that I owed him three times. Three times? I owned him nothing, I insisted, and demanded an explanation. He claimed that he had beaten me in fair combat twice (well, I certainly didn't count that time in the forest as "combat"), and he had just finished bribing a guard to keep me out of jail, as I had caused a public brawl and would have been arrested. As for himself, Gaar claimed innocence in that he was strictly defending himself, and the villagers helped him with this, too!

I had had enough of this. I turned away as quickly as I could and continued walking through the alley, trying my best to ignore Gaar's calls.

"Why, Mara?" he cried, still following me. "Why do you torment me this way? Why do you despise me as you do? It's all I ask!"

I gave him no answer and walked even faster. He kept pace with me, however, and wouldn't give up yet.

"Mara, please, all I ask is a reason!"

I gritted my teeth and fought off tears, but kept on going. Then Gaar made his next big mistake by grabbing my arm and turning me to face him.

"I'll not let you run from me without an answer!" he spat. I gritted my teeth harder and tried to ignore him further, but I finally had to give in and speak, but not before wrenching myself out of his grip.

"Don't touch me again," I growled. "I 'owe' you nothing *for* nothing, and I need give no 'explanations'!"

"You *do* owe ne for that guard—"

"The guard? Fine, then!! How much did it cost you? Four coins? Five? Eh?" I cried, fumbling through my pouch for money. I grabbed four coins or so and threw them onto the ground in front of him.

"There!" I screamed. "There's your payment! Now leave me be! That's all I ask!" I said, and stormed away while he fumbled to pick up the coins.

"Wait! Please!" I heard him call after me. "I didn't really mean—! Mara!" By that time, however, I was becoming lost in the nighttime crowds.

I spent an extra few days in that town to rest up from our fight. I was staying in a fairly good inn—meaning one without too many thefts or barroom brawls.

I walked through the marketplace one day, noting the unusual amount of business for such a small town. I later found out that the people were preparing for a festival that began that night—a celebration of summer's beginning.

I was bored, nevertheless, and watched and listened to customers and keepers of shops and booths haggle and argue. Few of their wares interested me, except for some of the more exotic foods, but most of those were too expensive. I mostly just pushed my way absentmindedly through the crowds, trying unsuccessfully to keep my thoughts away from a certain individual.

It took me a few moments to notice a particularly violent argument taking place directly ahead of me. Curious, I pushed my way deeper into the masses of people until I saw a rather large man arguing with a rather spindly potmaker. I heard a few choice words about somebody owing someone money when the large customer fellow started kicking some of the potter's wares around. The potter was furious, of course. As the customer picked up a large vase and made as if to shatter it on the ground, he was suddenly knocked down by an even larger man who also caught the vase before it fell.

I immediately recognized the third man as Gaar. I intended to leave before he turned around and saw me until I saw that, while the potter was thanking Gaar profusely, the customer had reached into his coat and pulled out a knife. I looked over at Gaar to see if he or the potter had noticed. Neither of them reacted as the customer slowly rose up, blood flowing from his nose and teeth gritted, and made ready to attack Gaar from behind.

The next thing I knew, the customer suddenly dropped his knife and desperately clutched at the dagger that was firmly embedded in his neck. He fell backward into the dust with a short gasp, and it was then that Gaar and the potter realized that they had missed something. Gaar bent over the man and looked him over while I silently made my presence known. As Gaar stared at me in surprise, I bent down and pulled my dagger from the man's neck, flicked most of the blood off, and resheathed it in my boot. Gaar stood and stared at me for a few moments.

"Mara!" he said. *"You* threw the knife?"

"Um . . ." I began, "yes."

"He thought he'd attack me from behind," said Gaar. "Blast! How could I be such a fool, I might have been killed! Mara," he continued, placing a hand on my shoulder, "I owe you my life."

"No. You owe me nothing," I said. "I didn't plan to do that. I saw a weapon, and . . ."

"So you're saying you would have done that for anyone?" Gaar prodded.

"I'm not saying anything but that you owe me nothing. We have no debts," I said, and tried to walk away, wondering why it was suddenly so hard for me to think, and why the impulse to save Gaar the way I had had been so strong. I hadn't even been aware of my actions until after the fact.

There might not have been any legal complications regarding the killing of a man in broad daylight—this was a fairly lawless sort of town, it seemed—but there were plenty of emotional complications for me.

Gaar dogged me through the streets that day, despite my best efforts to avoid him. He had cornered me by a booth somewhere when I noticed a rather richly dressed man leading his pack mule toward us. It wasn't until he was right beside us that Gaar stopped talking and looked up.

First he asked Gaar if he was a mercenary, which Gaar was, of course, and then he introduced himself as Arem, a "wealthy man" from the nearby city of Castrill. He said that he had stayed too long where he was now, and thus had only one day to get back to Castrill or possibly be faced with the wrath of the magistrate for whom he worked. Normally it took two days to get to Castrill, but there was a short cut that took only one day. Unfortunately, that route was notorious for its bandits and cutthroats, and Arem needed a bodyguard to make sure he got through the short cut safely.

At this point, I was torn between leaving Gaar and staying to find out what the man wanted Gaar for. I ended up staying, in spite of myself. I was surprised to see that Gaar had accepted a dangerous job like that, and even more surprised to see that he would only do the job if I were hired, too.

I knew exactly what was on Gaar's mind then, so I started to walk away but he grabbed my arm and held on tight, his eyes never leaving Arem's gaze. I was going to wrench my way free but was held in place by the incredible shower of words in praise of me that Gaar suddenly erupted into. Naturally, Arem had never intended to hire a woman— of all creatures—to protect his hide; only Gaar's words soon convinced him that I was some great warrior. I almost believed him myself.

The next thing I knew, we'd been hired to protect a fat, rich man for ten pieces of gold each, with two given us in advance. We were to meet him next morning, at the stables. I was almost in a daze by the whole affair, but not so much that I couldn't pocket my money and start walking away while Gaar was still distracted. Naturally, he wasn't distracted for long, and he was soon keeping pace alongside of me while I tried to ignore him.

"It feels good to work again," he said cheerfully. I kept my silence.

"It's been too long since I've had decent employment," he continued. "As long as this Arem doesn't try to cheat us . . ." Gaar was silent for a few moments himself, then he continued. "We'd best stay together for the day. It wouldn't be wise for either of us to get lost around here and not make it to the stables tomorrow."

"Only an idiot could get lost in this place," I muttered.

"What?"

"Nothing," I said. I walked on in more silence, Gaar still following.

"So—where are you staying?" he then asked, still trying to make conversation. I laughed to myself.

"I'm surprised you don't even know," I said. "You find me wherever I am, whether I tell you or not. And I'm yet to tell you."

"I'm staying at the inn near the town well," he said.

"I'll be sure to get my water elsewhere, then."

"That was cruel, Mara."

"I intended it to be."

"Why are you always so cruel to me?"

"You don't know when to give up, that's why."

"No. No, I suppose I don't. When I want something, I don't give up until I get it."

"And of course you want me."

"You might say that."

"Why?"

"Why what?"

"Why do you want me? Why do you hound me endlessly, like you are even now? Why won't you leave me alone?"

"Why do you always want to be alone?"

"Because . . . that's just the way I am! I like being alone."

"I don't think anyone really likes to be alone."

"Well, I do."

"Always? You never want to talk to anyone?"

"No, I don't mean—" Gaar's questions were quickly becoming annoying, and I very much wanted to avoid answering them by running away.

"I just want to be alone *now* . . ." I began. "I don't want you to keep following me. I just want to be alone; why won't you understand that?"

"But we can't split up now," he said. "We'll be meeting Arem tomor—"

"Yes, we *can* split up," I insisted. "I won't forget about tomorrow. I'll be there."

"But—"

"Just leave me be!" I said, and walked faster to lose him. As usual, he kept pace with me, only he then made the mistake of grabbing my shoulder to stop me. I whirled around and stopped him in his tracks with a vicious glare.

"Don't you ever do that again," I growled.

"Mara—"

"Don't you *ever* touch me again! Do you hear me? Never! Now leave me alone!!" And with that, I whirled around again and sped through the crowd at top speed, at last leaving Gaar far behind me.

Gaar surprised me by not showing himself for the rest of the day. I had run back to the inn and my room and remained there until sunset when the festival was to begin. I decided to spend my last few hours in town wandering about and taking in the sights of the festival, Gaar or no Gaar. Mostly people were simply eating and drinking, but every now and then, I spotted someone entertaining a crowd with a song, poem, or some bit of physical dexterity.

I was engrossed in watching a juggler when I felt a familiar presence nearby. I looked to my side, and, sure enough, there stood Gaar right beside me. I sighed in annoyance. I heard him reach into his pouch and pull out some coins and then hold them in front of me.

"These are yours," he said.

I eyed him quizzically. "Mine?" I asked.

"Your money. From last night," he said. "I wasn't asking for your money when I told you about that bribe."

I shook my head. "I want no debts to you," I said.

"No debts," he said. "You owe me nothing. Here. They're yours."

"Spend them on the festival," I said. Gaar sighed in frustration before taking my hand and dropping the coins onto my palm.

"I wasn't asking for your money that night," he said. "I just . . . I just want you to stop running from me, that's all."

"And what would you do if I stopped?" I asked.

"Well . . ." he began, "I'd stop chasing you, for one thing. Then I'd like to take you someplace quiet, away from everyone else—"

"What?"

"And talk. That's all I want from you, Mara. I just want you to talk to me. To stop running and . . . talk."

"Really," I said. "And talk about what?"

He shrugged. "I don't know," he said. "Anything. Anything you like."

"We'll have plenty of time to 'talk' tomorrow," I said.

"And then what will you do afterward? Run from me again?"

"I don't know," I said. "I suppose I would. But I'm getting so tired of it all. Why don't you just leave me be? Why must I be a part of everything you do? You even got me employment just so I'd be near you all day!"

"That's part of it," he said. "But then, you need employment as much as I do. I only thought—"

"I'm used to getting it myself."

"I'm sorry about that, then," he said. "But, um . . . you still mean to be at the stables tomorrow, don't you?"

"Yes," I sighed. "Yes, I'll be there. But until then, I want to be by myself. I'm tired and I need to rest for the job. So I'll see you—"

"Wait," he said, trying to move in front of me. "We really should be together tonight . . . that is, if only to make certain we both arrive at the same time. So neither of us becomes lost."

I sighed and looked down. "I won't become lost, Gaar," I muttered. "And I will be there tomorrow, and we'll be 'together' all day. That's all you want, in spite of what you say, to have me around all day, knowing I won't try to run from you? Well, you'll have that tomorrow. But I want things my way tonight, and that way means to be by myself. Will you at least grant me that?"

I thought this time he would stay where he was when I left his side. He did stay in one place, in fact, only he was not silent about it.

"All right, then, go!" I heard him roaring at me from the crowd. "Keep on running! Run from everything! It's what cowards are best at!"

I froze in my tracks. What was that he had just called me?

"Keep running, Mara," I heard him calling still, his voice getting calmer, not to mention closer. "Keep running from everything! What better way to deal with your fears than to run from them, eh?" He was almost right next to me now. I stood with my back to him and clenched my fists. Then he pounded me on the back.

"I asked you a question! It's the best way to deal with your fears, isn't it?" he roared, and I only gritted my teeth and shook with rage. There was a silence, and then Gaar ground out of anger, "Ahh, why did I even expect you to answer?" he said, to himself more than to me. "Why did I even expect you to have common decency and actually talk to someone in a civilized way? But you know why you can't?" he said into my ear. "Because you're a *coward,* that's why!"

I whirled about instantly to glare at him, and I tried to speak, but tears were threatening to choke me, and I could only make a quick noise in anger before whirling about again to storm away from him. Gaar followed right alongside me, of course.

"Yes, Mara, I said a *coward!*" he continued. "A cowardly, spoiled little she-wolf who wouldn't know a thing about human feelings if they stabbed her in the heart!"

"Shut up!"

"But would a stab in the heart help? No! That's because you don't *have* one!"

"Shut! Up!"

"No wonder everyone hates you. No wonder everyone spits at you when you walk by. Because even if they didn't, even if they tried to be kind to you, you'd only spit at *them!*"

"I'll kill you!"

"You've already tried, remember? And when you lay on the ground, at my mercy, did I kill *you?* No! I bought your way out of jail!"

Suddenly I found that we had wandered into a dead end, and I ended up walking around in circles, too angry, dazed, and confused to find my way back out. None of this seemed to bother Gaar, who continued his brutal barrage of words.

"I was a fool to think you were even capable of gratitude! To think you were even capable of feeling! You're no warrior; you're a heartless monster!"

"Shut up!" I screamed at the top of my lungs before sinking to my knees in a sobbing, tear-covered heap. Gaar hovered over me, tall and dark, his verbal attack never ceasing.

"When I first saw you, I thought there was something special about you," he said, "something spirited. I thought that underneath those men's clothes was the heart and spirit of a woman. A kind and, yes, even *gentle* woman who only needed someone to look for her and bring her out. Now I know that I was a fool to think there was anything there. You don't even have a heart of stone, Mara; you just don't have a heart!"

I reacted the way I always did whenever my father had yelled at me; I said nothing. However, Gaar had done something my father had never been able to do; he had reduced me to tears.

"Why don't you say something, damn you?" Gaar demanded after some silence. "Why don't you just speak the truth and say that I'm right?"

"I have . . ." I started, but was stopped by more tears.

"Have what?"

"I—I—" I said, but could say no more. Gaar made a noise of frustration and turned to leave.

"Wait!" I called, and he stopped and slowly turned back around.

"What do you want now?" he growled, which made me cringe, but I gathered enough strength to stand shakily onto my feet. For a while I said nothing, and could not meet his gaze.

"Well, out with it," he said.

"I have—I have feelings," I finally managed to say.

"I find that hard to believe now," he said.

"It's . . . *Everyone* has them."

"Then why don't you show them?" he asked. "Or are hate, anger, and fear the only ones you have?"

"No," I said. "Not the only ones."

"Then what's the matter with you, girl?" he cried, making me wince.

"Why do you repay kindness with hatred? Why do you run from those who only want to be your friend? Why try to kill me because I want to talk to you? Why? Why, Mara?"

"I don't know!!" I cried out in a new burst of tears. "I don't know . . ."

I turned away from Gaar, repeating my last words over and over when I felt his arms pull me toward him. Soon he held me in a full, tight hug, which I struggled against.

"No . . . stop this. Let go . . ." I said, but he ignored me. Then I wrenched myself free and stepped away from him.

"Don't—don't touch me . . ." I whispered. "Leave me—"

But then I felt his hands again, and before I could get away, he yanked me into another hug, this one much tighter than the first. New tears came while I struggled, only he put one hand on the back of my head and held it in place on his shoulder.

"Shut up," he whispered. "If you struggle, I'll kill you. That's all you understand, don't you. All you know is killing, and death, don't you."

I said nothing, and eventually I gave up struggling and let Gaar hold me in place.

"You must know there's more to this than killing, Mara," he continued. "You must know that—that a warrior isn't supposed to enjoy death; he's supposed to fight it."

"I don't understand," I said.

"No. No, you don't know," he said. "But I'm sure you will someday."

After some silence, I spoke again.

"You made me cry, Gaar! I said. "No one's ever done that to me before."

"Well, maybe it's good that you did, then," he said. I looked up from his shoulder but still didn't meet his gaze.

"Don't mock me," I said.

"I don't," he said. "I mean, it's not good never to cry. You mean you've never cried before?"

"I don't remember the last time I did. It's something only women and weak people do."

"Whatever you say, Mara," he sighed. Then he let go of me, but I did not run from him now.

"And what about tomorrow?" he asked.

"What about it?"

"Do you feel up to our job?"

"Of course I do," I mumbled.

"Putting up a front won't help if we're attacked," he said. "I said, do you feel up to the job?"

I looked up at him abruptly, insulted, but I kept calm.

"Killing is still all I know, Gaar," I said. "I'd worry about yourself more than about me."

"Ah, yes," he said. "I suppose that's true."

Somehow, Gaar managed to talk me into staying in his room for the night. I think I was just too tired and frustrated to argue with him about it. He promised that I would be "perfectly safe" with him, which meant he wasn't going to try anything. Fortunately, he didn't; he must have been just as tired as I, for all I got was a quick "good night," and then he crawled onto his bedding. I slept on the other side of the room.

The next day, we had a very small breakfast and headed for the stables. Arem was waiting for us there, and we put our gear onto his mule and headed off. Arem rode his horse while Gaar led the mule up front and I brought up the rear. The short cut was mostly through a forest, which might have been another reason people avoided it; there was always the threat of wild animals, even if no bandits were around.

We didn't rest much on the journey, nor did we talk much, and Gaar and I were much more tired than Arem, considering that we walked the entire way. I was also very hungry, and could hardly wait until we were paid so I could find the closest inn and eat to my heart's content.

We were walking along an embankment toward the end of the day, and it was becoming quite dark. The shade from the trees didn't help our light much, either. I was beginning to wonder if Arem was going to let us bring out any torches, when I thought I saw a little movement in a distant tree to my left. The tree was above the embankment and at a different angle to see it clearly, so I stopped and peered at it as intensely as I could. I noticed that Gaar and Arem kept on going, but I ignored this until I could get another look at the movement.

It was a silhouette—about as large as a man, about thirty feet away from us, and moving very slowly and very silently. It moved what I was certain was an arm, perhaps for a weapon, and that's when it happened again. Before I knew it, my dagger was out of my boot sheath, into my hand, and flying through the air into the bandit's neck. I heard a soft grunt and watched his silhouette fall from the tree. And it was only after all this that Gaar and Arem noticed something was amiss.

About ten or twelve bandits were soon leaping from the embankment in an attempt to surround us all, but Gaar foiled that by slapping both Arem's pack mule and horse to make them gallop away to safety before unsheathing his sword and running to join me.

Well, maybe he didn't really foil anything; the bandits surrounded the two of us, instead. Gaar and I stood back to back, weapons drawn and teeth bared, hoping to size up the bandits' strength. But I was never very good at intimidation; that's something my father certainly never taught me. He was a berzerker when he fought, and as I mentioned earlier, so was I. I spent some time sizing up the bandits, all right, but I began the fight by roaring and throwing myself at the nearest bunch of them.

To some extent, the ploy worked, for they were hardly expecting us to attack first, considering how outnumbered we were, and no doubt they didn't expect a woman, of all things, to be slashing away at them like a maniac. I'm certain Gaar would have preferred letting them make the first move, but then there wasn't very much he could do about that now.

I took out three of them before the bandits could even get their bearings. But once they recovered from my surprise attack, there were still at least eight others who we had to deal with. Fortunately, there were only so many of them that could attack us at one time, and I believe there were no other snipers in trees. That, and the bandits were not used to attacking people who could fight back, so we were able to make short work of those who attacked us directly. Nevertheless, Gaar and I were quickly becoming exhausted from fighting so many at one time. I received several superficial cuts and one of the bandits succeeded in almost slashing Gaar's vest in half in a rear attack. I was relieved that it wasn't Gaar's back that was slashed, but, in any case, the man was eliminated long before he could dare attack again.

And the next thing we realized, all of the bandits were either dead, dying, or had fled. We wasted no time sticking around to see if any of their friends would stop by, and, out of breath as we were, we raced into the forest in order to catch up with Arem—if he hadn't decided to run away without us.

We were fortunate; Arem was waiting for us some one hundred feet away, in a small clearing near a pond. Gaar and I practically threw ourselves into the pond to wipe the sweat from our faces. But we couldn't rest, not when the bandits might be regrouping, if there were more of them. I could have slept forever myself, but nevertheless, we both had to drag ourselves to our feet again and prepare to press on.

Meanwhile, Arem was rattling off questions about the attack. What had happened? How many were there? Were they dead? Were they following us? Gaar answered his questions politely enough, but he also insisted on our hurrying along and getting out of that forest. Arem was amazed at our proficiency at handling the thieves, or rather, I should say, at *Gaar's* proficiency. Again I noticed Arem's tendency to ignore my accomplishments, and he continually praised Gaar alone for his incredible defeat of the bandits.

I expected Gaar to stick up for me and make certain that I got credit, too, but he remained unusually silent the rest of the way to the city.

Three

Although I had been in cities much more prosperous than Castrill, I could not say that the place was exactly destitute. Most of the homes we passed were relatively modest; even the places belonging to the rich had a certain air of frugality about them. The lack of any real night life also contributed to the frugal atmosphere of the city; the people seemed to prefer staying at home to squandering their money, carousing through the night.

We passed a small temple, built mostly from wood with some stone columns and statues lining the outside walls. Public baths lay directly across from the temple, and directly ahead was a large building of bricks of stone, and wood. Arem indicated that it was our destination—the center of the city government—but he veered off to the right of the building, where the stables were.

He was in a hurry to get to the magistrate once he had his horse taken care of, and he motioned us to follow. Gaar let me pass ahead of him, and I hesitated before following Arem. He had been unusually passive that day, and I wondered if he had been humbled somewhat by the experience with the thieves.

The central building had endless rooms and chambers. I had seen larger buildings before, but only from the outside; now I was actually inside one of these ancient "mansions," and its size and complexity were impressive.

Several servants bustled by us as we walked past room

after room. Most of them recognized and greeted Arem cordially, and he returned the courtesy. Gaar smiled at those who greeted Arem; I was grimly silent, as usual.

Finally, we reached the administrators' wing, where the "important" bureaucrats slept. Arem had us wait while he ducked into his room and deposited his belongings. Shortly, he returned and shut the door.

"When do we get paid?" asked Gaar. "And by whom?"

"Pray, don't worry," Arem answered. "You'll be paid very soon. And out of my pockets, I'm afraid. Please follow me, though."

He waved us on, and we had little choice but to follow. Soon we reached a shut door. Arem knocked, and a voice inside bade him enter.

The magistrate sat up in bed, reading a book. He looked just past his middle years—midsixties, perhaps—but his hair was not as thin as that of most men his age. His face showed many years of worrying and fretting in its lines, however, and his body would have done well to have more meat on it.

He watched Arem sternly as the quaestor gave him greetings. He was in a bad mood because Arem had got back so late at night and also because he had wasted money hiring "thugs" to see him back safely. Neither Gaar nor I liked that comment, but we kept silent while Arem babbled on about what a great fighter Gaar was, and how he should join the Army. Meanwhile, we just wanted our money. Finally, he and the magistrate finished their chat, and we glowered at Arem as he shut the door. Gaar spoke my mind for me.

"If you don't pay us right now, we—"

"Shh! Yes, yes, I understand!" Arem whispered, and pulled out two sacks from his robe. They clinked as he placed them into our waiting hands. I put mine away immediately, unconsciously mimicking Gaar's behavior. But I also didn't trust the man completely and wanted to count my money right there.

"That's eight for each of you, to complete the payment," he told us. "I simply didn't wish to pay you in front of him, that's all. He is every concerned about money and all, and—"

"We thank you, Arem," Gaar said. "But as for my joining the Army—"

"We pay our men," he interrupted. "And citizenship is easy to acquire in this city. Unless, that is, you belong to another already?"

"I was born in Actium. But I won't be returning there."

"Ah. Well, perhaps you should think about it. I know that warriors live as wanderers by nature, going from city to town to city, selling their services—mercenaries, in other words. But you, you have the air of a soldier about you."

"My father served in the Roman Army," Gaar stated. "Others have said I have his temperament."

"That may be," Arem said. "Perhaps you will give it thought, then. And you are welcome to stay in Castrill for any length of time. We are not Rome, but we are proud of our city. Tell me, will you be staying for the night?"

"I should hope so."

"Yes, that was a thoughtless question. Your wounds must weary you much now. You're welcome to stay here, then, if you wish."

"Oh? You mean, here in the magistrate's house?"

"Yes. We should have more than enough room for you and your wife."

"His *what?*" I interjected. Arem ignored me and called over a servant girl. I looked over at Gaar, who either hadn't heard Arem's comment or was pretending not to have heard. Meanwhile, Arem bade the girl to show us to an empty room and give us bedding and things. I decided to wait until we got there before I said anything.

"Are there any other rooms?" I asked the girl when she showed us the one room.

"Any other? Ummm . . . I don't think so."

"Mara . . . Mara . . ." Gaar kept calling to me until I turned around and glared at him.

"Let's not tax their hospitality," he said, then to the girl: "Thank you. This is a fine room."

"But—!" I started, only she quickly bowed and left the room. "But—!"

Gaar took my arm gently, which startled me at first.

"Never mind, Mara," he said. "At least we're getting a free room for the night, let's not try for two."

"He thinks that we're married," I said. "Did you hear what he said? He said I was your wife!"

Gaar muttered something almost inaudibly.

"What did you say?" I asked.

"Nothing."

"Wait, I heard you! You said, 'What a horrible fate that would be.' Are you mocking me?"

"It's late, Mara. Why don't we just go to bed?"

He said no more, but threw his pack off into a corner and started taking his boots off. I watched him a few moments before dropping my own gear into another corner. Meanwhile, his boots off, Gaar was unbuckling his sword belt. I copied his actions, only much more slowly.

Gaar threw his bedding onto the floor and started spreading it out. I took my own and did the same. The room was very small, so I had to put my bedding right next to his. Then Gaar plopped down and pulled his blanket over him.

"Good night," he mumbled.

"Oh . . . good night," I whispered. I left on all my clothes, but my boots and sword belt; Gaar had on the same, but had taken off his nearly slashed vest. He was bare-chested now, that is. He hadn't done that on any of the other nights. I found myself staring at his back, and a slight chill crept down my back after I caught myself at it.

I climbed onto my own bedding but sat up. I covered my legs with my blanket and let out a deep sigh. There was a long silence then before I gathered the courage to speak.

"Gaar?" I whispered.

"Mmm," he said. He didn't move, however.

"What is it?" he then asked.

It took awhile to speak, but finally I gathered the courage.

"You hate me now, don't you?" I asked.

Gaar sighed and rolled over onto his back. He was looking right up at me now.

"No," he said finally. "I don't hate you. Gods know you've given me good reason to, but I don't hate you."

"I wouldn't blame you if you did," I continued. "I can be very cruel sometimes. I suppose . . . I suppose you're right, what you said before."

"About?"

"Well, you know, about my having no heart. I mean, I—"

"Oh, no, no, no," he said, sitting up now. "I'm sorry for those things, I didn't mean them."

"But—"

"I'm sorry for what I said, Mara," he continued. "I was angry and tired and—maybe a little drunk, too, I don't know. I'm sorry. Please forgive me."

"Forgive you?" I asked, looking him in the face now. "But—it's all true, all of it."

"You have feelings, Mara," he said. "Everyone does. You just don't show them very well."

"No, I suppose I don't," I mumbled.

"Do you want to be that way always?"

"No," I said after some deliberations, "I don't think so."

"I didn't think you did," he said quietly, and then put an arm around my shoulder. I looked at him quickly, and then at the hand on my shoulder, but I did not struggle or pull away from him. He started absentmindedly squeezing my shoulder gently, which I found strangely relaxing.

He whispered something then which I couldn't make out. "What?" I said.

"I said, 'Gods help me.' "

"Why?"

He didn't answer right away, but sighed and looked over at me. After a time I met his gaze.

"I said, gods help me, Mara; I think I'm in love with you."

I remember mouthing the word "Wh-what?" to him, only not even I could hear it. I found myself unable to look away from him, not even in fear. He returned my gaze some moments longer before slowly pulling me toward him.

I had almost no strength to stop his kiss. He pressed his warm lips firmly onto mine, which were quivering in fear, and held me with both arms and pulled me even closer. I was stiff all over: my arms, my neck, even my lips were almost rock-hard.

The kiss must have lasted only a few seconds, but it was an eternity, really. He finally parted from me, and I'm not sure if I had begun breathing again.

"I love you, Mara," he whispered. "Fool that I am, I've tried to hate you, but I can't. I can't!"

"Uh," I said, and he pulled me forward again into another kiss. And another. And another. Scores of kisses all over my lips and my face and my neck. My head was spinning and my spine threatened to leap from my back and do flip-flops across the room, but I fought to remain conscious.

"Relax," he kept whispering over and over in what ended up to be a rather rhythmic chant. Kiss, "relax." Kiss, "relax," until I closed my eyes and let my head fall back as he worked his way to my neck again.

"Gaar . . ." I whispered. "I don't— Please . . ."

"No words," he said. "Just relax. Follow me."

His lips glided back to my face again, to caress my chin and cheeks and then my lips. I was still trying to voice protests, but he kept pressing his lips to mine over and over until the protests stopped, and I did as he said and followed him.

And then, just as suddenly as he'd begun, he stopped. I let out a great sigh and leaned back against the wall, breathing heavily, eyes shut. Gaar did the same, and we lay there, wordlessly, with only our breath breaking the silence. And then, after an eternity, he spoke.

"Mara . . ." he whispered.

"Yes."

"Stay with me. Stay with me always."

Before answering, I leaned toward him and wrapped my arms around him and let my face rest on his shoulder.

"I've never been so afraid as just then, Gaar," I said.

"I'm sorry," he said, "I couldn't take it any longer. I don't know what it is, what kept me going after you."

"You are a fool to love someone like me," I said. "You need a woman, not a killer."

"Silence," he said.

"What am I supposed to be feeling right now, Gaar? Am I feeling the right things?"

"I don't know. Are you?"

"I can barely breathe; I can barely think; I don't understand. I know no man was ever supposed to touch me, and now look at me! Look at what I've done!"

"You're doing just fine, Mara," he whispered. "You're only doing what's in your blood to do."

"I don't understand . . ."

"You will. I promise that. You're going to stay with me now. You'll never run from me again."

"No . . ."

"And I won't leave you, either," he continued. "I'll always be with you."

"Gaar? What . . ."

"Marry me, Mara. Be my wife."

Somehow I expected those words, but even that paled next to actually hearing them spoken. I looked up at him, my mouth trying to form words, but it was no use. I was paralyzed, unable to move or speak or do anything.

"Be my wife," he said again. I still couldn't answer. So he brought his face close to mine and started kissing me again, and that snapped me out of my trance. I pushed him away gently.

"No, not that again," I said. "Please."

"Marry me."

"I don't know if you mean that, or if you're just saying it."

"I mean it. I would never joke about something like this. I want you to be my wife."

"Gods, you are serious. But—but why?"

"Why not?"

"Why not, why, there are dozens of reasons. Y-you can't want to marry someone like me. I'm not a wife. All I know is killing, Gaar. You told me that yourself."

"It's not as if you can't learn anything new."

I said nothing after that, but unwrapped my arms from him and leaned back against the wall and looked down at my lap. Gaar watched me a moment and then placed a gentle hand on my shoulder.

"You don't have to answer me right away," he said quietly.

"Good," I said. "I mean, I *can't* answer you right away. Not something like this. Every part of me wants to run from you now, to get away and forget any of this ever happened. But I can't: not now, not . . . feeling this strange way. You keep saying you're in love with me, but I don't know what I'm feeling right now, or what I'm supposed to feel. Maybe that's why no man was supposed to touch me. It just confuses things."

"I'm sorry, I've probably only made you miserable."

"No," I said. "No, not now. I'm not miserable now, but I'm not happy, either. I'm not anything. I just need time to think about this. Will you give me that?"

"Of course."

"You won't follow me around, or—?"

"No. No following. I promise. I'll leave you be for as long as you like."

"Oh, you don't have to stay away completely," I said. "I mean, I just . . . don't want you to push."

"All right, no 'pushing,' then. I promise."

"Good," I said. "Uhhh—thank you. I mean, thank you."

He laughed once, then leaned over to kiss me on the forehead.

"You're welcome," he said.

Four

Gaar was true to his promise to me, for the most part. We were together for two days while I tried to decide whether to accept his marriage proposal. We walked and ate together and shared the same room at a cheap inn, but we didn't talk much during this time. Gaar kept his hands to himself, never even tried to kiss me good night—kept his distance. Meanwhile, I was still in a daze.

Naturally, I started watching married people and observing how they acted around each other. I tried to discover if they were any happier than unmarried people, or if they were actually miserable. It was hard to tell by observation alone, and I was too afraid to just walk up to someone and start asking questions. I did try to ask Gaar some subtle questions about what he thought a marriage was supposed to be. But besides the usual cooking, cleaning, and baby-making wife, I learned that he wanted a wife he could talk to, and who would listen to him, who would stand by him and his decisions, but who would never be afraid to tell him when he was genuinely wrong. He didn't like vain or conceited women who asked for jewels and servants and wealth. I knew he was in no danger of that from me. But then, he must have known that, too. My only obstacle seemed to be that he liked women who were feminine, but then every man in that time felt that way, too. Feminine was the last thing I thought I was. After all, I'd fought my entire life to avoid that. But if Gaar's interest in me was that great, then apparently I had failed miserably.

I made my decision late the second night, after I had spent our entire dinner staring at the table. Eventually I ate the food, but it was horribly cold by that time. We said little to nothing during the meal, but as usual, Gaar would look up at me a lot and smile quickly. Sometimes I felt his feet touching mine under the table, and our hands brushed against each other, and not just once.

Finally, we left the table and headed back to our room. Gaar unlocked the door and let me enter first. He yawned and stretched after entering and locking the door again.

"Long day," he said.

"Yes," I agreed. "Very long."

He took his gear and tossed it off near his bedding and slapped and rubbed his chest quickly.

"There isn't much in this town," he said, now reaching down for his boots.

"No, there isn't," I said. Then: "Gaar?"

"Mmm hmm," he said, still struggling with his boots.

"I've decided."

He stopped and looked up, one of his boots in hand.

"You have?" he said. "Why, that's— Tell me, Mara! Tell—no, wait," he said, and sat down to put his boot back on. When he finished, he stood up again and slapped his hips.

"Yes, well," he said. "If my heart's to be broken, I want to be fully clothed."

I laughed once and looked down.

"You like that," he said. "And that's the first time I've ever seen you smile."

"Uh . . . well . . . I don't smile much, do I?"

"No. But—your decision. Tell me, Mara."

"Um . . . yes. My decision," I said, and started fidgeting. "You know that . . . well, I've been watching married people and unmarried people. People with children and people without. People who—who touch each other in public and people who . . . don't seem to like each other."

"Yes?"

"It's hard to tell, you know," I said. "I mean, it's hard to tell if people are happy because they're married. A lot of them seemed miserable."

"People aren't happy just because they're married," he said. "It's best if they're happy while they're married. You should remember that."

"Yes. Well," I said, not quite understanding his meaning. "Meanwhile, you say you want a wife who will cook and clean and all that."

"Well, it does go with the job," he said, and smiled.

"I . . . believe it or not, I *do* know how to cook and clean and some other things. I mean, my father still made me do all that, even if he didn't want me to be a girl."

"So he got two in one, boy and girl. He must have been a splendid father," Gaar said sarcastically.

I shrugged. "He didn't like me much, actually," I said. "He was always telling me how stupid I was."

"That's too bad. Because you're not stupid."

"Well, I know I'm not very smart, either," I said.

"Your decision, Mara," he said.

I looked up at Gaar and fidgeted some more. "I still don't understand why you want to marry me," I said.

"To be honest, I don't understand why myself. But I do. And that's what's important in the end, isn't it?"

"Um . . . yes. It must be."

"Your decision, Mara. No more stalling," he said. "Will you marry me? Will you be my wife?"

"Yes."

We both wore our warrior vests for the ceremony, but I also wore a garland of flowers, which Gaar had made for me, in my hair. I had refused to wear it at first, but after

I saw how my words stung him and he became sad, I complied. He also wanted to buy me a dress for the wedding, but I wouldn't let him, stating that I had met him as a warrior and I would marry him as a warrior.

It was a simple ceremony, with no one else present but ourselves and the priest, as we knew virtually no one in the city. It lasted fewer than fifteen minutes, I think, and took place three days after I had accepted Gaar's proposal. The priest invoked the gods of marriage, the hearth, and the family to seal our bond for all time. As part of the ceremony, one finger from Gaar and from myself was pricked, and the priest brought them together, where our blood was to mingle and flow as one. Our bond was complete.

The priest proclaimed me to be Gaar's forever. Gaar then bent over and swept me off the ground into his arms. I screamed.

"Gaar, what are you doing?! Put me down!"

"I want to show you to the world!" he cried. "I want everyone to see my joy this day!!" He began carrying me to the door leading outside, and I panicked.

"No! Put me down! Gaar, have you gone mad? I beg you, put me down!" He burst through the door with me still in his arms, and laughed for joy, despite the passersby who eyed us curiously. I knew if I struggled too much, I would simply drop to the ground with a thud, so I was forced to be content simply yelling.

"Put me down now!" I commanded.

Laughing still, Gaar lowered me onto my feet and stood facing me.

"I'm sorry," he said, even though he really wasn't. He smiled and held my head steady with his hands, and leaned forward to kiss me. I wrapped my arms around his neck, and we embraced for an endless time, or at least I wanted it to last that long.

I couldn't stay angry with him for long in that moment,

not when I, too, was basking in joy. But Gaar had amorous tendencies as well as occasional urges to show off.

He insisted on holding my hand as we walked through the streets, and he took to greeting nearly everyone we passed. I turned away in embarrassment any time he announced our recent nuptials to friendly strangers, which was often.

We returned to the inn and dined from late afternoon to well past the sunset; he ate heartily, but I became full early on and took to watching him and other inn-dwellers feast. Alcohol never did take well to me, a tendency I also noticed in my father, although he drank often, anyway, which usually made him vomit all over the hut later on. Gaar, of course, could take his liquor like any self-respecting man, but he took care that night after I made my extreme dislike of drunkards quite clear to him. He wasn't going to vomit all over the floor in front of *me*.

Late in the night, many of the inn-dwellers took to singing raucous drinking songs, and Gaar joined them in several. Often he urged me to join in, saying that they needed "the sweet trill of a lady's voice," but my singing voice is similar to that of a cow's in labor, and I wisely declined. Come to think of it, Gaar's voice was nothing to brag about, either.

Reveling and celebration, for all the fun they may be, can take their toll on one's stamina. While I was hardly exhausted when we returned to our room, my heart beat a little faster at the sight of our bedding. Gaar held me in his arms, gazing at me dreamily, and then he reached out and removed the garland I still wore. The flowers had long ago wilted in the summer sun, and many of the petals had fallen away; it surprised me that I had even kept it on for that long, it was so ugly by now. He dropped the flowers and brushed my hair back behind my ears and cupped them.

"Have you enjoyed yourself this day, my wife?" he asked.

I couldn't help smiling at him. "Yes," I answered, "but it's been such a long day."

"Aye, it has," he agreed. "But the best is yet to come." I wasn't sure what he meant by that, but it pleased me to hear it. Gaar poked my cheeks playfully.

"It's good to see your dimples in a smile again and not a grimace," he teased.

I pushed his finger aside and looked away in embarrassment. "You mock me," I said.

"Oh, stop saying that," he said. "I only tease you. You have a beautiful smile, you know."

"I do?"

"You certainly do," he said. "And the loveliest eyes I have seen on any woman."

"Stop that," I said, no doubt turning bright red. He only laughed and pulled me toward him into a kiss. I started giggling and tried to push him away, only he growled playfully and held me tighter. I gave in eventually, and we kissed several times before ending in one long, deep kiss.

Gaar moved to a corner of the room after we parted, and I opted to collapse, fully clothed, onto the soft bedding.

"Ahh," I moaned. "Sleep at last. Good night, Gaar," I murmured, pulling the blankets over me.

"Hmm?"

"I said, 'good night.' "

There was a strange pause before Gaar finally answered with his own "good night."

I shut my eyes and waited for sleep to overtake me; Gaar seemed to be taking a while to prepare himself for bed, but eventually, I heard him blow out the lantern and climb under the bedding beside me.

I was facing away from him, toward the wall opposite the door. My thoughts were becoming hazy, and I welcomed the coming of slumber to rescue me from that long, warm day.

I felt a hand touch and begin caressing my shoulder, and I was forced to stay my sleep to see what was the matter. Then I felt Gaar's hot breath on my neck, and I turned my face toward him slightly.

"Good night, Gaar," I repeated.

"Aye, it *is* a good night," he agreed. "But it has not yet ended."

"Aren't you going to sleep yet?" I asked through a yawn. "Surely even you must be tired."

"We can't go to sleep yet," he announced.

"I'm not leaving this room again tonight," I mumbled. "Let me rest now. Revel more if you want, I don't care."

"Not reveling, my love," he whispered. "Our night is not yet through. For now, we must consummate our marriage."

" 'Consummate?' " I yawned. "What's that? Mayn't we do that tomorrow?"

"Tomorrow? Nay, it must be tonight, if we expect our bond to hold true."

Gaar continued rubbing my shoulder, and a chill suddenly crept down my spine.

"Uhhh—Ohhh . . ." I began, opening my eyes now. "You mean . . . c-*con*summate, don't you?'

I waited for him to answer, but he squeezed my shoulder gently and kissed my neck, instead. I still lay facing away from him, and he held my shoulder and started to turn me onto my back. He didn't need to explain himself anymore. I gripped the floor and stopped myself.

"Gaar," I whispered, swallowing hard, "I think I would much rather sleep."

"You will—when we're done," he cooed, and kissed my forehead. I covered it with my hand and held my breath. He took my hand and kissed the palm, and then continued working his way down my arm.

"Perhaps," I gasped, "perhaps it's only s-superstition. I mean, perhaps it doesn't matter when one, when we—'consummate.' " Gaar ignored me and followed my arm up to my shoulder, and then my neck. I grabbed his head and pushed it away from me. He moved to my side and made a sound in frustration.

"Mara," he whispered, "you'll not run from me again."

"Who's running?" I gasped. "I only . . . Perhaps we . . ." I fought for the words that would sum up my fear without revealing it, but could find none, and I was forced to opt for the truth.

"I'm afraid!"

"Shh," he whispered, moving a hand to my cheek. "There's no reason to be afraid. Just relax."

"Why don't we just kiss a lot, and—and that'll be it?"

"Don't be silly."

"Oh, that is me," I said. "Always . . . always silly . . ."

"It's too late to be modest, Mara. You're my wife now."

"I'm not 'modest,' I just . . . I mean this is more than just kissing! I'm used to *that* now, I—I mean I like it now, truly! But—*this* . . ."

"Gods, Mara, don't you ever want any children, either?"

"Ch-children? Gods, we never even talked about that."

"How do you think people have children? Do you think they buy them?"

"Of course I know how people have children," I lied. "But what does this have to do with—what you want?"

"Then you *don't* know," he said.

"I must not, then."

"Enough talk," he said. "Come, my wife . . ."

He started kissing me on the neck again, and I lay there, breathing quickly, terrified. Soon he was kissing my face, and then pressed his lips onto mine, only they were stiff.

"Relax," he whispered as he worked his way back to my neck. The same rhythm began again: Kiss, "relax."

Kiss, "relax," and Lord knows I tried to stay my fear, but it wasn't working well.

Gaar stopped kissing me and rolled away to start taking his vest off. My clothes stayed on, however.

"Gaar . . ." I said.

"Hush," he said. "And take your vest off."

"My vest? But—no, no, I couldn't."

"Clothes only get in the way."

"But this is my warrior's vest," I protested. He turned and dangled his own vest above me.

"And this," he said, "is mine," and he tossed it away into the darkness and rolled over to put his arms around me. I was still stiff, until he reached over to start pulling off my vest himself. I grabbed on to it and held it shut tightly.

"This is foolishness, Mara," he said. "You're no warrior."

"What?"

"I said, you're no warrior. And neither am I. Not tonight. Tonight we are only man and woman. Husband and wife."

He stayed on his side and waited for my response. I held my vest shut tightly for almost a minute, but my grip was loosening all the while. Eventually, I very slowly sat up, watching him the whole time, and slowly took my vest off, and handed it to him. Gaar took it gently and then tossed it off into the darkness to join his own vest. I couldn't see where it landed.

"Come, my wife," he said again, and I lay back down slowly to be taken up into his arms. He held me tight and kissed me several times before I reciprocated, and eventually, I put my own arms around him, and he began moving his body onto mine.

"It is time for you to learn what it is to be a woman, my love," he whispered.

* * *

Eventually, my fear faded away into nonexistence. I had rarely felt so free as on that night. Everything that I'd ever had, every suppressed and repressed feeling that I'd ever had poured out of me and into our lovemaking as our passion got heavier and sweatier. I practically ripped up my own clothes in my haste to get them off. It was the most basic, most primal pleasure I had ever known that night, and my eventual climax was but the tip of my ecstasy.

I feel very fortunate now that my first encounter with passion was so wonderful for me, considering some of the horrible stories I've heard since. There was never any pain, and no discomfort once I was able to open up and enjoy the experience. That night Gaar told me that he'd never been with a woman who made love as well as I did; he wasn't a virgin before meeting me, in other words. But I didn't mind; after all, it was acceptable, sometimes expected, for men to be "experienced" before marriage. Not for women, of course.

During a pause in lovemaking, Gaar had kissed my neck and shoulders over and over, which stimulated me quite a bit, but then he began kissing those places more slowly and gently, until he was resting his lips on my neck. He began sucking very gently. I felt strangely relaxed then, almost to the point of falling asleep, and my arms went limp and fell away from his back, and I lay there silently, lips slightly parted, as my husband gave me my first "hickey."

I was completely relaxed by the time our lovemaking came to an end, and Gaar hovered over my face for a time, breathing softly and gazing into my eyes in the darkness. I remember seeing a flash of light reflect from his eyes, and then he bent down and kissed me long and hard one last time before he moved off me and lay by my side. I shut my eyes in contentment and sighed softly.

"Good night, Mara," he whispered.

"Good night . . ."

Five

We decided to remain in Castrill. It was actually better off than most other "Romanized" cities; it had relatively good crops year round, and a bustling trade with other towns. It only seemed poor at first sight—probably due to the magistrate's "frugality."

After consulting with Arem again, who helped us obtain citizenship (or rather, helped *Gaar* obtain citizenship—women were fifth-class people, after all), Gaar joined the Castrillian Army. Unfortunately, it was not the best of militias. There was enough wealth in the city to sustain an army through taxes, but the general, Tetulius, was getting on in years and could not lead the men in combat or drills as efficiently as in his youth, and the magistrate didn't seem to show much concern for the lack of discipline that resulted from this. Tetulius relied more on his right-hand man, Taran, for training and other practical matters, but more men of leadership were needed to keep the Army from deteriorating.

Tetulius was one of the wealthiest men in the city, but he had no male heirs to his estates. It was expected that Taran would "inherit" the generalship once Tetulius died, and might even inherit some of the wealth. But there was little indication as to the general's beneficiary; in fact, it was assumed that he would simply leave his estate to the city itself, and a rather large estate it was, too.

Gaar was treated well in the Army; soldiers that needed

them were given small two-room hovels near the training camp, and we promptly moved in. He was paid the usual salary, which wasn't much. Fortunately, years of being completely without funds had helped both of us learn how to live frugally.

Gaar was at first rather disappointed in the men of the Castrillian Army, whom he considered sorely lacking in training and discipline. This was particularly disconcerting to him, as we learned that Castrill had a history of tense relations with its neighboring city, Westmont. Apparently the economy there was not as stable as Castrill's, and Westmont had often begun raids to take the city but had not yet been able to wear the military down. It had actually been a few years since hostilities had been taken up on either side, which was probably why Castrill's Army had been allowed to go lax. Many of the citizens were also uncomfortable about this, but Tetulius's requests for more support from the magistrate went largely unheeded.

Tetulius's right-hand man at the time was Taran, a former mercenary who had officially joined the Castrillian Army and quickly rose through the ranks due to his fighting abilities. He seemed to be next in position to gain the general's army, but he was not rich and would not be able to maintain it unless the general willed all of his wealth to Taran. But then, as I mentioned, the general hadn't made public the beneficiary of his will, and I personally paid little attention at the time to the politics of this particular army. Nevertheless, the Army was in need of repairs if it was to survive the Westmontians, should they decide to attack again.

Meanwhile, Gaar was working on getting to know Taran as the man to speak to regarding training. It seemed that Gaar believed himself able to help train the men, if possible, and quite frankly, it occurred to me that if anyone could accomplish that feat, Gaar could. But first he had to demonstrate his own abilities, which he was able to do during combat training. Taran was pleased with what he saw, and soon he and Gaar were working together to see if discipline and technique could, indeed, be resurrected in the men.

It bothered me that I couldn't join the Army myself, if only to fight by Gaar's side if I was called to. I might have been hired in the past by people desperate for fighters, but an official army wasn't going to let any women join, period.

We had been married about two weeks before Gaar gave me my wedding ring. I was quite surprised to get one at all, considering how poor we were. And a ring wasn't really that important to me, anyway. He made a big fuss about it, though, making me close my eyes and hold out my hand. It wasn't just some gold or silver wire; it was a specially made band of braided gold. I was quite flustered, and even tried to remove it because I didn't think we could afford such a ring. But Gaar made me promise never, ever to take it off until the day I no longer loved him. I haven't removed it since, except to put it on my right hand, where I have it to this day.

One thing that naturally bothered Gaar was the fact that I was still wearing my vest and shirt and not a dress. At the time, I was still stuck on my "warrior" routine, even though I hadn't been a warrior since we'd been married. After all, as Gaar's wife I was busy cooking, cleaning, and so on, and had barely any time to even practice swordfighting, let alone get money for it. So some resentment was brewing about my situation. Also, I had some respite because, even if Gaar wanted me in a dress, we had little to no money to buy me one, and I wasn't skilled enough to make my own. I guess my wedding ring set us back more than he would tell me. I did ask him why, if it was so important to him for me to wear a dress, he had bought a ring, instead. He said something about how important it is for married women to "look" married, whatever that meant. He also reminded me that I wasn't going to be dressing like a man for the rest of my life, either. I changed the subject.

One of the hardest things I ever had to do was to tell Gaar that he was going to be a father. Oh, it wasn't because of him; no, my hesitation came from those damned fears that my father had crammed into my brain with such a vengeance. Before I met Gaar, I was pathetically ignorant of virtually anything that had to do with the differences between men and women. Now, in less than a year, I had felt love for the first time in my life, married a man, had experienced lovemaking, and was now on the road to motherhood. Who, me? A mother? No, no, *women* get pregnant, not me, not a warrior. What did I know about being a mother? I'd never had one myself, after all, nor did I know anything about babies, for that matter.

I gathered the courage to tell Gaar, knowing full well that he would be ecstatic about it, but still fearing that he'd become angry, anyway. He *was* ecstatic, of course, and grabbed me and hugged me and kissed me and generally made a big fuss about the whole thing. He wanted to tell the whole Army the news before I protested and made him limit himself to just a few friends. I also didn't want anyone coming over and staring at my belly or fondling it or whatnot—excepting Gaar, of course.

That same day, I was in the marketplace to gather our daily supply of food. My appearance in public, as usual, was met with curious glances and mutterings as I walked by, as I was yet to obey the unwritten laws for female attire. I probably looked sillier on this day, what with my vest open at the bottom and sticking out away from my belly. Not that it was particularly large, since I was only about four months pregnant, but I knew, much to my worries, that it was only going to get worse.

So I usually took to side streets and other mostly empty walkways to go about my business in the marketplace. That way I could be away from gossipy neighbors and thus be more undisturbed in my thoughts.

I was strolling through an empty alleyway when I was suddenly sent tumbling into the dirt by someone slamming into me. Furious, I grabbed whomever it was who had accosted me, and saw the face of a terrified girl, no more than fourteen, I'd wager, as she struggled to escape my grasp. We fought for a few seconds before I saw the cause of her panic: three boys barreling down the alley, apparently in hot pursuit of her. In blind panic, the girl kicked my shin and scrambled to her feet just as the boys caught up to us. They grabbed her and flung her down, shrieking, and one of them was so base as to pull out a knife and hold it to her throat. That was enough for me.

"Bitch!" he screamed at her. "Thought you'd run from us, eh? Thought you could hurt me and then get away with it?"

"Leave her alone," I said. The other two boys spun around, and though they might have been intimidated by my height, they gritted their teeth and acted tough.

"This is none of your business, girl," one of them growled.

"Go on, before you get hurt, too," the other added, and was stupid enough to give me a rough shove.

Without hesitation, I caught his arm and spun him into the wall. The other boy I simply kicked once in the groin. Then I stepped to the side of him and slammed his friend in the face with my elbow before he could recover.

I waited for the boy with the knife to take notice of the mayhem I was causing, which didn't take long. He saw his companions holding themselves in pain, gave me a take, and then a double take.

"What—?"

"Get away from her," I ordered.

"Who the hell are you?" he demanded. "What happened to them?"

Too angry to argue with him anymore, I kicked the knife from his hand, and he fell away from the girl and held his wrist in pain. I took a step back and whipped out my sword, just to ensure they would make no more stupid moves. His friends, who were by now struggling to their feet, froze in place when they noticed the blade.

"All of you," I growled, "leave her alone and get out of here."

None of them moved, however, apparently too shocked to react.

"Go on," I commanded. "Leave!" Finally their minds registered the seriousness of my command, and the boys fell over themselves in their haste to leave. I sheathed my sword and stood over the girl, who looked up at me with terrified eyes.

"You can get up now," I assured. "They're gone."

"Uh—" she said, but remained where she was.

"Did they hurt you?" I asked, bending down to see her better. "What did they want from you? Can you stand?"

"Uh—" she said again, but nothing more.

"They're not going to hurt you now," I reassured. "See? They're gone." The girl looked around her, eyes still wide with fright, to test the truth of my words. I only wished that I was as good at calming others as Gaar was.

"They're gone," I repeated, and held out my hand to her. "Can you get up? I'll help you." Cautiously, the girl took my hand, and as soon as she had done so, I hefted her quickly to her feet and dusted her off.

"Are you all right now?" I asked after finishing.

She nodded quickly. "Yes. Yes, I am," she said finally.

"What did they want from you? They acted like thieves."

"They were, I think. They were boys—ones that have

always been tormenting me, for some reason or another. They tried to take my money today."

"Oh. So you ran from them?"

"Yes. But I kicked Gareth first."

"Who?"

"The one who held the knife to me. Oh, such anger in him! I think he really meant to kill me!" The girl turned away from me as she started to sob; the experience, no doubt, was catching up with her. I felt especially awkward before this girl, inexperienced as I was with comforting others. I looked around and fidgeted somewhat.

"Well . . ." I began, "they're gone now. They didn't get your money, did they?"

"No," she said, sniffling. "No, they didn't, thanks to you. Yes, I must thank you for this. I think they surely would have killed me if I hadn't— Oh, I'm sorry for knocking you down, but—"

"That's all right," I insisted. "At first I thought you were some thief yourself, or a drunkard."

"I was running, and I didn't see you, and—"

"I said, it's all right," I repeated. "I'm not cross with you. They were the ones who angered me," I added, referring to the boys.

"I should repay you, somehow," she insisted.

"You don't need to repay me—really," I said, now a little irritated with her. "So if you haven't been hurt, I need to finish my errands . . ."

"Yes," she said. "Yes, that's what I need to do, also."

"Well, perhaps you should stay by me, in case they want to get their revenge on you," I suggested, not really sure why I was actually saying this to her.

"By *you?*" she asked.

"Uh—" I said, suddenly aware of my words. "Um— Oh, why not? They could be waiting for you to be alone. At least this way they won't dare attack you again."

"You mean you would give me escort through the streets? After you've already saved me?"

"Oh, stop dwelling on that. Just—well, either come with me now or just sit here in the alley, I don't care."

"Yes," she said, smiling. "Yes, I will go with you, stranger. Yes, thank you." I made my way toward the end of the alley, and the girl followed me like some merry puppy.

"But tell me; what is your name, if only to let me know who to thank?"

Strange, this girl, I thought. Nevertheless, there was something about her, something that sparked some interest in me about her. "Mara," I replied.

"Maaare-a," she repeated, letting my name roll around on her tongue. "I like that name. I like it much better than mine."

"Which is?" I asked.

"Leta," she replied. "Not a very nice name, is it?"

"I see nothing wrong with it," I said matter-of-factly.

"Oh, it's all right, I suppose," she said. "But yours is pretty."

Pretty. I had never heard my name referred to as "pretty," and her word struck an uncomfortable chord in me. We continued on in silence for a few moments, I lost in my thoughts, and the girl, Leta, kicking sand and rocks around as we walked.

"I was wondering, ma'am," the girl broke in suddenly. "You don't wear the normal garb of other women here. Are you from Castrill? If not, is this how the women dress where you're from? Surely, you couldn't be a soldier."

"No, I'm not a soldier," I grumbled, irritated by her prying questions. "But I *am* a warrior."

"A warrior," she repeated. "Are they better than soldiers?"

"I think so," I muttered.

"Ohh," she said in wonderment. "And your husband doesn't mind this?"

"Of course he doesn't mind!" I snapped. "He's a warrior himself. And by the way, I don't like— Say, how did you know I was married?"

"Well, you have a ring," she explained. "And—well, you show other signs of wedlock," she added, pointing out my belly.

I touched it in embarrassment. "Is it really that obvious?" I asked.

"I don't think so," she said. "But I have many younger brothers and sisters, so I can see it in women early on, I think. And you know, I was even with my mother at her last birthing!"

"Really."

"Yes; it was my youngest brother. It was very exciting, but messy, I thought."

"Oh," I said. "And how is she now?"

"Who?"

"Your mother."

"My mother? Oh, fine, fine. She jokes that she's used to it by now. But there's always so many of us at home that I'm glad when they send me on errands."

"Really."

For reasons which were not entirely clear to me at the time, I invited this strange puppy-girl over to our hovel for supper. She declined at first, arguing that she "owed" me too much already, but after arguing with her for some time, she eventually gave in to my insistence. It surprised me later that I had actually been so adamant about being nice to someone, but I chose to put it out of my mind and fret about it some other time.

Leta insisted that she receive permission from her parents first, but only after she had rattled on and on to them about the aid I had given her, and had received a promise from me that she would be escorted home, did they comply. The idea that there would be one less mouth to feed probably helped sway them, as well.

When we returned from our errands, Leta insisted on helping me prepare the dinner, saying that she was the one who always helped her mother the most in this. But reluctant as I was to perform the "woman's work" of the household, I was even more reluctant to accept help from others when I didn't feel that I needed it. This girl was a hurricane of enthusiasm and helpfulness, however, and soon I found myself standing away and watching her do all the work.

I was in the bedroom, puttering over something or other, when I heard Gaar return home. I decided to finish what I was doing before greeting him, but then I remembered that Leta was in the other room, and that he hadn't met the girl.

"Uh—hello; what is this? Who are *you*, girl? What are you doing here?" I heard him say in surprise. Instantly, I bolted into the room to save her from having to defend herself.

"Oh! Gaar! Hello!"

"Hello," he answered, then pointed at the girl. "Mara, who—?"

"Leta," I jumped in. "This is Leta. I invited her over."

"I didn't mean to startle you, sir," she interrupted. "I . . . I only thought to help your wife cook for you."

"I invited her," I said again.

"Oh," said the confused Gaar, "uh, certainly. If you were invited, then stay as our guest. But why are *you* preparing the meal?"

"She won't let *me* do it, that's why," I shrugged.

"I feel I at least owe her that, for saving my life and all," she added.

"I told you to forget about that," I protested.

"Saving your life?" he asked her, then to me, "Did you, really?"

"It was only these three boys," I explained.

"They meant to kill me, I'm sure of it! They're horrid boys who are always tormenting me, and today they tried to steal from me. But I kicked one of them and fled. Then I ran down the alley where Mar—I mean, your wife, here—was walking, but I wasn't watching where I was going and knocked her down."

"Leta, he doesn't need to know this—"

"No, no, it sounds interesting," Gaar interrupted. "Go on, girl."

"I didn't mean to hit her like that, but they were chasing me, and—"

"I'm not angry with you, Leta. I asked you here, didn't I?"

"Yes. Yes, sorry. Well, those three boys caught up to me then, and Gareth—the eldest of them—held out a knife to me! And then your wife took them all, and tossed them around like dolls, and frightened them away with her sword! And then she even escorted me around the city so they couldn't try and take vengeance on me!"

I was tired of hearing this girl babble on about me, but Gaar stood and faced me; only I noticed he wasn't smiling.

"Knives?" he said. "You got into a fight with boys with knives?"

"Oh, only one of them!" the girl cried. "But she defeated all three of them so easily that—"

"How could you let yourself get into a fight, of all things?" Gaar continued.

"Why so angry all of a sudden?" I asked. "There were only these three stupid boys—"

"But you can't be fighting in your condition!" he cried.

"What? What 'condition'?"

"You know exactly what I mean, Mara!" he roared, and was about to roar some more when he realized Leta was there. Quickly, he grabbed me by the arm and dragged me into our bedroom.

"How could you be so stupid as to get into a fight in your condition? What if you'd been hurt? Eh? What would happen to the child, then?"

"What was I supposed to do? Let them cut her throat and steal her money? Let them steal mine, too?"

"No, I don't mean that, I mean—!" Gaar stopped in midsentence, sighed in frustration, and then began again in a different tone. "You just have to be careful while you're— how you are now. No more fighting. Understand?"

"You think I'm helpless, don't you?" I said. "You think I'm some feeble-minded invalid, don't you, Gaar?"

"I didn't say that! I never said that! You know exactly what I mean! So long as you carry one of my children, you're not to go running around looking for fights!"

"I didn't look for any fights! *They* attacked *me!*"

"That's besides the point! Just don't— Please just promise me that you'll be more careful from now until the baby is born. All right? Will you promise me that?"

It's too bad Gaar was too much of a butthead then to understand what had happened, but I promised him to "be more careful" just to keep him happy. *So this is what marriage is all about,* I thought.

Leta was understandably worried when we emerged from the bedroom.

"I hope I haven't caused any trouble for you," she said to me.

"No," I said. "You've done nothing wrong."

"Sir? I didn't mean to get her involved with those boys. It was all my fault. She was really very brave—"

"We blame you for nothing, girl," Gaar said. "I suppose she only did what had to be done. But it won't happen again, right, love?" He put his arm around me, but I gave no answer.

"Well . . ." Leta began, "I think the food is ready. I can serve for you, if you like . . ."

"No," I replied. "No, really, you don't need to help me like this. I only need to prepare the table," I said, opening our rinky-dink cupboard where our too-few plates and dishes were. I took out the number we needed, but Leta took them all from my hands as soon as I had them out and began placing them around the table. I made a noise in protest, but then Gaar cleared his throat and waved me over.

"This has always been my job at home," she explained. "It's no trouble for me."

"But—"

"Oh, let her do it, love," Gaar interjected. "She only wants to pay you back for helping her."

"This isn't even paying back my debt," she insisted. "This is light work, compared to trying to feed *my* family."

"You have a large family?" asked Gaar.

"Yes—seven children in all," she said. "That, and my grandfather, my father, and my mother."

"Ten mouths to feed," said Gaar, impressed. "Perhaps we'll have as many children." I stared at him in shock at these words, but he seemed to take no notice of my consternation. He wanted ten kids from me?

"There always seems to be so much busyness at home," she continued. "You may not want so many children, in the end."

"You are not unhappy with so m any at home, are you?" he asked.

"Oh, no," she insisted. "No, not really. I love everyone in my family. It is only—only that I often wish to be alone, and it's so hard to be alone with so many about."

"Ah," he said, then turned his attention to me. "You always wanted to be alone when I was around," he said. "Does this hold true now?"

"Uh, not really," I replied. "Not anymore, at least. But this girl makes me feel both lucky and unfortunate."

"How so?"

"Well, I never had much trouble being by myself, when I wanted to be. But then, when I wanted someone to talk to, there was usually no one there. At least she has a family to talk to."

"Yes," he agreed, suddenly solemn. "She has a family."

"But I have you now," I added.

"So you do," he agreed, coming out of his suddenly solemn mood. "Yes, you know that you can always tell me your troubles, and secrets," he assured, patting my stomach, "especially the important ones."

"I'm sorry," I said, holding my belly, "I meant to tell you soon—really I did. It's just—"

"Well!" the girl interrupted, slapping her hands together once. "All is ready, I think. You can eat whenever you like, sir—ma'am."

All *was* ready. With maniacal speed, this bouncing, enthusiastic puppy-girl had laid out the entire table—the plates, bowls, cups, food, serving implements—everything was ready. Smiling, Gaar took me by the hand and led me to my chair, where he let me sit first. Leta waited for him to be seated before seating herself.

As we feasted, I quickly took notice of how polite this girl was. She waited for each of us to serve ourselves first, and even after this, she ate tiny portions compared to ours—especially Gaar's. She would not take extra helpings until she had obtained our permission first, and she continued to call him "sir" and me "ma'am" or "lady," even after I tried to tell her that I wasn't used to such formalities.

After our dinner, she asked to be allowed to help clear the table and clean the dishes. I explained that only one person could clean the dishes with the tub we had, so she offered to do it herself. I tried to protest all this doting and fussing over me, but Gaar called me over to him. I watched her lug the tub outside to clean everything; then I sighed and shook my head in frustration.

"That girl is mad," I remarked. "What sort of guest is she, who won't even let us treat her like one?"

"It seems to me she's just gotten caught up in the events of today," Gaar offered. "You did risk life and child to save her, after all."

"I wish you'd stop belaboring that," I protested. "I only frightened off some stupid boys. They were probably half my age."

"But old enough to carry knives with them. Besides, it looks like the girl admires you."

"Admires me," I grumbled. "What's there to admire about *me?*"

"Oh, you have some qualities," he said, brushing the hair from my eyes. "You just don't notice them yet."

"Such as?" I asked.

"Oh—perhaps later," he said. "Meanwhile, I'd say this girl is about as stubborn as you are. Perhaps even more so."

"Impossible," I denied. "No one's as stubborn as I am."

"That's true," he said. "That's why she's outside, cleaning our dishes, and—" he continued, poking my nose, "that's why you so stubbornly agreed to marry me."

He sat there laughing at me, and although I knew he was right, I slapped him in the chest for teasing me.

Six

Relations with Westmont were faring poorly. The harvests there had not gone well, and the denizens of Castrill were becoming more worried about possible raids, and the city grew tense. Taran and Gaar continually beseeched the magistrate for more money for the Army, but to little avail, as usual. The magistrate's answer was that the city's taxes just couldn't support the increasing demands of the Army. Gaar and Taran's position was that the Army was barely at subsistence level with its present funds—little more than a militia. Tetulius did what he could for his Army, but it was not his job to support the military entirely on his own wealth; his job was to run it.

Nevertheless, working with Taran, Gaar was able to achieve minor miracles with the motley assortment of soldiers. Having been a wanderer for some years, Gaar had seen the best and worst of combat techniques, and he succeeded in passing on the best of them to the men, including Taran. Gaar was an incredible teacher: patient, enthusiastic, friendly, but always firm. The men took to him and looked up to him, and, while Gaar's official rank was not equal to Taran's, he might as well have been the general himself, for all the respect they had for him. Under Gaar's training and discipline, the men were more willing to work under the worsening conditions. Unfortunately, this only reinforced the magistrate's belief that the Army was doing well enough on its own; why give more money if they were improving already? But then, the improvements also caught the eye of Tetulius, who then took on Gaar as the Army's official trainer. This was basically little more than the position of drill sergeant, but Gaar also received a nice increase in pay out of the general's own pocket, which suited us just fine.

Meanwhile, the days went on, and my belly got larger. Leta borrowed an old maternity smock from her mother, and I had little choice but to wear it, even though it was far too short. Leta by now had taken to joining me once a week in my errands, and we wandered about the marketplace together. We must have made the oddest pair: the giddy puppy-girl skipping around with the pregnant woman whose smock barely went below the knees. I'm surprised we weren't laughed at as we went about our shopping.

In my eighth month or so, Leta started carrying everything for me. Despite my size, I felt far from helpless, but she usually just snatched my sack from me and lugged it over her shoulder. I think I gave up protesting her politeness the first night I met her.

Along with the increasing size came increasing anxieties. People were treating me as though I were helpless, and I was increasingly frustrated by the physical problems that came with pregnancy. I was sick of the backaches, sick of having to sleep on my back all night without moving, sick of not even being able to stand up without using my arms or a helping hand. And Gaar was the worst of all about my "helplessness." As far as he was concerned, I should have lain in bed all day and have Leta do everything for me. We got in many arguments about this; he suggested that we simply pay her to help out, but I knew that she had her own problems without having me to worry about. I also knew that she would have helped in an instant if I'd asked her, but I refused to take advantage of her kindness.

Another concern which I was never able to voice decently was that I was terrified that I wouldn't survive even my first child. My own birth was so complicated that it killed my mother, and how was I to know the same thing wouldn't happen to me? The only way I could know for certain was to actually give birth, and pray that I lived. So the bigger I got, the more anxious I became, and I began making some silent prayers to my mother, begging her forgiveness for what I'd done, and I even pledged to raise her grandchild the very best that I could in her name, if only she'd let me live.

Westmont decided to attack the city. Fortunately, spies had been sent on both sides, and the attack did not come as a surprise. The Castrillian Army knew when the other side was forming, and Tetulius was to lead the men out to meet the enemy and thus spare Castrill any pillaging and plundering. If Westmont won, however, the pillaging would come, anyway.

There was much brouhaha in Castrill before the men left. Wives and daughters and such wept and bawled and carried on as their husbands, brothers, sons, and fathers prepared to leave the city. I resolved not to carry on in such womanly fashion and, instead, bid my farewell to Gaar in the privacy of our home. I watched him silently as he assembled his armor and equipment, but I felt my lips quiver as I fought off tears.

He finished his task, and stood tall before me. He looked especially strong and handsome when wearing his black armor, sword at his side and shield on his arm. He moved toward me and brushed my cheek, and that made some tears come.

"Don't cry so, love," he said. "You make me want to join you."

"I'm sorry," I sniffled. "I only— I just—"

"I know," he said. "In times like these the tears come easily. And yet you've wept many times before this. Are these tears for the same reason?"

"No," I whispered. "I just—I just wonder if I'll see you again."

He tried to hug me, but it wasn't easy wrapping his arms around that bulk of mine. I was at least eight months with child. We parted, and he smiled and rubbed my belly gently.

"Try not to think of such things. I will come back to you—and the child. I promise you that." Comforting words, but then, I wasn't worried about *his* survival. I sniffled for some moments as he gazed at me and continued rubbing my belly. Then he drew himself up, leaned over, and kissed me.

"I must go now," he whispered. "Remember my promise. But if I must break it, and you know only death could make me do so, then remember my love for you. And always remember to tell the child of me, and of how much I loved it—son or daughter."

Warrior or not, my tears fell out in a waterfall, and Gaar sniffled and wiped away one tear, but he wept no more. I followed him to the door, bawling and carrying on like those women I had sworn not to imitate, and I was ashamed of my childish behavior, though I could not stop it. I watched him hurry away to the other men, and I longed to join them in the battle, if only to fight by Gaar's side as I'd done before.

He was nearly to the bottom of the hill, and I thought of shouting a last good-bye to him, but that would have been too embarrassing if anyone else but he had heard it. So I leaned against the doorway, sobbing, until he disappeared into the distance.

Leta began staying at the hovel a week or so after the men left, as by now I had to break down and admit that I needed help. None of her family had gone to fight, as they were farmers, but the crops would be one of the first things to go if Westmont defeated us and plundered the city.

I let her sleep on Gaar's side while she stayed over. Occasionally I would wake myself and her with my nightmares about the baby; Leta thought it was "my time" each time I woke with a start, and I had to assure her (and myself) that I wasn't ready yet. For myself, I wondered if I would even know when it really *was* "my time," as I had no idea what the signs would be.

I dreamt one night of the baby, huge and looming above me, with enormous teeth and evil eyes, pushing me into a corner and holding a bloody sword over my head. I screamed as he swung it toward me, and my eyes flew open, and the horrible image was replaced by the darkness of the room. I sat up, sweating and panting, and my legs were drenched in water. I almost cried out, wondering where it came from, if I'd actually wet myself during the nightmare. Leta was still asleep, and I was glad that I hadn't cried out. I tried to relax and forget the nightmare and that awful water, but it was becoming harder to breathe, and my stomach was tight, and my back ached. I felt a pushing and jostling inside me, and my breath quickened in fear. Then the feeling stopped, and I sighed in relief and lay down to sleep again, water or no water. At last I calmed down and was nearly in slumber when it happened again: a tightening and a pressure in my belly and back. I held my stomach and tried to relax, tried to slow my breath down and ease the pain, but it kept on and on, and I looked around wildly in the darkness. I flung my left arm to my side and hit Leta, who groaned once and moved.

"Leta!" I whispered harshly, and hit her again. "Leta!"

"Wha—? What? What?" she moaned, struggling to sit up. The pain increased, and I grabbed my belly and groaned.

"Mara? What is it? Another nightmare?"

"No, it's—! Leta, I think—!"

"Think what, Mara?" She suddenly gasped, and I felt her hand on my belly. "Oh, no. Are you—? Is it the baby?"

"I—I think so!"

"Oh, no," she muttered. "Not now. Why now? Why in the middle of the night?" I heard her stand and fumble around in the darkness. "Where is that lantern?" she cried.

A small light soon appeared, and Leta crawled over to me, lantern in hand, and felt my stomach.

"Yes, I can feel it," she said. "Final labor!"

"I . . . if you say so," I wheezed. "It must be— OOOOOOOO!"

"Try not to think about the pain," she said. "I need to get, uh— Uh— What? What do I need? Blankets! Water! Y-yes, I remember!"

"I don't know what to do!"

"Just relax, Mara," she said, taking my hand. "Just—just start breathing slowly, in . . . out . . . just breathe, calm yourself. I'll be right back—"

"Where are you going?"

"I need to get everything ready! Water, blankets, everything! Just stay here, and try to breathe slowly, easily . . ."

"Where else am I going to—OOOOOOO!"

Leta ran from the room, and I heard her stumble into something in the darkness. *Breathe slowly and easily, she says,* I thought. *I've never felt such pain!* There was even more pain, and I screamed. It felt as if the baby would burst straight from my stomach itself.

"GAAAARRRR!" I screamed, and Leta ran into the room and shouted at me again to keep calm. She threw down all the things she'd brought in, then took my hand again.

"It's going to be all right, Mara," she said. "You're going to be fine."

"Where's Gaar?" I asked.

"He's not here right now, Mara. But I'm here. You'll have your baby."

"It hurts so much. It's killing me!"

"Breathe slowly, deeply, Mara," she continued. "I know the pain is awful, but you have to bear it."

"I knew this would happen," I said. "I knew I would—OOOOOOO!"

"Keep calm, Mara! I'll be right back! I just need to get the water! I'll never leave your side once I get back!"

I fought the pain as best as I could while she ran from the room again. The pain was one thing, but I hated her seeing me like this, like some weeping little girl. But the pain was beyond anything I'd imagined it would be, and I was terrified, and Leta was all I had. I needed her.

She came back in, lugging a big bucket of water. She set it down and dipped her hands in it and then shook them dry.

"Please don't cut me, Leta; whatever you do, don't cut me open!"

"I pray it will never come to that, dear friend," she said. "I'll do whatever I can to avoid it. Meanwhile, you must open your legs. Come on, Mara; open!"

I obeyed her, and she crouched down in front of me and tried to peer in. I tried to sit up so I could watch, but she held me down gently.

"No, no, you have to lie down," she said. "Yes, your water has broken. It's almost time, my friend!"

"I want to see—OOOOOOOO!"

"I can barely even see! I need a light." She took our little lantern and held it in front of her.

"Yes," she said, "yes, good . . ."

"What? What is?"

"You're getting bigger," she said. "Your opening is big now."

"My what?"

"Keep breathing, Mara," she said, "and start pushing! Start pushing the child!"

"I—I— Help me, Leta!" I said in despair. I was certain I had only a few moments of life left.

"I'm helping you! Here—take my hand!" I reached out and felt her grab my fingers. I squeezed again, and she cried out. She bade me squeeze gently and regularly, and I did this the best I could, which wasn't all that good, but Leta encouraged me with enthusiasm.

"Yes! That's it! Slowly—regularly! Breathe and push, slowly, in rhythm! Work with the baby, not against it!"

"I'm trying! Gods, Leta, it hurts!"

"Shhh—just breathe regularly—squeeze gently. You're getting it!"

I wondered when the pain would end, when it would be all over. I wondered if my mother felt this way when I was coming, or if my pain was even worse. I shut my eyes and grimaced, and I pushed with all my might in the hopes that I might avoid her fate.

I lay there, drenched in sweat and fluid, frightened, tired, and feeling completely helpless. I pushed and breathed to the best of my abilities under Leta's advice, wishing it would all just end, wishing that Gaar were there so I could see him one last time.

I resolved that I would not hate the baby for what it would soon do to me; I vowed not to seek vengeance on it.

"Leta . . ." I said.

"Yes. Keep pushing . . ."

"Leta, you must promise me . . ."

"Of course, whatever it is, breathe . . . push . . ."

"You must promise me that if I die, you must tell the baby I don't blame it. You must tell it that I did not die hating it . . . Promise me . . . !"

"I'd rather not talk about your death while you're still alive, Mara—"

"Promise me!"

"Yes, I promise, I . . . of course, keep on—! Mara! I see it! Keep pushing!"

"What? See what?"

"The head! I can see the head! The baby's coming!"

Leta crouched down even more and peered more intently between my legs. I tried to sit up again, but couldn't, of course.

"No, no! Stay down!" she said. "Just keep breathing and pushing!"

"A-are you sure it's coming? Th-the right way?"

"Yes, of course the 'right' way! Oh, Mara; Mara, my dearest friend—you're about to become a mother! It's—one last push, Mara! PUUUSH!!"

An explosion erupted from between my legs, and more goop and blood and flesh came out, and I feared that the child had taken my insides out with it in some last attempt to destroy me. I heard Leta scream, and I wondered if it was from joy or horror.

"Mara! Mara it's out! It's here! It's, uhh—it's a boy! You have a son! Mara—you have a *son!*"

I had no words for her. Tears flooded my eyes, and I let my head slowly sink into the blankets, crying and laughing at the same time.

I woke up to the sun shining in my eyes, and I wondered if I was still alive. Shielding my eyes, I looked around and recognized the cramped space of the bedroom, where I'd been all night. Leta was gone, but I caught sight of a wooden thing lying to the side of me. I recognized the cradle Gaar had made some months before, but it had not been kept in the bedroom until now.

I heard some clanging of dishes in the next room, and I assumed Leta was cleaning or preparing a meal or something. I looked at the cradle again, but I could not see over the top and into it, and I was afraid to sit up and look. I was afraid of what I might find.

The dishes stopped clanging, and I heard footsteps coming toward the bedroom. The door opened slowly and quietly, and Leta peeked in, and I struggled to sit up. She opened the door wide and entered, her face beaming.

"Hello," she whispered. "How do you feel?"

"Awful," I said.

"You look tired," she said. "Did you rest well?"

I nodded, although I could have used quite a bit more rest. Leta stood silently for a moment, fidgeting her hands.

"You had a son," she whispered finally.

"A son?" I repeated, glancing at the cradle. "Yes . . . I remember you saying that."

"Yes," she said. Then: "Have you held him yet?" I shook my head. Leta moved to the cradle and peered in.

"He sleeps now," she whispered. "Would you like to hold him, though?"

"Uh—I don't know," I murmured, my spine suddenly shivering.

"I placed him on your belly soon after he came out," she said. "But you'd fallen asleep. Before the afterbirth, even; I was surprised.

"Afterbirth? Y-you mean I had *two* children?"

"No, no, the afterbirth. You know, the womb and the rest of the cord. Don't you know about that?"

"Um . . . no," I said.

"Oh, it doesn't matter. But are you certain you don't want to hold him?"

"Um . . ."

"When you're feeling more rested, then?" I stared at the cradle and nodded quickly. Leta moved over to me and then sat beside me. She sighed and shook her head, smiling.

"Such a night," she whispered. "I thought it would never end."

"Me, too." She turned and smiled at me.

"You kept saying you were going to die," she said, and laughed once. "The pain was that bad, eh?"

"That's part of it," I murmured. "I thought you'd have to cut me."

"No," she said. "No, and I'm glad I didn't. Sometimes that happens, though, and the mother must be sacrificed. I thank the Lord that He spared you."

Myself, I was busy thanking my mother.

Then, again: "Are you certain you don't want to see him?"

The shivering started again. I looked at the cradle, and then back at her.

"Well," I said, my lips quivering slightly, "maybe—maybe if you held him—and . . . I just looked . . ."

"Certainly," she said, rising and moving to the cradle. She reached down and slowly drew out what resembled a big lump of blankets. She knelt beside me and moved some blankets aside, and there was the ugly, wrinkled, sleeping face of my son. I drew back slightly in disgust, but then was drawn to it again in a blend of curiosity and fear.

"Your son," she whispered, holding him closer to me, and I drew back again, eyes widening. Leta smiled and laughed softly.

"You fear him?" she said. "There's nothing to be afraid of. Look at him, Mara; look—your child."

I looked at the boy, then at her, then at the boy again. I reached out with my hand—slowly, cautiously—until I touched his cheek, and then pulled my hand back quickly.

"Hold him, Mara," she whispered. "Go on; hold your child." Leta held the baby closer to me, and, my hands quivering, I reached out to it and slowly took the boy from her arms. He began to move, and I became afraid that I would panic and drop him, or hurt him somehow. He was so small, so fragile-looking, and I wondered how such a little thing could make me so big.

"Here," Leta said, reaching for the baby, "keep his head up, and hold him under here." I sat passively while she corrected my hold, and then she sat back and smiled.

"Newborn babes are beautiful things. Don't you think so?" she cooed.

I looked at his face again. "No," I answered.

"What? Your own son?" she said in surprise. "I'm surprised at you. You should be bursting with joy; you've had your first child!"

I stared at the child some more, and slowly, very slowly, the realization that I was alive—the baby was alive!—I had had a son and I was alive—crept into me, and I began to smile, then to chuckle softly. The more I looked at him, the more I accepted that this was real—this was not a dream—I was alive. I threw my head back and closed my eyes, crying tears of relief and joy. Leta laughed with me, and I opened my eyes and smiled at her through my tears.

Seven

It was just past sunset, the same day Ran—Gaar and I decided on that name before he left—was born. Fortunately, Leta had prepared a hot meal for the two of us. I was still weaker and more tired than I wished to be, but I had moved to the other room to dine, and we sat around the hearth rather than on the chairs. Leta had suggested that we bring the baby in with us, and he lay beside me in his cradle, resting.

At one point, Ran woke up and started crying, and all of Leta's efforts to quiet him failed. She suggested that he was probably hungry, and handed him to me. After much stalling and hesitation, I finally had to admit that I didn't know what to do, which Leta didn't believe at first. I wasn't actually *that* ignorant; I did know about mother's milk, but I had blocked that sort of knowledge from my mind for so long that I might as well never have learned it.

At first I was afraid to open my robe in front of Leta. It was then that it occurred to me that she probably knew far better what to do than I. She had delivered my first child; now she was helping me cope with it. I broke down and asked for help, and basically let her show me everything, including how to hold the child.

We sat there silently for a long time, the only sounds coming from the hearth, and, of course, Ran's suckling. I felt very calm then, very much at peace just from watching him feed. It was all so strange to me, not just the baby, but my entire life thus far. In less than a year's time, I'd been married and had a child. I even had a best friend now . . .

"Leta," I said, still looking at my son. He had finished the first breast, and I started to move him over to the other.

"Yes," she said.

"I—I just wanted to thank you," I said. "For everything. I wouldn't know what to do at all with him without you." Ran resumed his feeding on the other side.

"You are my friend, Mara," she said. "You know I would do any of this for you again and again."

"I've never had a friend like you before," I whispered. "Or actually, I've never had a friend before, for that matter."

"Ohhh," she said. "You must have been very lonely."

"Yes," I said. "But back then I would never have admitted it."

"I'm very glad to be your friend now, Mara."

"And I'm very glad to be your friend," I said. "You know that I am, don't you?"

"Of course I do," she laughed. "You have some strange thoughts sometimes."

She then offered to help me in any way she could with Ran. She even suggested that I ask her mother for help, should I need it, as the woman had seven children of her own, after all. I insisted that I wouldn't be troubling them so; I wanted to deal with my own problems on my own.

Ran soon finished his feeding, and I held him up to my face and watched him. I watched his eyes close, and soon the boy had drifted into deep sleep. It wasn't hard for even me to understand why people often see children as small miracles. My own miracle was that I had survived. I wondered if I had been forgiven, and silently renewed my pledge to raise Ran as best as I could in my mother's name. Because even then, terrified as I was of this tiny thing, somehow I knew that my mother couldn't have died swearing revenge against me. Even I couldn't have summoned up such hatred against my child if he really had forced Leta to cut me open. Even I couldn't have . . .

I soon thought of Gaar, and the war he was fighting, and I missed him then. I wanted him to see that I was still alive, and that he was now the father that I knew he longed to be. Tears threatened to cloud my eyes, but I fought them off, for I didn't wish my friend to see how sad I was.

In spite of Leta's generous words, I tried to work with Ran by myself for some time before I finally had to break down and admit that it was a hopeless cause. I visited Leta and her family, and especially her mother, and admitted to her that I needed help—a lot of it. Fortunately, Leta was correct about her mother, and the woman gave me all the advice she could think of, and then some. And for once, I was willing to learn something, listened to everything she said. She showed me how to clean, bathe, clothe, and feed him (or that is, the most comfortable way for *me* to feed him!), and gave other advice as how to keep Ran happy.

Three months later, the word came back that Castrill had won the war and was now looting Westmont, apparently to end its threat once and for all. I had taken part in raids and pillages before, but I rarely enjoyed them, much preferring to destroy soldiers over unarmed civilians. Word also returned that Tetulius had perished in the combat, but no information was available on Taran's life, or most importantly, on Gaar's.

The men returned some three days after their victory was made known, and rarely have I seen so much rejoicing as on that day in Castrill. It resembled the day of the men's departure, only this time the tears were shed in joy and relief. Except for the tears for those who did not return.

As in all wars, along with the triumph of Castrill was the inevitable grief and sense of loss for the brave ones who died defending the land.

I searched for Gaar the day they returned, but could not find him among the throngs of soldiers and their rejoicing families. I carried Ran with me in a pouch that I wore in the front, and the awful noise and confusion distressed him and he screamed and bawled incessantly. His distress only echoed my own as I tried to search for my husband and to comfort the boy—both efforts in vain.

I gave up after several hours, and trod solemnly home, hoping that I might see him waiting for me there and I could show him my joy in private, as it was meant to be.

I searched both rooms of our hovel thoroughly, but he was not there. Ran, meanwhile, had wet himself and was crying, and I silently removed him from the pouch and cleaned him (and myself), hoping to lose my thoughts in this activity. The sun was setting when I finished, but I didn't bother to light any candles or lanterns, preferring to hold my son close to me and to try to soothe my own tears by soothing his.

It was time for both of us to eat, but I cared for neither food nor drink. Ran would not be deprived, however, and I took him to my breasts until he became limp in my arms, and I carried him into the darkness of the bedroom and placed him into the cradle. After covering him with his blankets, I lay on the bedding next to him and wished for sleep to come soon.

I grabbed my pillow and swung behind me at the one who was nudging me. I was in no mood for games, and I wanted to be left alone in my tears of bitterness. But the pillow was snatched from my hands, and I rolled over to confront my tormentor. It was morning, and the sun shone behind him, making him little more than a silhouette. But it was a familiar silhouette.

"Gaar!" I screamed, and sat up, throwing my arms around him and kissing him and holding him tight. "You've come home! You've come back . . ."

"Yes," he whispered. "It's over."

"I thought you were dead—"

"It was close sometimes—"

"I looked for you—"

"I tried to get to you, but I couldn't—"

"I waited here for you—"

"I missed you, my love. My wife . . ."

"I wanted to go with you. Fight with you—"

"I know. I know that, but it wasn't possible—"

"Oh, Gods, you've come back . . . you've come back . . ."

Slowly, he pushed me from him, and neither of us could hold back our tears for long. We laughed and wept together. Soon afterward, I took Ran from his cradle and handed him to his father, who at first held him awkwardly until I corrected him. Gaar nodded his head and smiled.

"A son," he whispered. "You've given me a son."

"Leta said that—that you'd be happy about having a son."

"Yes," he said. "But son—daughter—it matters little. What's important is that you've made me a father."

"That's all you wanted?" I asked.

"Yes," he whispered. "Or—no. I wanted a family; that's what I wanted most." I sensed some sadness in his words, and I meant to ask him about his family in Actium, but he leaned over and kissed my lips gently, and handed me the child. Then he scooted closer to the two of us and brushed my hair with his fingers.

The rest of the day was spent just being a family for the first time. It was one of the best days of my life.

* * *

The next day, the magistrate produced Tetulius's will, after all the proper funeral ceremonies had been performed. Over a thousand citizens crowded around the platform near the marketplace, hoping to hear of the city's newfound wealth. Taran, who had returned alive, was given a small portion of Tetulius's wealth in recognition of his friendship and devotion. The magistrate continued reading the will, and the people waited for some statement indicating that the rest of the estate would be open to them. But it was not to be. According to the will, the beneficiary of all the rest of the estate was the magistrate himself. The stunned silence that followed allowed the magistrate to continue in a lower voice as he announced his intention to ask the governor to appoint Arem as their next leader, for the current one (himself) had decided to retire and settle into his new home.

The uproar as he left the platform was tremendous, and many cried "Fraud" and "Hoax" to the magistrate and his men. Others tried to snatch the will from his hands, only to be pushed aside by brutish bodyguards. Taran followed the magistrate determinedly through the crowd. Though I was disappointed in the general's will, I was not interested in following the crowd to the bureaucrats' building; but Gaar elected to continue on, out of curiosity. I agreed to wait for him at home.

Eight

Gaar was not home terribly often over the next few days after his return. He found the whole controversy over the will to be rather exciting, and he was spending a lot of time with Taran, trying to figure out what was really going on. Gaar mentioned to me that I shouldn't talk to anyone about what he and Taran were doing, but since I didn't really understand what they were doing, anyway, I had nothing to talk about. I spent most of my time with Leta, whose parents were trying to marry her off. I think she was fifteen by this time, which was about the age when parents began the search for a suitable husband for their daughters with a vengeance. So far, they hadn't found one. Leta put up a good facade about how she wasn't wise enough to choose her own husband, but I knew her too well by this time.

Gaar came trodding home one day, his head down in what seemed to be near-despair. I guided him to a couch and rubbed his shoulders while I asked him his troubles. He said that he and Taran had exposed Tetulius's will as a fake and had spent the past few days looking for the authentic one. In it, a good portion of his estate had been given to the city, not the magistrate, and they had exposed *him,* as well, to the Army. I thought that was wonderful news, until Gaar pointed out that some half of the Army had rebelled and stormed the magistrate's house. Gaar, Taran, and other men tried to bring things under control, but the rebels won, and killed the magistrate for treason. I saw nothing wrong with that, but then Gaar reminded me that the city was left with no leader. Well, better than a rotten one, I said, but Gaar disagreed. He'd never been a real follower of anarchy.

This was one time when local politics had a very direct effect on me. I should have paid more attention then. But this is what happened: Gaar became the magistrate.

We certainly were surprised. Gaar expected Taran to take the position, even though he didn't want it, but it was not to happen. Not quite, but almost behind our backs, Taran sent Gaar's name to the governor and praised Gaar to high heaven, apparently, for the recommendation returned saying "yes."

The soldiers liked Gaar, and were quite happy with his appointment. The people's reaction was mostly "Gaar who?"; after all, we had only lived in Castrill for about a year. The people had little power to decide on their leaders, unfortunately, but at least those who did know Gaar were not displeased.

Leta and her family were ecstatic for us, of course, and Leta offered me a blanket she had made as a congratulatory gift. I declined as graciously as I could, but she insisted I take it; Leta is not the easiest person to turn down, and I soon owned a new blanket.

A new house, too. We moved into the magistrate's house almost immediately, and I don't think I need compare it to the hovel. Our bedroom alone was larger than the entire hovel, and there were plenty more rooms where that one came from. There were private eating rooms besides the huge banquet hall, conference rooms, servants' rooms (not to mention the servants that occupied them!), a huge kitchen, and I could go on, but I'd much rather concentrate on more important things. I must say, however, that even the humblest of today's homes are much more comfortable and cozy than the magistrate's house was, but by fourth-century standards, this was one luxurious place!

We even had a separate room for Ran. I rarely, if ever, used it, however, at least not while he was a baby. I insisted that he sleep in our room during that time. Gaar wasn't exactly thrilled about that, but he soon learned that it wasn't a good idea to argue with me as far as taking care of Ran was concerned.

Gaar criticized me for spoiling Ran so. I always dropped everything and ran to him whenever he cried and insisted that he be near me at all times, which often caused quite an inconvenience, as one might imagine.

But Gaar had more important things to worry about besides my spoiling his son. As magistrate, he had an entire city to worry about, and since he was new, it would take him some time to solve the basic problems and learn all the intricacies of Castrill's politics. All this work, under the shadow of the will scandal! Gaar set himself to settling everything once and for all, including all sorts of legal problems, changes in staff, and so on.

There were also a few other problems that were not ironed out so quickly or easily, and they, for the most part, came from me. For one thing, I was still dressing in my ten-year-old vest and shirt—and the sword, of course. At first, when he began his magistracy, Gaar simply gave me some money to go buy some dresses. After all, now that he was magistrate, he couldn't be a warrior anymore, either—at least, not in practice. To me, he would always be wearing his vest.

I would make excuse after excuse, at first, for not buying any new clothes. Usually they had to do with my being too busy; I had to settle into our new home, after all. Too much to do. Gaar was clearly frustrated but didn't push me, considering that he had so many problems already. Meanwhile, I made sure to offer him a loving ear whenever he had a problem, so he couldn't complain much, could he?

But then *I* started becoming one of Gaar's major problems. My attire became more than a personal issue between us. Gaar was now a public figure. He was the magistrate of a city that had just killed its previous leader and killed or banished his closest associates. Gaar had to clean up his predecessor's mess, and, because of this, criticism of anyone replacing the old leader would be especially severe. Severe for him, for his associates, and for his family. Now I was more than some strange woman who dressed like a man; I was a shadow, a blot on Gaar's reputation. I knew about the gossip, I even heard some of it directly, but I'd been hearing gossip about me for my entire life, and my reaction had always been to keep on doing whatever it was that bothered the talkers, even do more of it, just out of spite. This was part of the reason why I always hated politics, and now that I was right in the middle of *them,* I hated politics even more.

We were arguing about everything. Mostly about stupid things; in fact, I don't even remember what we'd been arguing about. But when Gaar brought up the dress issue again, and especially all the gossip that not only I, but he, too, was the subject of, I lied and told him the gossip didn't bother me at all, so he called me selfish and tried to explain about our responsibility to all the denizens of Castrill. And then he said that many people were saying I wasn't even a woman, which I knew about, anyway, but then he also said that he was beginning to wonder that himself! Now, considering that I had wondered that for some time myself, one would think that such a comment wouldn't really bother me. Wrong! I was already angry enough, since we were in the middle of arguing, but that last comment made me furious. I struck Gaar in the face. I don't mean a nice womanly slap, either. God forbid I should do that; that wouldn't be like a warrior at all. I planted a good, hard fist right onto the side of his face, and it wasn't until the deed was done that I realized what had happened.

This was not the brawl I'd started outside the inn; this was a wife striking her husband. And I knew that, and I was horrified at what I'd done. Gaar was horrified, too, but not so much so that he couldn't react. Before I could blurt out any apologies, he sent me sprawling across the room with an even stronger counterblow to *my* face.

"Wench!" he roared. "How dare you strike me! How *dare* you? You know I could have you killed for that, don't you? Don't you?"

I was too full of tears to apologize or fight back or beg forgiveness or do or say anything at all. All I could do was continue holding my face in pain and sob and listen to him roar some more.

"Do you think I'm some lowly beggar living in the streets, to do that to me? Get away from me! Get away until you've learned to act like a decent human being! Go on—get out of here!"

I paid no attention to where he was actually pointing, but I raced out the door as fast as I could, avoiding his gaze the whole way, and burst into our bedroom and slammed the door. I dove onto our bed and buried my head in a pillow, thinking only: *What have I done? Oh, Gods, what have I done?*

When Gaar entered our bedroom, my tears were just beginning to stop flowing. It was obvious that his anger was only just beginning to cool, as well. He came in noisily, slammed the door shut again, and gave me several angry looks while he dug through drawers and cupboards for something or other. At last he found what he was looking for, and he came over to me and loomed above me, arms akimbo. The sight of him made the tears flow again, and I looked away to cry.

"Look at me when I tell you this," he commented. I turned toward him but still couldn't bring myself to look him in the eyes.

"I know how important being a warrior is to you," he said. "I was one myself; I know what the vest stands for. But you just don't understand, do you? You just can't get it through your stubborn little head that you don't need the vest to be a true warrior. What are you afraid of, girl? Are you afraid to be a woman?"

I still couldn't answer him.

"I have been as patient with you as a man could possibly be, and this is how I'm repaid! Was I right about you, girl? *Are* you capable of feelings?"

"Yes . . ." I sobbed.

"Well, then, prove it!" he snapped. "Show you have even the least bit of consideration for other people, and take the money I've given you and buy those damned dresses!"

"I'm sorry," I whispered into the pillow.

"What?"

"I'm sorry," I repeated. Gaar said nothing, but reached out and pulled the pillow from my hands and threw it to the other side of the room.

"Now . . ." he said. "What were you saying?"

I sniffled and wiped some tears away.

"I'm sorry," I repeated.

"Sorry for what?" he demanded. "Sorry for dressing like a man all the time? Sorry for what?"

"For . . . for hitting you . . ." I forced out. "For . . . for everything, I—I'm sorry . . ."

"So what's to be done about that, then?" he asked.

"Everything I do is wrong," I said. "All wrong . . ." Then my words were buried completely under tears. I heard Gaar sigh and start pacing back and forth.

"You're my wife, Mara," he said, his voice strangely calm now, "and I love you. You know that, you know that I don't hate you. But you just"—he made a noise in frustration—"you just can't be this way for the rest of your life! Don't you understand that it's not just—just wearing a dress . . ."

"I know that . . ." I blubbered. "I know. I've ruined things for you . . . I've messed up, as usual . . ."

"You haven't ruined things for me," he said. "But no later than tomorrow, I want you to fix this problem. Is that clear?"

"Yes . . ." I whispered. "It is. I'll do as you say, Gaar. No more arguing, I'll just do what you say."

"I'm not asking for total obedience," he said. "Only in this case. All right?"

"Yes . . ." I whispered. "All right."

"Good," he said. "In the meantime, dry your tears. You're an odd girl, and a terror, too, sometimes, but Gods help me, I still love you madly."

I smiled bittersweetly, but kept my gaze on the floor.

"I'll see you at dinner tonight, then, my wife," he said, and turned to leave. It was then that I had a great urge, greater than I'd felt before, to tell him something. Something I'd never told anyone else before—ever.

"Gaar," I said so softly that I was afraid he wouldn't hear. He stopped and turned, however.

"Yes?" he said.

It took me a long time to say it, but I wouldn't let him leave before I'd forced it out.

"I love you."

There was a long silence, and then he walked slowly toward me, and then bent over to kiss me gently on the lips. When we parted, he kept his face very close to mine.

"I know," he whispered.

That night Gaar gave me even more money to go into the marketplace and buy some clothes. I promised to buy plenty of dresses, and I even considered asking Leta to help me.

She was thrilled to help me shop for new clothes, and I lost count of all the dresses and material she ended up thrusting in my face all day long. I had no concept of what was fashionable at the time. By the end of the day I was exhausted, and only had two outfits to show for it. That satisfied Gaar, however, and from then on, when Leta had the time, she would direct me to things that she thought suited me. She even got me to start arranging my hair in different ways; usually it was just pinned up, but sometimes I let her practice her braiding technique on me. She seemed to really like playing with my hair—no doubt because it was long and straight and took easily to many arrangements. I've worn my hair short these days, however.

Also, the night I bought my new clothes, I brought Gaar to our family hearth, and threw my vest into the flames. This startled him, and he tried to pull it out, but I wouldn't let him. I told him that I had decided I was no longer a warrior—period. He tried to go on about how I could always be a warrior in my heart, blah blah, but he was missing my point. I was rejecting what to me had always been the warrior: the mercenary. The killer for pay. That was a fruitless, empty life for me now. It had caused far too much pain and heartache, and it was time to put aside that pain and embrace a new life. From then on, I would be a wife, a mother, a friend—but never again a killer.

So I became the most devoted, loyal, and obedient wife that a woman could be. From then on, I lived to serve my husband and family and was proud of it, too. I never had any regrets about my decision. For the first time in my life, I felt happy and fulfilled, even redeemed for the life I once led.

We had another son, Tirell, two and a half years after Ran was born. I wanted Gaar to witness the birth, but that was one thing I couldn't change his mind about. He just wouldn't watch, period. By this time Leta had also been married and was working on producing her own children. She'd had her first child—a daughter—by the time we had our own daughter, Kiri. I must admit, I was a bit apprehensive about Gaar's reaction to Kiri. In fact, before he learned that he had a new daughter and not a son, I vowed to myself not to allow her to grow up hating herself or fearing men as I had. Fortunately, he was thrilled with Kiri, although I know that he really would have preferred another boy. Nevertheless, Gaar was a fine father and loved all of us deeply.

A little more reminiscing, if you'll allow me. Besides being extraordinarily patient and understanding, Gaar was also the most generous man I'd ever known. He couldn't seem to help buying gifts for me. Sometimes he didn't even need an occasion, such as when he surprised me one day with a beautiful emerald ring—"to match your eyes," as he put it. I wasted no time showing it to Leta and some other friends.

Another time, he arranged for me to have one full day at the public baths. That is, he paid in advance for every service they had so that I could choose whatever treatment I wished in the entire place. I'd never been there before and wasn't certain what to expect, but I ended up taking a private spring bath, a full one-hour massage (which put me right to sleep), and a manicure. I avoided the frilly beauty things like the mud packs and face-painting sessions. I had a wonderfully relaxing and freshing time there, and when I returned home, I treated Gaar to the best and longest lovemaking he'd ever had. He more than deserved it.

BOOK II

BOOK II

Nine

Eight of the best years of my life (not counting my present life, of course) ensued. I was thirty-one, Gaar was thirty-four, Leta was twenty-three, Ran was seven, Tirell was four, and Kiri was two. Leta's two children were Gwendolyn and Jonathan, ages four and two, respectively. Castrill prospered fairly well under Gaar's magistracy, or at least more so than under the former magistrate. For one thing, Gaar wasn't afraid to spend money or invest it, either. Gaar also alleviated the problem of Westmont by setting up a partial trade with them—partial because they really didn't have much to trade, and the city was still recovering from its defeat at our hands.

Gaar was always willing to expand Castrill's boundaries or extensions if possible. He was very interested in starting up trade with more coastal cities in Gaul if he could, but it wasn't always easy negotiating with the magistrates there.

Then one particular magistrate took an interest in setting up trade with Castrill. His city had wheat and other crops to share in exchange for our wood and coal.

His name was Agyar, and he contacted us first. He sent several messages inviting Gaar and me to come to Clovaine and talk. Gaar initially responded by sending other men to speak for him, as he was rather busy at the time. But each of the men were sent back with the message that Agyar would speak only with the magistrate. And he insisted that the magistrate's wife join him to "keep him company," as it might take a while to reach an agreement.

Quite frankly, the thought of having to sit through a bunch of trade negotiations gave me the heebie-jeebies, but Gaar talked me into going along with him. He didn't want to go, either, and thought it rather arrogant of Agyar to *demand* that he go. But if Gaar was to go, then I would go along with him.

I surely wanted to be with Gaar, but I also didn't want to leave all my friends and family behind. Leta certainly couldn't go, and it would have been terribly inconvenient and even rude of me to take my own children with us to Gaul. They were so young, you see . . .

Kiri cried because she knew Mama and Papa were leaving, but I did my best to assure her that we would be returning to her. I promised her we would come back; I promised all of the children. But I was unable to say goodbye to Leta when we left; actually, I gave her my good-byes some time later in Gaul. You'll understand what I mean later.

We reached the other side of the Channel around late afternoon, and by the time we reached Clovaine, the sun was just setting. Agyar sent a carriage to take us to him, but I can't say I felt all that comfortable with our driver; a rather creepy-looking fellow, he was, all pale and emaciated.

I could tell right away that the nightlife here was about as dead as Castrill's before Gaar took over the magistracy. Nearly all of the homes and hovels we passed by were shut up tightly, and only if one looked closely was it possible to see any light coming from shuttered windows.

I was not awestruck by Agyar's home when we arrived. Gaar was a magistrate himself, remember, and I was now a bit spoiled by our very spacious living quarters. Agyar's home may not have been as wide or long as ours, but it was taller, with three stories as opposed to our two. It was also rather brightly colored and well lit. Our creepy-looking driver soon pointed out the obvious—that it was Agyar's home—to us, and headed us for the stables.

We were directed to the main entrance, where we were to wait for someone to take us to our room before meeting the magistrate. Gaar was pleased that Agyar wanted to make sure that we felt comfortable before business commenced. I was momentarily distracted from what he was saying when I felt as though someone were watching us, or if not both of us, then me.

We were soon joined by one of Agyar's servants, who quickly summoned some other servants to carry our things to our room. Gaar was clearly enjoying the attention, and taking my arm, we followed the servant to our quarters.

They were only slightly larger than our own room, but with the pleasant addition of a balcony overlooking all of Clovaine. I was drawn to the balcony immediately and went outside, ignoring Gaar's chatter.

"The magistrate would like to know if you have eaten dinner, and, if not, a feast will be prepared for you immediately, if you wish," said the servant.

"Yes. Yes, we'd like that," said Gaar. "I'm starving. Mara? My wife, are you hungry?"

"Hmm?" I said, tearing myself away from the view beyond the balcony.

"Agyar has been kind enough to offer us dinner," Gaar said.

"Oh," I said. "Yes. Yes, good; I'm half starved," I finished, and then turned back to the view.

Soon after the servant left, Gaar crept by my side and placed an arm around me.

"These quarters are marvelous," he murmured. "I've always wanted to sleep in a room with a balcony."

"Mmmhmm."

"Aren't you cold?" he asked, rubbing my shoulders. "Hmm?"

"Your arms are so cold. Can't you feel it?"

"Mmm. No, I suppose I didn't," I said, but now felt the cold once I'd been reminded of it. Gaar left my side to bring me a cloak, and we stood silently in the almost-full moonlight, breathing in the night air.

"We'd better see what they're serving us," Gaar said suddenly.

"Aren't they going to call us?"

"Mmm. I suppose they will. But I'm so hungry . . ."

"I've been much hungrier than this," I said.

"In the old days," he said. "Yes, I suppose we've both been spoiled by wealth. It makes one forget about those who still struggle, but it doesn't make one forget hunger," he joked, slapping his belly. Then he sighed loudly and leaned onto the balcony wall.

"This place *is* lovely," he whispered. "Even at night."

"How do you know it looks good in the daytime?" I said. "You can't see very much now."

"There you go, spoiling things," he scolded.

I shrugged. "I'm sorry; I don't really know why I said that. I've always been that way. You know that."

"True," he said, and stood up straight. "But I love you, anyway, complaints and all," he added, and began kissing me, slowly at first, but then harder until he was practically tearing my clothes off in the moonlight. I put my hands between us and pushed him away.

"Gaarius!" I cried (I called him that when I was upset with him). "Stop that; what if they announced dinner all of a sudden?"

"Mmm, food isn't the only thing I'm hungry for," he growled playfully.

"Later, Gaar, later," I teased. "Gods, you know I don't like it when you're like that."

"Then perhaps you'll both be in higher spirits after

you've dined," a voice called suddenly from behind us. Gaar and I both whirled around, startled, as a silhouette stood in the doorway. It moved slowly toward us into the candlelight, and then we could see that it could only be our host.

He was tall, but not as tall as Gaar or even I. His dark, curly hair only made his somewhat pale skin seem that much paler. He was leaner than Gaar, but not thin—more like wiry, if anything. Agyar greeted us in fancy Roman dress, no doubt to impress us. Our own clothing was fancy, too, but dirty from the long, dusty trip to Agyar's home.

He moved quickly to us and extended both hands to Gaar in greeting.

"Welcome, sir," he said. "I am the magistrate here—Agyar. I hope you enjoyed the trip here."

"It was well enough. And I am the magistrate, Gaarius," he said.

"Please accept my apologies for refusing to see anyone but you," Agyar continued. "It's the way I am, you see. I've had too many problems with bumblers to trust anyone less than the top man."

"I see," said Gaar. "Well, let's just hope we can work quickly, then. I *do* have—"

"Of course, of course," Agyar interrupted. "We both have cities to run. I assure you all this will take only a few days at best."

"Good," said Gaar. Agyar then diverted his attention to me.

"And this . . ." he began. "This must be your lovely wife."

"Yes," said Gaar. "My wife, Mara. Mara—the magistrate, Agyar."

I said nothing at all. I didn't realize it until later, but I had been staring at Agyar from the moment he entered the room. He was not blindingly handsome; nor did he strike me down with charm or wit. But I couldn't help just staring

at him, even while he bowed slightly in greeting. Then he
motioned for us to follow him, and it was only after Gaar
nudged me once that I snapped out of my trance and took
his waiting hand into mine.

Dinner was marvelous. Or maybe it was because I was
so hungry. Gaar ingested three servings of roast pig, vege-
tables, bread and butter, and two cups of wine. I ate less
than he, but enjoyed every bite. Agyar, meanwhile, had only
a few chunks of meat and a carrot on his plate; he explained that he had eaten most of his meal already and
wasn't terribly hungry. But he insisted that we pay no heed
to his own measly servings and eat our fills, and then some.

I paid little attention to the majority of the table conversation; it was mostly Gaar and our host chatting about their
respective cities. I don't think they were trying to compete
with each other, but they each occasionally exaggerated the
good features of their lands. A natural thing, I suppose.

I made an effort not to stare this time, as the realization
that I had been doing so earlier embarrassed and shamed
me. I had never stared at anyone other than Gaar like that
before, and I felt myself suppressing the notion that Agyar
might actually have fascinated me.

After dinner, Agyar offered to give us a personal tour
of his home, but Gaar and I were exhausted from all that
traveling and had to postpone the offer. So Agyar simply
escorted us back to our room to bid us good night.

"Sleep well, sir—and lady," he said. "And may you have
lovely dreams, as well," he added, but looked at me as he
spoke those words. I shifted a little uncomfortably and
looked down out of nervousness.

"Thank you," said Gaar. "Thank you. And the same to
you."

"Uh—" Agyar suddenly said as we were about to shut
the door, "I'm afraid we cannot meet tomorrow."

"What?" said Gaar, a little annoyed.

"Not until the evening, I'm afraid," Agyar clarified. "I

have business in town all day tomorrow and can't be back here until the evening, you see. You will forgive the inconvenience, won't you?"

"Uhh, certainly," said Gaar.

"Good," he said. "Until tomorrow evening, then, my home and my servants are at your disposal. Do what you wish with them, until we meet again."

"Thank you, Agyar," Gaar said as politely as he could. "Until tomorrow, then." Then he shut the door, and we were alone, finally.

Gaar sighed once and shook his head. "Arrogant," he grumbled. "First he demands that I come personally and then we must wait for him all day."

"Well . . . maybe he can't really help having business in town," I offered.

"I think he can. If I demanded to see another magistrate I would make certain I had no other business to distract me."

"I know that," I said. "But then—"

"And I don't like the way he looks at you."

"What?"

"I said, I don't like the way he looks at you. Gawking at you all night. Does he think I wouldn't see something like that?"

"Gawking at me?"

"Yes!" he said. "*You* certainly noticed it. You've been gawking at *him* all night, too."

"I haven't."

"You have. You were practically in a trance when he first greeted us."

"A trance?" I cried. "But I—but— Well, I wasn't really looking at *him*—"

"Then what *were* you looking at?" he demanded.

"Nothing," I lied. "I was only thinking. You know—you begin thinking, and then you start staring . . . ?"

"I see," he said. "So you're saying you see absolutely nothing in the man?"

"Of course not!" I cried. "I can't believe you would accuse me of that! I've been faithful to you; I have *always* been faithful to you, and I always will—"

"All right, all right," he interrupted. "I'm sorry, love. I only—I'm just exaggerating. But only for *you;* Agyar has no excuse. He *was* gawking at you all night."

"Well . . . I should tell him not to, then."

"No. *I'll* tell him, if he continues," he said. Then he moved to my side and kissed me on the temple.

"You're right, love," he continued. "You've never been unfaithful to me, and no, you never would be, either."

"Thank you," I whispered.

"Thank *you,*" he insisted. "For always being there when I needed you—for standing by my side. And I'm glad you're here now, to keep me company."

"I wish the children could be with us."

"So do I," he said. "But they'll be fine. We'll only be gone a week, at most. We'll see them again soon."

We passed several minutes embracing and kissing before climbing into bed. Agyar had provided us with a wonderfully comfortable bed, which was exactly what we needed to end an exhausting day.

Gaar, being the friendly fellow that he was, spent a good portion of the next day chatting with some of Agyar's servants. I noticed that there didn't seem to be too many around—maybe some stable workers, and of course the people who prepared our food. I really wondered if those people ate enough themselves; not a chunky or fat person within miles of us, it seemed, but they certainly pulled out the stops to feed *us.* Agyar's orders, no doubt.

Meanwhile, I took to aimlessly wandering about the house. It was quite richly decorated. Every room had an entire wall painted, statues, vase collections, or some other fine work of art within, and I noticed a few busts and paintings of Agyar himself scattered throughout the house. And I caught myself staring not a few times at these, as well. *What am I staring at?* I wondered. *There's nothing so wonderful about him, is there? I must stop this; Gaar is right. He doesn't deserve this from me, after he's been so wonderful to me all these years . . .*

I went back to our room before lunchtime. Gaar was off, still talking with Agyar's people, I surmised. And I was tired and not a little bored, trying to pass the time away all day long. And then I looked on our bed, and there lay the finest suit and finest dress I'd ever seen. *How did these get here?* I thought. *Whose are these?* And then I noticed there was a note on the dress, and it said in Latin: "Gifts for the magistrate and his wife. Your humble host, Agyar." I was enthralled. He had had his servants lay these clothes out for us as a surprise. Immediately, I swept up the dress into my arms and held it in front of me before our mirror. *I can't possibly accept this,* I thought. I become so embarrassed when I'm given gifts. *And Gaar will probably be furious to know that Agyar is giving me gifts now. But wait—he gave Gaar a fine suit, too. He's just being generous, that's all. But I couldn't accept this; or— I could at least try it on quickly, just to see if it fits. I'm certain it doesn't fit . . .*

It fit perfectly. He either knew my size before I even arrived there, or he was an excellent estimator. I opted to believe the latter explanation. The dress was green, with blue-and-red trim, and it emphasized my modest hips perfectly while deemphasizing my broad shoulders. I didn't really want to admit it, but it looked lovely on me, and I decided that Gaar had to see me in it, if only for a little while. Just during lunch, at least.

Gaar had tried his suit on and liked it. He was angry, but also pleased that Agyar was giving us gifts, especially such expensive ones. Gaar was always generous to his own guests, but not to the point of excess. I commented that he was probably just being extra nice to us because our trip there was an inconvenience, and Gaar agreed that I was probably right. And besides—I had seen that look in Gaar's eyes when he first saw me in the dress; he was definitely pleased.

Agyar joined us after we had already started dinner. He mentioned that his business in town had been tedious, as usual, but then announced that it was not going as well as he wished, and he would have to leave us for the day tomorrow, as well. Gaar was naturally not very pleased with this news, but there wasn't much he could do about the situation. Then Agyar complimented us profusely on how our gifts looked on us and thanked us for accepting them. Again I noticed him lingering his gaze on me, and I felt more uncomfortable than before, not so much for the idea of being stared at as for Gaar's potential reaction to it. But Gaar kept calm about the whole thing, commenting later that he was more interested in getting the trade set up quickly so we could leave than starting any diplomatic incidents.

And despite their short times together, Gaar and Agyar seemed to be getting along well enough in the negotiations, even by only the second night. But once they got started on that topic, I knew it was time for me to leave them alone in their business and go elsewhere. At first I meant to just go straight for our room, but then I decided to just wander around a little more. I ended up on the third floor, where there were mostly storerooms and such, but just above that was the roof, and I decided to look around up there.

There was nothing particularly special about the roof. It was flat and spacious—perfect for just walking back and forth in the night air, if one so chose. I made my way toward a wall and leaned forward to see the grounds below.

I could see nothing, as it was practically pitchblack now. It was just one day away from the full moon, however, and the light from this made some shadows visible every now and then. Mostly, I just sat and listened—listened to the sounds below, and some even coming from the small forest nearby. Again, I became so lost in my thoughts that I scarcely noticed the cold, until I heard some strange noises. They came from below, toward the stables a little bit, and I assumed it was the animals skittering around a bit. But then, I know the sounds of horses and pigs and cows and sheep and goats, and these sounds didn't seem like they were coming from any of those animals. I actually thought rather little of what it might be, when I heard another sound, directly behind me. It was my name; someone had whispered my name, I was sure of it, and I whirled around immediately, startled.

I could see nothing. The roof suddenly seemed blacker than before; I could barely even see my own hands before me. And I was afraid, that much I knew, but as Gaar had taught me, I was no longer letting my fear rule me.

"Who said that?" I whispered harshly. "Who's there?"

No answer. Not even the sound of the wind.

"Gaar?" I continued. "Did you call me? Gaar?"

Dead silence. Now I was becoming worried for myself; I seemed to be hearing things. Then I remembered that it was almost the full moon, and that it can make people hear and do strange things. I needed to get inside, then, away from its influence, and I especially shouldn't go out the next night, either.

Almost the same activities ensued the next day while waiting for Agyar, only Gaar was a little chummier with Agyar's people this time. He talked a few of the friendlier ones into playing card games with him after that night's negotiations. They were too busy to join him during the day, they had told him. Gaar asked if I wanted to join, but I had never really been interested in gambling games, and I declined his offer. This, and I was still a little frightened by my experience on the roof, not to mention what happened as we slept that night, as well. You see, I was awakened later on that night by the same feeling I had experienced on the roof; I thought I had heard—no, not heard, *felt*—my name being called, and when I sat up in bed, I saw no one. At least I think there was no one there; I saw nothing, but then I definitely had the sensation that someone was watching me, someone who was either too cowardly to show him or herself, or too devious. It took me some time after that incident, but I eventually fell asleep again and was undisturbed the rest of the night.

Dinner was exquisite as usual, and I excused myself to return to our room after the business talks started up again. Gaar had brought some books to read for our trip, and since he had long ago taught me to read Latin and Greek, I had something to do to pass the time away.

I read as much as I could handle by the dim candlelight without going mad from boredom—most of the books were about philosophy, you see—before I closed up the books and headed for our balcony again. It was the full moon now, and one could see Clovaine off in the distance quite well, and the silhouette of the little forest to the east. I began thinking about Castrill, then, and the people we had left behind for all this, and I began to miss them all: Leta, the children, even Leta's children. They were all so dear to me, and I wanted them there with me, or better yet, that Gaar and I could go home.

Then I heard my name again, and I almost fell from turning around so quickly, I was so startled. This time someone was there.

"Oh!" I cried. "By the Gods, Gaar, please don't . . . oh . . ."

I could see as he came from the shadows that it wasn't

Gaar. It was Agyar. Silly that I could ever mistake the two, considering how little they resembled each other. His face became clear as he moved under the moonlight, and he smiled.

"No, it is not your husband," he said. "Only I. Gaarius is entertaining my people, it seems."

"Oh," I said, still a little flustered. "Oh, yes. He told me about that."

"I'm glad that he can enjoy himself here," he continued. Then: "And you? Are you enjoying my home?"

"Hmm? Oh, yes. It's very nice," I said. "You've been very generous to us."

"I try to treat all my guests as well as I can," he said. "Or at least the important ones."

I smiled a little, embarrassed. "Thank you again for the dress," I said. "It's lovely."

"Think nothing of it," he said. "It was only to make your stay more comfortable. But what else might I do for you, to make your stay better?"

"Better?" I echoed. "No, really—everything here is just fine. There's nothing more you need do for me . . ."

"If you insist."

We were both silent for a long time. Agyar stood closer to me than I felt he should, and it then dawned on me that I wasn't supposed to be outside during the full moon.

"What are you thinking of?" he asked suddenly.

"Hmm?"

"What are you thinking of?" he repeated.

"Oh—nothing, really," I said. "Just of home. Friends, and family."

"Do you have many?" he asked.

"Friends or family?"

"Either."

I sighed once and leaned over the railing.

"Neither, really. Only Gaar, and our three children. And my very good friend and her children. Beyond that, I have only some acquaintances. But that's all I need, really. I've never needed to be surrounded by hundreds of people."

"Neither have I," he said. "We are alike that way. We like to be alone."

"Only sometimes," I said. "I've learned that always being alone breeds loneliness. And I hope I never have to be lonely again."

"I, also," he said.

I sighed again and propped my head up on my arm. "And I do miss them," I whispered. "Ran and Tirell and Kiri. And Leta."

"Your children?" he asked.

I nodded. "And my friend," I added.

"Well . . . it ought to be all over soon," he said. "Then you may see them again."

"Yes."

We stood in silence for an even longer time before either of us spoke again. Agyar began staring at the moon, as I was, too, I then realized.

"The moon," he whispered. "How it seems to stare at us always. I like to think of it as an eye, almost, that can gaze at us, wide-eyed, as it does now, or that can wink at us, as it does at the crescent."

"I've never really thought of it that way," I said.

He laughed once. "One can think of the moon in any way, really. As an eye. As a great white flame that flickers over a month's time. As the sun of the night, giving life to those that live by night as the sun gives life to all other things."

"But the moon can be dangerous," I said. "It can make people go mad."

"Do you truly believe that?" he asked, turning to face me.

"Me?" I said, moving back a little. "Well, that's what they say, anyhow. Stay away from the full moon, they say; it can make you go mad."

Agyar began staring at me for so long that I was beginning to get nervous again. Then he slowly opened his mouth to smile.

"You stand in its light now," he said. "Do you feel . . . mad?"

"No," I said. "I don't think I'm mad. But it could still happen, I think."

"I think . . ." he began, turning toward the railing again, "I think the moon only brings out what is truly inside us. We are animals, all of us, and perhaps the moon only brings that out. But man, vain as he is, doesn't want to believe that he is an animal. He wants to be so much more than that. But when others come along to prove otherwise, they call them mad and lock them away somewhere, or put them to death."

"Umm . . . yes, I suppose that could be true," I said.

"But for all man's incredible accomplishments, for all his knowledge and philosophy and science and art—he still must eat, he must sleep, drink, and breathe, just as all animals do. And he must die."

"I know," I whispered, now becoming a little uncomfortable. I had always avoided talking about death whenever possible.

"And he has even fought and struggled to avoid having to do all that," he continued. "To eliminate his hunger and thirst and need for sleep. And especially—his need to die."

I said nothing.

"Even I once fought and struggled to eliminate all this," he added. "But that was many years ago. Then I stopped searching."

I remained silent.

"Do you want to know why I stopped?" he asked. I said nothing, but only looked at him in curiosity.

"Because I found the answer," he announced. Now I gave him an incredulous look.

"It's true," he insisted, sensing my confusion and disbelief. "I have fought hunger and thirst and even death, and I have defeated them. I know how to avoid death now."

"That's impossible," I said.

"As I expected you to believe," he said. "But it is all true. I will not die—not from age, not from disease, not from starvation. I know the secret to immortality. And I can offer it to you, if you wish it."

"Wait a minute, wait a minute," I protested. "What do you mean, you won't die? All men must die. You just said that yourself."

"Not I," he insisted. "I cannot die. I am immortal."

"Only the Gods are immortal," I said. "And you're no god."

"You must be wrong, then, for I *am* immortal," he said. "Perhaps I am even a god."

"You should be careful. They often punish people for saying things like that."

"Oh, I am careful," he said, then cocked his head a little and threw me a wry smile.

"How old do you think I am?" he asked.

I shrugged.

"Give me a guess, anyway," he insisted.

"Thirty . . . five?" I said. He smiled even more and chuckled a little.

"Yes, I *do* look that age, don't I?" he said. "But I'm not thirty-five; not anymore. I'm more like . . . three thousands years old."

I didn't believe him for a minute.

"You're lying," I said.

He then moved his mouth right up to my ear and whispered, "I don't lie to you, wife of Gaarius. I am over three thousand years old, and I can easily be three thousand years older still. I will never age. And neither will you, if you wish me to share the secret."

"This is nonsense," I said, preparing to leave now.

"All right," he said, standing up straight now. "All right.

You're correct; it *is* nonsense. All of it. It was only a jest, as you said. After all, how could I possibly be three thousand years old? Not even Methuselah lived that long; no one could. Right?"

"Right."

"Then only answer me this, wife of Gaarius. What do you fear the most?"

"Excuse me?" I said.

"What is it that fills your sleep with nightmares, that haunts your almost every waking moment, that threatens to drive you almost mad because you know it's out there, waiting, and there's nothing you can—"

"I don't think I like this conversation anymore, Magistrate," I interrupted.

"Forgive me,"he said, bowing slightly. "But could you tell me the answer, if only to satisfy my curiosity?"

I frowned at him once and leaned over the railing again.

"I've . . . never really thought about my 'greatest fear,' " I said. "I've been afraid of so many things for too long. Only thanks to Gaar have I been able to conquer them and put them out of my mind."

"But they will always be there, whether you acknowledge them or not,"he said.

"I know that. But I'm not really sure what frightens me the most."

"Perhaps it is death which fills you with the most dread."

"Um . . . that may be so . . ."

"As I said, it's what men have been fighting since the dawn of time. It's only natural that it would be most men's greatest fear."

"I suppose that's true."

"It was *my* greatest fear. That's why I fought it for so long. But I need fear it no longer."

"Because you're 'immortal' now," I said.

"Let's not get into that. My question to you is this: do *you* want to be immortal?"

"Living forever?" I asked.

"Yes . . ."

"Never getting old . . ."

"Forever young . . . and beautiful . . ."

"It's only a fantasy, of course . . ."

"But is it something you want?"

"Nobody wants to die, really . . ."

"And neither do you, I'm certain . . ."

"No. No, I don't want to die. But—"

"I can make certain you never will. I can make you ageless."

"You told me you were jesting."

"I was lying. What I said before is the truth. Look at me. Look at me, wife of Gaarius. And let me show you what it means to live forever . . ."

Curious, I looked at him. And then I realized what had made me stare at him so often before. It was not his face; it was not his body or his manner of moving or his clothes. It was his eyes. It was his eyes that I had been so drawn to. It was his clear brown eyes that so fascinated me. No; they were not brown now. They were red. Like a red star that shines in the night, or the sun just after sunrise and just before sunset, Agyar's eyes glowed a bright red that burned clean through all the thought in my mind and went straight for the soul. I heard his voice in my mind, but not the words. They were only sounds—gentle, soothing sounds.

He kept on talking in that comforting way of his, and began touching me. I remember having no strength of my own to stand; he must have been supporting me completely. I remember that he began kissing me, and then I felt the slightest prick of pain that was just as quickly replaced by a gentle sucking, a soothing rush of warmth that felt as though warm water were being slowly poured over my shoulder. I shut my eyes and let my head fall back more and more as I began to feel an almost dizzying sensation of pleasure. All conscious thought was slowly leaving me, and I was ready to fall asleep in his arms.

Then I felt an awful tearing at my shoulder, and then I saw Gaar's face, peering at me worriedly. I could no longer see Agyar, and I wondered if he had ever been there at all. *Was I talking to Gaar the whole time?* I thought. *What is he saying?* But I could make out few of his words, only snippets of "—Attacked? —t's wrong?"

I meant to answer him, but my legs suddenly rebelled against me, and I began to fall. Gaar caught me up in his arms before I reached the floor and carried me immediately from the balcony.

Ten

My next memory was of Gaar again, seated in front of me and looking very worried. I felt somebody putting something onto my shoulder, and I looked up to see a thin, middle-aged woman wrapping bandages around my neck and shoulder. I recognized my surroundings as Agyar's kitchen. Gaar had carried me there, apparently. He then placed a hand onto my knee, and I looked at him.

"How do you feel?" he asked.

"Gaar?" I said.

"Yes. It's me. How do you feel?" he repeated. I breathed loudly once and shut my eyes. Then I reached my hand up to my shoulder and made to rub it, but Gaar took my hand gently into his own and shook his head.

"Don't touch that," he said. "You've been hurt there." The woman was now tying the bandages in place—firmly but not too tight.

"Do you remember what happened?" he asked. "Were you attacked?"

"Attacked?"

"Yes. Did someone attack you? Or some-thing?"

"Attacked . . ." I echoed distantly. "I don't . . . I don't remember."

"Was anyone in the room with you?" he asked. The woman made as if to leave the room, and Gaar called her to him quickly.

"Wait!" he cried. She looked at him vaguely. "Where is Agyar?" He asked.

"The master?" she asked.

"Yes. The magistrate," he said. "Where is he now?"

The woman shrugged. "I know not, sir. The master is where he wishes to be, as always."

"Well, not this time," he growled. "He needs to be found—*now*. He's going to hear of this."

"But I know not where he—"

"Then look—for—him," Gaar ordered. "I want to speak to him now. Can't you see what's just happened here? My wife has just been attacked by someone or some-*thing,* and he'd better do something about it!"

"I—" the woman stammered, "I— He will know, sir. He will know."

"Good," he grumbled. "Off with you, then."

He returned to my side as the woman scrambled hastily from the room.

"Weren't you a little harsh with her?" I asked.

"Considering how I feel now, I think I was very civil to her," he muttered. "That something like this would ever happen to you . . ."

"But I don't remember anything . . ."

"Try to, Mara," he said. "Try to remember. What did he look like? What did he say to you? Did he do anything else to you?"

"But I don't remember," I whispered. "I don't even know what happened . . . What happened? Why was I being bandaged?"

"You've been cut," he said, placing a hand on my shoulder. "Right here. Somebody cut you—no, more like punctured you—on the shoulder. It was—almost like a bite. That's why I wonder if it was an animal. Was it an animal? Did an animal attack you?"

I ignored Gaar's questions while I tried to piece together what few images remained in my memory. I remembered the moon, sometimes glowing white, sometimes red, and then some red eyes occasionally appeared. And I remembered hearing someone whispering, "Immortal," but that was all. I couldn't make sense of it, and I knew Gaar wouldn't be able to, either.

"I'm sorry," I said finally. "I can't remember who—or what—did that. I don't even know if I *was* attacked. Maybe I did it myself."

"Are you trying to say that you bit yourself?" he asked.

"No, of course not," I said. "Maybe I . . . I just don't remember, Gaar. Could I rest now? I'm so tired . . ."

"Yes," he said. "Yes, you'd better rest now. But I'll be damned if Agyar doesn't hear of this monstrosity. He has some madman or mad animal running around his house, and I won't sleep until he's done something about it!"

"You're not coming with me?" I asked.

"I'll come with you," he assured. "I'll make certain you're safely in bed, and all the doors and windows are locked tight. But I won't rest myself until I've seen him tonight. All right? Will you promise me to keep everything shut tight until I return?"

I nodded. "I'm not afraid, Gaar," I said. "I'll be all right."

"Good," he said, and rose to his feet and offered a hand to help me up. "This will not go unavenged," he said. "I'll kill the man or creature myself, if I find him."

I decided to say nothing.

We were on our own during the day, as usual. Gaar had apparently found Agyar the night before and demanded that he find the "madman" before sunrise. A servant informed us during lunch that "the one responsible"—some crazed servant, he claimed—had indeed been found, killed, and had his body thrown out into the forest for the wolves to get. Then he offered his sincerest apologies on behalf of the magistrate, who was of course horrified that something like this could ever happen in his home. I think Gaar was only vaguely satisfied by all this. For one thing, we were still made to wait around all day for Agyar to finish his "business" in town. I still had few memories of the night before, however.

"Now we can't leave," Gaar announced after lunch. "At least not until you get better."

"I feel fine, Gaar," I insisted. "We can easily leave once you figure out these trade problems. I'll have no trouble traveling."

"Hmph," he grumped. "Trade problems, indeed. We're coming along well enough, I suppose, but we could be done by now if Agyar weren't trying to do two things at once."

"Well . . ." I said. "He's just very busy. You're a magistrate, you know what it's like . . ."

"Of course I get busy," he said. "But I never leave guests waiting. And you know that."

"That's true," I said. "But not everyone is like you. He seems to be doing what he can, love."

Gaar said no more on that subject, and walked over to a small bookcase and browsed through some of Agyar's books.

"Many books," he muttered. "The man is well read enough." He skimmed a few more titles with his eyes.

"And many of them are in different languages," he continued. "I can't even recognize most of them . . ." he added, flipping through one book that looked to me like it was written in nonsense symbols. Then he quickly shut it, put it away, and sighed.

"You still don't remember what happened last night, do you?" he asked, going back to a familiar subject.

"No," I said. "No, I don't. I'm sorry. I really have been trying . . ."

"I know," he said. "I know. It must have been a horrible

experience for you, for you to forget it like that. People can do that, you know—forget things that are too horrible for them to remember."

"I guess that's what happened," I said.

Gaar placed his hand on my shoulder and leaned over to kiss my cheek. "I'm so sorry, my love," he whispered. "This should never have happened to you. I feel so ashamed that I wasn't with you—"

"It's not your fault."

"But if I'd only been there, instead of wasting time playing games . . ."

"I blame you for nothing, Gaar. You don't have to be by my side at every second. Besides, I was a warrior once. I know how to fight, I can defend myself—"

"But you weren't able to this time, remember?" he interrupted. "You were attacked by surprise, right?"

Again I tried to think back to the night before, to piece together my sparse memories and answer his question.

"I don't think so," I answered finally.

Gaar turned away from me momentarily and leaned onto the back of a chair. "I saw no one else in the room when I found you," he said. "No one leaving, trying to escape before I got there. Just you—with blood all over your shoulder. You weren't even beaten."

"Maybe I was, but don't remember."

"Where?" he asked. "I saw no bruises or other marks on you anywhere. Just some small cuts near your neck."

"Small cuts," I echoed. "They ought to be fine now, then. Can I take these bandages off, then? They make me sweat."

"Well . . ." he began in protest, then: "All right. I know you've had worse wounds before. Here; I'll take them off for you . . ."

He had to remove the top to my dress to unwrap the bandages, and I stood patiently for him while he worked, but not before he had shut and locked all the doors to the room—just to keep out the Peeping Toms, of course.

"Ah, you look all right now," he announced. "It's just that you had bled so much, for such small holes . . ."

"I do feel a little weak still," I said.

"You just need more rest now. I'll take you back to your room, and—"

"I don't want to sleep now," I protested. "Then I'll be wide awake all night."

"Not if you're still recovering like this," he said. "You lost a lot of blood; that's what's made you so weak. You'll sleep fine tonight."

"If you say so," I muttered. "I just . . ."

"Just what?"

"Just . . . I just want all this to be over with. I just want to go home. I miss everyone—Leta. Kiri. Ran and Tirell . . ."

"So do I, love," said Gaar. "So do I."

Gaar only spoke to Agyar on business matters now. No small talk, or idle chatter, or even friendly conversation. He was angry with all the things that had been happening to us, especially to me, and wanted to make that quite clear to Clovaine's magistrate. Agyar might have picked up on Gaar's discontent, but I don't believe he ever made it noticeable.

Gaar was pleased enough that he had almost reached an agreement with Agyar when he entered our room for the night. But we still had one more day to get through before they could finish up once and for all, and that made Gaar more than a little grumpy.

"All I care about is going home," I said.

"Me, too," he agreed. "But despite all the aggravation, this would be a good agreement to make, if we could only agree on it all a little faster. That's the only reason I've put up with this."

"Mmm," I said. "Well— Will you be coming to bed now?"

"Hmm? Oh, yes, I'd say this day is through for me," he said, and walked over to the balcony doors and shut and locked them tight.

"Couldn't we leave them open?" I asked.

He shook his head. "I'm not taking any chances. Agyar says some mad servant attacked you, but I'm not taking his word completely."

"Well, nothing else has happened . . ." I said.

"Doesn't matter," he insisted. "We weren't even shown the man. If you'd only been allowed to see him, perhaps you would have remembered what happened."

"Perhaps . . ."

"And besides," he continued. "The full moon is out. I've never trusted the full moon. It makes men and animals go mad."

"Yes . . ." I whispered. "Yes, I suppose it does . . ."

I had a strange dream that night. I was lying in bed, and Gaar was asleep beside me, when I felt my name called. Then I felt my name again. It was merely the faintest whisper of my name, floating to me (on the wind?), and I heard it not with my ears, nor even with my mind, but in my soul. My eyes opened themselves, and my body rose from bed of its own will, not mine, and I felt my legs being pulled toward the bedroom door, which even now was slowly and silently opening, seemingly of its own will.

I gave no backward glance toward Gaar, made no effort to reach out and hold on to a wall or some heavy furniture to stop myself; it would have been futile to even try. I knew there would have been no use resisting.

When I reached the main hallway, I knew that I was not

alone. But no one was actually there; at least, no man or woman was there. I continued walking steadily through the hallway, never stumbling into furniture or corners or walls, because it was not I who guided my body through the blackness. My eyes were not needed here. I felt cold hands taking both of mine into their own, and I sensed figures around me—man or animal, I couldn't tell—or perhaps neither—but I didn't look to see who or what it was nor did I try to pull them away.

At the edge of the forest, Agyar removed his cloak and placed it about my shoulders. Then he placed his cold lips over mine again and only pulled away after many minutes passed. There were more shadowy shapes hovering around him, and the light of the moon flashed once in his red eyes before he spoke. I could do nothing but listen.

"For years now . . ." he began, "for so many years. Centuries. I have searched—searched for one who would be mine for all time. Who would share all my nights, all my power—all my love with me. For centuries I have searched. And then—and then one night as I searched, reaching out with my mind and my heart, I saw your face. And I knew in that moment that I had found her. After waiting so long, and hoping, I had found the one woman who was destined to be mine—forever.

"You are that woman, Mara. And when I finally located you, found your city and your home, and I asked you here, you came. And when you came, and I saw you face-to-face, and looked upon you not in my mind but with my own eyes, I knew that I had truly found my immortal queen.

"The magistrate—Gaarius—your husband—he is not meant for you. Fate has played a cruel joke and given you to him before you met the one you were truly destined for. But that is only a small inconvenience now. I will have you, Mara. You will be mine, even if it means his death . . ."

I listened to every word. I understood every word. His eyes were burning into my soul again, flooding my mind and all its thoughts again, and I couldn't even struggle to keep from drowning. I watched silently, passively, as Agyar pulled a small dagger from his belt and held it to his finger. He pricked it quickly and held it out to me. I watched the small blood spot grow as he continued his speech.

"Taste it, Mara," he said. "Take this blood from me, as I have taken from you. We will then finish what we have begun tomorrow night—the last night of the moon. Come, taste . . ."

Amidst Agyar's thoughts within my mind was a memory—a small memory, one from years past. It was the image of my finger pricked, and Gaar's, and we were bringing them together in a symbolic bond. Our wedding. I hesitated to obey him.

"Taste my blood, Mara," he urged. "Help complete our bond. Then, tomorrow night, it will be over. And you will be mine forever."

I was not consciously resisting, but my hands were trembling as I slowly raised my arm to take his waiting finger. And slowly, ever so slowly, I brought it up to my lips and licked the spot once with my tongue. Agyar pushed it gently forward, however, and soon I held it completely into my mouth and began sucking.

There is little one can take from a finger, but I could taste his blood clearly, and I am ashamed to admit that I liked it. It was not like human blood; there was no "rusty" flavor; it was sweet, and thicker than human blood, and I continued sucking, for how long I do not know, before Agyar pulled the finger gently from my mouth. He straightened himself up and breathed deeply once. Then he brought the small dagger before his face and spoke again.

"You will be allowed to return to bed soon," he whispered. "But first you will take this with you," he added, taking my hand and placing the dagger into it.

"Tomorrow," he continued, "as I sleep, you will use it. You cannot be mine as long as Gaarius lives. You think you love him with all your heart, but I know that it is I whom you love with all your *soul*. So it is your task, Mara—your task to remove him.

"Before sunset . . . before I return to you, you must kill him with this. Take the dagger, and embrace him, and send it into his heart as he holds you. Before sunset, Mara. You must kill him. You must kill Gaarius!"

Those shadowy things were around me again, removing the cloak and returning it to Agyar, and they took my hands into theirs again.

"But until then," he said, "return to him. Return to your husband and lie by his side and sleep by him through the night. But dream of me."

"Please close that, Gaar. It's too bright out," I said the next day. Gaar turned around to give me a quizzical look, but then complied with my wishes and closed the shutters he had just thrown open.

"It's not very bright at all," he said, sitting beside me now. "In fact, it's gloomy in this room without some light."

"I just don't want any shutters open," I said. "Everything just seems so bright to me today." Gaar leaned toward me and placed a hand over my forehead.

"You look paler today," he said softly. "Do you feel all right?"

"I feel . . . weak, still," I said.

"You'll need to keep resting, then," he said, sounding not a little worried. "Eat and drink as much as you can for lunch, and then lie down."

"I'm not very hungry," I said.

"But you don't eat enough, love. I don't want you to

get worse; I don't think I could take—" he said, and cut himself off in midsentence. Then he cleared his throat once and smiled nervously.

"Try to get better, love," he whispered. *"Make* yourself get better. You were bleeding so much that night . . . You've lost so much blood, but you will get better, if you only eat enough and rest . . ."

"All right," I whispered. "I will . . ."

"Perhaps . . ." he continued, "perhaps if you've lost so much blood, then perhaps I can bring you some from the servants who slaughter the animals. Perhaps that will replenish what you've lost."

"Blood?" I said. "From the animals?"

"Yes," he said. "You've never done that before? When you've lost blood, you take some from an animal?" He waited for a reply, but I was inexplicably lost in strange, new thoughts from his suggestion.

"You never have?" he continued. "Well, perhaps you've never been badly hurt before. That's probably for the best, then. But you wait here; I'll find someone who can bring a fresh cup to you . . ." Gaar rose and kissed me quickly on the cheek and bade me to wait for him until he returned. I nodded slowly but never raised my head to look at him as he left. I was too busy thinking—thinking about his suggestion, and wondering why my mouth was watering so much over something I had never tasted before . . .

Gaar was pleased to see some color return to my face after I had drunk the cup of sheep's blood—or pig's—or whatever animal it was. And it tasted good—richer and sweeter than I had imagined, and I wanted more, but one cup was all Gaar had brought for me. A servant found us at that moment and announced our midday meal, and Gaar held my cup for me while we made our way to the dining room.

We had to eat elsewhere, it turned out. There were so many windows in the room, and the light was so bright that my eyes were in pain until we finally took all our plates, trays, and so on and moved to one of Agyar's guest rooms—meaning a room where he could talk to guests privately, if he wished. We sat by ourselves on couches and put all the food and plates on a small table at our feet. The room itself, fortunately, had only one small window, whose light shone on a particularly lifelike bust of Agyar in the corner. I caught myself looking at the bust and tore my gaze away before Gaar took any notice of it.

"It really bothers your eyes that much?" asked Gaar as he sat himself. He referred to the sun's light, of course.

"Yes," I whispered. "Yes, it does. I can't understand it. It's never bothered me before. I've been out all day on days like this, and it's never bothered me . . ."

"Maybe you looked at it too long," he suggested. "Hurt your eyes."

"Yes, I suppose I did," I agreed, pulling my gaze away from the bust again.

We ate in silence for some time; Gaar was satisfied, eyeing Agyar's books and artworks as he ate, and I struggled to keep my gaze on my food and not on that bust. It was so real; it captured his essence perfectly. It was as though the man himself were there. Even the eyes were perfect; no, especially the eyes . . .

I needed to cut some of my food, but when I picked up a knife, horrible images suddenly shot into my mind—images of blood, of organs lying at my feet, of a jumbled mess of a man lying before me, and I held a bloodied dagger in my hand, and the longer the images played in my mind, the more vivid and gory they became, and I was powerless to stop them! I yelled once and dropped the knife and covered my eyes; the images disappeared.

Instantly, Gaar was by my side, asking what was wrong, what I'd seen, and so on, and he had to pry my hands from my eyes before I would look at him. And the moment I looked at him, and realized that the "jumbled mess of a man" I had imagined was *him,* I burst into tears and covered my face again.

But I couldn't tell him what I had imagined, for it was too horrible for *me* to take, and I couldn't possibly explain why he was the one I had "killed." I didn't even know where those images came from, and I was terrified. Gaar then did what came naturally to him—holding me in comfort—only that made the images come back.

"No!" I cried, pushing him away. "Don't hold me! Please don't hold me!"

"What—? Why—?" he gasped, reaching out to touch me again.

I pushed his hand away. "Horrible things!" I yelled. "I think of horrible things and they won't stop!"

"What—? What horrible things?" he begged.

"I—I can't tell you!" I sobbed. "I could *never* tell you! You'd lock me away for even daring to think those things!"

"What things, Mara?" he pleaded. "I'm not going to 'lock you up'; I want to know what's wrong! Why did you cry out before?"

"Please," I begged, "let me leave. Let me go back to our room. I'll lie down and sleep, I can't hurt you then."

"Hurt me? How would you hurt me? Is that what you were thinking about?"

"No!" I cried. "Or—I don't know what I was thinking about! They just came out of nowhere, and I couldn't keep them out of my mind! Please let me go, Gaar. I want to go back to our room . . ."

"Uh . . . yes," he said. "Yes, all right. But aren't you finishing your meal?"

"No, I'm not hungry. I'll be fine, I promise."

"I'll walk you there, then."

"No!" I snapped, then forced myself to calm down. "Or— I'm sorry, Gaar. I didn't mean that. I just want to go alone, that's all. You finish your meal, don't worry about me."

"I worry about you, anyway," he said. "You haven't been well, Mara. 1 only—"

"Really; I'm fine now, Gaar," I said softly. "I just need a little more rest than I thought. I'll be even better in a few hours, when we have dinner. You'll see. All right? Will you stop worrying about me?" I watched him for some moments before he smiled a little and nodded his head in agreement. But his eyes told me a different story.

Eleven

I woke up to Gaar holding and kissing my hand. He stopped and held it when he noticed my eyes had opened.

"Feeling better, love?" he asked. I nodded solemnly.

"Good," he said, patting my hand quickly. "They're serving dinner now. Still not hungry?"

I shook my head. "Starved," I said. He smiled and pulled me into a sitting-up position. I could see through the corner of my eye that sunset was still about an hour away. I started shaking inexplicably. Gaar had let go of my hand in the meantime and was putting on a different shirt—one of his good ones, for when he and Agyar met again. Meanwhile, I sat placidly by the bedside, partly still trying to wake up and also staring vacantly at my bedclothes lying nearby on a chair. I decided to put them away somewhere, and I rose to grab them when I saw a dagger lying just underneath the clothes. I knew it was neither mine nor Gaar's, and then I remembered that dream I'd had the night before, and almost gasped in horror. Suddenly, I felt the clothes being taken from me. Gaar was there.

"Am I supposed to do something with these?" he asked.

"Hmm?" I asked.

"You were handing these to me, weren't you?" he asked, indicating my bedclothes.

I eyed him quizzically and shook my head. "No," I said, "I was just . . . uh . . ."

He then looked at the chair and saw the dagger there.

He tossed the clothes onto a chest and picked up the dagger, examining it.

"Where did this come from?" he asked. "Is this yours, Mara?"

"Uh . . . n-no, I . . . I . . ."

"It's not mine, either," he said. "I wonder where it came from."

"Um . . . yes," I murmured. "I do, too."

He continued examining the knife—checking the sharpness of the table, the knife's balance and design. He seemed rather pleased.

"It's a good dagger," he said, thinking out loud more than talking to me. "Well—" he continued, "we'll find out whose it is later. And if not . . . well, we may just have to keep it," he said with a wink.

"Yes. Of course . . ." I said.

I was not lying at any time to Gaar. I couldn't explain the dagger, as I still thought the whole thing had been dreamed. And yet, there it was, and there were still those horrible images that kept forcing their way into my mind. They hadn't reappeared since that last attack, but I could feel them in my mind still, just waiting for the first chance to torment me again.

Gaar, unknowingly, was a fool at dinner. He kept the dagger by his plate so he could show it to Agyar when he joined us and ask of its origin. I could scarcely keep my eyes off it all evening, something which Gaar eventually noticed.

"Something wrong?" he asked suddenly, startling me.

"Uh?" I snapped, looking up abruptly.

"What are you staring at, girl? You've been like this all day."

I raced through my thoughts for an explanation of my actions, and then only vaguely gestured at the knife.

"Oh, it's . . . uhh . . . It's a good knife," I muttered finally. "That's all."

"What? This?" he asked, holding up the dagger. I could feel those images pushing against my thoughts again, but I gave Gaar no answer to his query. Then he held it out to me suddenly.

"It's yours, then," he said. "My gift to you. You've always appreciated daggers more than I, anyway."

"Uh . . ." was all I said as Gaar lay it before me and went back to his meal. I looked at the blade, then glanced at Gaar, then back at the blade, until I shut my eyes and forced myself to finish my meal.

"Kill him," a voice called in my mind, and I started and glanced quickly around the room. No one else was there but my husband. He had his back turned to me.

"Did you say something?" I asked him.

"Hmm?" he said, turning around. "I didn't say anything."

"Are you sure?"

"Yes. I'm sure," he said after a quick pause, then turned away again. I sat back in my chair and bit my lip. Someone outside, then, I thought to myself. Someone outside.

"Kill him," the voice said again, and I sat up quickly.

"The dagger . . ." the voice continued. "Use it. Kill him." I folded my arms tightly across my chest and tried to ignore it.

I felt something making me turn my head, turn my gaze toward a small table where the dagger lay. Sweat began forming as I resisted the force, but it was little use. My gaze was locked on to the blade, the blade which barely reflected the dim light of the setting sun.

The sunset! It was almost here. *So what?* I thought. *The sun sets every day, so why should I fear it so much now?*

"Kill him," the voice continued, and I felt my hand

reaching out for the knife. I soon held it in quivering hands, and my eyes were then made to look upon Gaar, who was engrossed in a book. Then I felt myself moving toward him, and I used every bit of my will to keep myself in place and call to him.

"G-G-Gaar," I shivered. "Help me." He quickly looked up from the book, then shut it without another moment's notice after seeing my distress. But I don't believe he saw the dagger as he came instantly to my side.

"What? What is it? What's wrong?" he pleaded.

"Hold me," I whispered, and he obeyed instantly.

"Shh," he said. "Calm yourself, love. Tell me what's wrong . . ." He was embracing me, and the images flooded into my mind like water rushing from a broken dam. I shut my eyes tight and let out an awful cry of terror and fear and anguish. I could feel my arms wrapping around Gaar, but not to hold him. To kill him.

"Tell me what's wrong—"

"NO!" I screamed, shoving him away with all my might. "I can't . . ."

"Kill him," said the voice.

"NO!" I shrieked. "I . . . can't . . ." My voice died out as my gaze fell toward the dagger—the one which still rested in my shaking hand.

"I can't kill you," I whimpered to him. Gaar looked at me in growing confusion and horror, and I looked at the dagger again. I could feel my arm raising itself again.

"Mara . . ." he whispered, and reached out to me.

"Kill him. Before the sun sets . . ."

"I'm sorry, Gaar," I said, tears choking my eyes and voice. "I . . . I . . . can't do it!" And with that, the knife dropped from my hand, barely missing my feet. I held my cheeks in horror and turned away from Gaar; I couldn't possibly face him now. Still, I felt a gentle hand rest on my back, but I would not let myself face him.

"Mara . . ." he whispered. "You were . . . going to kill me?"

My voice was lost in tears, however, and I could not answer him. Suddenly, I felt myself being whipped around to face Gaar. His expression was not sympathetic.

"Answer me!" he yelled. "Were you trying to kill me?!"

"I don't know!" I screamed. "I *don't*—know . . ."

"Damn your 'I don't knows,' girl! You were going to kill me, weren't you? Weren't you?"

"YES!" I screamed, and tried to turn away again, but Gaar held me fast. His fury was slowly changing to a look of hurt, of anguish, of unpardonable betrayal.

"Why?" he asked, surprising me with his calmness.

I shook my head slowly. "I—I thought it was a dream . . ." I started.

"What was?"

"In a forest . . . Gave me that . . ." I said. "He gave me that . . ."

"Who?"

"T-trying to remember . . ." I said. I sat down slowly, and Gaar knelt down to listen better. "These shape-things . . . creatures. I remember a voice . . . a voice telling me to kill you, Gaar. It was telling me to kill you!"

"Whose voice?" he asked.

I shook my head vaguely, unable to look at him. Then suddenly he grabbed me by the shoulder and shook me hard.

"Answer me!" he roared. "Whose voice?"

"I don't know!" I roared back, and my voice was lost under a barrage of tears. "I don't—know . . ."

"Was it someone here?" he demanded. "Someone in this house?? Mara—who was it?"

"I— I don't know, I— Wait . . . I can remember a little bit, I—"

"Tell me, then," he said. "Tell me everything you remember."

"S-somebody . . . was talking to me . . ." I said. "Something about the moon. About men being hungry, and dying. I remember I was upset . . ."

"Who were you talking to, Mara?" Gaar asked, much calmer now. "Try to just let it all come back naturally . . ."

"W-well, he—he said things about . . . three thousand years, and . . . the moon is an eye. Did you know that, Gaar?"

"You're not making sense, love," he said. "Just . . . try to remember who you were talking to."

"But—wait," I said. "I—I thought it was you."

"I wasn't talking about eyes and the moon, Mara. Was—was this the night I found you?"

"Yes," I said. "It had to be you. I remember you picking me up."

"But this was *after* you were attacked," he said. "I found you barely conscious, bleeding. Who did it, Mara? Who? Tell me—was it Agyar?"

I looked at Gaar, and a light dawned in my mind.

"Yes," I said. "Yes, it was him. He was telling me about the moon, and—and how he was immortal."

"What? Immortal?"

"And—and he said I could be, too . . ." I continued. "What does he mean, Gaar? I looked at him, and—and then you were there."

"But he wasn't there when I was. No one was there when I found you. What did he do to you, Mara? How did he get away?" he asked. I could tell his anger was growing by the second.

"I can only remember his eyes . . ." I said.

"What about his eyes?"

"Burned through to my soul. Dark red . . . like glowing embers . . ."

"Now you're making no sense again," he snapped, and snatched up the dagger from the floor and thrust it in front of my face. I tried to back away from it, but the chair didn't give me much room.

"And what about this, eh?" he demanded. "Did he give you this and tell you to kill me with it?"

"Please . . . I can't look at it . . ."

"Well? Is that what he did?"

"Yes!" I cried. "But—but I thought it was a dream! I dreamt that he gave me a dagger, and—and he pricked his finger, and—and I drank from it, Gaar . . ." I said, looking up at him in great fear. Then I fell forward into his arms and wept with renewed tears.

"Gods, Gaar, help me!" I cried. "Please . . . please, forgive me! I don't understand this; what is he doing to me?"

"That's what I'm going to find out, and this minute!" He tried to pull away, but I held on tightly.

"Don't leave me," I said. "I'm afraid!"

"Nothing's going to happen to you. Come, let me go . . ."

"I would never want to hurt you," I continued. "I love you, Gaar, I—I would never think of killing you . . ."

"I know, my love," he said, rubbing my head. "Now take my hand; we're going to find that monster and make him answer to what he's done to you!"

"I'm afraid this is one 'monster' who answers to no one, Lord Magistrate," a slightly contemptuous voice called from the door. Gaar stood and whirled around the moment he heard it. I looked away from the sound of it, however.

"Agyar," I heard Gaar growl. "What you have done to my wife . . . you deserve death!"

"I'm afraid that's not possible, Lord Gaarius," Agyar continued in the same tone as before. "You see, your wife was telling you the truth. I *am* . . . immortal."

But Gaar was being carried away by his anger. I heard him whip out his sword, and I felt myself letting out a quick whimpering sound.

"I would never kill an unarmed man," I heard him growl, "but by the Gods, I may do so now . . ."

"Fool . . ." he said. "You haven't the merest idea of what you're dealing with!"

"I need none," Gaar said. "I need only to know that you're some . . . some witch who's been twisting my wife's mind about! I should kill you this very moment, right where you stand!" he growled.

"You may try, Lord Gaarius," Agyar continued in an infinitely calm voice, "but it will accomplish nothing. Look at me. Watch."

"Watch your 'dark red eyes,' I suppose?" he taunted. "I'd rather—uhh . . ."

Curious as to what stopped Gaar's speech, I turned my head slowly toward the door, expecting to see Agyar's hypnotic eyes working on Gaar now. His eyes had, indeed, become red, but they were not glowing; they were simply red. Agyar seemed larger than usual—fuller, more muscular, and he held his arms high, majestically, before Gaar. Then he opened his mouth in a hideous smile—a smile made up of inhuman, fanged teeth. He began to make a noise—a low noise at first, almost like a moan, but it grew in intensity and pitch until it became a horrible shriek, and I saw Gaar cover his ears an instant before I began screaming myself.

Soon all I could hear was my own scream, and I was being shaken by someone. I opened my eyes wide to see Gaar desperately trying to shake me back into calmness, and it worked for the most part, until I saw all the creatures that had suddenly joined us in the room.

They were pale and naked and dirty, mostly hunched over and shuffling back and forth in place as they appeared to be studying us. At first, they had looked completely inhuman—like demons, even, before I noticed disturbingly human features in their now-distorted, red-eyed, fanged faces. There were at least five of them, and Agyar stood directly in the middle of their group.

"What . . . what . . . ?" Gaar flustered.

"The word is vampire, Lord Gaarius," his voice boomed. "And I, Agyar, am the first vampire! I am the first to unlock the secrets of our power. Far more power than any mere mortal can possibly contain."

"A . . . what?" Gaar said, eyeing the creatures around us nervously.

"A vampire," he repeated, "and I have chosen *her* to be mine forever," he added, pointing at me.

"Whatever you call yourself, dog," Gaar growled, "she is not yours to take. Mara is *my* wife, and she always will be!"

"Do you truly believe that, human?" his voice boomed. "Why don't you ask her yourself? Why don't you ask *her* who she wants to have her?"

"Filth!" cried Gaar. "I'd rather have your head!" He took a threatening step forward, but was stopped in his tracks as Agyar's creatures snarled and moved forward, their eyes burning brightly.

"Gaaaarrr . . ." I whimpered, and he lowered his sword and jumped back to my side.

"What are these . . . things?" he murmured.

Agyar smiled coldly. "My most faithful servants, Lord Gaarius," he said. "Creatures with hardly my power, but each one of them more than a match for any human. They are without thought, without will. They obey me completely, totally. And they are here to finish what Mara was unable to. They are here to kill you."

"No!" I screamed, leaping to my feet. Agyar seemed a little startled by my ferocity. "You can't kill him! I won't let you! I don't want you! I don't want you!"

Agyar was taken aback by my words, but Gaar was only made stronger by them as he placed his arms around me. I buried my head into his chest as he spoke.

"It seems she *has* chosen who will 'own' her, vampire—or whatever you are. She won't be another one of your mindless creatures. And neither will I!"

"True, Lord Gaarius. Neither of you will join my creatures. Mara—she is to become my wife—my confidante, my lover. And she will be just as intelligent, just as independent of spirit, just as beautiful as always. Only she will live forever. And you, Gaarius? You'll just be dead."

That was enough for Gaar. Creatures or no creatures, he released his hold on me, brought up his sword again, and lunged straight for Agyar. Creatures grabbed at him from all sides as he completed his attack, and I almost screamed, but then a cry came out from Agyar himself. Slowly, surprisingly, the creatures drew away from Gaar and their master, and I could see the faces of Gaar and Agyar barely an inch away from each other. Gaar still held the hilt of his sword, and it was buried deep into Agyar's chest. I knew Gaar would hold his sword in place until Agyar collapsed, but the vampire suddenly gripped Gaar's shoulder and pushed him away, almost right into me.

He stood there silently for an uncomfortably long time, the sword firmly embedded in him, before he very slowly and very calmly reached up to the handle. His face concealed any pain quite well as he calmly pulled the bloody blade from his chest, and then, to Gaar's and my horror, ran his finger along the edge and then licked the blood that came off of it. He then held the sword out to Gaar and smiled coldly.

"Like to try that again?" he asked. Gaar reached out for the sword, hesitated, glanced at Agyar and his creatures, and then suddenly ripped the sword from his hands and threw his body straight into the vampire, knocking him almost but not quite off his feet, and raced through the room to the door, towing me with him all the while. Everyone involved was caught completely off guard, especially me, who now had to catch my second wind as we raced through the endless halls and rooms of Agyar's home.

We heard him shouting behind us, no doubt ordering his creatures to catch or stop us. Even Agyar's human servants knew about us, and those who saw us rush by sometimes tried to stop us, and a few even threw things at us.

I had no idea where Gaar meant to run or hide, but I offered no protest or suggestions as he held my hand tightly and dragged me through the house with him.

We soon reached a door leading outside, and Gaar pulled me through, and we started to run across the grounds until I looked up, and I saw the full moon rising into the night sky, and I couldn't help stopping dead in my tracks. I stopped so dead, in fact, that Gaar was jerked back to my side.

"What are you doing?" he cried. "We've got to get out of this place!"

"No," I murmured. "No, we can't. We can't leave here . . ."

"Keep moving, girl!" he yelled, tugging at me. But I wouldn't budge.

"We can't leave, Gaar! We can't . . . We can't go out into the night!"

"What are you talking about, girl? We can't just sit here! Come on!" Gaar cried, pulling me toward the open air.

"No! This way!" I yelled, and yanked him toward our new direction—back into the house. I couldn't explain why I had felt the way I had; I only knew that the night would be even less safe for us.

I led the way this time, dragging Gaar up and down the halls, turning corner after dark corner. Then one of the creatures spotted us, and we spotted it, and it pointed and shrieked at us before lumbering its way after us. Then there were more of them. One appeared just ahead of us as we rounded a corner, and I screamed once and dove back the other way, Gaar still in tow.

We reached the kitchen at one point, and some of the servants in there pointed and made as if to chase us, only they decided otherwise once they saw the creatures bounding in after us. *Let them do the dirty work,* they no doubt surmised. Gaar let go of my hand once and yanked a knife from a wall and continued on with me, never stopping or slowing down at any point along the way.

We were running for our lives; but what didn't quite register at the time was that, if Agyar was so powerful, and this was his own house, and everyone in it was after us, then why were we not caught during all of our running? Any of those creatures could have caught us quite easily, I figured out much later, only they seemed to be holding back. I believe we were only being toyed with, then. It was his way.

We ran for hours, it seemed. In and out of every room, every hallway, sometimes chased by human and nonhuman alike, sometimes chased by nothing more than our fear. We were exhausted, but still we had to keep going. We found stairs going to a lower floor, under the normal one, and decided to take our chances there.

The hallways were lit, surprisingly—with barely flickering flames, but light, nonetheless. I expected to find dungeons or old cells with rotting corpses stashed away or I don't remember what else I expected to see, but in fact we found only storerooms—wine stores, meat stores, wood and brick and weapon stores. We picked a room and flung the door open and threw ourselves inside. And it was pitch-black in there, so Gaar was forced to creep back outside and swipe a few lanterns from the hallway and rush back inside, shutting the door quickly but quietly behind him.

It was a room like the others, really. This one was for furniture, evidently. Old chairs and tables and dressers were piled one on top of each other all along the walls and in the corners. Even a small bed was positioned by the wall before us, and I wanted so much to lie in that bed, but

Gaar suddenly thrust the lanterns into my hands and began pushing a larger dresser toward the door. He placed it directly in front of the door, and then went back to get more furniture. I understood his intentions immediately and placed the lanterns onto the bed and helped him with a large table.

We continued piling furniture in front of the door as quietly as we could, sometimes rearranging what was already there to make room for heavier or larger things. Finally, we had done our best, and we both lumbered over to the bed and placed the lanterns off to the side on the floor and let ourselves fall backward onto the bedding.

"They're going to find us, Gaar," I breathed. "It's just a matter of time."

"Maybe. Maybe not," he said. "But if they do, they'll have quite a time trying to get in here."

"And what if they don't?" I asked. "What if they just walk right in?"

"How could they? They have to go through all this," he said, waving toward our blockade.

"I just . . ." I said. "I don't know. You saw Agyar; you saw those . . . slaves of his. They're not human, none of them are. You can't kill them with steel. Who knows what else they can do?"

Gaar reached over to me and brushed the hair from my eyes.

"I don't know, Mara," he murmured. "I just don't know. These creatures . . . these 'vampire' things. I've never seen anything like them. I wish I knew what to do . . ."

"I'm afraid, Gaar . . ."

"So am I, love. So am I. But there's nothing we can do right now. We can only sit here, and wait . . ."

"You—you mean, just wait for them to get us? That's all we can do?"

"Or perhaps . . . until they go away. Give up on us."

"You're not—giving up, are you?" I asked.

Gaar sighed and patted my arm. "No," he whispered. "No, I'm not giving up. We'll keep on fighting, even if they do somehow get past the door. And if we're to die tonight—I'm going to make sure it hurts him."

"I don't want to die."

"Neither do I, love. But it's something that *will* happen eventually, regardless."

"But I don't want to die *now*."

Gaar offered no comfort or advice to my lamentation, but silently sat up onto the edge of the bed. I watched him quietly pat his knees in a particular rhythm, and I wondered if he had a song going through his mind at that moment.

"Gaar?" I called softly. He turned an ear toward me.

"I think . . . I think, if we can stay in here all night, then we'll be safe in the daytime."

"We can stay here all night," he said. "They won't find us."

"We can leave after sunrise, and they won't follow us," I continued. "I . . . I just know that. I'm not sure why."

Gaar gave me no answer for a while, but first patted my knee gently.

"Go to sleep now," he said. "I'll keep watch."

"But you need to sleep, too," I protested, sitting up to join him.

"Later," he insisted. "Right now, I want you to be rested."

"But—"

"No buts, Mara. That swine has cast some sort of spell over you, I think, and you've been weakened for it. Now go to sleep," he ordered, simultaneously trying to close my eyes with his hands. I pushed his hands away from me but then lay back onto the bed.

"You'll be my lookout later," he whispered. "But until then, just rest. That's an order," he added, and bent over to kiss me.

But I couldn't sleep. Oh, I was exhausted, all right, but

I was also terrified, not to mention a little hungry and thirsty. I tried my best to calm down and lie quietly, but too many thoughts and feelings were cascading through my mind.

"Gaar?" I said after an extremely long silence.

"Shh," he said. "You're supposed to be asleep."

"Sorry," I whispered. "I can't sleep. I'm too frightened."

"Well . . . at least try and rest, then," he whispered back. "Don't think about all this. You'll have nightmares."

"I won't have *any* kind of dream, Gaar! I can't sleep!"

"So what do you want to do, then?" he asked, only I gave him no answer.

"Ohh, very well . . ." he grumbled, and took my hand and pulled me into a sitting position. I put my arms around him and buried my face into his chest and just sat there, holding him. He put his powerful but gentle arms around me and quietly rubbed my head with one of them.

"It makes no sense," he whispered. "It just makes no sense . . ."

"To think I was such a fool as to come here," he continued. "To think that—that I could be tricked like this!"

"It's not your fault, Gaar," I mumbled. "Nothing that's happened here is your fault. It's mine."

"Noooo," he said. *"I'm* the one who accepted the invitation. *I'm* the one who—"

"But it's me he wants," I interrupted. "It's me he's wanted all along. He never cared about you. He never cared about any trade. He just wants *me.* And I don't know why!"

"Hush now, love," he whispered. "Keep your voice low."

"I didn't know what was happening when he kissed me, Gaar! I swear to you by my mother's grave I—"

"Keep your voice down!"

"—By my mother's grave I would never ever be unfaithful to you of my own free will," I finished in a whisper. "Ever!"

"I know that," he said. "I know that now, love. Even I

felt some of his power—his influence—in that room. It was almost overwhelming!"

"He uses his eyes to do it, Gaar," I said. "That's how he did it to me, I remember now. His eyes glowed, and I couldn't stop looking at him, and I swear I might have done *anything* for him, anything at all that he asked. And it's not because I love him, Gaar, you must understand that!"

"I understand," he whispered. "You never lied to me about that night, I can see that now . . ."

Tears were clouding my eyes, but I did not bother to wipe them away.

"You forgive me then?" I asked. "It's *you* I love, not him. I never loved that . . . that . . . I don't even know *what* he is! I love *you,* Gaar . . ."

"I forgive you," he whispered. "And I swear to you that he will not have you. We'll make it through this; I promise you that . . ."

Twelve

I woke up in Gaar's arms, and I could see that he, too, had fallen asleep in *my* arms. I had no idea how long we had been asleep. It could have been morning already, for all we knew, when it would be safe to leave . . .

I felt my name. Just the merest faint whisper of my name, but it came crystal clear to me. I felt my eyes widening a little, and my arms pulled themselves away from Gaar, who began to fall behind me before he woke up. I was rising from the bed and couldn't stop myself, and I clutched its edge in a desperate attempt to keep myself from walking to the door and leaving.

I was resisting with all my might, and I still felt my name being called in my mind over and over again, getting louder and stronger each time. It was now becoming painful to resist, and I had to cry out.

"Gaar, help me!"

"What—?" he gasped, still trying to wake up. "What is it? What's wrong?"

"Hold me! Hold me tightly!"

Without hesitation, he threw his arms around me and held on. But then—against my will—I began struggling with him.

"I have you, Mara," he said. "But why are you fighting me?"

"I can't help it!" I cried. "It's—it's *him!* He's making me try to leave! Hold me!"

"I'm holding you; I'm here" he said. "What is he doing to you?"

"I'm not sure! I'm being . . . I'm being called! He's calling me to him, and I can't fight it! It hurts!"

"Keep fighting it, Mara!" he cried. "Ignore the pain! He has no power over you! Just keep thinking that!"

One of the unfortunate effects of the calling was to increase my strength. Gaar is strong, but in that moment I became far stronger, and soon I was onto my feet from the bed and inching my way toward the door.

"For someone who doesn't want to leave, you're certainly doing a good job of it!" huffed Gaar, trying to hold me back with all his might.

"I can't help it! I'm being . . . pulled! Don't let go, Gaar! No matter how much I scream!"

But just then, Gaar released me, and I stumbled forward again, pulling at the furniture in my way. I had pushed away a large dresser when I felt Gaar again, this time grabbing one of my arms and tying a rope to it. He yanked me back and tied the other end to the bed, and struggled to catch hold of my other arm and tie that up, too. I did my best to help him, but in this case, it was the vampire's strength we were fighting against, not mine.

Soon, I was completely tied to the bed, which fortunately was too heavy for me to drag along the floor. And I was still being called. The pain was becoming unbearable, and I threw my head back and screamed and screamed while Gaar desperately tried covering my mouth. Eventually, he resorted to tearing off a portion of my dress, wadding it up, and shoving it into my mouth. I could no longer scream, but the pain was making my eyes blind with tears, and I was certain I could take no more of it unless I passed out or died.

And then it stopped. I shut my eyes tightly and let my head slowly drop. It wasn't easy breathing with that wad in my mouth, and I raised my head to face Gaar and begged him with my eyes to untie me. He understood that I was no longer being called, and pulled the wad out. I let out several loud, long breaths as Gaar hugged me, but he did not untie me.

"It's stopped," I whispered. "He's stopped calling me."

"Thank the Gods," he whispered back.

"I'll thank them if we survive this," I said. "Please let me go, Gaar . . ."

"What if he tries again?"

"He won't. I'm sure of it. He knows where we are now, Gaar. He's going to come here . . ."

"How do you know that?" he asked.

"I felt him . . ." I whispered. "In my thoughts. He was everywhere in my mind. He's coming here now, Gaar, I'm sure of it! We have to get out of here!"

Gaar let go of me and reluctantly began untying me—slowly at first, just to make certain, no doubt.

"We're not going to make it, Gaar," I continued. "He's going to kill us both."

"Kill *me,* you mean," he corrected. "You're supposed to live forever."

"But I don't want to! Not without you! If I must live forever while you lie in the ground forever, then I don't want it! I don't want him!"

"He won't have you, my love. I promise you that."

Brave words from a brave man.

"We can't stay here!" I said.

"I don't think we could get out in time," he said matter-of-factly. "We'd need to move all this junk first."

"So what do we do?? Just sit here?"

"No," he said. "We'll fight him to the end. And we can even win."

"How?" I cried. "Stab him to death? Your sword did noth—"

"We'll use something else, then," he said. "Something

like—" Then Gaar reached down and snatched up one of
the lanterns from the floor and smiled triumphantly. "Fire!"

We sat on the edge of the bed and waited. Gaar had
hastily smashed up an old chair and set fire to some of
the legs to make torches. I held one while Gaar armed
himself with his sword and another torch. I also had the
knife that Gaar had swiped from the kitchen, but if the fire
didn't work, I knew the knife would be useless, too.

I couldn't take much more of the tension as we waited.
I began rubbing my neck in anticipation, and it made me
think of Agyar again and what he'd done to me there. I
didn't understand; was that part of his "secret"? Making
me bleed like that? Out of habit, I slipped my arm into
Gaar's, and he looked at me with an expression of helplessness that shattered what little hope I had left. Eight
years of happiness . . .

I heard nothing, but Gaar suddenly stood up and brought
his torch into a ready position. I rose up and stood close
to him, and he glanced at me long enough to motion for
silence.

There was an unbearably loud smashing against the door
before us, and our entire blockade was moved forward at
least one foot. Then another smash, and the door shattered
into a thousand pieces, followed by a horrible gust of wind
that blew dust, splinters, and other pieces of wood into our
faces. It also blew our torches out.

We were barely recovering from that attack when horrible, inhuman shrieks filled our ears, and I felt seemingly
hundreds of cold, dry hands and arms grabbing, pulling,
clawing at me, and I fell backward and screamed.

I heard cries from Gaar, too, and I think I also heard
some of the creatures shrieking in pain; perhaps his sword
was doing something to them. Meanwhile, I could only

swing wildly at the creatures in the blackness, hoping to dislodge them from me.

I clutched the end of the bed and pulled myself up, ignoring the hands ripping at my hair and skin. I stabbed directly ahead of me over and over, sometimes hearing a shriek of pain, sometimes striking nothing. I wanted to help Gaar so much—I couldn't bear to hear him crying out so— but there was nothing I could do.

I felt a hand grip my face, and I raised the knife to strike at it, but I was shoved backward, the back of my head smashing into the wall behind me. I was dazed . . . dizzy . . . disoriented, but I would not let myself fall unconscious. I meant to try to strike again, but more hands and arms gripped my arms and pressed them firmly against the wall. They had immobilized me.

"Enough!" a voice roared from the darkness, and the creatures parted from me enough to let me see the doorway, but none of them dared release its hold on me. I heard Gaar struggling still, and a creature occasionally cried out in pain as he stabbed them, no doubt.

"I said *enough!*" Agyar roared, and all sound ceased. He stepped slowly over the threshold, his face partly lit by the lantern he carried. He let his gaze pass slowly over the total chaos in the room until his eyes met mine, and I meant to look away, but then they began to burn again.

No; it wasn't Agyar in the doorway; it was Gaar. It had to be. It didn't matter that he was being held onto the bed next to me by hellish things, he was right in front of me, waiting for me to go to him. I felt the creatures release my face and arms, and we faced each other silently, neither wanting to destroy the moment.

"Fight him, Mara!" I heard somebody say just behind me, but I couldn't quite place the voice. "Look away from him!"

"Come to me, Mara," he said. "It's all over now. You don't need to be afraid anymore . . ."

"Don't listen to him, Mara!" that person said again. I wanted to listen to Gaar, though.

"She can't hear you, 'Lord Magistrate,' " he said. "And if she can, she isn't listening." That's right. Gaar was the only one who mattered then. I was halfway across the room to him, and he opened his arms to greet me. The knife dropped from my hand, and I raised my arms in anticipation of meeting him.

"It's over now," he repeated. "You're safe now."

"No! Fight him, Mara! He's lying to you!" That annoying voice again.

"Silence him!" he called, and the person made some noises in protest, but then was silent.

I reached my wonderful, beloved husband and sank into his arms. Now I was safe; it was all over, he said. I was safe now.

He felt different. He seemed smaller and thinner, and he was so cold. I made a promise to myself to feed him better and warm him up with a nice big fire by the hearth. I would have done anything for him; I loved him so much . . .

"Take him away," he said, and I heard some shuffling noises behind me. Then some people moved past us, carrying a large man, whose hand suddenly gripped my shoulder as he passed by. I looked up abruptly and into this man's faintly red eyes, and he had such a look of sadness and hopelessness as I'd never seen. And he was beginning to look familiar to me . . .

Gaar flung the man's hand away from my shoulder and waved all the people away. We were alone now. It was all over; I was safe now. He held my head against his shoulder and patted me gently as he spoke.

"It needn't have been this way," he whispered. "You needn't have caused yourself so much pain, if only you'd come to be before . . . But now it's all over. Look at me, Mara. Look at your destiny . . ."

I obeyed him without hesitation, and my look of bliss

was instantly replaced by betrayal and horror. Agyar! I was in Agyar's arms! Where was Gaar?

I yelled and tried to pull away from him, but his grip was inhumanly strong, and all my kicks and pummels that would have hurt any normal man bothered him not at all. He held me out before him in both arms, and he opened his mouth to show needle-sharp teeth within.

I opened my own mouth wide and tried with all my might to scream, but nothing escaped but a few quick gasps. And those eyes began to burn again, only this time I was too panicked, too angry, too hysterical to succumb to them completely.

"It's no use struggling, Mara," he said very calmly. "You *will* be mine."

Not if I could help it. But then, I couldn't. Slowly, he pulled me toward him, toward his smiling, fanged face and made me kiss him. I did my best to keep my lips shut tightly, but I could not shut my eyes—not while his were burning so.

I was completely immobile in his arms, and I tried to scream again, but no sound would come out. Soon I felt his face pressed against my shoulder, and I shut my eyes out of sheer terror as the pain came again.

I think I whimpered a little while he sucked. Only the prick itself hurts; the rest is warm, soothing, calming— almost euphoric, even if the victim is not willing—and I was certainly not willing.

I heard a scream, and I couldn't tell if it was coming from me or from my soul. And the rest was oblivion.

Thirteen

I awoke to the sound of stone grinding against stone. I could not yet open my eyes, for they felt so stiff, and I was still so sleepy.

The grinding stopped, and I felt a light rush of cool air falling onto my face. I breathed in softly and wondered why my chest felt so stiff, as well.

A minute passed before I could open my eyes again, and when I did, I saw the face of a strangely familiar man peering over at me. I said nothing to him, but only blinked over and over again, trying to force the cobwebs from my mind and remember who he was.

I opened my lips a little to speak but was stopped by an extremely dry throat. I tried to swallow, but there was nothing to swallow, of course. The man smiled slightly at me and reached his hand out. I still couldn't remember who he was, but I raised my own hand to his and let him pull me up into a sitting position.

"Welcome back," he said. "I hope you've slept well." I still would not speak, but only threw him a confused look and cast several furtive glances around the room.

I had never seen this place before. It was a strange room, with walls entirely of stone, only visible due to several torches on each wall, casting an eerie glow with their flames. But what struck me was all the boxes that lined each wall. There were about six of them in all, each of them large enough for a man to lie in. And I? I was sitting in a huge stone container, on an even larger stone platform in the center of the room. An identical container lay just to my right. I was confused. *What are these things, and what are they for?* I wondered.

"You've gone through quite a lot these past few days, Mara . . ." the man started again. He knew my name, too. "You might not . . . remember very much of it."

"I don't . . ." I began, but had to stop and cough due to my dry throat. I continued coughing as the man reached into my box, lifted me out, and put me gently onto my feet.

"Are you all right?" he asked over my coughing.

I nodded. "Just confused," I whispered. "I don't remember anything. These past few days? What past few days?"

"You ought to remember some of it soon, my dear," he reassured. "Weddings can do things like that to women, it seems."

"W-weddings?" I stammered. "Um . . . whose wedding?"

He laughed a little. "Whose? Why, yours, of course!"

"M-mine?" I asked. "You mean . . . I was just married?"

"Of course, darling," he said. "And oh, what a spectacle you made of yourself!"

"Uh . . . yes," I whispered. "Yes, I suppose I did." He began guiding me toward a small stairway behind me, and I wasn't certain what I was supposed to be feeling at that moment: Fear? Shame? Joy? Horror?

"My husband, then," I whispered as we ascended the stairs. "You're . . . my husband."

He said nothing, but only nodded emphatically.

"I'm . . . I didn't know," I said. "I mean—I didn't remember. I'm sorry, sir. Everything's so confused."

"I understand," he said. "As I said, you will remember me. Soon."

The stairs led up to what apparently was a kitchen. I

saw some servants bustling around us, and some of them left the room as soon as we entered. They seemed so strange to me then—I couldn't quite figure out why. My mouth was starting to water as I watched them go back and forth about their business, and it reminded me of how thirsty I was.

The servants who had left earlier soon returned, carrying a tray of mugs. And the strangest-looking things were following them. I thought they were animals at first, but then they were walking upright. They were those pale, hairless, dirty things with bright-red eyes and nasty-looking teeth, and they smelled awful. They raced for the tray of mugs as soon as it was set down and gulped down the contents.

I should have been frightened or even horrified at the sight of these vile creatures, but, instead, their "inhuman-ness" fascinated me. I wanted to look at one more closely, perhaps even talk to one, if they could. I began moving toward them but was stopped by a hand at my shoulder. It was my husband, and he shook his head at me. Then he said something.

"Huh?" I said, snapping out of my fascinated trance. "What was that?"

"I said we'll be eating elsewhere," he said. "And far better food than what *they* eat . . ."

"Oh," I said. "Oh. Yes. Of course," I said, letting him lead me from the kitchen by my hand. But I didn't really want to leave. The smells in there were so good, and the aroma of whatever those creatures had drunk was just start-ing to drift into my nostrils. I hoped my husband would at least let me have some of that.

I was led through endless hallways and up one flight of stairs, and through even more hallways, until we arrived at a beautifully decorated guest room. He sat me down onto one of the couches and kissed my cheek quickly.

"You'll be dining any moment, darling," he murmured. "I only need to fetch your wedding gift . . ."

"My wedding gift?" I echoed. "You've gotten me a wedding gift? That's so generous of you."

"More than generous, darling. It was . . . necessary, in a way."

"And then we'll be dining together, right?" I asked. "I think I may faint if I don't eat soon. And I'm so thirsty."

"It'll only be a few moments, dear," he murmured. "And then it'll all be over." And with that, he bade me wait for him until he returned with my gift. I could hardly contain my excitement waiting, either. I felt so strange about everything that had happened, so far; here I wake up one day and find that I've been married! And if I could only remember my husband's name. It was disgraceful that I couldn't even remember my own husband's name when he obviously remembered mine. But he didn't seem to mind; he acted as though I shouldn't be remembering anything until it "all came back to me." I wonder what had happened over those few days. He said I'd made a spectacle of myself. Oh, Gods, I had probably had been drunk out of my skull or something, which seemed odd to me, considering that I never was much of a drinker. Maybe they were especially strong drinks . . .

I didn't recognize the dress I was wearing. It was a long, bright-red thing, and if it was my wedding dress, it certainly was an unusual one. I glanced around the room for some sort of looking glass to see myself in, but I could find none. Oh, why couldn't I remember anything??

There was a quick knock at the door, and it opened before I could rise, and my husband stepped inside. And behind him stepped a young lady—perhaps thirteen or fourteen—and he waited for her to stand before me before he shut the door again.

"This is Lara," he announced, placing a hand on her shoulder. "She is my gift to you."

Now that was confusing.

"My . . . gift?" I asked. "Her?"

"Yes" he said. "She'll see to all your needs from now on. Forever."

"I don't understand," I said. "My gift? I don't—" Then his intentions dawned on me, and I gasped quietly.

"Oh," I said. "You mean she's to be my . . . servant?"

"Yes," he said. "Exactly. And she'll see to it that you dine tonight." Then he moved to my side and kissed my cheek again.

"Enjoy your gift, darling," he whispered. "May she serve you well."

"But I—"

"And . . . I'm sorry to tell you this, but we won't be eating together tonight."

"But why not?" I protested. "This is our first night together. Isn't it?"

"It is," he agreed. "But I think you might prefer to dine alone. It . . . *is* your first time, after all."

I gave him no reply, but only watched him quizzically as he nodded his head once and, giving the girl a quick look, left the room. And then we were alone, just me and this girl, my "gift" that I knew I couldn't actually accept. She was supposed to be my personal slave, it seemed, and I wasn't given the opportunity to explain how I felt about that to him. So now what? Do I order her to fetch some food, or do I get it myself? *I don't understand why this husband of mine refuses to dine with me; is he angry with me? Does he—*

"Will you be . . . eating soon, mistress?"

I snapped out of my thoughts and looked at the girl. She watched me with big, sad, almost frightened brown eyes, as though she would be afraid of my answer, somehow.

"Uh . . ." I stammered, clearing my thoughts. "I . . . certainly hope so. I take it you're suppose to bring it to me?"

"Yes," she said. "I am . . . supposed to supply your first meal." She had the most interesting smell. I was very tempted to just stand up and start sniffing at her, but then restrained myself immediately, wondering where in the world such a bizarre notion came from.

"Well . . ." I began, "I don't really like the idea of having a slave, of all things—oh, nothing personal to you or anything. You smell like—uhh, look like—a fine girl, I'm sure. But perhaps if you could bring me something—if only as a favor to me."

"I don't understand, mistress."

"Well, what I mean is, is, umm . . . I just don't . . ." Her smell was almost beginning to overwhelm me, and my throat was becoming so dry. I coughed a little to see if I could wet it.

"Could you just bring me something?" I asked. "Anything? I feel as though I haven't eaten in days!"

"No," she said. "No, I suppose you haven't, mistress."

"Please, not 'mistress,' " I said. "Just Mara. But please get me something, anyway, and I'll do you a favor later. All right? And something to drink, too! My throat is parched!"

I turned away from Lara and was about to become lost in other thoughts, when I realized that she was still there. I meant to chastise her for still being there, but then calmed myself and addressed her in a civilized way.

"Lara . . ." I began very calmly. "I must—have—some food."

"I know that, mis—uhh, Mara," she said. "Um . . . that's what I'm here for."

"Then why are you still here?" I queried.

"Because I am to supply your food," she muttered, a slight quiver in her voice. *Had I made her cry?* I wondered.

"I know that, Lara," I continued as calmly as I could. "Which is why I'm asking you to bring me something. Isn't that what my husband told you to do?"

"Um . . . no," she murmured, biting her lip.

"He didn't?" I asked. "Then, what *did* he tell you to do?"

"He told me . . . to supply your first meal here," she said, her voice quivering even more. Now I was really becoming angry with her, but I was also still confused. And that smell of hers! It was becoming stronger, clearer, the more I talked to her. My mouth began watering and I didn't know why, but at least it was not so wretchedly dry anymore.

I realized suddenly how cold I was, and I looked around the room for a cloak or blanket or some kind, but could find none.

"Fine," I said. "Then I ask you to 'supply my first meal.' And bring me something warm to wear, too, if you could."

"You're cold, mistress?" she asked. I nodded, and she walked over to a dresser and pulled a wool cloak from one of the drawers. I made to stand and take it from her, but she came over to me and put it on herself. But *she* was much warmer than any blanket. I remembered how much warmer I had always been on winter nights when I had snuggled next to . . . next to . . . Why couldn't I remember?

"I'm ready, mistress, whenever you want to begin," Lara said suddenly, and I heard under her breath, "I hope."

"Uh— " I said, but wasn't sure at all what to say. I looked into her sad, worried eyes, and my mouth was watering more, and I couldn't figure out why. And for the first time, it occurred to me that yes, I was half starved— But for what? What was I so desperate to eat? The images of food flashing through my mind did nothing for my appetite, and, yet, I couldn't help staring at this girl. And she watched me, too, with her frightened eyes, and she opened her mouth a few times as if to speak, but said nothing, and she rubbed her neck nervously several times.

"I think . . ." she said at last, "I think I'm supposed to help you out, first."

"Huh?" I said, still watching her. She did not repeat herself, but reached into a small pouch at her side and drew out a large needle. She held it before her and bit her lip and fidgeted her hands a little before speaking.

"In case you're not sure what to do," she whispered, and shut her eyes and quickly pricked one finger. I was taken a little aback, and meant to question her actions, when she held her finger out to me, the blood spot growing, and smiled weakly.

"Just so you know . . . what I taste like," she said. "Mistress."

But I wasn't really listening to her. I was mesmerized by her finger—by only a simple little spot of blood. I had seen far worse before; so why couldn't I help looking at it? I could even smell it now, and I had also smelled blood many times before, but never had it made my mouth water this way.

She began to bring it even closer to me, and I felt my hand rising seemingly on its own to meet it. Soon her finger was in my hand, and I squeezed it a little, and my lips began quivering as the spot grew bigger.

I yanked her finger into my mouth and sucked. I think I almost pulled the girl over in my enthusiasm, but I didn't care. I was starved; I had to have something, anything, to eat. Or no—not just anything. But I didn't comprehend just what, yet.

I sucked and sucked until no blood came from her finger. I released my grip on her and let her pull her finger away from me. It was not enough. I was starved; I had to have something to eat. I looked up at the girl, who seemed even more worried than before, and she took a step away from me. I rose from the couch and let the cloak drop to the floor. *Fear me, girl? Why fear me? I wouldn't think of harming you. I only want some food.*

Her skin was beautiful. So white and smooth, and she

was neither too lean nor too plump. She took another step away from me and rubbed her neck nervously.

"Does it hurt, mistress?" she asked.

"Does what hurt, Lara?" I asked, still moving toward her.

"When you . . . you . . ." she said, gesturing a little, but I still didn't know what she meant. She was moving away a little faster now, and it wouldn't be long before she'd reach the wall.

"When I—what, Lara?"

"When you . . . um . . ." She had to stop now. She had reached the wall. I was only a few inches away from her; I could feel her warmth from where I stood, and wanted to be closer to it.

"Spit it out, girl," I said very calmly. "When I what?"

"When you . . . bite me," she said, swallowing once.

"Bite?" I asked.

"Yes," she said, nodding her head rapidly. "The bite. Will it . . . hurt?"

"Hurt?" I echoed. She nodded again.

"Oh," I said. "The bite. No . . . I don't think so," I whispered. "In fact, I remember it feels quite—"

I stopped because *I did* remember. I remembered the flash of pain, then the gentle, soothing sucking, and I remembered the face of a man who had made me feel all of those things, and it was the man who was calling himself my husband. And his name sounded again in my memory; it came back in a flood of recognition, of images, of awful memories. Memories of my arrival there; memories of a moonlit night on a balcony; memories of talking about immortality, and hypnotic, glowing eyes, and that pain followed by the sucking. Then memories of myself and a man whom I loved more than my own soul, locked up together in a dismal room, frightened, tired, hungry, near the point of despair, because we knew that it would be our last night together. Then hideous, shadowy creatures attacking us both, driving us to the ground, killing us both. Or at least killing *him*. I was saved for the most hideous of them all. Agyar. He had done this to me. But done *what?*

I threw my head back and screamed, and it was a scream such as I never knew I could make. Tears began flooding my eyes as I looked back at the girl, who was clearly more terrified of me than before. And I was just as terrified of her, for I now understood what I wanted from her—what I was so hungry for—what "meal" she was supposed to supply me with . . .

I leapt back a full ten feet and screamed again. Lara cringed and doubled over, covering her ears from the noise. I had to force my own mouth shut just to stop myself, and I accidentally bit my tongue in the process. I yelped in pain and felt my tongue with a finger. Blood was there. I had bitten pretty hard. Or so I thought. My finger brushed against needles in my mouth, and I pulled it out quickly and very carefully used my tongue to feel my teeth. Sharp! Each one of my canines was sharp—needle sharp!

I raced over to a dresser and searched desperately through the drawers, throwing out piles of clothes and papers and other bits of junk all over the floor until I found what I was looking for—a mirror.

I was almost afraid to look. But without hesitation, I thrust the glass before me and barely kept myself from crying out again in horror.

My lips were already parted to reveal a mouthful of hideously sharp teeth—or at least, hideously sharp canines. My face was pale, sunken, and drawn, and it only made the eyes look that much worse. They were bright red—perhaps redder than Agyar's even, only they did not burn as his did when he used his power. I looked on this horrible image that could not be me—I would not let it be me. I tried to wish it away, but my face only got worse—paler, more sunken, more drawn—the harder I tried.

I screamed again and let go of the mirror and heard it

shatter at my feet. I was a monster. I was a hideous monster, with hideous thoughts going through my mind, and there was nothing I could do about it!

"What's happened here?" a familiar voice called at my side. "Mara, did you cry out? Lara! But you should be—"

"YYYOOUUUUU!" I roared, whirling to face Agyar. "YYOOUU did this to me! YYOOUU made me a monster! I'll kill you for this! I'll kill you!" I screamed, and threw myself at this thing that dared to call itself my husband.

I went straight for his throat with my hands, which had actually become claws without my knowing it, and hoped to squeeze the life from him. He was taken by complete surprise, and I managed to catch hold of his throat and push him back, slamming him hard against the wall. His eyes widened in surprise and, I hoped, terror, and I listened for the sounds of his wheezing and hoped to see his face turn red.

Neither came to pass. His eyes widened, all right, but only in surprise. If he was in any pain he did not show it, as he slowly brought his arms up to my hands and forced them away from his throat. I tried with all my might to hold them in place, but I was too weak then, too hungry, and I'm certain he had already dined and, therefore, had all his strength about him.

"Die, you monster!" I screamed. "In Gaar's name—*die!* DIE! DIE! DIE! . . ."

I repeated that command over and moved again, kicking and struggling at him all the while. But he remained completely calm, holding me firmly where I was, his eyes smoldering again, and my concentration was slowly being broken by his thoughts replacing my own.

"DIE! Die! Die . . . Die . . . die . . . die . . ." I continued, each command growing softer and weaker as I watched his eyes. Soon I said nothing, but only watched him, and waited.

He released my hands finally, and I let them drop limply to my sides.

"I thought you would understand . . . by now," he said, shutting his eyes and letting his head fall back in exhaustion. "I thought you would see we are not—'monsters.' "

"Monsters," I whispered. He brought his head back up and smiled helplessly.

"What has happened is part of the past now, Mara," he said. "You can change nothing. Killing me will change nothing.

"I knew," he continued, "that you would remember, eventually, but not—everything. I tried to prepare your mind myself, but your memories . . . they must have been burned into your mind irreversibly. But that will not stop me; I can still teach you to love me."

"Love you," I echoed. He nodded his head and smiled.

"Yes," he said. *"You will* love me. No matter what you believe about Gaar, you will understand soon that you were never meant to be his wife."

"Yes . . ."

"No," he said firmly. "Not his. It was never his destiny to be immortal. It was yours. Yours, Mara; yours, and you will never die, but spend eternity with me, my forever young, forever beautiful companion. My immortal goddess . . ."

"I wanted . . . blood . . ." I said. "Wanted to kill her . . ."

"You would not kill her, Mara," he said. "When you feed, she will not die, but—only seem to. And when you are finished, she will rise again and be your servant forever."

"Want to wake up . . ."

"This is no dream, Mara," he said. "It's real. And resisting your hunger is quite pointless now. There's no turning back now. The longer you resist, the more ravenous you'll become, and—the more dangerous, as well."

He turned me to face Lara, who was cowering by the dresser. She was shivering and covered in sweat.

"Look at her, Mara," he whispered into my ear. "Smell her. Feel the blood flowing in her veins . . ."

I was shivering and sweating now to match Lara. I don't know who was more frightened: the victim or the monster.

"It's not a horrible thing, this hunger," he continued. "It's part of the price we must pay, that we must feed on the living. But does that not make us master of those we feed from? To fight it, to reject this hunger, only makes it worse. It makes *us* into *its* servant, and that must never be. If you cannot enjoy it, Mara, you must learn to accept it. So go on. There she is, Mara; there she is, waiting for you. Go on, Mara . . ."

Tears were forming in her eyes, and my own tears were matching hers. I was almost convulsing now, I was shivering so hard.

"Take it," he kept whispering to me. "Take what is rightfully yours, Mara!"

I started to whimper, and Lara's tears and mine were flowing freely now. I felt my leg move forward, and I could not stop it, and soon both legs were forcing me forward, hesitantly, and Lara tried to move away, but she was too afraid of Agyar's wrath to try.

Spit was dripping from me when I reached her; I touched her cheek gently with my hand, and I let it caress her face down to her neck. She gasped quietly and cringed a little, but could not get away. I heard Agyar say "Yesssss . . ." while I pulled her toward me slowly, very slowly, until my teeth were almost at her neck, and then

"NOOO!" I screamed, and turned away from her and tried to rush at Agyar again, but all my strength left me, and I fell to the floor onto my hands and knees. "No! No! No! No!" I cried over and over, feebly striking the ground at each cry.

Fourteen

I refused to take any of Lara's blood. And Agyar promised me that I would eat nothing at all until I did. Taking from an animal, as his creatures did, was "beneath" me, he explained, and I was only to take from people. I still refused, and I could tell that he was sorely tempted to just hypnotize me and force me to convert Lara, but he did not do so. No doubt he meant to "master" me without having to cheat, whenever possible.

I asked to see Gaar's body. I wanted to see him for myself, to see if he really and truly was dead, and, if so, to ask his soul for forgiveness. I had betrayed him, and to this day it is something I must carry in my memory. Again I was refused; Agyar claimed that his body—what was left of it—had been thrown to the wolves. For the time being, I chose to believe him, and asked if he would at least allow me to be alone for a few moments. Naturally, he was suspicious.

"I shall not try to escape," I said.

"You couldn't if you tried, anyway," he said. "For I could call you back at any time."

He spoke the truth. "Calling" works not only on people but on the vampire whom one has converted, as well.

"I only want to be alone right now," I said, rubbing my hands together. Agyar nodded slowly and made as if to leave, gesturing to Lara to follow him, when I noticed something different about my hands. They felt . . . naked.

"Where are my rings?" I asked. He stopped and turned to face me.

"Elsewhere," he said slowly. "I assumed they might bring back old memories too well."

"I want them back," I said. "One of them was my wedding ring. I want it back."

"That part of your life is over, Mar—"

"Both of them, Agyar," I said slowly, firmly. "I want—them—back. Please."

"Very well," he sighed. "I shall have them"—then he stopped and cocked his head defiantly—"brought to you when you decide to comply with my wishes."

"What?"

"You heard me, woman. You'll have them back when you do as you're told, and accept my gift," he said, referring to Lara.

We glared at each other for several long, tense moments before I broke away.

"Fine," I said softly, sitting daintily onto a couch. "So be it, then."

"Then you will do as I ask?" he asked a little eagerly.

"No," I said firmly. "I said nothing of the kind. Keep my rings. Keep everything that ever meant anything to me. Keep my soul, even! It's what you want, isn't it?"

I turned away from him, but I could hear him open his mouth several times to speak.

"No. It's not what I want," he said finally. "You do this to yourself, Mara. I want you to be happy here, yet you won't let me or anyone else help you—"

"Help me?" I said. "Help me be happy? Leave me alone, then. Let me fend for myself from now on. Give me the things that belong to me and let me out of here!"

"Don't be a fool, Mara. There's so much you don't understand about yourself yet, you'd be destroyed in an instant!"

"Destroyed?" I said mockingly. "You said I couldn't *be* destroyed! I'm immortal now, right?"

"Ageless, yes," he said. "But not—invincible. Steel will not destroy us, no, but there are . . . other things that can end our lives. So go out on your own, without understanding your weaknesses, and your first mistake would be your last."

I folded my arms and looked down.

"So . . . it seems that being a vanper—"

"Vampire," he corrected.

"Vampire . . ." I continued, "isn't as glorious as you made it seem. So what is there, Agyar? Fire? Cold? What will end our so-called endless existences?"

I waited for the answers, but he only smiled coldly.

"Those things . . ." he began, "will be made known to you in time. Some much sooner than others. Some will be obvious. For instance, yes, fire will burn us. But that's all I'll tell you for now."

"I see," I sighed. "To keep me from trying to leave."

"To make you understand better."

"I'd still like to be alone, regardless."

"Indeed," he said. "I'll give you that, then. And we'll see how long it takes before your hunger conquers your will."

"Go to hell, my 'dear husband.' "

He smiled again.

"I already have, my dear wife. I already have."

A predictable thing to say, but true. You see, as the first—the original—vampire, Agyar had gone through all sorts of horrors on his quest for immortality. Alchemy. Black and white magic. Bizarre, horrific rituals and journeys that apparently included a trip to hell and back. And finally, he reached his goal. He was ageless, immortal, but at the cost of his soul, not to mention a few other "inconveniences," as he put it.

I was, indeed, still half starved by the end of the night, but I wasn't about to give in to him yet. I made plans to sneak away to where the servants slaughtered the animals for the next day, perhaps when Agyar was "in town," as he always was when Gaar and I were still together. But now he never seemed to be "in town."

Morning was coming soon, and it took a while for it to sink in that I had really been up all night. I had never done that before, but apparently I had slept through the whole day after Agyar attacked me. He had told me earlier to be ready to go back to bed soon, but I knew I'd have a hard time, as it was, sleeping through those hunger pangs of mine, nor was I particularly interested in joining him any time soon for anything.

I wanted to watch the sunrise before returning to bed. They were much nicer in Clovaine than in Castrill, in my opinion, which was actually about the only thing I liked better about this city—besides our balcony, of course.

I was alone by the window, but somehow I felt as though Agyar were watching me from somewhere. But I couldn't tell from where; I eventually dismissed the feeling as silly suspiciousness.

The sky was becoming lighter, and the stars were slowly disappearing, flickering out, a sight that never ceased to fascinate me. The characteristic blood-red of the presunrise sky filled the atmosphere, and I am ashamed to say that it was reminding me of the food I had missed.

It was becoming so bright now, though. I couldn't understand it; the sun hadn't even risen and my eyes were starting to hurt. I held an arm up to help shade them, but as time went on, my arm began feeling hot. I pulled it away from my face, and, without such protection, my face was heating up, too. *But the sun is not up yet,* I thought to myself. *How could it be so hot?*

The first ray of the sun poked over the distant mountains, and I couldn't help crying out as it stung into my eyes. I covered them with my hands and doubled over in my chair. Then I felt the heat on my scalp, and it felt as though my whole back was getting ready to burst into flames.

Somebody grabbed my arm and yanked me off the chair, away from the window, away from the light. I remained doubled over, still covering my eyes and whimpering softly. The figure hefted me back onto my feet and brushed off my dress while I dared to find out if my eyes would still see.

My blurry vision revealed Agyar before me, watching me expressionlessly.

"Danger number two," he said. "Stay away from the sun."

"Why?" I asked. "Why does it burn? Why didn't you tell me?"

"I really don't know," he said. "I only know that it burns. And I wanted you to find out for yourself. That's what *you* wanted, isn't it?"

"That's why you only saw us after sunset," I growled. "You were never 'in town' at all. Ohhh, if Gaar had only known that before—"

"But he didn't," he said. "And now you're as I am. Unable to see the light of day ever again. So unless you'd like to stand here and wait for this whole room to be flooded, and die painfully, you will come with me—to our beds. To sleep in peace."

I had little choice then but to obey him and keep my rage inside me, and let it boil.

Fifteen

The next day—excuse me, *night*—was much like the first. More confrontations. More threats, more refusals; only I knew I couldn't fool myself for much longer. I was ravenous and still was not allowed to eat. As far as Agyar was concerned, I was surrounded by food. And my first meal was already selected for me.

I was not left with much time to myself that night. Agyar made certain to "call" me to him several times. Obviously, he wanted me by his side, and I was far too weak to resist, even with vampire strength.

It was all to make sure I didn't sneak away to the stables and take blood from the animals, you see. Two nights in a row I had to watch Agyar's creatures take their fill from their mugs, and two nights in a row I was not allowed to touch any of their food. I was breaking down, too, I could feel it, but I'd be damned if I'd let Agyar know that. He might have been closer to breaking than I was, for all I knew.

"I'll starve myself, then," I threatened him after I'd been called. Agyar angered me even more by smirking.

"You can't," he said. "You won't die."

"I'm weak now. I'm sure I'll only keep getting weaker until I can no longer move, and that'll be the end."

"No, my dear," he murmured. "It'll only be the beginning. You see, you'll grow weaker, all right, even to the point where you haven't the strength to move. But you will not die. You'll simply lie there, immobile, until by some miracle, blood is given to you. Or perhaps it never will be. Perhaps you'll never feed again, and be forever immobile, an ageless, unliving statue."

"How do you know this?" I asked, a chill going down my spine.

"Because I have reached that point of immobility before," he said. "You forget, Mara; I have existed for some three thousand years, and I have seen and experienced far worse things than any mortal mind could imagine. I assure you. As to starvation, the feeling is not pleasant. It was centuries before I came into contact with blood again."

"How?"

He smiled coldly again.

"A rather long and disturbing story," he said. "Perhaps I'll tell you some night. Needless to say, I wouldn't advise self-starvation."

Defeated again. I considered facing the sun—to burn myself to death—but I was certain Agyar would call me to him or pull me away before it killed me. But not before I'd suffered; I was certain of that, too.

The stone lid of my sarcophagus wouldn't budge. I took another breath, braced my hands against the lid, and pushed. No strength remained in my arms. My throat was absolutely burning with thirst, and it was agony for me to make even the slightest noise. It felt as though my tongue would crack in two if I dared move it, and I could swear that my cheeks had become brittle. It was over. It was all over.

I heard a soft knocking from outside the coffin, and I tried again to lift the lid, but could barely make a sound. I threw my hand out with what little strength I had left to knock on the lid, but it didn't seem like any sound that could be heard.

Some moments passed before I heard stone grinding against stone, and I opened my eyes to watch the lid move away from my sight. It was removed completely, and I lay there passively, waiting. Soon Agyar's face peered over the edge at me, but he said nothing, as though waiting for me to make the first move.

I watched him for a time, gasping for breath and vainly trying to lick my lips. It was time now.

"You win," I croaked, and almost coughed from the pain, but I couldn't even do that.

"What was that?" he said, bending an ear to me. Bastard. He knew exactly what I had said.

"You win, damn you . . ." I whispered. "I give up," I added, and shut my eyes in pain. I felt hands and arms move under me, and I was lifted completely from the coffin and hefted up into his arms. I didn't want him to even touch me, but I had little choice at this point. He carried me up the steps and into the kitchen, past wide-eyed servants who hastily made way for "the master" and his nearly unconscious wife.

I was carried through endless hallways, up the flight of stairs, through more halls, and back into the room I had been brought to that first night. He lay me gently onto the couch, and I could barely keep myself up as he left me there.

My back was to the door when I heard it open, followed by the sound of somebody being shoved in; and then it slammed shut again. But I remained where I was. There was a brief pause before a familiar voice sounded behind me.

"Mistress?" Lara said. "Are you all right? The master said—you needed me."

I needed her, all right. Oh, gods, how I needed her. I remained where I was, and the girl—the foolish little girl— moved around the couch to face me. She even dared to sit beside me. I had my head down and my eyes shut, and I felt her hand reach out to my chin.

"Mistress?" she said as I raised my head and opened my eyes to look at her. Gods, she was just a child . . .

"For-give me," I croaked, and lunged forward with everything I had. She screamed once and fell backward, and my teeth searched for and found her throat, and the vein that would feed me.

Blood poured into my mouth—hot, fresh, young blood, and all of it was mine. Despite my weakness, horses could not have pulled us apart in that moment. I was beyond rational thought the moment I tasted the girl's thick red life juice, and I just kept on sucking and sucking and sucking, and I imagined that I could have sucked her completely inside out if I'd wanted to.

I hadn't bothered hypnotizing her first. I had not learned to do that yet, and I was too ravenous to care, anyway. I simply dove in and drank. But she did not fight back. Yes, she screamed once, but more out of surprise than horror or fear, I'm sure. Eventually, she started making soft, sighing sounds the way I had when I had been bitten, and they grew weaker, and softer, the more blood I took.

Then she made no sounds. No movement. No pulse. Nothing. She was dead now; I had killed her, but that was what she had been prepared for all her life, it seems. She expected it, and I suspect that she even wanted it, in a way. Damn him, I thought. Damn him and his grotesque world of blood and death.

I finished the feeding. I drained her dry in less than five minutes, and I let myself fall off the couch and onto the floor in exhaustion. And there was still more blood—on the couch, on the floor, on her, on me. I shut my eyes tight and gasped for breath. I wanted so much to sleep now.

The door opened again—slowly, quietly. I kept my eyes shut; I already knew who it was. He knelt beside me and placed a hand on my chest. I sighed loudly to let him know I was awake.

"I'm sorry it had to come to this," he said. "It could have been such a pleasant experience, if you'd only let it."

"You're right," I said, my eyes still shut. "Everything that's happened to me is my fault. All my own."

"It is," he agreed. The idiot. "But I hope you've learned your lesson."

"Do whatever you want to me, Agyar," I said. "You win. There's nothing worse you could possibly do to me."

"As I said before, you do these things to yourself. But here," he said, taking my hand and placing something in it. "You wanted these. They're yours now."

I rolled my rings over and over again in my hand while the door opened again, and I could tell by the stench that his creatures had come in.

"She's over there," said Agyar. "Take her and prepare her."

I opened my eyes to see some of the creatures taking Lara from the couch and heading for the door.

"Wait," I murmured. Agyar motioned for them to stop. "What is it?"

"Not like them," I said. "I don't want her to be like them. Like those creatures of yours. I want her mind intact. I want there to still be a Lara that I can talk to. Please."

"Very well," he said, then: "Leave her mind!" to the creatures. The door closed again, and we were alone.

"Well," he said. "Are you just going to lie there all night?"

"For a while, at least."

"Very well," he said. "But only for a few minutes. Then I want you to wash yourself off and join me on the roof. I have many things to show you there. Wonderful things," he whispered.

"As you wish," I said in a dead tone. The war was over, and Agyar was the victor, that much was certain.

Sixteen

I changed into a bright green dress that was laid out for me. I had assumed that my clothes for the night would be chosen by him at all times in the future—I was right, too.

He stood by one of the towers on the roof, in the darkness, and waited for me. I approached him silently, my eyes to the ground. He leaned forward and kissed my cheek lightly, but I gave him no reaction.

"You look lovely," he said.

"Thank you."

"So . . ." he said, "now is the time for you to learn the wonders of what you are. You seem to think only of the disadvantages to being a vampire. But tonight you'll see how glorious it can truly be."

"As you wish."

"Watch me, Mara. Watch me, and learn."

I watched him, and he stepped away from me quickly and lowered his head slightly, and his eyes turned up to gaze at me intensely. They began to smolder, and I assumed he meant to hypnotize me again—for whatever reason, I didn't care anymore—but my mind was untouched. Instead, I watched as his features and form seemed to begin melting, shifting, and I furrowed my brow in disbelief, wondering if he really *was* playing with my thoughts.

His face was growing longer, thinner, his dark hair spreading all across his face and body. His hands shortened and his feet lengthened, his body contracted and grew leaner, and a *tail,* of all things, was growing from his rear. He let his body drop until he stood on all fours, like an animal, but then, he was an animal. A wolf.

I should have cried out in horror, least of all surprise, but I made no noise. The entire transformation lasted some five seconds, and my gaze never left it for an instant. I had seen all of it, he couldn't have tricked me—or could he? I didn't know yet how subtle his mind manipulations could be.

Our eyes locked together for an endless time, this wolf's and mine, yet nothing was said, no sound was made. And then—much faster than before—he transformed back. Transformed back into Agyar. He moved close to me and placed his arm around my waist, much to my revulsion.

"You share this power with me, Mara," he said. "You, too, have power over the animals of darkness, of the night. Come. I'll help you through your first change."

"I'd rather not."

"But I want you to, Mara. You *will* change."

I shut my eyes slowly and sighed.

"As you wish," I whispered.

"Think of the wolf, Mara. Think of its form, its shape. Think of its color and smell. Now think of yourself. Think of *your* form, *your* shape, *your* color and smell. Now think of you and the wolf, coming together, joining, merging, until both of you remain, but as one. As the wolf, but with *your* thoughts, *your* mind. That's it. Breathe deeply, and think of the wolf. Now you—now the wolf. Bring them together, Mara. Let them be one!"

I did exactly as he told me. I thought of wolves, limited as my knowledge of them was at the time, and concentrated on making my form match its. Then I would feel a strange, quivering sensation at the back of my skull, and I could feel my eyes glazing over and a trancelike feeling beginning to set in. Then I would feel parts of my body begin to move, and once that began, I panicked and broke concentration. I would then have to start over, trying to make myself get used to that unsettling feeling of physical metamorphosis.

This was my fourth attempt. I was beginning to change again, and I almost panicked again, but I shut my eyes tight and bit my lip—or at least tried to, and let myself fall onto all fours. I continued thinking of wolves, and thinking of myself as one, until I heard Agyar's voice again.

"Excellent," he said, and I opened my eyes wide.

It is difficult to understand what it is to see as a wolf unless one has directly experienced it. It is an entirely different world. Colors mean virtually nothing here, for they are not as clear as in human vision. Here, shapes and forms make up the wolf's world, or at least of the vampire as a wolf.

I found myself staring at two dark columns directly ahead of me, until I raised my head, watching the columns join together and thicken, ending some four feet above me in a spheroid shape. It was Agyar, and here I was, seeing him as he actually was—a joining of columns and spheres and box-shapes of different sizes and thicknesses. His body was black, his skin gray, and his eyes white, but no other colors were noticeable to me.

"You make a beautiful wolf," he said. Even his voice sounded different—much sharper and clearer. And louder. "Fur of the purest gray, and silver. This is what you were meant for, Mara," he continued, and I watched his shape begin to blur and shift, until within a few seconds, we were watching each other eye-to-eye. Two wolves standing beside each other in the moonlight. If I hadn't loathed him as I did, I might have considered it romantic.

"We shall run together in the night," I heard him say directly to my mind. *Ah,* I thought. *We can think to each other.* I made a promise to myself to guard my thoughts whenever we transformed.

"Come with me," he thought, and turned away to head for the stairs. I followed him silently.

He led me to a hill overlooking the town. As usual, only the barest flicker of light escaped some of the homes as we looked. They were quite distant from us, but I could see much farther, much clearer as the wolf.

I heard the howls of other wolves far off near the mountains, and even contemplated answering them, but I fought off the urge, realizing how silly that would make me look. Then Agyar opened his mouth and howled himself. It was a long, low howl, and when he stopped, a dead silence followed, until, from the mountains again, more howls came. I wondered if Agyar was going to answer again, but he turned and looked at me expectantly.

"Me?" I thought to him. He nodded:

"I'd . . . rather not," I protested.

"Answer them, Mara."

"But I don't even know what they're asking."

"They're not 'asking' anything," he thought. "They're taking each other's measure. And they need to be reminded that we are still their masters. Answer them!"

I licked my lips once and cleared my throat—or at least as much as a wolf can clear its throat. I looked at Agyar again, who was sending flashes of anger and impatience to me, and then opened my mouth and howled.

I had to stop myself and try again, the first howl was so feeble and high-pitched. Agyar rolled his eyes in exasperation, and I tried again, but for my sake, not his. My second howl showed improvement, but I doubt if it would have made any wolf turn tail and run in terror. It probably would have laughed, instead.

We waited under the moonlight, and soon more howls sounded from the distance.

Agyar shook his head. "They don't even acknowledge you," he thought.

"But they howled back."

"Not to you, fool. They're back to measuring each other."

"How do you know that?"

"Because I've been doing this for centuries now, remember? I've learned the ways of the wolf, and I've mastered them. And you will, too, if I can help it. I don't want them to start thinking they can come here and terrorize my people."

Personally, I wanted to cause him more trouble by being the most incompetent wolf I could, but then I began thinking of what else he might be able to do to me. He knew what we could and couldn't do, what hurt us and what didn't, and I knew barely anything. I had little choice but to obey him—at least until I, too, learned "the ways of the wolf."

"As you wish, Agyar," I thought, and I felt a twinge of pleasure and triumph coming from him.

I wondered if we were going to have to run all the way back to the house, and I believe I sent this question to him as we listened to the wolves. He shook his head slowly, however.

"We're going back as humans?" I sent.

"Not humans, my dear," he thought. "We'll be flying back soon."

"Umm . . . I thought wolves couldn't fly."

"They can't. But *we* can. Watch," he thought, and I turned to see him transform back into his old self. Then he held his arms straight out and leapt into the air, and in an instant, his form shifted again—a smaller, darker form, and one with wings. If I had been able to catch all the details of his transformation, I would relate them to you, but it was quite fast and the lack of light did not help my vision.

Agyar shot away from me like an arrow, and I heard a horrible, high-pitched shriek come from him before he soared back around to head for our small hilltop. I expected him to land, but first he shot over my head, forcing me to duck, and flew away to circle back again.

When he landed, it was obvious that this form was not well equipped for standing or squatting on flat land. He spread his wings in an attempt to balance himself, and from this pose I was able to determine the shape of a huge, black bat.

He transformed back a little slower, perhaps because he didn't have to worry about falling to the ground as when he first transformed. I was still a wolf, and he knelt down and lifted my chin to face him better.

"Change back," he said.

"Don't know how," I sent.

"The same way you became the wolf," he said. "Only picture yourself as you were, and make your form fit that image."

I nodded in comprehension and concentrated. I had forgotten about the unsettling sensation of my body shifting, but I stayed any panic and allowed the metamorphosis to complete itself. However, I forgot to stand up while changing and was on all fours still when the process was done. I heard Agyar chuckling a little as he helped me up.

"This time will be a little more difficult," he said, "because it must be quick. Otherwise, you won't change before you hit the ground, and you'll be stuck, flapping about like a dying fish."

I nodded again in comprehension.

"Now take a deep breath, close your eyes, and hold your arms out. That's it. Now do not think of the wolf this time, but of the bat. Think of leathery wings forming from your fingers, your body becoming smaller and leaner, a winged tail forming below. Think of your features changing, your nose lengthening and flattening, your ears pulling up and back on your skull, enlarging themselves. Are you thinking of all of this?"

"Yes," I whispered.

"Good. Now, do not break your concentration for an instant, but when I give the word, think of the bat as I described to you, hovering over your form, covering it, enveloping it, transforming it. And leap as high as you can into the air, and at that instant, change, and soar into the night."

I kept all the images in mind, and waited for his signal. Strange how I felt no fear or anticipation in that moment; I was simply waiting. In retrospect, I believe Agyar may have been much subtler at manipulating my mind than I had given him credit for. Perhaps he had suppressed my fear for me.

"Fly!" he cried suddenly, and without hesitation, I leapt as high as I could, which to my surprise was some fifteen feet, and concentrated. I felt my hands and fingers stretching and webbing up, my nose pulling out and pushing up, ears lengthening, teeth shrinking and sharpening, tongue thinning and lengthening, my whole body molding itself to the image I held in my mind.

For an instant, I felt lighter than air, until I realized I was indeed falling, and must do something about it quickly. Instinctively, I began flapping my arms about, and the falling stopped and I felt myself shooting forward into the air.

It was then that I finally opened my eyes, and I shrieked in terror as the dark ground rushed beneath me in a blur. And my panic only made me flap faster, which made me fly higher and faster. *Now what?* I thought. *How am I supposed to get back? I don't know how to steer!*

"Slow down!" I heard in my mind. It was Agyar's voice.

I dared not turn to look, but I knew he was close to me, flying after me with his own leathery wings.

"Slow down or you'll drop from exhaustion!" he sent. I could only send him sensations of panic, however, and I shrieked some more. A second later, I heard a faint shriek come straight back at me from the distance, and I wondered just how many bats were flying about here, anyway.

"Stop that screaming and slow down!" he sent again. I could feel him trying to send sensations of calmness, of control, but my mind was not acknowledging them very well.

I shifted my weight to the side a little, and found myself turning at high speed toward the forest. *Nothing like a good, solid tree to stop one's maniacal flying,* I thought to myself. I shifted my weight again to turn away from it, which worked fairly well. I skimmed by the edge of the forest, fortunately missing any trees in the process. Agyar was still behind me, still strongly suggesting that I calm down. Well, I had no idea where I was by now, anyway, which I related to him as best as I could.

"Follow my voice," he sent, and I heard a quick shriek to my left. I turned as best as I could toward the sound, and more shrieks followed, sometimes to the left, sometimes directly ahead or to the right.

At last we reached the hilltop, but then I still had no idea how to stop. Agyar landed gracefully, transforming as he hovered and setting gently down onto his feet. I, on the other hand, went screaming by the hill and had to circle around to try again.

Apparently we cannot use telepathy while in human form and I heard him shout "Lift your—!" Uncertain as to what I was supposed to lift, I decided to at least try and slow down. I dropped my tail and headed for the hill in what might as well have been a dive bomb. Agyar was flailing his arms about, probably to get me to stop, no doubt, but it was too late. I was coming in fast, and, much to my chagrin, had no idea how to stop myself.

Ahh, thank God for soft ground. Of course, it felt like a stone wall when I hit it, but I knew it could have been much worse. I plowed into the hill face first, rocks and sand flying into my eyes, ears, nose, and mouth and scraping me up a bit, too. When I finally stopped skidding along, I just lay there in the dirt, wondering what I had done to deserve this existence. I had never asked for what Agyar offered me—at least not willingly.

I felt myself being lifted from the dirt and turned over. Agyar had knelt down and laid me onto his knee. I felt like a baby, then, and I wasn't sure if I liked it, either.

"I said, lift your tail," he said. "You let it drop."

He could have asked if I was all right, at least. I stuck out my hideously long tongue and tried to lick the blood off my face.

"Your wounds will heal quickly enough," he said. "But I want you to change back now."

Now *that* I could understand. I assumed that the reverse was similar to changing from the wolf form, and I began concentrating on becoming human again. Or rather, human *form*. I keep forgetting.

I began changing right on his knee before he pulled it out from under me. But the transformation was complete before I thudded to the ground. Always the gentleman, that Agyar.

"I can get up myself," I said, refusing his outstretched hand.

"You must change again, now, before we return to the house."

"You realize, of course, that I'm exhausted," I said.

"That is your own fault," he said. "I told you to slow down. Now this time listen to my commands, and flap your wings slowly and steadily! And another thing: you can glide, you know."

"Whatever you say, dear husband."

"Don't get uppity with me," he snorted. "I learned to do all this the hard way—by trial and error. You should appreciate that I'm trying to spare you the indignities of doing it yourself."

"Oh. Of course. Forgive me, then. I've always been too ungrateful for my own good, I suppose."

"You are forgiven," he said. "Now get ready to change."

Agyar made me join him in his study when we returned. He was browsing through some book of his while my thoughts began to drift to memories of my old life. Keston. My father. Then Gaar and Castrill. His magistracy. Leta. And the children . . .

"Agyar," I said quietly after a while.

"Mmmhmm," he said, not looking up from his book.

"I want to see my family again."

"You know that's impossible," he said. "I can't allow you to leave here."

"I see," I whispered. Then: "How long has it been . . . since Gaar and I first came here?"

"About three weeks now," he said.

"Three weeks," I echoed. "You realize Gaar is the magistrate of Castrill."

"Was," he corrected.

I nodded. "Was the magistrate. So what message have you sent to Castrill?" I asked. "Have you mentioned that Gaar had been fed to wolves, and I have been changed into a monster?"

"I'll have none of that from you, woman," he snarled. "I did what had to be done."

"Naturally," I said, and looked him square in the face.

"I want to see my family again," I repeated. "My children—all of them. Tirell, Ran, little Kir—"

"I told you, that's impossible!"

"It's not impossible!" I cried. "Look at you! You and your immortality, and power over animals and let's not forget me, and your power as a magistrate, and you tell me I cannot even see my own children!"

"You could never make the journey—!"

"Then bring them here! Send a letter asking that my children be sent here, so I may see them again! I want to see their bright young faces again. Please . . ."

"That would be possible," he said quietly.

"Just for a little while," I said. "For a few days. To . . . say good-bye to them . . ."

"Is that why you want them here?" he asked.

"Yes," I said. Agyar turned away from me to contemplate my suggestion. Then he whirled around after a few moments of silence.

"I have a better idea," he said.

"I may go to them?" I asked excitedly.

"Don't be foolish," he said. "I meant that you need never be parted from them again."

"I will not let them live here," I said.

"And why not?" he said. "Would you rather they live out their lives as orphans?" he asked, then leaned much closer to me and said, "When they could be with their mother for all eternity?"

"All eternity?" I said. "I don't—" My mouth dropped open in horror as I understood the full meaning of his suggestion.

"No!" I cried. "No! I would never—!"

"Then let them be orphans, Mara," he said. "Let them live out their brief, miserable existences with neither mother nor father to care for them, to hold them, to love them—"

"Stop it!" I cried.

"You would allow them to live amongst filth and disease and poverty, never knowing where their next meal will come from, subject to all fears and horrors that plague each and every human for—?"

"Not my own children!"

"And why not, Mara? You are their mother! And every mother lives in fear and dread that her children could die before her, and she will be alone, forever alone—"

"No more, Agyar! I beg you—no more!"

"But think of what you can give them, Mara! You have already given them life, and now—now you can give them *eternal* life! What greater gift could a mother give her children?"

"I would rather they *do* live in poverty than . . . than . . ."

"So you want them to die?" he asked. "You *want* them to rot in their graves while you live on . . . and on . . . *and on—?*"

"Stop this!" I cried. "I've changed my mind! Forget I said anything. You were right, it's impossible for me to see them now—"

"It's too late, woman, I've decided now," he said. "And what I say is law to you. You yourself said you would obey me from now on."

"Not in this!"

"Mara!" he said, his eyes smoldering again. He gripped my chin and made me look at him. My thoughts were swimming again.

"You love your children, don't you, Mara?" he said softly.

"Yes . . . oh, yes."

"Then you will do what I ask because you love them! They are your children; you cannot bear to be parted from them, can you?"

"No . . ."

"Could you bear to be parted from them for all eternity?"

"No . . . !"

"I will send for your children, Mara. And then you may give them eternal life, because you want to. Because you love them."

"I . . . love them . . ."

He released me, and then left the room in a hurry, no doubt to write his letter and send for my children. And I was alone, alone to contemplate the horrible fate that their own mother would be dealing them.

Seventeen

One night I watched the stars twinkle from the roof. Leta and the children would be there in a few days. Leta was coming as their chaperone, and also because I had asked for her. The same fate was intended for her, of course. We could be best friends forever, she and I, running or flying every night together while the children wrestled at our feet as wolf cubs. What an idyllic existence.

A familiar presence had joined me on the roof. The smell was the same, but now there was just a trace of a death stench to it. I shivered as it drew nearer.

"Mistress?" she called from behind me. I kept my back to her.

"Hello, Lara," I said.

"The master told me you were up here, and I should join you."

I smiled weakly. "How thoughtful of him," I said. I could think of nothing else to say to her, nor did I turn around. I wanted so desperately to beg forgiveness for the thing I had done to her, but I could not find the courage to do so.

"The night air is wonderful, is it not?" she said.

"Wonderful."

"I woke up only a few moments ago," she said.

"Oh, really," I said. "And how do you feel?"

"A little hungry," she said. "But they gave me some blood already. I didn't know how good it would taste, either!"

I laughed once to myself, but then was silent.

"Um . . . mistress?" she said, moving to my side.

"Yes."

"How did *my* blood taste?" I could hardly help smiling to myself. The girl could ask even the most horrific questions in the most innocent way. She reminded me so much of Leta when we'd first met. That puppy-dog enthusiasm and innocence.

"Good," I said finally, reaching out to pat her on the back. "Very good."

"I'm glad," she said. "Although . . . you took me a little by surprise, when you bit me."

It amazed me how casually she was taking the hideous thing I had done to her. What did Agyar do to his servants to make them think this way? It only made me hate him all the more.

"And what was it you said to me, just before feeding?" she said.

"I said . . . I asked your forgiveness," I said.

"Oh," she said. "Well, you needn't ask that of me, mistress. It's what you were supposed to do."

"You claim he treats you well, and yet your lives mean nothing," I murmured.

"What was that?" she asked.

I smiled and turned to look at her. "Nothing," I said, rubbing her head. Her face was a familiar sight. Lara had a drawn, thin face, bright red eyes, and glistening white fangs. I had since learned to eliminate those features from myself, and I now looked like my old self, but paler. But apparently, all vampires share the same awful appearance when they first "wake up."

"I'm glad you're not really dead," I said.

Her fangs flashed as she gave me a cheerful smile. "Oh, no, mistress," she laughed. "I can be your servant forever now."

"You take all this so well," I said. "You have great courage for such a young girl."

"Thank you, mistress," she said. "But now I can frighten everyone else! See?" And with that, she raised her arms and let out a horrible hiss, shifting her features slightly until she looked even more monstrous. Her new existence was just a wonderful dream come true for her, and I watched her hiss and lumber and stalk all about me, acting out her nightmares for real; only now *she* was the nightmare.

She stopped her lumbering and began laughing, at first much like a human laugh, only it was becoming higher and rougher, until it more resembled the screech of a bat. Then she ran over to me gleefully and tugged at my arm, pulling me away from the roof's edge.

"Oh, mistress!" she cried. "Will you teach me to fly? Will you teach me how to become a bat, and to run and howl as a wolf? Please, mistress?"

"What! Now?"

"Could you?" she cried. "I would be forever grateful, and I would never cease praising your kindness and generosity! Could you, mistress?"

"But I—I—" I was flabbergasted by the girl's enthusiasm, and, reluctant as I was to venture out into the night, I finally agreed to teach her what little I knew.

Lara was thrilled by the sensations of flight. She was rather shaky during her first try, but hardly as much as I had been, and she also expertly avoided the hard fall that I had experienced my first time. Upon landing, she clapped her hands together and laughed with glee after transforming.

"I can fly! I can fly!" she shouted, dancing all over the hilltop as I watched, amazed. "Oh, mistress, I can fly! I've always wanted to be able to fly! Isn't it wonderful?"

"Uh—yes. Yes, it is," I said. Then she stopped her dancing and ran back and threw her arms around my waist.

"Thank you, mistress," she said. "Thank you for teaching me."

"Uh, it was nothing, really—"

"And to think I was chosen for this," she continued, parting from me. "The master really must have thought I was worthy."

"Yes, it seems he did."

"Could I become a wolf now?" she asked. "And howl to the ones in the mountains?"

"Of course—"

I felt my name again, and that irresistible pulling that follows a calling. I was wanted back at the house, it seemed, much as I wished to remain with Lara.

"I'm afraid we must do that later," I said, feeling myself walking away from her. "I think Agyar wants me back."

"The master?" she said. "Oh. Are you being called?" she continued, chasing after me.

"Um, yes, I think so," I said, and was forced to turn toward the house and begin running at top speed. Lara kept pace with me as best as she could.

"Couldn't we fly back?" she gasped. Good suggestion. It would be a lot faster. I kept my running pace and began to concentrate. Once I had formed the bat image, I ran a little faster and took a flying leap, transforming as I went. Now it was time to give my legs a rest and make my arms do all the work.

Fortunately, Lara was able to follow, beginner that she was at flight. It turned out that Agyar only wanted to make sure I was nearby, as morning was little more than an hour away. Well, I knew that already. I was perfectly able to take care of myself.

They were already unpacking in their rooms when I was able to join them. Apparently Leta and the children had arrived about when Gaar and I did—in the early evening—and were just settling in when I greeted them at the door.

I had asked Agyar to allow me to be totally alone with them—no mental eavesdropping, no calling, no walking in at inopportune moments. He reluctantly agreed to busy himself on the other side of the house while I finished with my own business.

I wore my best green cotton dress and my prettiest smile as I greeted them. Leta had her back turned to me, but the children saw me in an instant.

"Mama!" they cried, and surrounded me instantly, smothering me with hugs and kisses and love. Even little Kiri toddled over excitedly and held on to my leg, jumping up and down to get my attention. I bent down and picked her up, holding her and kissing her over and over, letting her aroma and her warmth envelop my whole being.

Then Leta was by my side, smiling and calling loving greetings to me, and I leaned over to hug her, making certain not to squash Kiri between us.

"You've been gone a long time," she said. "Have things been going well for you?"

"Oh . . . well enough," I said, holding Kiri closer.

"Will you and Gaar be home soon, then?"

"Um . . . not that I know of."

"Oh," she said, disappointed. "Well, we left as soon as we got your message. Are you certain everything is all right?"

"Yes. Yes, all is well," I lied. "I just . . . wanted to see you all again. I've missed you so."

"We missed you, too, Mama," said Ran.

I smiled at him and then laughed. "Well," I said, "now that all of you are here . . . have you eaten? Do you have your rooms yet?"

"Here is my room," she said. "The children are next door. But we have not eaten yet."

"And we're hungry, Mama," said Tirell. "Can we eat now?"

"Of course you can," I said. "And the food here is wonderful. You can have as much as you want, too!" The children cheered at that. Then Kiri unburied her head from my chest and looked up at me with her big, round eyes.

"Mama cold," she said.

"Uh—well, the nights are cold here, you know. I just haven't been by the fire."

"No?" said Leta, reaching out for my cheek. I drew away from her touch.

"Are you sure you're all right, Mara?" she asked. "You look . . . different. You look pale."

"I'm fine, Leta. I told you that. I just haven't been out in the sun lately."

"I'm sorry. I was only concerned."

"Yes, well—there's nothing wrong with me."

"Sorry."

"Would you like to eat now?" I asked, changing the subject.

"Yes!" the children cried. I laughed again and held Kiri closer to me. Her warmth was so comforting—her aroma much stronger now, threatening to overwhelm me. I could hold her like this forever. But then, that's what I was planning on doing.

"Be sure and put all your things away," I announced. "And then ask one of the servants to show you where to eat. All right? Leta and I will be with you soon." Ran and Tirell cheered and rushed out the door to their room. I was alone with Leta and my little one now.

"I'm glad you'll be joining us," she said. "We have so much to talk about. So much has happened since you've been away."

"A lot has happened to me, too."

"I'm sure it has," she said. "Both of you, away in a new

land, seeing new and wonderful things. So tell me, what is it like here? What are the people like?"

"It's . . . different."

"I can imagine," she said, turning away to continue her unpacking. "I'd like to see the whole city tomorrow. Could we do that? Walk together through the town, and you could show me all the sights? Or will you be too busy tomorrow?"

"I— think I might be too busy tomorrow. Sorry."

"Oh, that's all right," she said. "I understand. I'm sure you and Gaar must be —"

"That reminds me," she continued. "Where *is* Gaar? We have not yet seen him."

"He's . . . around."

"Oh, I know," she said, turning back to her work. "He must be busy with the other magistrate now, with their trade business, and all that. What was his name again?"

"Gaar."

"No, silly, the *other* magistrate."

"Agyar."

"Ah, yes. Agyar," she said. "Almost akin to Gaar, I notice. Did you notice that their names are a little similar?"

"Umm, no. No, I hadn't."

"Oh. Well, it hardly means anything, I'm certain. But I hope he can join us later. I do miss him . . ."

"So do I," I whispered.

"Hmm? Did you say something?"

"Nothing." Kiri had fallen asleep in my arms. Leta and I were silent for a while, and during that time, I found myself watching Kiri, listening to her soft breathing, smelling her young, fresh aroma, feeling the warm blood pulsing in her young veins. My mouth began to water, and I parted my lips slightly, ready to kiss my daughter, or perhaps to—

"I'm ready," Leta said, startling me. She moved toward me and stroked Kiri's head tenderly.

"Do you want me to put her to bed for you?" she whispered.

"Uh—" I stammered as a tiny drop of spit fell from my mouth. "Yes," I said. "Yes, I'd be grateful if you did."

My friend reached out and took my child from my arms. I was grateful that she had been taken from me. But then there was also the deep, unacknowledged feeling that someone had just stolen prey that I had captured personally, and my nose quivered slightly.

I could wait no longer. If I didn't do it now, then I never would. *We'll be friends forever, we'll be together forever,* I told myself over and over. *I can be with the children for all eternity . . .*

Leta returned without Kiri and smiled warmly. We were alone.

"She was so tired," she said. "I saw that the boys have gone to supper. Shall we go, too?"

"Not yet," I said. "I'd, um—like to show you something first."

"Oh? Show me what?"

She waited patiently for an answer, and I opened my mouth to speak, but then turned away quickly, instead.

"How was the trip here?" I asked.

"Good," she said curiously. "It went well. Not as long as I thought it would be at all. Do you know this is the first time I've ever left Castrill?"

I nodded. "There was money sent to you, wasn't there? To pay for the trip?"

"Yes. Enough for all of us. That was very generous of you. But . . . I can't pay you back until—"

"You needn't worry about that," I said, whirling around and smiling. "Accept it as my gift to you."

"Oh, Mara—"

"Ah-ah!" I said. "My gift. I want nothing in return. Only . . ." I continued, leaning toward her a little.

"Only what?" she asked innocently.

"Only . . . that you stay for a while," I finished. "You will—stay for a while, won't you?"

"Um . . . certainly," she said. "But not too long, you know. Won't you and Gaar be returning yourselves soon? You've been here so long now."

I could play with her no longer. I was tired of lying. I had to get it over with.

"Gaar's dead, Leta," I said.

"What?" she said quietly.

"Gaar's dead," I repeated. "Agyar killed him."

"No . . ."

"Yes."

"Do you know what you are saying?"

"And do you know what has happened to me, Leta? Do you *want* to know?"

"I . . ."

"I'm dead, too."

"What—?"

"It's hard to explain, really . . ." I began, moving around her now. She watched me as I went. "But I am dead, too. Only not really dead. Agyar says that I am *un*dead. Something about being dead but still alive. Perhaps that's why I'm going to 'live' forever. After all, people are dead forever, so if they're *un*dead, instead, wouldn't they be that way forever, too?"

"What—what are you saying, Mara?"

"I'm saying, Leta, that I am not human anymore. Gaar has been brutally—coldly—unjustly—murdered, and I've been . . . changed. Changed into a monster bride of a monster. Agyar, that is. Feel my cheeks, Leta," I commanded. "Go on—feel them."

"This is blasphemous, what you say, Mara!"

"What's happened to me is blasphemous, Leta!" I roared. "Yet you speak as someone who believes in your religion, and I never did! Tell me I'm being punished for that, Leta! Tell me that!"

"I . . ."

"I called you here to make you just like me, Leta! Will your God save you from that? Will He save my children?"

"The . . . children?"

"Yes! The children!"

"Mara, your face! What . . ."

"It looks horrible, doesn't it?" I said. "I'm sorry you ever had to see me this way."

"Mara . . . my dearest friend, what has happened to you? What . . . *are* you??"

"You haven't heard of it," I said. "I don't know if anyone has, really. Gaar and I didn't know. That's why he lies in the woods as food for wolves, and I stand here before you, ready to drain you of every drop of blood you have."

"You . . . *what?*"

"That's how it's done, Leta. A little prick—a tiny bite from this monster's teeth—and then I just drink and drink—and—"

"No!" she yelled, and I rushed forward to cover her mouth.

"Silence!" I hissed. "It'll only be that much worse for the both of us, if you resist! I get no joy from this, Leta; I have no wish to take blood from my own best friend, my own *children*, but it will mean you can live forever!"

She tried to scream again, but I held my hand firmly in place, and she kicked and struggled in vain against my strength. I hardly even felt her blows.

"Please stop struggling, Leta!" I continued. "I'm far stronger than you now. You couldn't possibly get away!" She stopped struggling and watched me with terrified eyes.

"I was against this from the beginning," I said. "I only asked that I be allowed to see you all again, if only to say good-bye to you all. I had no intention of ever making you what I am now, of ever . . . taking your very blood from you! But then Agyar talked to me, and made me think about what it would be like to be an orphan forever, as my children would be if I never saw them again. I was an orphan, too, Leta. It's a miserable existence: no one to talk to you, no one to care for you or wipe away your tears when you're hurt or afraid. I never had a mother, you know; she died as I was born. And Kiri is only two; she may as well have never had a mother, either, if I leave her now."

"What—?"

"I'm going to make you immortal, Leta; I'm going to make all of you immortal! Just think of it; none of us will ever age, never die of disease or hunger. We can be together forever, a family for all time!"

"No!"

"What's wrong, Leta? Does that bother you?" I asked, pushing her down onto her knees and hovering over her. "Believe me, I fought against it, too. I kicked and screamed and I think I even died screaming, too! And for what? I'm still here, walking and talking to you, and to the children. I love them, Leta! I love *you*, too! That's why I want you here with me!"

"It's blasphemy!"

"Why do you keep saying that?" I roared.

"We were offered immortality in the beginning, but sinned against God! Death is our punishment!"

"But you're a good person," I said. "Why should you die for someone else's mistake?"

"It's . . . it's just the way it is!" she cried. "You mean to deliver me from death by drinking my blood? That is the way of witches and demons!"

I dropped to my knees and watched her crawl backward up against the wall. She reached the corner and cowered there, watching me with tear-stained eyes.

"Have I become a demon, then?" I asked quietly.

"I don't know, Mara!" she sobbed. "I don't understand any of this! Why, Mara? Why has this happened to you? Why have I come to visit my dearest friend to find she has become a . . . a . . . I don't know what she has become!"

"Vampire," I said.

"What?"

"A vampire," I repeated. "That's what I've become."

"And you will now . . . drink from me," she sobbed. "You say I'll become immortal if you may only kill me first. You say you do this out of love for me, for the children."

"Leta, I . . . Yes. Yes, I do."

"And what of Gaar?" she asked. "Was he offered this 'immortality,' too?"

"No. He never was. He was always meant to die."

"I see," she said. "And you do not grieve for him?"

"I do," I said. "I grieve for him. I cry for him each night; he has never left my thoughts, Leta. You know I loved him with all my heart; how can you think I didn't?"

"Because you seem to be hiding it so well."

"That was cruel, Leta. You don't understand. You don't understand what that creature has done to me! What he's done to my body, to my mind, and I'm certain my soul, too! I'm nothing now! I have nothing left of me! He's destroyed all that ever was in me, everything that meant anything to me!"

"Who?"

"Agyar, you fool!" I cried. "He's taken my husband, he's taken my home, he's taken my life away from me! And it seems . . ." I said, kneeling onto the floor in front of her, "he's taken my will from me, too. I can't resist him any longer, Leta. I have to do what he says, when he says it. He tells me I must convert all of you, and I no longer have the strength to say no."

"Convert?"

"It's just the word he uses," I said. "To make you like me. Make you all vampires."

"I don't think I like 'convert' being used that way."

"Oh, what does it matter, Leta? I'm going to take your blood! I'm going to take *all* of your blood!"

"No, I beg you—"

"I have to do what he says, Leta—"

"But you don't want to! You don't want to kill us! That's what you said before—"

"What I want makes no difference anymore—"

"It does, Mara! What you want will always make a difference!"

"Shut up!"

"Oh, pray with me, Mara! Pray with me that God will hear, and deliver you from this!"

"I was never a Christian—"

"It's never too late for that! You only need to repent what you have done and ask His forgiveness! Try it, Mara! Please pray with me!"

"I can't . . ."

"You can, Mara! Here," she said, reaching into her coat and withdrawing a small silver cross. "Take this! Hold it and—"

"Aaaaaowwwwww!" I screamed, falling backward onto my fanny. It was so bright! And the heat from it—like flames rushing onto my face and into my eyes! Leta put the cross down and crawled to my side and gripped my hand.

"Don't be afraid, Mara! It *can* work! Just listen to what I say, and repeat after me—"

"Oh, Gods, what have I done? What's happened to me?"

"Your gods cannot help you! They're not real!"

"It almost blinded me!"

"What has?"

"Your . . . thing! Your cross!"

"My . . . ?" she said, and reached behind her to pick up the cross again. She held it before her, and I had to cover my eyes to keep it from burning them.

"It is only my cross, Mara. See?"

"I can't look at it, Leta! It hurts! Please—put it somewhere else!"

"But—but . . . Oh, stop this, Mara! Hold it while I—" I screamed the most horrible scream as she tried to put it into my hand. The flesh on my palm began to burn and scorch the moment she touched it to my skin. She pulled it away instantly and looked at my nearly blackened hand in wide-eyed horror.

"Oh, my God . . ." she whispered. "Oh . . . my . . . God . . ." I scrambled away from her as quickly as I could and cowered by the bed, holding my hand by my bosom and whimpering. She watched me in horrified silence for many moments, then slowly brought the cross up between her and me. I could only glance at it before it threatened to blind me again. My eyes were filling with tears now.

"Mara . . ." she whispered. "You truly are lost. You truly have been . . . rejected," she said.

"It sees your god does not forgive . . ."

"Mara . . ." she said, placing the cross on the floor and crawling to my side. I tried to turn from her, but she gripped my shoulder and turned me back.

"I wish I knew how to help you now," she said.

"You can't. There's no help for me, at least not from your god."

"He is the *only* god."

"So you believe," I said. "It doesn't really matter. I told you I'm lost. I told you there was nothing left of me."

"And do you still mean to do this to me, and your children?"

"I have to . . ."

"Do you want God to reject me, too? Would you make Him cast me out? Cast out your children, too?"

"I didn't know, Leta . . ."

"I have always tried to be a good Christian, Mara," she said. "Please don't take that from me. Immortality? What good would it be for me, without God with me, always?"

"I'm sorry, Leta . . . I only thought it would mean living forever. I had no idea of the consequences . . ."

I began sobbing again, and Leta dared to lean forward and embrace me. I tried using her warmth to comfort me, her human warmth, but it did little good. Suddenly, I gripped her shoulders and forced her to look me in the eyes.

"Kill me," I said.

"Wh-what?" she gasped.

"You must kill me, Leta. I can't continue like this!"

"Mara, what are you—?"

"You yourself said there's no hope for me. Well, there isn't! You must kill me!"

"Oh, no, I . . . I could never—"

"Leta, I do not ask this lightly. If I could do it myself, I would, but I cannot! I don't have the strength or the will to!"

"But neither do I!"

"Yes, you do!" I cried. "You're strong, Leta, and I know you can do this! In the morning, when I'm asleep—"

"Oh, please, Mara, stop this!"

"In the morning, while I sleep, you must take some wood—a sharp piece of wood—and plunge it into my heart! That's how I can die, Leta!"

"No, no, I can't—!"

"You *can!* You *can* do this—for me, for the children— you must kill me!"

In a panic, she thrust her hand over my mouth to stop me.

"No!" she cried. "There must be a better way, there *has* to be!"

I yanked her hand from my mouth and unintentionally bared my fangs at her. She shrank back in fear.

"Does it look like there's a better way?" I hissed. "Do you still think your God will 'save' me? I can't even look at His symbols! There *is* no other way!"

I could feel my eyes burning, the skin tightening on my

face, the drops of spit falling from needle-sharp teeth. Yet the monster was just as terrified as the human.

"Please kill me, Leta," I pleaded. "Please end this existence. Do it for Gaar, do it for me, do it for the children, but most of all, do it because you love me as your best friend!"

"And as my godsister," she said. "Even though you were never a Christian . . ."

"Will you do it, Leta? Will you kill me?"

She closed her eyes momentarily and let her head drop. I saw her lips moving a few times in silent prayer, and then she crossed herself and looked up at me.

"What must I do?" she asked quietly. I threw myself forward and hugged her long and hard, wiping away tears all the while. I kept my arms around her as I told her exactly what to do.

She was to wait until morning, and, without even stopping to eat breakfast, was to pack all of her things up again, the children's, too, and put them all into a carriage. The children were to wait for her there while she sneaked into the kitchen and went to a large iron door there and climbed down the stairs to Agyar's and my sarcophagi. She was to take her sharpened piece of wood and open the left sarcophagus, where I would be sleeping, and plunge it into my heart, then run from the room, out the door, out the kitchen, out of the house as quickly as she could. She and the children were to speed away in their carriage and not stop until they reached a boat leading away from there and go back to Castrill and never come back. I asked that the children be told that Gaar and I had died in the night, from some illness, and they had to get away before they caught it. Leta wanted to tell them the truth, but I asked that she not do that until they were older, when they might be able to understand. I left it up to her to judge when that time had come. She promised to raise my children herself as if they were her own, and I thanked her over and over for all she had ever done for me, and would soon do for me.

"I promise," she said through tears, and I held her in my arms for how long, I do not know, thanking her again and again.

"I pray that God forgives me for this," she said.

"He'll probably reward you, considering how He feels about me right now." For the first time that night, we were able to laugh together as friends, until I begged her to leave me and join the children for supper and tell them how sorry I was that neither I nor Gaar could join them that night. And to tell them how much we both loved them; I made her doubly swear to that.

Eighteen

Agyar was disappointed that I had not completed my "business," but I appeased him by saying that all would be accomplished soon. I was simply letting them rest for the night. It would be all over tomorrow. He smiled coldly and kissed me on the cheek, and I climbed into my sarcophagus and let him cover it up for me.

I did not hear the lid being removed, but my sleep was disturbed by a sharp stick being placed slowly onto my chest. I swallowed once as inconspicuously as I could and waited for my dearest friend to do what she had to. Then the stick was removed, and I heard a quiet sniffling.

Do it, Leta! I cried to myself, but the stick was not placed back.

Do it!

Still nothing, and I opened my eyes ever so slightly to see Leta's shadowy figure crossing herself again and to hear her whispered prayer. Then she loomed over me again, and I forgot myself and opened my eyes all the way, and she gasped and stepped back.

I rose up in the sarcophagus and reached for her arm. She almost cried out when I grabbed it, but I shushed her and took the stake from her hand and held it firmly against my breast. She began shaking her head, and I pulled her toward me and whispered into her ear.

"You have to, Leta," I said. "You have to!"

She started making whimpering sounds, and I covered her mouth quickly and decided to take drastic action. I concentrated and felt my eyes begin to smolder, and I peered straight into her eyes, into her thoughts, into her soul. I watched her own eyes fade from brown to red, and in that moment her mind was hers no longer. It was mine.

"Kill me," I whispered, and guided her hand to the stake by my chest. "Plunge it into my heart, Leta . . ." I commanded. "It's the only way . . ."

"The only way . . ." she echoed, and I lay back down into the coffin, never letting my gaze drift from hers.

"With all your strength, Leta," I whispered. "Push it in!"

"All my strength . . ."

She placed both hands over the end of the stake and bent over me. I shut my eyes then and clenched my fists, and braced myself for the pain.

My head flew back, and I opened my mouth wide but did not scream as she plunged it in. My chest was on fire with pain, and I felt cold blood spilling out all over my chest, but I refused to scream for fear of putting her in danger. I struck the bottom of the sarcophagus several times to help me take the pain, and then she pushed it all the way in. And my body went rigid, I let out several short, loud gasps, and then everything was still. And black.

I heard stone being moved against stone again. I felt my body laid out as it usually was, rather than frozen in agony, as I thought it would be after I died. A cold, wet cloth was placed on my forehead, and my eyes shot open to see Agyar looming over me, his face expressionless. I opened my mouth to speak, but could think of nothing to say, and, besides, my throat was terribly dry.

Agyar reached down and lifted me into a sitting position,

and I watched him, totally confused, as he held out a mugful of fresh, hot blood to me. I hesitated to take it, however.

"Drink," he said. "You lost a lot of blood today."

Silently, I took the mug from him and drank it all in one gulp. He took the mug from me, and I returned to watching him in confusion.

"It seems your 'friend' was not such a friend after all," he announced. "She tried to end your life."

"Really," I said, swallowing once. "And . . . what exactly did she do?"

"Tried to kill you with wood," he said. "Tried to stab you in the heart with this," he added, holding up the bloody stake.

"But fortunately, I pulled it out," he said.

"Pulled it out?"

"Yes," he said. "I told you we can be killed by wood through the heart, as well. But only as long as it remains in place. Otherwise, the wound shall heal, and—" he said, leaning over to kiss my cheek, "—we'll be as good as new."

I looked down at my bloodstained dress and felt my chest hesitantly. No pain. No hole, no wound of any kind. He was right; I was "as good as new."

"All for nothing," I whispered.

"All for nothing," he repeated, smiling pleasantly. "Your 'friend' escaped with your wretched children after this bungled attempt at your life."

"Where are they now?" I pleaded. "Back in Castrill?"

"Probably," he said. "To live out the rest of their wretched lives. I told you it wasn't a good idea to see them again. You should have put your old life completely behind you, as I told you to."

"Yes," I whispered. "I'll have to do that now."

They lived. They all lived. That alone comforted me. But I began sobbing again quietly, and Agyar moved to my side and placed a sympathetic hand on my shoulder.

"She was no friend, Mara. Remember that. What friend would try to kill another friend like that, when you could have given her eternal life?"

"She was a good friend . . ."

"Was a good friend," he said. "But obviously not anymore."

Wrong again, Agyar. She was the best friend anyone could ever have.

I gave up trying to kill myself after that incident. Agyar knew I wanted to die, but he also knew all the ways he could foil my attempts. Usually he used his "calling" power to keep me around so I couldn't try anything. Or hypnosis, when I was being especially cranky. I never bothered to try resisting him at that point; I had no hope anymore.

Another surprise awaiting me was the arrival of the full moon, which came shortly after my children's visit. I noticed that before it arrived, I was getting more and more hungry, but not for blood. As the time grew nearer, I often caught myself unconsciously . . . well, rubbing myself. And then the full moon itself arrived.

I was in a daze. Not just every man, but every *thing* looked attractive to me, at least those that had the right shape. Even Agyar started looking appealing, and before I knew what was happening, we were both running from the house and into the forest, where we threw ourselves to the ground and gave in to our passions.

Gave in completely. I had barely a rational thought in my head as we lay on the ground all night long, relieving ourselves, as it were. What intelligence was still there was so thoroughly repulsed by what I was doing that the only way I saved my sanity was to make Agyar faceless. I made his face, his name, everything about him a blur, for once I realized who I was with, I might have gone completely mad from disgust. There was no love here, only blind, savage lust. And through the night, we were surrounded by wolves, who had been called to us by our passions, and they copulated all around us, as though we were some undead Aphrodites who caused the animals to mate. And this happened all three nights of the full moon.

Afterward, I was certain the whole thing had been a nightmare, but Agyar delighted in telling me it was real, all of it. I wouldn't look him in the eye for two weeks afterward and only spoke when forced to. Eventually, I told him that he had raped me. That got him a good laugh. Raped? As though I had actually been resisting him. *See what happens next moon, and see if you are "raped" again,* he told me.

I shed no more tears over him. They had dried out long ago. I couldn't even cry for Gaar anymore, and that's what really hurt. I had numbed myself to nearly all feelings just to help me cope with Agyar's abuses. Now I am able to mourn for him; it's simply that while with Agyar, I had no choice but to keep it inside.

I had some consolation in knowing that Leta and the children were safe, that they would never succumb to my fate. Unless Agyar had lied to me about that, and they had been captured and killed, but I doubt it. It is more likely that he would gloat about something like that rather than cover it up. But I never saw any of them again, so I choose to believe that they lived out full and happy lives.

I liked to pretend that Ran and Tirell had grown into great soldiers like Gaar had been, and they would come with a huge army, equipped with sharp wooden spears, and skewer Agyar and his wretched creatures and take me away from there. And then we would all find out that Gaar was not dead at all, but was living in a cave somewhere in the forest until we came and found him. And we would be a family again at last.

Yes, it's true; my fantasies were those of a helpless female dreaming of rescue by a dashing hero. But they were my only defense against Agyar for many, many years. I certainly could not kill him myself, much as I dearly wished to, for he still had too much power over me, in addition to all those creatures to protect him should I ever misbehave. Oh, they obeyed me, too, all right, but Agyar's word was always law over mine.

I had difficulty with Lara. She was cheerful, energetic, enthusiastic, and always willing to obey me, but she was also a strange girl. She enjoyed being a vampire far too much for my tastes. Even her mother was proud of her for having been "worthy" of the Great Gift of immortality. *Gods, what sort of mind manipulation does Agyar perform with his servants,* I wondered again.

Some number of years had passed by, when it occurred to me that I had never seen anyone else from Clovaine except those people of Agyar's home. The town was always there, every day and night, but nobody came out at night, or at least no one I could see. And of course, I couldn't watch the town when the sun was up.

Agyar had come to ignore me for the past part, fortunately. No doubt he felt safe that I wouldn't try to escape, or kill him, or even kill myself. I spent most of my nights sitting up on the roof, by myself, watching the sky and just thinking. Very boring. I had to do something different.

So I decided to pay a visit to the town, people or no people. I knew they were there, they were simply locked away for the night. I was pretty certain now why this was so, mind you, but I was dreadfully curious about what they were like, anyway.

I did not tell Lara what I intended, for I knew she would tell Agyar if he happened to ask about my whereabouts. She may have been my servant, but I was *his*, so his commands were above mine. If he asked, she had to tell.

So one night, while on the roof, I spread my arms, leapt over the wall, and transformed. The town was not far at all; only a few minutes' flight away. My only fear at the time was that Agyar would decide for some reason or another, to call while I was visiting the people. But he wasn't doing that very often anymore, fortunately.

I landed in the outskirts, using the shadows to hide my descent as best as I could. I hardly think there was much need for such secrecy, considering how deserted the place was, but I didn't want to take any chances.

I walked calmly and silently through the town center, keeping my gaze mostly straight ahead but occasionally throwing side glances into alleys and other dark corners. The hovels I passed were modest enough—most of them about the size of Gaar's and mine all those years ago. They were rather dull and drab, also, much like the Castrillians' homes before Gaar took over. He had encouraged the people to make their hovels more festive—make them look more like homes.

I stopped at a hovel near the edge of the town and decided to give those people a try. *But how to go about it,* I wondered. *Simply walk up and knock on the door? Or perhaps I ought to call to them from here; I could call to no one in particular, perhaps asking where everybody was.*

I walked up and knocked on the door. They were not asleep inside; light was peeping out through the shutters, and I heard some muffled voices arguing with themselves, and then shushing themselves quiet. I sensed that they were near the door but would not answer, and I knocked again quickly, pretending to be frantic.

"Who is it? What d'you want?" a male voice called from inside.

"A traveler," I called back. "I'm coming from across the sea and need a place for the night."

"We have no room here!" the voice said.

"I'll sleep somewhere else, if you like, sir," I answered. "But I just need to rest my feet for a while. Could you lend a hand to a stranger, sir? Just for a while?"

I hoped that speech would be enough to get me in, and

sure enough, they began arguing with themselves again, until they stopped suddenly, and I heard a lock on the door being undone. Then, after a pause, the door opened, and a woman was there, a short plump woman, which was a welcome change from those anemic, scrawny servants back at Agyar's. I smiled as pleasantly as I could to her.

"Thanks to you, mistress," I said. "I only need a warm fire and a place to sit." She did not return my smile, but silently looked me up and down, taking in my appearance, seemingly looking for some flaw in me. But I knew I looked human.

She seemed satisfied with my appearance, and opened the door wider, stepping aside a little to let me pass. Her husband stood off to the side and near the back of the house, eyeing me suspiciously. I smiled again, and bowed my head quickly, and stepped forward.

My entrance to the house was abruptly stopped by—something. I'm not sure how to describe it, really. It was sort of like an invisible wall, but not really; it was more like—a force of some kind. A force that was there, but not there, and could not be passed. Agyar had told me of it, but I had never encountered it before. I stopped where I was and smiled at the man.

"But I wouldn't want to come in, knowing the master does not welcome me," I said. The man tilted his head a little in apparent contemplation, and then nodded to me and gestured to a small table at the center of the room. And the force disappeared; I was free to enter.

I seated myself at the table and sighed, still smiling at the family. Several small children toddled over to me slowly, apparently curious to see a new face. I patted the head of one of them, and his mother reached out and brought him close to her. I smiled a little weakly at her then. All eyes of the household were upon me, and I shifted a little uncomfortably.

"It feels good to rest," I said, trying to break the ice. "I've been walking a long time."

"You say you're from across the sea," the man said slowly. "From what land?"

"Umm . . . Castrill," I said. "Across the Channel, really."

"Oh," he said. "So what brings ye here?"

"I was . . . I am making my way to the East," I said. "To rejoin my husband."

"You poor thing," the woman said. "Making such a long trip all by yourself?"

"Yes, well . . . I am used to it. We've been separated before. But he tells me he's become very rich there, and I'm to join him now."

"Found a fortune, has he?" said the man.

I smiled and shrugged.

"But ye shouldn't be wandering about so here," the woman chastised. "It's too dangerous for one like—"

She was stopped by her husband barking at her, and she seemed ashamed at what she had said and walked away from the table. But this was what I had come to town for; this was what I really wanted to talk about.

"Dangerous, you say?" I said. "How so?"

"She means nothing by it," the man said quickly. "Pay her no mind."

"But if I'm to be traveling about here, I ought to know what I'm in for," I insisted. "I have no one to protect me but myself. Oughtn't I know?"

The man glared at his wife quickly, who looked away in shame, and then he moved toward me carefully and pulled out a chair. He motioned me forward, and I leaned over to let him whisper into my year, "No one goes out at night. Not while . . . those *things* are out there."

"Things?" I asked innocently.

"Things!" he repeated. "Awful things . . . these horrible monsters, pale and dirty, with evil eyes and teeth and claws that'll tear your throat from you right where ye stand!" No doubt he had told this tale to his children before, for they became frightened rather quickly, and ran over to their mother, who held them close to her and tried to comfort them.

"They'll steal the life from you, take yer soul!—and you'll be a livin' corpse, walking the shadows of the earth for eternity!"

Even I began to shiver at his words. And what frightened me most was that none of it was just old wives' tales; it was all true. I licked my lips slightly and leaned back.

"I saw . . . no such creatures," I whispered.

"Ahhh, ye were lucky!" he said. "But ye might not be so fortunate, if ye stay in this place, walking about unprotected at night. They can only strike at night, ye see, for the sun'll burn them to a crisp!"

"I'm sure I can make it out of here safely if I just find an inn—"

"No inns in this town," he said. "You'll have to find someone who'll take ye in for the night."

"Oh," I said. "Well . . ." I said, rising from my seat, "I should trouble you no longer, then—"

"Jacob!" the woman called. Jacob turned to his wife, and I stopped to listen. She threw him a few curious looks, gesturing toward me a little with her shoulders.

"We can't let her go walking about all alone like that," she chastised. Jacob rose and cast me a quick glance before rushing over to his wife to argue with her.

"No, really, I can take care of myself," I protested over their disagreement. I certainly couldn't afford to stay there all night, after all. They ignored me and continued arguing, she for me to stay, and he, to not get involved.

"I'm certain they won't bother me, good people," I continued. No use. They were really going at it, and I had little choice but to think of a way to get away from there. Then I was momentarily distracted by a wide-eyed little girl who stood before me, watching me intently with round blue eyes. She made me think of Kiri, as I remembered her, and the sound of her parents' arguing was soon drowned out by my own fascination with the girl.

We watched each other unblinkingly for some time, and then I couldn't help slowly beginning to smile at her, perhaps hoping she would smile back. But then she broke away her gaze and ran from me, rushing up to her mother and clutching her leg. I stopped smiling and looked down, a little sad now.

The adults finished their "discussion," and it was rather obvious that the woman had won. She came toward me, smiling and extending her arms. I moved back a little, but she took my hands into her own and began leading me toward the back of the room.

"It's far too dangerous for you," she said. "You'll be staying with us tonight, and then you'll be safe to move on. And . . . Why, you're chilled to the bone!" she exclaimed. "You'll be by the fire tonight, as well."

"No, really, I . . . I ought to find someplace else," I protested.

"Oh, no," she said. "Not with those monsters out there! It'd be inhuman of us to let them loose on you! You're so young and fair—ye don't deserve the fate they deal out to travelers . . ."

"Don't I?" I said.

"Of course not," she said, leading me to a pile of bedding. "Now you just lie here for the night, and you'll be safe that way—"

I broke away from her and backed off, shaking my head.

"I'm sorry, mistress, I . . . I really can't stay," I said. "I'll find somewhere else, and I'll be safe. You needn't worry about—"

"I'd never forgive myself if something should happen to you—"

"I've imposed myself too much on you already—"

"No, no, you'll stay here," she insisted rather firmly this time, reaching for my hand again. I was near panic by now; what was I to do? Staying was out of the question, but how to get away from there? The only solution I could come up with was simply bolting for the door and running away. But what would that make them think? That might very well frighten them even more than they already were.

"She don't want to stay," Clairisse," Jacob then intervened. I thanked the gods silently. "Why don't ye just let her go, then?"

"You know that wouldn't be right!"

"She's trying to leave, Clairisse!" he said, more loudly this time. "Why don't we let her?"

"I'm quite certain I'll be safe," I said quietly, smiling as pleasantly as I could. I could sense Clairisse's frustration in having to give in to us. She alternated her glances first at him, then me, then him, until she sighed loudly and walked away, shaking her head.

"I'm sure someone else'll be happy to take you in," said Jacob, placing his hand on my back to turn me toward the door.

"Wait," Clairisse called suddenly, and Jacob turned to chastise her, only she stepped boldly past him and stopped in front of me. She held a small bag in her hand.

"Take this with you, then," she said, closing my hands around the bag. "It'll give you some protection."

"But *we* need—"

"We have plenty of it left, Jacob!" she called to him curtly. I was curious as to the bag's contents; its smell answered my question before I opened it to peer inside.

"Garlic?" I said.

She nodded quickly. "It's said to be protection against the creatures," she whispered. "Keep it in your hand while y'walk, hold it in front of you always. And walk quickly!"

"Umm, thank you," I said. "Thank you, mistress— master. I'll even rub it all over me, if I have to!" I added, and made many quick bows on my way to the door. Finally I could get out of there. Clairisse followed me to the door and even watched me walk out into the night, holding the door slightly ajar all the while. I stopped some yards away from the house and looked over at her and smiled and waved a little. Then I pulled out a bulb and held it up for her to see, and began walking away.

As I continued walking, I heard the door shut swiftly, followed by the sounds of locks being pushed and turned into place. I stopped and dropped the bulb back into the bag and closed it up and sighed. If these people were using garlic to protect themselves, no wonder they were so frightened . . .

Nineteen

"I forbid you to return to that town," Agyar said after he had discovered my little escapade.

"They're terrified of you, you now," I said, ignoring his anger. "They're terrified to even leave their homes at night."

"They are not afraid of *me,*" he insisted. "They fear my servants, I'm afraid."

"Then why don't you do something about it? Or do you *like* them running around terrorizing your people?"

"I cannot waste my time keeping track of every servant I have, Mara," he growled. "What they do on their own, once they have been fed—"

"—is go out into the village and frighten everyone, that's what they do!" I interrupted.

"You listen to me, woman," he warned, his eyes fading into red now. "I don't like my servants frightening the villagers any more than you do. But I can only control them so much; they're wild creatures! They know only hunger, thirst, cold, heat, and comfort; beyond that, they have no conscience—no sense of decency or morality. I can only do so much with them—"

"And whose fault is that?" I interrupted.

Agyar stiffened. His eyes began to glow a little, and I felt my will being drained slightly.

"They are the way they are," he said in a low growl, "because I wish them to be the way they are. They may be animals. They may possess no minds, no wills of their own, but that is exactly as I wanted them to be. And I think you ought to bear in mind—in case you decided to criticize my judgment again—that I could just as easily have made you the same way. Understand . . . dear?"

He watched me intently, waiting for my answer, but I returned his gaze for some time before I decided to respond.

"I understand," I whispered finally. "Dear."

"Kiss me," he said one night in his study. I hesitated for a second or two, and then leaned over to peck him on the cheek. I leaned back to continue reading my tome, and he sighed once in frustration.

"That's not the best you can do," he said.

"I think it is," I said, not bothering to look up.

"Put the book away," he said.

This time I looked up at him, doing my best to keep my face expressionless. "Why?" I asked.

"Because I want you to."

"Ah," I said. "Of course." I closed the book and set it aside, clasping my hands together and waiting for whatever was next. Agyar moved toward my chair silently and took my hand and yanked me onto my feet. He smiled coldly and pushed my hair from my eyes and forced his lips over mine. I resisted him by keeping my lips "dead"—that is, letting his do all the work while mine did nothing. Finally, he pushed me away in frustration and turned away.

"Why do you do this to me?" he complained.

"Do what, dear?" I asked calmly, seating myself once again.

He whirled around and glared. "You know perfectly well what I mean!" he cried. "You refuse me! No matter what I do for you, always you refuse me."

"Do I?" I said. "I'm sorry. I didn't know I was doing that. You know I only wish to please you."

"You wish to torment me, is what you wish!" he said, leaning so close to me I could feel his breath on my face.

"Why?" he continued. "Why do you torment me, and yourself? Why won't you simply come out and admit it?"

"Admit what, dear?" I asked, feigning curiosity. He leaned close to me again, and I had to resist shrinking back in disgust.

"Why won't you admit that you love me?" he whispered.

It was all I could do to keep from laughing in his face. Love him? We had been together for some thirty years or so, and he still knew nothing about me! He was either too stupid or too stubborn to realize how much I hated him—or both!

"Because I don't," I said very calmly. He made a quick sound of anger and frustration before standing up and impulsively raising his arm as if to strike me.

"Liar!" he said. "I know you love me, and you always have! You're only too stubborn to admit it!"

"If you say so, dear," I said.

"I know you at least loved me once," he continued. "And do you know how I know that?" he asked, now hovering over my face. I raised an eyebrow in mock curiosity.

"If you never loved me," he said, "then why was I able to seduce you so quickly, so many years ago? Why did you give your will so quickly to mine, back when you thought you were oh-so-happily married? Answer me that . . . dear!"

And then he had to strike the ultimate blow. And then he had to imply—no, he *insisted*—that I had never really loved Gaar at all, but had only pretended to be happily married, until he came along and "showed me otherwise."

That was too much. He could insult me, taunt me, beat me, torture me, and destroy my mind and will—I no longer cared—but he could not insult Gaar's memory and get away with it. Without hesitation, I stood up and hit him as hard as I could, and I felt no horror, shock, or guilt at having done so. I felt good.

Agyar nearly lost his balance and had to grip a small nearby table to keep himself from toppling over. I tensed my muscles slightly in preparation for any counterattack he would no doubt make. Perhaps it had been a long time, but I still remembered all my combat techniques and could still defend myself if necessary.

Surprisingly, he did not counterattack but only turned his head quickly to look into my eyes. His own eyes burned bright red, and I could feel him assaulting my mind, trying to get in and drain my will away. But I was far too angry to allow him to win. That, and I had been becoming much better at resisting his hypnotic powers; in fact, it had become rather rare for them to actually work on me.

He gritted his teeth—now needle-sharp—in a vicious snarl and shook with rage. And still his eyes tried to burn through to my soul, but I would not let them. I'm not sure how long we stood that way, our eyes and minds locked in a fierce, silent combat that neither of us was about to lose.

It did have some effect on me. I could not move, as all my concentration was focused on defending my mind from his control, and he was thus able to reach out suddenly and grip my shoulder. I was startled, but my concentration remained intact, until he suddenly shoved me away from the chair, where I smashed backward into a table and almost fell over.

"Get out of here," he growled. "Get out of my sight, you witch! Get away!"

I was only too happy to leave the room, released from that mental battle as I was. And just in time, too, for I had been only a few seconds away from giving in. Agyar's powers were still far greater than mine. A vampire's powers increase with age and experience, you see, and he had at least a three-thousand-year head start on me. But I would never stop trying.

Twenty

I chose to spend my time in the stables the rest of the evening. I know what you're thinking: it's a noisy and smelly place, so why bother going *there* of all places? Well, I knew that Agyar never went there himself, and that alone was good enough for me.

I didn't expect to find Lara when I entered, but it was good to see her, anyway. I needed somebody to talk to, and Agyar's creatures wouldn't do.

She was crouched low in a far corner, eyeing a cow lumbering back and forth in its stall. I saw her fangs flash as she smiled, and she began creeping slowly and silently toward the big animal.

She didn't seem to notice me, so I crept up to the other side of the stall and knelt down, waiting for her to approach. She was quiet enough, but my ears are much sharper than a human's, even more so than most vampires', and I popped my head up the moment I sensed she was near. She caught sight of me and yelped once and nearly fell backward in fright.

"Mistress!" she cried. "Don't frighten me like that!"

"Sorry," I said, coming around the stall to join her, "I was only teasing."

I reached her and took her into my arms in a tight hug and kissed the top of her head. She looked at me curiously when we parted.

"Have you and the master fought again?" she asked.

"Yes," I said. "You're getting very perceptive. That, or I've become very predictable."

"You're predictable," she said.

I laughed and rubbed her shoulder. I couldn't take the smell in this place much longer, though.

"Umm . . . Lara," I said, "do you really like being in here? The stench is unbearable."

She smiled and shrugged. "Your senses are much better than mine," she said. "But we can leave, if you like."

"Oh, thank you!" I said, and I put my arm around her and led her from the stables. We walked a bit before finding a storage room, and sat beside each other on the floor.

"If you hate the smell, then why go to the stables, mistress?" she asked.

I sighed. "I was just trying to find a place to be alone. But what about you? What were you doing to that cow?"

She looked down, apparently ashamed. "Oh . . ." she said, "just . . . um . . . playing. That's all."

"It looked like you were charming it."

"Oh, well, that's . . . um . . . yes, I was just charming it. I do that with all the animals. Just for play. I'm not allowed to charm people, remember?"

"Oh," I said, nodding. "I see."

"I mean, it's not as though I take blood from them, too, or . . . anything." Too late for her words. Lara and I were bonded by blood; I could sense her stronger feelings.

"Lara . . ." I said warningly, "I don't think you're telling me the truth."

She laughed nervously and shrugged. "What's there to tell?" she asked. "I was only playing."

"Lara . . ." I said in a gentle tone. "If you're afraid of my finding out anything, well, don't be. I don't care what you do, and do you really think I would tell Ag—er, the master anything?"

"Um . . . no," she said. "No, I guess you wouldn't. I mean, of course you wouldn't. We're friends."

"We're *best* friends," I corrected, and patted her knee. "So tell me; you weren't cheating, were you?"

"Oh, well . . . only a little, really," she said. "Only sometimes. I mean, I don't take that much, really I don't. You can even look at them, you'll see I'm not making them anemic or anything."

"That's fine, love, that's fine," I said in my most reassuring voice. "I'm not angry. But then, if I were you, I'd stop 'cheating' like that. Sooner or later, the master will find out."

"Well, maybe he'll think one of his smelly vampires did it."

"Maybe, but I wouldn't hope too much. Meanwhile, I'd rather not spend all night talking about blood. It bothers me."

"Yes," she said, "Makes *me* hungry, too."

Must she always spell things out so bluntly?

"Umm, well . . ." I said, and put my arm around her. "Maybe we'll play a game or something. Do you know any games?"

She shrugged. "We could play 'Charm the Cow,' " she said.

"Uh, no, that's all right," I said.

Lara sighed. "Mmm, no, I'm bored with that, too," she said. "I wish I could practice on people, though."

"Why?"

"Oh, I don't know, make them do funny things, or something. Give them after-commands. For instance—"

"I don't like being charmed myself, Lara," I said. "I don't think other people do, either."

"Oh, I wouldn't hurt them," she insisted.

"I know that, but it's just not very kind, that's all. I'd rather you charm *me* than some other poor soul. After all, the master would—"

"May I?" she cried suddenly. "May I practice on you, mistress?"

"What?"

"I promise I won't make you do anything you don't want, and I won't make you—"

"Wait, wait, *wait*, love . . ." I said, but she grabbed hold of my arm and tugged it. The real blow was when she gave me that look which never failed to make me give in to her requests, the look that put lonesome puppy dogs to shame.

"Aaaack!" I cried. "Stop that, stop making that face!"

"Oh, pleeeeease, mistress?" she said, loving every minute of this. "Please let me charm you?"

"I hate it when you beg like this—"

"Pleeeeease?"

She flashed me another one of those looks of hers and soon I had no choice.

"All right!" I cried, throwing my arms up in surrender. "All right, you win! Do as you wish!"

She shrieked and clapped her hands in glee, then scooted around so we were facing each other.

"Oh, thank you, mistress!" she cried. "Thank you, thank you!"

"I wouldn't be letting you do this if you hadn't cheated."

"Oh, I promise not to make you do anything you—"

"—wouldn't want to, I know. I trust you, love," I said. "But you ought to calm down first."

"Oh, yes," she said. "Calm down." She started taking slow, deep breaths until she had calmed herself sufficiently. I suppressed my laughter in the meantime.

"I'm ready now, mistress," she said. "So . . . what must I do?"

"You do pretty much what you do with the cows, I suppose," I said. "Do you look at their eyes, and feel for their thoughts?"

"Mmmhmm . . ."

"And, after that, you make your thoughts into theirs?"

"Umm . . . yes. Yes, that's what I do."

"Well, just do that, then."

"That's it?" she said. "It's not different, or harder?"

"Oh, it's certainly harder than charming a cow," I said. "But don't worry; I won't resist you."

"Please don't," she said. "You'd end up charming *me,* instead."

"I promise not to do that."

"Secret promise?"

I laughed. "All right, secret promise," I said, and we reached out to grab each other's noses.

"I secret promise not to charm you, instead," I said, and we let go.

"Good," she said. "I know you won't break *that.*" As though we ever had any real punishment for breaking "secret promises"! I was getting impatient, though.

"I think you're just stalling, cub," I said.

"I'm not," she said. "I'm starting right now."

"Of course. Start, then."

She was silent, and she took more deep breaths. I relaxed and reminded myself not to resist in any way. Then we looked each other straight in the eyes, and Lara started to giggle, until I slapped her playfully on the thigh. She forced herself to stop giggling, and then her eyes started changing . . .

I almost started to resist, but then forced myself not to. It wasn't easy, as she was inexperienced and was a bit rough getting into my mind. I ended up guiding her in myself, until she got the feel of it, and then her thoughts became mine. All she needed do now was give a command.

Most of it was a blur after that. I remember she was very excited about having charmed a person for the first time, and her former mistress, no less. She clapped a lot and told me how she could feel my mind and all. I already knew what it felt like to charm someone, though.

Then I became overwhelmed with fear—not mine, but Lara's, and there was an awful tearing sensation as she tried to pull her mind from mine too quickly. I almost passed out, when suddenly another mind smashed its way into my thoughts, and I was back to being someone's servant.

Agyar's.

"W-we were only playing, master," Lara gasped. "W-we meant no harm."

"You've done quite well, Lara," he said, his gaze never leaving mine. "I'm actually rather proud of you."

"Y-you are, master?" she gulped.

"Yes," he said, still watching me. "You've controlled her when I could not. I thank you. You may go now."

"Sh-she asked me to, master," she continued. "We were just playing, you see, so it's not as though—"

"You may go, Lara," he said, and she stopped babbling instantly and ran from the stables in terror. And I wanted to do the same, but could not. Agyar smiled again and gestured silently for me to stand, and I obeyed. I had become fairly competent at resisting his charming, but if a vampire actually succeeds in charming someone, the victim might as well stop resisting. It's almost impossible. I was his to command.

He reached a hand for my chin and cradled it.

"Kiss me," he said. "Kiss me like you mean it."

I wrapped my arms around his neck and kissed him exactly as he wished—like I meant it. Then he let me part from him, but I could only wait for more orders.

"Why do you despise me, Mara?" he murmured. "Why do you loathe me so? You loved me once, I'm sure of it. Tell me you loved me!"

"I loved you," I said, trying in vain to resist. He would not let his concentration falter, however.

"But you hate me now, much as I tell myself otherwise. This should not be; we were destined for each other! But destined for each other in love, not hate! Yet you hate me. Why, Mara? Why do you hate me?"

I had plenty of reasons for hating him, and I struggled

to let them escape my lips, but he didn't truly want to hear them. He held my mind in his own; he ought to have sensed my reasons, if not understood them outright. But he didn't want me to actually say them, and I remained silent.

"Love me, Mara," he pleaded. "It's all I ask of you. Love me, and I swear you shall live as a queen. I am magistrate now, and could be so much more, but your hatred holds me back. It cripples me, Mara! I offer you so much, yet you'll take none of it! Is love so much to ask for? Is it truly such a torture for you to take me in your arms and hold me and kiss me and stay with me forever? Is it?

"Please try to love me, Mara," he pleaded. "I don't want to have to keep commanding you to kiss me or hold me. It wearies me to have to charm you always, as I'm certain it wearies you. If only to make things better for both of us—try to love me," he said, and his eyes stopped glowing, and I could feel his mind pulling out of mine, and my own will growing as strong as it ever was. Love him of my own free will—that's all he wanted, he said. He would be so happy if I only loved him, he had said, and I would be a queen.

Twenty-one

Agyar did find out about Lara's playing in the stables and practicing on the animals, which I feared would happen. So he tried to punish her.

He *tried* to punish her. He ordered her to be whipped ten times; only I intervened and prevented any lashings. I told him that if the end of a whip came within ten feet of her, I would kill him. He knew I meant it, so he ordered the lashings for me, instead. I never told Lara what had happened, and wouldn't let her give me any rubdowns or baths until the scars went away. That didn't take too long, fortunately.

Obviously, I made no effort to love Agyar after he had commanded me to, which only drove him to further punishment. He must have believed that fear and pain were important parts of love, or he wouldn't have expected me to learn to love him after being beaten. I did fear him, I'll give him that. I was terrified of him. But I wasn't going to let that fear make me give in to him, either.

He was always trying all sorts of tricks to have his way with me, besides the hypnotizing, blackmailing, threatening, and other such things. As an instance, some decades into our "marriage," I spied him talking with an old woman for a few days in a row. Later on, I watched her leave the house for the last time, and before I knew it, she had van-

ished in a big flash of light and smoke! A witch! I thought.
He's associating with witches now?

Oh, why not, I thought. We are creatures of magic,
after all, just as they are. Anyway, I thought it was amus-
ing that he was associating with old hags, so I thought
little of it.

Then Agyar called me into his study. I asked him about
the witch, only he came defensive and ordered me to just
drink the blood he'd brought me. To my surprise, it was
animal blood; or at least, it wasn't human blood. But whatever it was, it was ghastly, and I almost choked on it. I
knew it wasn't the blood, though; he had put something in
there. Agyar feigned innocence and ordered me to finish
the drink. Eventually I forced it down and made many faces
afterward. Then Agyar started questioning me again—the
usual questions, such as why I hated him so. I gave him
my usual curt answers, but he kept on asking, and I started
to feel very strange. The more he talked, the more questions
he asked, the more I found myself unable to answer them.
I started to become confused—confused about why he
would ask me why I hated him; why did he think—?

"I . . . I don't hate you, Agyar," I remember saying to
him under clouded thoughts. "Why do you think
that . . . ?"

"You mean, you don't hate me, Mara?" he asked somewhat cautiously.

"No . . ." I said. "I . . . I love you."

I remember he smiled that cold smile of his, but it
looked so wonderful to me then. I sighed and fell into his
arms and kissed him again and again.

"A love potion," I said after we parted. "You've given
me a love potion."

"I don't know what you mean, darling," he said. "You've
simply come to your senses, that's all."

"If I didn't adore you so right now, Agyar," I whispered,
"I'd despise you for this."

* * *

And so it went for some twenty years. That's how long the potion lasted. During those twenty years, I was utterly in love and hate with him. Both, really. Let me explain something. Love potions work, but only on the surface. They only cover up what feelings are really there, only those feelings are crushed down so tight that the potion's effects reign supreme. Until they wear off, that is. I knew that deep down I still despised Agyar with every part of my soul, but the potion wasn't letting that come out. It tried, though. While I was giving him rubdowns, shining his boots, dressing him, bedding down with him, combing his hair, and so on, I would occasionally remind him that once the potion wore off, I would go back to despising him.

Lara couldn't quite understand me the whole time. I asked her to be patient with me while she could, for he had me under a spell which would wear off eventually. She had to be patient because Agyar took the opportunity to chastise me for not treating Lara the way I was supposed to, meaning as a servant. She was supposed to be tending to all my needs, not playing games and such. Under normal circumstances I would have lashed out at him for saying such things, but I sat and listened to him, all smiles and nodding my head vigorously. But each time I gave Lara an order, I asked her forgiveness under my breath, and asked her again to please be patient.

Twenty-two

I ought to be fair and give an update on Clovaine's situation. It was becoming poorer and poorer each year, just like the rest of the Western Empire. And Agyar was not exactly known for keeping up friendly contact with his people or offering support or advice regarding their situation. The wheat crops were still decent enough—no one died for lack of bread—but Agyar was having a harder time getting taxes from his people. The little existing militia was practically disbanded, and our own wealth within the house was suffering. No more pretty new dresses for me, it seemed, which I didn't really care about, anyway. I worried much more about the suffering of Clovaine's people than about my own lack of wealth.

Naturally, it bothered Agyar. He loved wealth and power, but he was quickly losing that means to happiness. He began talking often of moving to the East and seeking wealth there. I thought it was a most wonderful idea (still under the potion's influence at this point), and did my best to help him prepare for our departure. But it ended up being a distant fantasy for him in the end, as he could never really seem to mobilize himself into action.

So the East became his ultimate goal for a while—his final dream, his lost cause. This went on for some seventy more years—long after the love potion wore off. Things then went back to normal for us. I continued hating him and he continued being desperate. I'm certain he would have liked to find his witch friend again, but she was either long gone or long dead by this time—though witches aren't supposed to be immortal, so she was probably long dead. Needless to say, Agyar never tried the love potion on me again.

My anger now was a lot more subdued. I stopped snapping at him at all times, and my sarcasm was much more subtle. Most of the time I'm certain he didn't even realize I was using it. I believe my change in tactics was partly due to the potion itself. Oh, not because there were still some residual effects involved, but simply because it was a rather humbling experience. I had effectively been his love slave for some two decades, and I lived in constant fear that he could make me be such again.

This time I truly had given up all hope of escaping him. Whatever he asked, I did it—no complaints, no snide comments or sarcasm . . . I just did it. If he had asked me to convert every servant in the house, I would have done it. If he had asked me to run around on all fours and howl at everyone—and in human form, no less—I'm certain I would have done that, too. I really didn't care anymore. And even Lara noticed my change in personality.

"Perhaps we could fly together, mistress," she said one night on the roof. "To help cheer you up."

"If you wish, love," I breathed. "But not too far. I'm a little tired tonight."

"You're always tired," she said. "Come—" she continued, tugging at my arm. "A good flight will make you feel a lot better."

We flew past the forest and soon turned back toward the house. I was ready to land, but Lara indicated that she wanted to do some more exploring in the Channel's direction, and I decided to follow. The Channel was still a good few hours' flight away, but we didn't really intend to travel that far. Besides, I was becoming tired again and meant to turn back soon, Lara or no Lara. Also, I remembered that Agyar had wanted me back long before sunrise; he had said he wanted to drink a glass of wine with me in honor of our one hundred fifty-third "wedding" anniversary. I couldn't afford to keep him waiting.

I indicated that I was going to head back to the house, when Lara screeched and bade me look down. And peering through the darkness, I saw a carriage—a small one, really, but a carriage that held two people. One was lying down in the back while the other drove, and I couldn't tell which sex either of them were, as they both wore large, heavy cloaks. And they were definitely headed for Clovaine.

Lara wanted to swoop down and frighten them, maybe even nibble at them a little, but I scolded her for that and insisted we return, instead. If they decided to visit us, then so be it, and if they passed right by us, instead, then so be that, too.

When I reached Agyar's guest room, I heard a servant mention that it had started to rain. I had seen the clouds when Lara and I were flying, and that was part of the reason I had wanted to return quickly. Running water and vampires do not get along very well, you see.

Agyar had a small candelabra lit on the room's center table, and he held out a small tray with two goblets on it, waiting to be drunk from. I took one silently and began to drink from it, but Agyar held it away from my lips and took his own goblet and set the tray down.

"We must drink together," he said, and touched his goblet to mine.

"As you wish," I said.

"To one hundred fifty-three years of marriage," he said. "To one hundred-fifty-three years of misery. You have always scorned my love."

"I have," I said. "And I plan to keep doing so."

"Yes, I would imagine you do," he agreed. "It's almost a game to you. You gain pleasure from making me miserable—"

"I think it's only fair. After all, you destroyed my life—and my will. Though, I may obey your every command, you shall never make me love you."

"I know that," he said. "And I have finally grown tired of trying. In fact, I have been considering—" He was interrupted by a frantic knocking at the door.

"We're busy!" he yelled, and tried to complete his previous sentence, but the knocking persisted. Making a sound of anger, he stood and stormed over to the door and swung it open quickly. A small, timid boy servant was there.

"I told you we were busy!" Agyar yelled.

"F-forgive me, master," the boy stammered, "but there are people who seek refuge here. From the storm. Should I send them away?"

Agyar towered over the boy, and, after casting several glances back at me, gave his final answer.

"No," he said. "Let them in. But have them wait for me in the first guest room. Give them something to eat, too, if they need it and we can spare it."

"Yes, master," the boy said, and turned as if to leave, but then stopped.

"Uh . . . one of them is very ill, master," he continued. "What should I do with him?"

"Ill, hmm?" said Agyar, rubbing his chin. "Have them wait in one of the bedrooms, then. I'll be down shortly."

"Yes, master," said the boy, and scampered away. Agyar turned to face me again.

"We have visitors, it seems," he said, and I nodded silently.

"Come," he continued, offering his arm, which I took obediently. "We'll go to greet them now. It will be good to see some fresh blood around here."

* * *

"We cannot thank you enough, good sir," the woman said as she drank from her mug of wine. "My husband has fallen so ill these past few days . . . And then this storm coming in— We had to rest. We thank you for giving us such fine shelter."

"There is little need for thanks," said Agyar, resting in his favorite chair. I stood behind him silently. The woman took a long sip from her wine and set the mug down. Then she drew her cloak more tightly about her and moved closer to the hearth.

"Oh, hospitality must always be thanked," she said. "But I fear we have little money with which to repay you. Perhaps a gift of some kind?"

"This is no trouble at all," Agyar insisted. "We're always happy to take in newcomers to Clovaine."

"Oh, we're really only passing through," the woman said. "My husband and I mean to travel to the East, you see. But he has fallen ill, and—"

"Where do you hail from?" Agyar asked.

"From Britain," she said. "Across the sea. From London."

I was hoping they had come from Castrill, instead, but I kept my silence.

"The land has become poor, and people are falling to plagues," she continued. "We are praying that we can find a new life in the East."

"They say there is much wealth there," said Agyar.

"So we hear, as well," she agreed. "But we only wish for enough with which to live comfortably. We have taken very little with us for the journey."

"I see," he said. "Well, perhaps you will both find wealth there—or what you deem to be 'comfortable' . . ."

"I pray so," she said. Finishing off the wine in her mug, she stared into it, apparently deep in contemplation. Then she put it down suddenly and pulled her cloak in tightly again.

"I should see to my husband now," she said. "He's very ill, you see, and I should be with him tonight."

"Yes. Yes, I understand," said Agyar, who then rose to his feet to offer the woman a hand up. She thanked him courteously and made ready to leave.

"Again, we can't thank you enough," she said. "You've been so kind."

"Please—we're always happy to have guests," he said. "Enjoy your rest tonight, Lady . . . ?"

"Oh . . . Heleyne," she said. "I am Heleyne, and my husband is Charles. And you, good sir . . . ?"

"Agyar," he said. "And my wife here, Mara."

Heleyne bowed courteously, and Agyar acknowledged her with a slight bow of the head. I only smiled at her weakly. She thanked us both again and left, and I noticed Agyar as he watched her leave. He had the same look on his face as when he had first met me.

Their door was shut, so I pressed my ear to the wood and listened. I had thought I'd heard whispering coming from Heleyne and Charles's room, and I wondered if it was actually those two, or if Agyar had decided to get to know Heleyne better.

There was still whispering, but I heard only one voice, and in Latin, no less. I recognized some of the words as things said during a prayer, and as I listened further, I realized it was a Christian prayer. And I smiled to myself then. Agyar couldn't touch her now—not without bringing down the wrath of God on him, anyway. But then, he might also consider that to be some sort of ultimate challenge; after all, Gaar and I had barely given him a run for his money, in the end.

And then the door opened suddenly, and I jumped back

as Heleyne began to step quietly outside. I startled her, though, and we both stood there a few moments, holding our chests, recovering from the fright.

"Oh!" she gasped. "You're Lady . . . uh, Lady—Mara! Yes! Mara, right?"

"Right!" I said, and reached over to shut the door for her.

"Your husband sleeps now, yes?" I said.

"Yes. He rests as comfortably as he is able," she whispered. "I was just finishing praying for him . . ."

"I see," I whispered. Then: "Well, I was just—walking by, when you opened the door, and—"

"You startled me so, too!" she whispered. "I didn't frighten you, too, did I?"

"Oh, it was nothing, really," I insisted. "I just wasn't expecting you, that's all."

We laughed nervously in the hallways, and when we stopped, there was an awkward pause while we both fought for our next words. And when we finally did speak, it was simultaneously. We made several false starts before she insisted that I go first.

"I was only curious as to why you're still awake?" I whispered.

"Oh," she whispered in return. "I cannot sleep. I worry so for him. I fear he may have taken the plague with him . . ."

"How awful . . ." I whispered. "Well, perhaps there is something we can do for him?"

"Do you know of a doctor here?" she asked. "One who can help him?"

"I know of no doctor here," I murmured. "I'm sorry."

"That's all right," she said. "I'll just have to keep praying for him, and hoping . . ."

"By the way . . ." she began again, "might you have a small, private room here? One I could use as a chapel, perhaps?"

"A chapel?" I asked.

She nodded. "Only if it's no trouble to you," she insisted. "I simply wish to be by myself while I pray. I don't want to disturb Charles's rest, but I don't wish to stop trying to help him, either."

"Oh," I said. "I see. Well, I think I can find someplace for you."

"Only if it's no trouble," she said.

"No, no, it's no trouble to me. I could use a way to pass the time."

"Oh, thank you, good Mara," she said. "Thank you. You are a good Christian."

"I'm—not a Christian," I said. "But you're welcome, anyway."

I know she wanted to be alone at the time, but I asked Heleyne if I could sit quietly in the back of the room and watch while she prayed. I had never seen any Christian rituals before, and apprehensive as I was, I was curious as to what one was like. I knew that its symbols could hurt me, but I couldn't understand why, and I wanted to see if I could determine the reason for myself. Fortunately, she didn't seem to mind my presence.

I expected something very elaborate—perhaps many trinkets or gadgets, or perhaps a bit of strange singing and dancing—but none of that transpired. Now, one may also wonder how I could have been so ignorant about Christianity, considering that my best friend had been a Christian herself. Well, that's simple; I never saw her go through any of their rituals or ceremonies. No, not even her wedding. Oh, I saw her pray many times, but I just assumed that that wasn't really authentic, just some quick little casual beseechment such as Gaar and I always said. But it *was* authentic, of course.

Heleyne removed a cross, which I had to look at at an

askew angle, and she held it close to her chest. Then she began whispering fervently. I tried not to listen, but my hearing is extremely sharp, and I couldn't help hearing most, if not all, of her prayers. All of them were in Latin, and I wondered if she could actually understand what she was saying. I knew *I* could; Gaar had taught it to me long ago.

The cross was not in view, so I didn't have to worry about hurting my eyes, but I soon noticed that my ears were starting to ache the more I listened to her pray. And the more fervent and heartfelt the prayer, the worse they hurt, until I had to resort to plugging them to shut out her voice. And I wondered, *Why? Why does one small woman asking her god for help cause me so much pain? Why does His symbol hurt my eyes, and even burn me at its touch? What have I done to deserve such punishment from a god I hardly know anything of?*

Heleyne finished one of her prayers, and I unplugged my ears before she could turn around and see my pain. I expected her to go on, but she put her cross away and rubbed her eyes. Then she turned and leaned tiredly against a heavy chair and sighed.

"I can think of no more prayers," she said. "I know not what else I can do for him. I can only hope that God has heard me, and will help us."

"He's very ill, isn't he?" I asked.

"Yes," she sighed. "Very ill. I think only a miracle could save him . . ."

"I'm sorry," I whispered. "It must be very difficult for you. You're very young to have such a hardship on you."

"Hardship can strike at any age," she whispered back, then was silent.

I decided to break our silence, finally.

"You seem very devoted to your god," I said.

"I try to be," she said. "But in moments like these . . . it's so hard. I know He listens to me when I pray, but sometimes I just wish I could just know that He has heard. Some sign . . ."

"Like your husband becoming well?"

"That would be the greatest sign He could give me," she said. "I would be so grateful for that." Then she sighed a little and shook her head. "But if He does not save Charles, I think I would understand," she said. "I am not as good a Christian as I ought to be."

"You seem very devoted to *me.*"

"Seem devoted," she repeated. "But I do not pray or visit church as often as I should. It's not right to pray only during times of sorrow and crisis."

"When else must you pray?" I asked.

"As often as possible," she answered matter-of-factly. "Times of sorrow—of gladness, too. It's easy to forget to give thanks when times are good, you see."

"True," I said. " I think I may be guilty of that myself."

"You seem very interested in my faith," she said suddenly. Uh-oh. "Have you ever been to a church?"

"Umm . . . no," I mumbled. "But my dearest friend was a Christian."

"And she never asked you to join her in church?"

"Oh, many times," I said, smiling nervously. "But I wasn't very good at listening to her." I started thinking of Leta again, and wondered if things would have turned out differently had I listened to her, for once.

"Well . . ." Heleyne said, breaking my thoughts, "you know it's only too late to listen when you have died. As long as you live, you can be saved."

"Um . . ." I said, feeling sweaty now. "Yes. But you must be very tired right now. You've been praying all day and night, haven't you?"

She shrugged. "What else am I to do?" she asked. "I know of no other way to help Charles."

"No, I suppose you don't," I said. "But you ought to

get some rest yourself. Else you'll become too tired to do anything at all."

"Mmm," she said. "Yes. I am very tired. But he needs the rest, not me."

"Come, Heleyne," I said, rising and walking to her with arms outstretched. "Let me help you up."

She took my hands wearily, and I hefted her to her feet quickly and dusted her off. She laughed a little, embarrassed.

"Oh, these clothes will never be clean," she said.

"Yes . . . Well, you'd better be off to bed, then. You're tired and need the rest."

"Thank you, friend Mara," she whispered.

"Hmm?"

"For letting me use this room," she explained.

I shook my head and meant to tell her it was no trouble, but—

"Ah—here you are, ladies," Agyar said. "I've been looking for you."

I looked at the floor then, afraid to meet his gaze, but Heleyne seemed undisturbed by his entrance and spoke enthusiastically.

"Oh, greetings, Magistrate," she said, bowing her head slightly. "We have only been in here, talking."

"As women are wont to do," he said cheerfully. "But I'd like my wife to come with me now, if she will. Mara?" he said, extending a hand out to me. I still would not meet his gaze, but I let him take my hand and lead me to the door. He stopped at the threshold and turned back to Heleyne before we left.

"I hope it was nothing important?" he said.

She smiled and shook her head. "Oh, no, friend Agyar, it's nothing we can't talk about later," she said. He smiled back and nodded once, and I looked up quickly enough to catch his eyes ever so briefly flashing red as he watched her and I began to feel a sudden chill.

Later, he commanded me to tell him what we'd been talking about, and I shrugged and said we'd only been discussing her church and how much she prayed. He was not angry with that, but fell silent afterward, as though taking what I'd said into consideration.

Twenty-three

Heleyne was by her husband's bedside the next night, as usual. I stopped by after feeding to see to their needs, but they had none. He did not look long for the world, and when I left the room, I couldn't get rid of the sickeningly empty feeling that enveloped me. Though I didn't even know the man, I knew exactly what Heleyne was going through. But I couldn't offer comfort. I didn't know how to. My feelings had been pushed down so deep I could scarcely reach them anymore.

Some hours later, I had decided to force myself to at least try to help Heleyne and was heading back to the room when I heard voices coming from a bedroom that was usually empty. The open doorway was still ahead of me, and I crept along the wall in perfect silence and stopped once I reached the door. One voice I recognized immediately—Agyar's—but the other took a few seconds longer to remember. Heleyne's. They were speaking in low, whispery tones—he, using his seductive, soothing voice, and she, sounding disturbed, almost confused.

I could not pick up everything that was said perfectly, but the few choice words I heard sounded over and over in my ears. Death. Disease. Poverty. Starvation. Immortality.

Immortality. Each time I heard it, I shut my eyes. Immortality. He offered it to Heleyne, and she resisted, of course, not really understanding his true intentions, and he offered it to her again and again. Never once was Charles offered it, something which she, too, did not pick up immediately.

How often had he spoken to her? I wondered. *How long have I seen the glances he'd been throwing her and have done nothing about it?* The looks he gave her had been burned into my memory for over a century and a half; they were what I had received so long ago, when Gaar and I had come to him.

I knew right away; I knew exactly what he wanted the moment she had left that room that first night, and why did I then do nothing? I hated him; I hated my so-called husband, lover, confidant, friend, and wanted him dead or myself free. I had fantasized about him finding someone else—some other hapless woman who could then be his wife. I would then be free.

I don't really care about her; let him make her a monster like him, and I'll be cast away and allowed to do as I please. I let Leta get away; I promised to let her "keep her god." But why worry about this woman, whom I barely even know? Let him take her.

I heard him ask her slowly, carefully, if she wanted to die, and there was a long pause before I heard in the faintest whisper, "No." Then he asked slowly, carefully, if she wanted to live forever, and there was another long pause before I heard in the faintest whisper, "Yes." And after that, I didn't need to hear; after that, I knew what he was doing, and I shut my eyes tight and tilted my head back against the wall, and fought against tears that I shouldn't even have been shedding.

She was sitting in one of the guest rooms, her back facing me as I stood in the doorway. I had already been to her other room and seen her husband.

"Heleyne," I whispered, but she did not turn. One of

Agyar's portraits hung directly in front of her. I moved closer to her silently and placed a hand on her shoulder.

"Heleyne," I repeated, and she turned her head slightly.

"I was in your room just now," I said, and squeezed her shoulder a little. "I'm sorry."

"I looked for you today," she said finally. "I couldn't find you."

"I was—elsewhere," I said.

She shook her head. "It doesn't really matter," she said. "There was nothing you could do."

I moved in front of her and sat on a stool and took her hands into my own.

"I should have been here, if only to comfort you," I said. "You see, I—know exactly how you feel. I have lost my own husband, long ago."

"Agyar is not your husband?" she said.

"Um—in a way," I said. "He— I was once married to another before he died. Agyar is—m-my second husband.

"But that's part of the past," I continued. "What's important now is that I—" and I had to stop, as it was quite a struggle to shake off Agyar's influence and tell her what needed to be told. Heleyne waited patiently for me to continue, and eventually I could only smile at her helplessly before looking down.

"What is this important thing, friend Mara?"

I looked up at her again, and it was then that I was able to see the tiny red markings on her shoulder. Two puncture marks. Teeth marks. I had to look away again, and I silently cursed Agyar over and over for all he had done to me, to what he had done to my will—my once infamously mulelike stubborn will. Now it was gone—nothing.

"I can't tell you," I murmured. "I—can't!"

"I don't understand," she said. "Are you unable to speak now? Or is it something forbidden to you?"

I nodded my head quickly to her last question.

"I can comfort you, Heleyne," I said. "Just let me do

that. I can comfort you. I'm certain you loved him deeply, as I loved my own husband . . ."

She said nothing, but continued watching me with concerned eyes. I smiled nervously again and released her hands, and she watched me again before turning away slightly and sniffling a little.

"I know you did all you could for him," I whispered. "I know how you prayed for him, talked to him, comforted him. There's nothing else you could have done for him."

She sniffled again and nodded solemnly. I bit my lips and fought for more words.

"It wasn't your fault," I said. "You did all you could . . ." And as I spoke, my own memories of Gaar came back to me, of the two of us running, running in terror and confusion, of hiding in darkness and cramped rooms and holding each other for comfort. I remembered how bravely he had fought Agyar and those creatures of his, and how in the end none of his strength or courage or skill had amounted to anything against him. And I had always blamed myself completely for everything that had happened.

"And all was in vain," Heleyne whispered. "All that I have done did not save him . . ." she added, and she began to gaze at Agyar's portrait ahead of her. I watched her in silence as she stared and stared, until her eyes seemed to glaze over in a trance. It was almost unbearable, what was happening to her. I knew exactly how she felt, what she was thinking, and I cursed myself over and over for not being able to help her. But I *had* to help her; I couldn't just sit and let him take another like he took me, not while she was grieving so. No one but me deserved such a fate.

The door behind us swung open, and Agyar entered the room silently. Heleyne barely moved her head toward the noise, but I jumped noticeably and moved off to the side, away from Heleyne. His face was expressionless as he moved toward us, and he stopped behind Heleyne and placed his hand on her shoulder. She still did not turn toward him, but continued staring at the portrait. Then he looked at me, and a chill shot up my spine.

"Come here," he said. I could only obey him.

"I was only comforting her," I whispered, my head down.

"No doubt," he said. "But I shall do so now. You may go."

"But Agyar—"

"You may go, Mara," he said, and I hesitated before moving around him silently toward the door. But when I reached it, I stopped and called to him again.

"Agyar . . ." I said as he began stroking Heleyne's head.

"I told you to leave," he said.

"I have seen your mark on her," I continued. "I . . . know what you plan to do to her. It isn't right, Agyar."

As I finished, he began turning toward me and glared. I shivered as he walked quickly to the door and stopped within an inch of my face.

"Sh-she's suffered enough," I stammered. "Sh-she would never want—"

He gripped my chin in a rough hold and held my head firmly in place. His eyes burned in anger.

"You'll do nothing to stop me," he growled. "Do you understand??"

"Y-you shouldn't do this to her—"

"Silence!" he hissed, and his eyes glowed brighter. I felt his thoughts crowding out mine.

"She *will* be mine," he growled. "Your purpose with me is done, woman. I grow weary of your constant whining, your nagging, your complaining. I offered you love, and you have given me nothing but hate. I offered you a paradise, and you have given me nothing but a hell!

"Heleyne is to be mine now. *She* shall be my bride for eternity, not you. You've had your chance, woman, but would not take it. Now let me be rid of you, and take the better choice for my own. And you will do nothing to stop me. Do you understand me? Nothing!"

"Nothing . . ." I whispered, and he released my chin in a rough jerk.

"Go now," he commanded. "Go to the roof, and sit and sleep there, and wait for the sun to rise. It will be all over when the sun rises, Mara; watch it rise . . ."

"Watch it rise . . ." I said, and left him.

"—stress?" I heard, but could not open my eyes. I was being shaken, first gently, and then rather roughly.

"Mistress?" I heard again, and made a supreme effort to wake and speak to Lara, but could only manage a quick grunt.

"Mistress, wake up; you shouldn't be out here," Lara said, and shook me again. Then the shaking stopped, but I knew she had not left me, because I was suddenly jolted from the trance by a painful slap on the check. I held my face and shook my head quickly to clear out the cobwebs in my mind. Lara knelt down to help me up.

"I'm sorry I did that, mistress, but it was the only thing that would wake you . . ."

"Uh . . . yes," I said. "It seems that way . . ."

"Why are you out here like this?" she asked. "Morning will be here very soon. The sun will be up."

"Um . . . um . . . I was—resting," I said. She began guiding me away from the roof edge toward the door leading downstairs.

"I'd say you were in a trance," she said. "I could barely wake you."

"A trance?"

"It seemed like one."

"A trance . . ." I repeated, and my memories flooded back to me, and I remembered what I had been sent there for.

"No . . . It's too late now," I whispered as we reached the door. "It's over."

"What is?"

"Heleyne. Heleyne and Agyar. She's his now."

"Oh, is that what he wants to do with her?" Lara said matter-of-factly. "They went into a room together only a few moments ago. She wouldn't be converted by now—"

"A few moments ago?" I said.

Lara nodded. "Something like that," she said. "I was wondering if you knew. That's why I was looking for you. Mistress, you weren't trying to kill yourself, were you? Is that why you were here, waiting for the sun to rise?"

"No. Agyar wanted me dead. That's why I was here."

"That's awful!" she gasped. "The master wants you dead so he can convert that other woman? That's awful!" she repeated.

"Never mind about that," I said quickly. "Where are they now? There may still be time to stop him, then!"

"Stop him?" she said. "The master does as he pleases, you know that!"

"I know," I said, "but—that shouldn't be! She doesn't want to be like us, he shouldn't do that to her!" I grabbed Lara's arm and pulled her down the stairs faster. She almost stumbled several times and began to protest.

"Mistress, stop this, I can't keep up with you!"

I stopped dragging her and tugged her forward to face me.

"Where are they?" I asked. "Please, Lara, I have to know where they are!"

"In the—the—" she stammered, and I don't think I made it much easier to continue by shaking her so.

"Where are they?" I demanded.

"In the guest bedroom!" she cried. On the second floor, remember?"

"I remember," I said, and bolted away from her to reach the room before sunrise—before it was too late. Lara darted after me, pleading with me to please explain what was going on, what was I trying to do, did I mean to hurt the master?

As I reached the door, I almost burst straight through, when I was suddenly stopped within inches of it by a nearly tangible force. The force was my own fear, Agyar's influence making my fear of doing anything to stop him so great that I was immobilized, and when Lara rushed up behind me, I was shivering in a cold sweat.

"No . . ." I whispered.

"What are you doing, mistress?" she cried. "What's this all about?"

"Shh!" I hissed, and clamped my hand over her mouth. "I can't do it!" I said, and pulled away my hand.

"Can't do what?" she cried. "Mistress, I don't understand this—"

"Hush!" I whispered. "Lara, we must be quiet! I have to get in there," I said. "But I can't! He won't let me!"

"The master won't let you enter?" she whispered, and I nodded quickly.

"He wants to convert that Christian woman, yes?" she continued, and I nodded again.

"It isn't right!" I said. "She doesn't deserve to be converted! But I can't stop him!"

"Do you want me to help you?" she asked.

I shook my head frantically. "No, no!" I cried. "I must do this myself!"

"That's too bad, mistress, because *I'm going* to help!" she said, and threw the door open.

The sun had not yet risen, but the sky was rather bright by now, and the blacks and grays of the night had become the muted grays of twilight. It was the room Gaar and I had originally stayed in. Heleyne lay asleep on the bed, and Agyar loomed over her, his teeth firmly implanted in her veins. I'm certain he must have heard us talking outside the door but had deemed us to be no threat. I had no way of knowing yet how much he had taken from her, but I assumed it was quite a bit already, and the anger I felt from that helped stifle my fear a little.

I started when Lara threw the door open, and I made a small noise in surprise, but once the deed had been done, yelling at her about it would have been pointless, at best. Agyar raised his head as the door slammed into the wall behind it, and I almost ran screaming down the hallway, only Lara stood behind me and blocked my way.

"Leave us, woman," he growled, and I almost obeyed, but Lara pushed me inside, and I desperately fought off the terror building up in me and stood my ground. Agyar raised his head higher until he was sitting up.

"I said, leave us, woman," he said even more firmly. I raised my chin in defiance and set my jaw, and remained where I was, despite the fact that I was almost ready to faint right there. Agyar rose from the bed and glided toward me, his face contorted in anger. I shivered as he reached me and stopped, and although I was taller than he, I felt as though he were looming above me.

His eyes began to glow, and for the first time, I thought to fight fire with fire and try to charm *him*, as well, if I could. We locked gazes and concentrated, each pair of eyes trying to burn through to the other's soul. Lara could do little but watch our mental battle, one which I was very quickly losing.

Agyar reached his hand out for my throat as my will began slipping away. And then, perhaps by impulse, perhaps by something else, I knocked his hand away from my face and leapt back. His concentration was broken, and I was terrified, but I was even more terrified to give up now.

He took a step forward and tried to grab me again, and I knocked away his hand and sent him sprawling with a quick counterpunch. Lara cried out in surprise and leapt away from the fight toward the bed.

"Lara!" I yelled. "Take Heleyne and—" I was interrupted by Agyar, who threw himself at me in utter rage, his fangs dripping with saliva, his hands extended into claws. I cried out and leapt to the side, making him fly out the door into the hallway.

"Get Heleyne away from here!" I yelled, never taking my eyes from the doorway. Whether or not Lara obeyed me right away I do not know, as Agyar flew back into the room as a huge black wolf. He flew straight for my throat, and I barely ducked down enough to avoid his deadly jaws.

And as I ducked, I turned toward the window, and was nearly blinded by the brightness. The sun was minutes away, and the sky was signaling for its entrance. But I couldn't give up yet.

The wolf landed squarely on its feet and turned back toward me, and I stood my ground before it and waited for its next move. I saw it glance to the side momentarily before howling in rage, and I looked to see Lara hefting Heleyne into her arms. Now my job was to keep Agyar away from her.

The wolf continued howling, and its cry became more and more human-like as it changed, and it became upright in Agyar's form. He pointed at Lara.

"Bring her back, wench!" he hissed, and Lara almost dropped Heleyne in terror.

"Keep going, Lara!" I cried, trying desperately to wave her on. "Take her out of here!" Time was running out; I could barely see in the brightness, and it was becoming hot. I continued waving the petrified Lara on, unfortunately turning my back to Agyar.

"Lara!" I yelled, pointing at her and concentrating on her mind. "I'M ORDERING YOU TO GO!" She looked at me quickly with great fear in her eyes before turning to leave, and I returned my attention to Agyar in time to see that he had torn a piece of wood from the windowsill and was holding it menacingly before me. Then he let out a horrible cry before thrusting it straight for my heart.

I screamed and turned away from the stake, making him deflect away from me and rush forward toward Lara. I raised my hand and was about to scream again, only Lara beat me to it as he plunged it into her heart, instead.

My ears rang from her cry of pain as she fell, and she dropped Heleyne in the process. I screamed again, too, but this time from my own pain as the first ray of the morning sun shot through the window. Agyar cried out, also, but I took most of the light at first, and it was not yet as painful for him.

Now there was no time. Victory for Agyar and myself now meant just getting out of there, away from the sun, and our battle quickly became a race to the door. Agyar held me tight and meant to throw me back toward the window and run from the room, but I held on to his cloak as he pushed me away, which made him fall backward, as well.

We rolled over each other, both crawling in agony for the door, both now beginning to smoke from the heat. And I had at least three goals, where he had no more than two; I had to escape, kill him, and get Lara and Heleyne out of there, too. Agyar wanted to escape alone, meaning that I was to be left behind to burn. Perhaps he also intended to take Heleyne with him—but certainly not Lara.

The pain was almost overwhelming, but I would not give up—not after coming this far. And if I had to die to make sure he did, too, then so be it.

His last attempt to break away from me was to transform into a bat. His changing form and size made it difficult for me to hold on, and he managed to leap away, and he was about to begin flapping his wings when I sprang up at him, grabbed him, and threw him under the bed. Meanwhile the light from the sun blinded me, and I screamed and covered my eyes, turning away to run for the door.

My eyes were still shut when I tripped over Lara or Heleyne's body—I couldn't tell which yet, and my flesh was burning too much for me to be able to tell from their smell. I collapsed to the floor and scooped up her body and crawled in the door's direction. She was warm—not bleeding. I could feel no stake—where was Lara? I reached back blindly and began groping about for Lara, when I heard Agyar's roar as he crawled from under the bed.

Now there truly was no time. I panicked and held on to Heleyne and crawled for the door. I could feel flames forming on me now, and I hoped that none of them were touching her. Agyar's roar sounded again—a grotesque blend of rage and pain, and it was getting closer, fast.

I reached the door's threshold and scrambled through, and I used the wall to help me stand as quickly as possible. I opened my eyes long enough to glimpse the door, not to mention Agyar's fast-approaching figure, and pulled it shut, fast as I could.

He reached the door quickly enough to thrust his seared hand into the crack, preventing it from shutting. And Agyar was stronger than I, so he began slowly pulling it back open, despite my putting all my strength into closing it. Then, without really thinking, I used the one weapon Agyar had been such a fool to give me—my teeth. I was in such pain, as it was, that my fangs were already well extended, and I bent over, grabbed his hand with my mouth, and bit down hard. He shrieked in pain and tried to pull the hand away, but I bit down even harder, until with a mighty jerk, he ripped it away from my fangs and released the door.

I slammed it shut and held the knob with all my might. Agyar began pounding on the door now, screaming the most horrible screams, and I wanted to let go and shut my ears, but I shut my eyes, instead, and gritted my teeth and bore the awful sound.

The pounding soon stopped, but the screams continued, only they grew weaker and weaker, until they were little more than a groan, and then they stopped. And I still held the door shut and would not let go until I heard absolutely no noise coming from that room; then I slowly released the doorknob and slumped back into the wall.

I could have slept forever, then, but I could not rest yet. There was still Heleyne to take care of; my own wounds would heal quickly enough. I also had to move away from the door, for the light coming from the crack at the bottom would soon be strong enough to burn me again.

She was still unconscious. I was a little thankful for that, as she was spared the ghastly scene which had just transpired. But I didn't know if he had taken enough blood from her to convert her. If I could have given her my own blood, I would have, but that would have done more harm than good.

I slumped onto the floor next to her and felt her face. Still warm, and I could hear and smell her breathing. She would live—she had to. I continued feeling her face and contemplated trying to wake her, but I was so tired myself, and my appearance would surely disturb her; and I didn't want to have to think of any explanations for her, either.

I remember telling myself that I couldn't just lie there in the middle of the hallway all day with some anemic woman, when the blackness of vampiric sleep overcame me.

Twenty-four

I awoke to the sound of one of the servants moving about near us. I sat up quickly and peered down the hallway. No one was in sight, and I remembered Heleyne. She was still unconscious; her breathing was shallow, but I was certain she would recover. Daylight was still poking out under the door to the ill-fated bedroom. I forced myself to rise and almost collapsed again, but held on to a wall.

Then the servant who'd been moving about came from a room and saw me.

"What's going on here?" he said. "Who— Oh! Mistress! I didn't see you!"

"Hello, Clarence," I said, bending over to pick up Heleyne. I was too weak, though, and almost fell over. Clarence grabbed me and steadied me.

"M-mistress, you're . . . you're not well," he said. "Your face . . ."

"I'll be all right," I said. "Only a little sun. Help me lift her."

"A little sun?" he said. "Is this . . . is this the woman with the sick husband?"

"Her husband has died," I said, "and she's . . . she's very ill. Help me with her."

Finally Clarence complied and scooped her up for me. I held my arms out.

"Let me have her," I said.

"But you're weak—"

"Let me have her. I have to make certain that she's safe before I rest." He obeyed, and now that I was standing, I had little trouble holding her.

"Does the master know what's happened?" I asked Clarence.

"He's abed now," he said. "Don't disturb him."

"No . . . no, of course not . . ." I said, and I bade him walk ahead of me and close any windows we came across. Some could not be closed, so I had to duck and run by quickly. It was painful, nonetheless.

Finally we came to the kitchen, where there are no windows, and Clarence cleared the main table while I laid Heleyne out on it. I checked her breathing and pulse again.

"Clarence," I said, "I want you to get her things, and fetch a wagon, and pack it up for her. She needs to leave here, and the sooner the better."

"But, mistress, I don't understand—"

"She can't stay here," I said. "This is a bad place for her. You understand that, don't you? This is a *bad place* for her."

"Oh . . ." he said. "Yes, I . . . I understand, mistress. I'll get everything ready. But she's too ill to leave, isn't she?"

"Being too ill is what doomed me and my first husband. It will not happen again. And the master does not need to know of this. Do you understand?"

"Yes, mistress," he said and made to leave, but I called him back. He approached me timidly, and I grabbed him in a quick hug.

"Good-bye, Clarence," I whispered. "Come nightfall, you shall never see me again. You were the only servant who would ever talk to me. Few words, yes, but it was enough."

"Th-thank you, mistress," he said, and I slapped his shoulder gently and smiled.

"Go on," I said.

After he left, I turned my attention back to Heleyne, who was as still as ever. I took her face gently and opened her eyes with my thumbs. That didn't rouse her, but I looked into her unconscious eyes and concentrated. It was difficult reaching her mind, but eventually I was able to find her thoughts and take hold of them.

I made her forget everything that had happened to her. She was only to remember that her husband had been sick but had died, and that she had done everything she could for him. Now she had to leave as quickly as she could, and go East, or wherever she was to go, and never come back to Clovaine.

She was starting to regain consciousness just as I was shutting the coffin-room door behind me. I paused long enough to see her reach out blindly before shutting and locking the door for the last time.

Agyar's sarcophagus was the first place I went. I opened it up quickly and peered in. Empty. I sighed in relief and replaced the lid, and then opened up one of his servant's coffins. There was one there, sleeping peacefully, or as peacefully as they're able to.

I shut the lid and opened my own sarcophagus. Also empty—no nasty surprises—so I climbed in, took one last look around, and then shut the lid over me and fell into dark sleep.

I willed myself to wake before any of Agyar's creatures did, and after more furtive glances, I crept from the room. There were only two servants in the kitchen when I came out, and they gave me quizzical looks, no doubt because of the burn marks on my face, but I said not a word to them and hurried out.

I ran up to my private room where all my clothes were and started to place as many as I could into a sack. The sun had just set, fortunately; no more burns for me. Then a knock came at the door, and I started.

"Who's there?" I called.

"Mistress?" a muffled voice said. "M-may I come in? It's urgent."

"Uh . . . Yes, very well," I said, stuffing my sack under a table. "Come in."

The door opened, and Clarence entered, carrying a lantern.

"Forgive me, mistress," he said.

"Never mind, what is it?" I said hastily.

"I . . . I only wished to say that I did as you bade me," he said. "The woman left soon after you went to sleep. She was very confused, mistress."

"I'm certain she was."

"But there was also . . . I found—"

"Found what?"

"There was a . . . someone's body . . ." he said. "In the guest room."

"Burned?" I said quietly.

He nodded quickly. "Aye," he said. "Burned. A girl, I think. She had a . . . She had been stabbed. By wood . . ."

"Oh . . ." I whispered, my memories fighting to overwhelm me now. But I couldn't let them.

"I . . . I took the body away," he said. "No one saw me. That was—that was your friend, wasn't it?"

"Yes," I whispered, my throat growing hard.

"Have I done a bad thing? Burying the body?"

I laughed quietly and fought off tears. Then I looked at him and smiled as best as I could.

"No," I said. "Thank you for that, Clarence. But you must tell me: you saw two bodies, yes?"

"No, mistress. Only the one."

"No, no, there were two bodies in that room."

"I swear to you, mistress, there was but one body in the room."

A chill went down my spine. I had checked his sarcophagus myself. Where else would he have been, if he'd been alive? I had to get to that room—

My thoughts were interrupted by a horrible screeching and howling coming from deep in the house. Without hesitation, I grabbed my sack and rushed for the door, leaving Clarence in my wake. I rushed out the door in time to see shadowy, misshapen, foul shapes barreling full tilt up the stairs and up the hall—and straight toward me.

I panicked and bolted from the room. Somehow his creatures knew—they knew their master had been slain, and they knew who did it. But I was searching my mind and could find no trace of Agyar, nothing of his influence. He had to be dead; *he had to be!*

But for the time being, that was the least of my worries. My main concern now was to get away from them in one piece. Our flight—Gaar's and mine—from them was being repeated all over again, only there was no Gaar this time. Now I was alone.

At least none of the human servants were after me. I doubt if any of them even knew what was going on, and even if they did, none of them would dare try to stop me. They feared me almost as much as they feared Agyar, even though I had never tried to make it so.

I didn't think I could get tired running anymore. I had once thought that a vampire's stamina was limitless, as it normally took me hours to begin to feel tired, even after constant physical exertion. That night, running from those creatures proved me wrong.

I ran through every inch of that house over and over again, dodging, hiding, even fighting sometimes, and everywhere I turned there was another one waiting for me. The whole mob of them or sometimes just one or two. But they were everywhere.

At last I reached a large, open window, and I leapt through it to what I hoped would be my freedom. But first

I had to fall two stories without my wings to stop me, and I managed to roll the moment I hit the ground to lessen the impact. I was dazed, but I couldn't rest or recover, not when several of the creatures were leaping right out after me.

I scrambled to my feet and ran again, smashing away one of the creatures who tried to grab me directly, and raced away, first for the village, and then shifted directions for the forest, instead. I thought of changing to the wolf so I could run faster, but then I couldn't carry the sack, and I couldn't afford to just drop everything. The creatures had no such problem with any belongings, however, and I was soon being hounded by wolves, bats, and lumbering monsters, alike.

And I couldn't concentrate enough to command any of them. I couldn't focus any attention on charming them, or commanding them, or anything. I may as well have been simply human, for all the power I had over them.

I think it was fear alone that gave me the speed and strength to keep ahead of them all the way up to the forest. But I could not use the cover of the trees to my advantage yet; in fact, the creatures did first. Some of them scrambled up the branches quickly and dropped down as I rushed by, forcing me to stay and fight for the chance to run again.

And then finally, I was surrounded. Everywhere I turned, everywhere I looked, smoldering red eyes peered out of the blackness, trying to reach into my mind and make me give up. And they were moving in closer to me, the circle closing up tight. But I wouldn't give up, hopeless as the situation seemed. My only chance was to force away my fear, to grab it and mold it into anger, or I would never survive this. I forced my breathing to steady itself, and I took a deep breath and let it out slowly in a low, inhuman growl. And still the creatures were moving in on me.

I gritted my teeth and let my fangs grow, and kicked my eyes into action to fight them on their own terms. And then it occurred to me—I couldn't fight them on their own terms. I couldn't allow myself to become like them, to fight them like some animal, for they could surely overwhelm me easily with brute strength.

I kept my fangs visible and made my eyes glow, but I stopped growling and slowly straightened myself up to my full height (and a rather substantial height, too, you remember). They were nearly on top of me now, but I held my ground and threw my hand out and cried, "Stop!"

The circle stopped closing, but the evil never faded from their eyes, and I knew this was no time to show any weakness. I turned around slowly in the circle, letting my gaze pass by all of them, and mentally knocked away their lame attempts to charm me. A few eyes stopped glowing, but most of the creatures stood their ground.

"Leave me be," I said quietly, but firmly, I hoped. "Go back."

I could see that many of them were at a loss as to what to do, and these began to take a few hesitant steps back. Unfortunately, one of them chose to ignore my command and hissed suddenly and leapt straight at me. I let it slam into me before regaining my balance and grabbing it by the throat and holding it up before its "friends."

"I said, leave me be," I growled, tightening my grip on the creature until tears came to its eyes.

"Goooo!" I roared, and tossed the creature I held into one of its companions, and they started to panic. "Get away from me! Go! I command you to leave!" I said over and over, scattering the wretched things left and right until they were scampering away into the darkness of the forest.

I dropped to my knees and shut my eyes. Alone now. No more creatures. No more Agyar. No more Clovaine and no more Lara, either. And I felt nothing in that moment—no relief, no joy, no triumph, not even grief for my friend. I was numb, and I don't know how long I just sat there, thinking of nothing and no one.

But I knew I couldn't sit there all night. I was cold and without shelter, and it was most important that I had somewhere to hide when the sun came up. I didn't know if the creatures might decide to come back, nor was I certain what sort of animals roamed about in Clovaine's forests at night. I needed to find someplace, and quickly.

Fortunately, my night vision is rather good, and I had little trouble examining all sorts of trees in search of holes suitable for sleep. Even if none of them were large enough for my normal form, I could always shift to my smaller bat form and sleep that way. But then, none of them were lightproof, either, which was most important.

I hadn't eaten. The forest was filled with the sounds of nocturnal creatures, but then, most of them are quite small—raccoons and rats and bugs, mostly. But I had something of an advantage. At least I wouldn't have to hunt, as far as, say, rats and other rodents were concerned. All I had to do was concentrate on summoning them, and soon I was surrounded by dozens of squeaking, scurrying rats. And disgusted as I was with the thought, I dined that night on rats and rat blood. At that point, I was hardly in the condition to find a bear or even a deer. Small animals tonight.

It was getting dangerously close to sunrise when I finally located a suitable hole to crawl into. It was on the side of an embankment, fortunately a dry one, and I had to shift to bat form to fit inside. I'm grateful it was dry, for the last thing I needed was for some river to overflow and flood the hole. As I mentioned before, running water and vampires do not get along very well.

Twenty-five

After feeding the next night (on rats again), I set about making my way to the Channel. I expected I could make it to the shore by morning, if I went on foot, and that wouldn't do. Flying was out of the question; my sack was too big to carry, and probably would be too heavy, too. Eventually, I ended up tying the sack to my back and then transforming into a wolf. The sack stayed on quite snugly after I changed. There was no more time for me to waste, though, so I immediately set off at full speed.

Wolves are already blessed with good stamina, and add to that the vampire's tirelessness, and I was able to reach the shore in half the night. I transformed behind some bushes and stepped out into a clearing, where I could see that a boat was docked, ready for a morning departure.

We vampires can see life auras—that is, living things literally glow in the dark to us—and no one seemed to be about. It was the middle of the night, after all, so I didn't have to be especially sneaky to reach the boat.

Getting on board and down below seemed too simple, but I could detect no one moving about, although a rat startled me one time. This was a cargo ship—wheat, it looked like, which was just fine with me. That mean no passengers.

It was only halfway through the night, but I was weary, following such a long run, but after snagging a huge rat and tossing the carcass overboard, I found a mostly empty crate. It seemed dark enough to sleep in, so I scrunched myself inside and fell uncomfortably asleep.

It was dark enough; I survived. That, and not much light got to where I was. Before leaving the crate, I listened for a long time for any voices or movement. All I heard was the creaking and rocking of the boat itself, so I slowly stood up and opened the top.

It was night again. But the same night or the next? I wasn't sure, until I noticed that many of the crates that had been there before had been removed. Ahh, thank the Gods mine wasn't, I thought, and climbed from the crate.

Still no voices, so I made my way across the room and crept up the stairs, and then listened at the door. I could hear other sounds, but they were too faint or muffled to tell what they were, so I opened the door and peeked out. There was the top deck, all right, but there didn't seem to be anyone about, so I opened the door wide enough for me to squeeze through, and then shut it behind me quietly.

I was almost at the edge of the ship when I heard a "Hey! What are you doing?" and I didn't even look back, but dove right off the boat. I had no intention of diving into the water, however, so I grabbed hold of part of the hull and scrambled off to the side, spiderlike, just in time to see someone poke his head over the bow. I was able to avoid further detection that way, and crawled over to where the dock was, plopped down from the hull, and ran off into the night.

It didn't take me long to figure out that I wasn't in Clovaine. I thanked the Gods for that. I knew I'd been in this place before, though, but when was it, I wondered? There didn't seem to be any familiar landmarks about, but damned if I didn't remember this fog and that enormous river that—

Oh, of course, London, I thought. The boat had come to London, and why wouldn't it? *Did you really expect Castrill, girl?* I remember laughing and crying tears of relief and joy then, for that meant Gaul and Clovaine was a whole Channel away. But London was still too close for me. I wanted to get as far away as I could, which wasn't very likely in a place like England. Just then, I had more immediate concerns, however, such as finding food and shelter before daybreak, so I slung my sack over my shoulder and crept into the fog.

Don't expect great descriptions of a Dickensian city. This was the sixth century we're talking about. I've been around long enough to stop seeing cities and towns as so incredibly varied and wondrous. Naturally, every place has its own local culture, distinctiveness, and flavor, but when trying to find a place to sleep, eat, or work, a shack becomes a shack and a pub a pub.

I had some money with me, but not much, and I intended to save it, so I spent the evening looking about for abandoned shacks, cellars, or whatever. Eventually I found an old wine cellar that no longer had any wine (it had the smell, though), but it had plenty of dust, dirt, bugs, and rats. There was a window level with the street, so I found some old rags to cover it up with. Then after a hearty feast of rats, I spread out some clothes and slept on the floor.

The next night, I found an old dog to feed on, instead. Hardly much of an improvement. Later on, I walked through the streets and started remembering Heleyne's talk of plagues and death. She wasn't lying, but then she never really described it to us, either. I had seen the effects of plagues in small cities, but not in one as large as London. They tried to be very discreet about it, of course. Bodies weren't lying in the street but had been stuffed off into corners and behind crates and into shadows. Small carts with bodies under the blankets collected them every now and then. Some were not dead, but were dying; they had been put off into corners as though they were already gone.

My one Good Samaritan act that night was to help one victim get away from the corner. He was covered with blotches and boils, and was not long for the world, but he begged me to take him away from there. I hesitated for a long time, but then hefted him into my arms and carried him through the streets in search of some comfortable place to put him. And people who saw us backed away, pointed, muttered to themselves, and one person even shouted at me to put him away. I would die with him if I didn't get away.

I ignored them for the most part and finally reached a church. I pounded on the door, and some time passed before a priest answered it, and crossed himself when he saw the man.

"Dear God in heaven," he mumbled, and then clearly: "Why have you brought him here, my child?"

"Um . . . he . . . he was lying in the street," I said. "Don't you have shelter for these people?"

"As many as we can help, but he . . ." the priest said. "He is almost gone from us now. Look."

"Please help me, priest," the man croaked.

The priest fidgeted and hesitated some more. "Um . . . um . . . well, child, have you been carrying him all this way?"

"I'm not tired," I said. "Please, couldn't you at least, um . . . take him and give him a cot to rest on?"

"Um . . ." he said, and then looked down, shaking his head. "Dear God in heaven, if you would deliver us from this," he muttered, and then looked up again.

"Come in, my child," he said, and opened the church door wide for me to enter. I took a step forward and then hesitated. A church? Wouldn't I—" Wouldn't it—?

"Come, child, come," the priest urged, and I took another

slow, hesitant step, and then entered the church slowly, cautiously.

No pain so far, I thought as I followed the priest off to a small room in the back of the church. *Still no pain,* I thought as we passed moaning, writhing masses of dying and dead plague victims. He gestured to a blanket-covered spot on the floor, and I knelt down and laid the man gently onto the blankets. I tried to stand, but he grabbed my hand tightly and held on.

"Thank you," he croaked.

"It . . . it was little trouble," I said nervously. I kept looking around the room like a frightened mouse, wondering when the wrath of God would fall on me. The priest tried to move me to the side, and I scooted over to let him kneel down and give the man a wafer, then some wine. The man swallowed the offering, then let his head fall back onto a blanket. He held on tightly to my hand.

"You'll be safe here," I said. "You won't need me anymore."

"Thank you," he croaked again. Then his hand started to weaken. His grip was loosening, and I watched his aura begin to flicker, and then start to fade.

"Priest, he is dying!" I said, but the priest had left the room. The others who were also there started to groan louder, and the man I'd helped lost hold of my hand as his life slipped away.

"Priest!" I called louder, only the aura was gone. Too late, the priest ran back in but could do nothing now. He was no doctor, I knew that, but I didn't know who else to call. He saw that the man was dead and then crossed himself. Then he started mumbling things in Latin like (translated) "God keep your soul, Let your journey into heaven be well," and other things like that.

Outside the room, the priest told me I was a good Christian for helping the dying, and he blessed me, which, I was quite surprised, did not cause me to burst into flames. Why is it that Christians kept thinking I was one of them, and yet all of their ceremonies and trinkets hurt me? But there I was, standing in God's own house, being blessed by a priest, no less, and I wasn't in pain. And when I finally left the church, I couldn't help wondering if God hated all vampires, or only some of them. I had never wanted to be evil, but Agyar never seemed to mind. Perhaps his influence on me had been stronger than my own will.

I'd already decided that I didn't want to stay in London, and wanted to get as far from Clovaine as I could. Next, I had to gather supplies, such as lanterns, more clothes, a wagon, and so on. I found a man who had a small wagon, but I didn't have enough money for it. He saw my emerald ring and offered to trade, but I refused and went on to other business. An innkeeper was willing to sell a few plates and bowls for a piece of gold, and eventually I managed to scrounge up most of the necessities (including a small wagon) through paying, begging, or even stealing.

The only reason I was considering a coffin as my place to sleep was its practicality. We don't *have* to sleep in coffins. Period. But—as a human-sized portable and light-proof vessel, a coffin is quite useful. Now I admit I had no money to buy one, and I knew no coffinmakers personally, so I was forced to take the third option. There was a coffinmaker near a church (naturally), so late at night, when not a soul was awake (save us vampires), I crept behind a local coffinmaker's shop, hoped it wasn't where he lived, too (else I wouldn't be able to enter), and concentrated.

After transforming to mist, it was a simple matter to slip through cracks and rematerialize inside. Good luck for me: the shop didn't double as his house. There were eight completed coffins along the walls and three in progress (plagues gave them a lot of business), so I chose a large one, lifted it, and struggled to strap it to my back. To me it wasn't heavy, but it was certainly bulky; I had quite a time getting it out the back door. Outside, I barely managed to get it onto the wagon and cart it away. It became easier once I put all my things into the coffin instead of the wagon.

I hadn't the faintest idea where I would go. But now that I had my portable bed, I knew I could sleep in the middle of a desert and not have to worry about the sun. If the coffinmaker was any good, that is. Fortunately, he was, or you wouldn't be reading this right now.

BOOK III

BOOK III

Twenty-six

I made very little human contact while traveling about England, which wasn't quite England yet, actually. There really were very few cities that even began to compare with London at the time; come to think of it, there were very few cities, period. What there were were a lot of tiny villages, chiefdoms, kingships, and bands of roving tribes. Travelers were not so uncommon that I was interrogated just by stepping foot into town, but I tried to keep my distance from people while I went about my business, mostly to avoid trouble. Especially when a full moon was near.

Once there was an actual full moon, I made it a point to be out of sight. Don't misunderstand me; I wasn't likely to start foaming at the mouth and raping the first man I came across, but I had never been with a man during that time, and I wasn't certain how much I could keep in. Maybe my eyes would become red, or a fang would grow, or something, if I hit my peak, and he'd be likely to throw me to the flames as a demon or witch or . . . a vampire?

Either way, I thought it wise to stay out of sight. Most of the time I had to satisfy the urge myself, or . . . all right, I'll admit that if there happened to be any big male wolves around, I'd . . . well. Yes. But I never harmed any man during a full moon.

I considered myself fortunate whenever I found a cave

or some abandoned lair in the hills. I could live in the caves for a while and survive pretty well off of the animals around there, including the bats who were often in the caves with me. Hares were the best, when I could catch them. It's much harder to make eye contact with an animal than one might think, so I usually had to chase my prey. If I came across a wolf pack, then the hunting was a little better. They always had a pack leader, but I was always alpha wolf for the time I was with any pack, so I got the first pickings. I only wanted the blood, anyway; the meat was all theirs.

Gruesome though it was, it's how I lived for centuries. At least I never succumbed to behaving like an animal; much of a night was spent in contemplation, not howling at the moon (except for full moons, that is). I don't claim to have become a philosopher during that time; I never made great intellectual discoveries, but I would just think. Usually about my old life, and old friends, and where I was now. Sometimes I fantasized, sometimes not, and sometimes I thought about nothing at all.

After four hundred years of this, I returned to London. I had seen more wars, more plagues, more famines and droughts, and occasionally something pleasant like a pagan festival, but on the whole, things were not good. It was the tenth century now. Many of the men before and after Charlemagne had tried to unify the land, but none were all that successful. The new economy was beginning: feudalism. Others call it the Dark Ages.

Well, none of it made much difference to me, either way. Remember that people in the Renaissance named it the Dark Ages, not the people living in them. I'll admit that the standard of living had dropped significantly from what I'd known before, even for the rich, but since I'd been living off weasels and hares for several centuries, it wasn't much different to me.

But I didn't start this just so I could give you a history lesson. Forgive me, I teach it in night classes now. Just wanted to set things up, really.

But once again, I was reduced to scurrying about, looking for old cellars and shacks to hole up in for the day (or two). Now that I was in a city, I couldn't skulk about all the time; I had to find a job, somehow.

Most women were supposed to be married, so they didn't need jobs, but I wasn't, so I walked the streets nightly, checking all the pubs and guildhalls and whatever, to see if anyone had a job for an unskilled woman. After a few months, I found one pub that needed a serving wench, so I took the job. Nights only, please, which the owner accepted grudgingly.

Not long after I moved back to London, I heard an odd and disturbing story. I was working a pub that night, and it was near closing time. One of the customers rose to leave and tipped his hat to all. But then one of his friends called out, "An' watch out for the Wagon Woman!"

"Aye, that I shall," he said, and left. I was curious.

"The Wagon Woman, sir?" I said, while wiping down his table. "Who be the Wagon Woman?"

"Aye, ye've not heard of her?"

"No, I have not."

"Well, then she might find thee as well, if'n ye're not wary!"

"Why, sir?"

"Why, ye've not heard her stalking the streets on many a foggy night, pulling her death box behind her?" he said. Now *this* was curious. I looked about to see if there was other work for me, and finding none, I pulled up a stool and sat down.

"I've not heard this sir," I said. "Tell me more." Another man spoke up.

"Some nights," he said, "when the fog's good and thick, the Wagon Woman walks the streets, pullin' her death box behind, and peeks into unfortunate homes, that she might find someone to fill the box with."

"Death box?" I said. "You mean—a coffin?"

"Aye," said the first man. "Ghostly pale she is, with a long white gown, an' she walks the streets with her wagon creakin' away . . . creeeak, creeeak, creak, 'til she finds a body she can fill the box with!"

"Umm . . . Are you certain that's what she wants?" I asked.

"That's what they say, wenchy," a third man said. "They say she died hundreds of years ago without a burial, for she was wicked, and now she's doomed to carry her coffin around and bury someone in her name."

"So that's why she needs bodies, eh?" I said, smiling nervously. The first man thought I was frightened and laughed.

"She'll be after you, wenchy, if'n you're not wary," he said.

"Aye, but I never seen her," the third man said.

"Oh, I have," said the second.

"Have you, now?"

"Aye, I have. Well—her creakin' has woken me before . . ."

"But ye never looked, did'ya, lad?"

"Well, I heard her."

The first man laughed and hit him in the back. "Ahhh, what a brave lad!" he said. "It was just an old man in an oxcart!"

"And how d'ye know it wasn't she, eh?"

The others waved him off and laughed heartily. I was called back to work by my impatient boss, so I politely took my leave of the men and got ready for closing time.

* * *

Well, I didn't own any long white gowns. Neither was I looking for bodies. But obviously I had not been so discreet as I'd thought while looking for places to live. I'd also thought putting a blanket over the coffin would conceal it, but people are more perceptive than I thought. At least no one in any of the pubs recognized me as their "Wagon Woman." Nevertheless, in the years to come I was always horribly nervous and self-conscious when it came time to "walk the streets, pullin' my death box behind me." The Wagon Woman needed a new wagon and death box, too; her old ones were antiques now.

About fifty years later, I was able to push in another version of the story, which was that the Wagon Woman was looking for a home, not a body. She had died hundreds of years ago, prematurely, after being forced from her home, so she was doomed to spend eternity trying to find a place to live. I thought that was more accurate, anyway. After a time, I started to enjoy the story myself, and even told it to travelers every now and then if they were going outside especially late. And only once did anyone ever confront me when I was in the streets myself. Not directly, but from his window. I heard someone shout, "Wagon Womaaaan!" I started to look up, and made myself slowly fade into mist all the while, until it seemed as though I'd disappeared into the fog. His window slammed shut tight. Just a good scare for him, nothing more.

A consequence of the new version was that people started putting up crosses all over their doors and windows on foggy nights. Well, I didn't go into occupied houses, anyway, so it never affected me. Neither did the crosses anymore. I've never taken my chances with holy water, though. No one's ever thrown any at me, to my memory.

Twenty-seven

My, how time flies. The fourteenth century already. London had survived fires, wars, plagues, and feudalism. Now it was time for Crusades, more feudalism, knights and lords in castles, and renewed Christian vigor. And it was always time for more plagues, as in bubonic ones.

Rats were still my usual meals, and they were hardly low in stock here; they're the ones who carried the disease, after all. My best hunting was in the alleys, where it was exceedingly dark, so I could summon them to me without anyone seeing me. I ducked into an alley where I'd been having the most success, and after looking about for onlookers, moved toward the back and stopped at a nice open area. I smelled death here, but then, I was smelling death just about everywhere in London, and I assumed whoever was in the alley with me was far beyond seeing or hearing anything.

I concentrated on the rats, and soon I was surrounded by hundreds of the squealing, crawling little beasts, and I got busy feeding right away. I only needed about ten of the creatures, and after taking my share, I sent them away again. I took out an old rag and wiped my mouth and turned to leave, when I heard the distinct sound of somebody trying to hold his breath but was no doubt too nervous to do so. I stopped and listened for more, and the breathing continued; I wasn't quite sure how old the person was. It sounded a bit high-pitched for a full-grown adult (which status few people were reaching in those plague-riddled years).

I was able to pinpoint where the breathing was coming from, only I could see no one, and I bent over to listen again for the sound. It was coming from under old rags and papers, and I reached out to touch them gently, and a quiet gasp came from them.

I got a good hold of a big rag and yanked it away, and the girl beneath them yelped and covered her face. I was startled, too, but I soon calmed myself and let the rag drop behind me. I looked at the girl again and reached out to touch her, but then thought better of it.

"Here, here," I said in my softest voice. "Don't be afraid; I'll not harm thee . . ." The girl peeked out from between her fingers, and then suddenly tried to bolt away from me. She plowed right into me, however, and I caught her and held her down gently but firmly.

"Here, here, child!" I cried. "Stay thyself! I'll not harm thee! I'll not harm thee . . ." I said over and over, until she became tired and let me place her back against the wall.

"I'll not harm thee," I said again, and sat down before her.

"Did I disturb thy sleep, child?" I asked, smiling. No answer.

"Surely thou dost not live here, with the rats and the filth?" I asked. Again, no answer.

"Where is thy home?" I continued. "Thy parents? Thy mother and father?" No words from the girl, and I was going to ask her the same questions again, when I was interrupted.

She mumbled something, and I leaned forward to listen better.

"What was that?" I asked as cheerfully as I could.

"God took 'em," she mumbled again. Hmm; enough

with the smiles, then. I let it fade and put my hand on her knee.

"Thy parents have been taken from thee," I whispered. "Fallen from the plague?" She only nodded.

"Poor thing," I whispered. "Living out here in the streets, sleeping under rags taken from the dead. How long hast thou been alone like this?"

She made an effort to look me in the eyes, but then hesitated and looked down again. I fidgeted with my hands while thinking of my next words.

"Hast thou a name?" I asked, and she nodded but did not speak it.

"I am Mara," I said, and held my hands out in greeting. She took them, but it was a feeble hold before she let go again.

"May I have thy name, child? I would call thee by it." "Elizabeth," she muttered. I smiled at her.

"Elizabeth," I repeated, letting my hand rest on her knee. "Well, Elizabeth, thou shouldst not be out here, in the dark, cold alleys where the rats can get thee. Dost thou want the rats to get thee?" She shook her head, and I laughed once.

"I can take thee where there are no rats, and there is no cold," I said. "Wouldst thou like that?" Again, she would not speak, but she nodded. I smiled and held my hand out to her.

"I can take thee there, Elizabeth. Wilt thou have my hand? Away from this place of death and darkness."

She looked up at my hand, and then up at me, and I gave her my gentlest smile, and she slowly brought her little hand out to take mine, but then hesitated.

"I'll not harm thee, child," I said, and she attempted a smile herself. Then she reached out again and touched my fingers, and I wrapped them about her wrist and began standing up.

Soon she was standing and looking up at me with anxious eyes, eyes that mirrored the anguish of the dead and dying she'd seen. She stood placidly while I brushed her off, and she yawned when I knelt down to speak to her again.

"Sleepy, child?" I asked, and she nodded. Then I wrapped my arms about her and stood up, hefting her off her feet. She gripped my collar in fright and yelped once, but I shushed her gently.

"It's a long walk, and thou art tired, child," I said. "Just relax . . . rest in my arms . . ."

She soon calmed down and quieted herself, and I carried her out of the alley and into the city.

"Where are we going?" she said sleepily.

"To my home," I said. "It's not far from here. It's no castle, but it serves me."

She did not speak, but looked back at the alley where we'd been and then let her head rest against my arms.

"Just rest in my arms, Elizabeth," I whispered, "and we'll be home soon . . ."

I gave her some water I had gotten from the Thames that night. She drank deeply and handed back the cup silently and yawned. I stood up and fetched my warmest blanket and wrapped it around her. Again, she said nothing, but looked up at me with her big, bright blue eyes. I smiled and sat beside her.

"Well, Elizabeth," I said, "it's no castle for a lord, but I call it my home. You may rest here tonight, if you wish. I'll be here to make certain no harm comes to thee.

"You say little, child," I said after a long silence. "Was it harsh, living as I found thee?

"Well, you can sleep now," I said after she nodded. "You have a warm blanket, and soft bedding, and a pillow there. Sleep now, Elizabeth; go on . . ."

Again, no words from her, but she watched me for many moments before yawning again. She looked down at the bedding I'm made for her, then back at me, then back to the bedding, and she closed her eyes and lay down. I took the blanket and pulled it up to her head, and tucked her in at the sides a little. Then I crawled over to sit near her head, and sat down to start thinking. I looked at Elizabeth again, who seemed to already be asleep, and touched her head gently, and soon found myself scratching it a little.

There is a child with me now, I thought to myself. *She ought to sleep through the night, if nothing happens. But nothing will happen, for I swore no harm would come to her. But why did I swear that? The child might have the plague already, and could die in a few days. Then for what purpose have I done this?* She was only one of thousands of children who live in the streets, eating scraps when they can find them and sleeping on the cold ground with the rats and the dead.

What on earth were you thinking when you took her here, girl? Do you really believe that you can take care of anyone, least of all a child such as this? You can barely take care of yourself, let alone a child! She cannot feed on rats and weasels as you do; she must have bread and milk and meat! You have none of those things, nor do you have the money to buy them! Stupid woman! So desperate for someone to talk to, anyone, *that you would take away a girl's chance to live by bringing her here?*

But she will die of the plague there!

Who can say it isn't here, also?

I only want someone to talk to, just for a little while—
Selfish woman!

Just for a little while, and if she doesn't like me, then she can leave anytime—

And she certainly will, *once she learns what you are!*
She doesn't have to!

Oh, and I suppose you'll be able to keep it from her?
I can always try . . .

Yes, girl, you do *that! You* try!

I buried my head in my hands and shut my eyes tight. *Selfish woman! Stupid, selfish woman!!*

I didn't hear Elizabeth lifting the lid or peering inside the next morning, but I was awakened by her quick yelp before she let the lid slam shut again. My eyes sprang open, and I furrowed my brow in curiosity. Then I opened the lid myself and sat up cautiously, at first peeking out over the side before sitting up all the way.

Elizabeth stood to the side of me and watched me wide-eyed. I couldn't tell if she was afraid, then; she seemed to be more . . . just confused and curious, really. We stared at each other for a while before I smiled nervously and pushed the lid back all the way.

"Good morning, Elizabeth," I said. "I'm glad you decided to wait for me."

" 'S not morning anymore," she said. I looked at the window, which was covered by a rag; but sunlight was fighting to shine through. The sun was up all the way, all right.

"Oh," I said. "Well . . . I have slept late, it seems."

"Why do you sleep in that box?" she said.

"Box?" I said in mock confusion.

"The box you're sitting in now," she said. "It's a coffin, isn't it?"

I laughed nervously. "Um . . . well, some people might use it for that. But really, 'tis only a bed, Elizabeth."

"Isn't it hard to breathe in that?" she asked. "How do you breathe?"

"I—it is not so difficult to breathe," I said, not wanting to tell her that I don't even breathe while asleep. "It's comfortable."

"Oh," she said, and looked about the room some more.

"Won't you be waking now?" she said suddenly, just as I was about to shut the lid again, as a matter of fact.

"Uh—no, child," I said. "I must rest still. I—I was up all night, keeping thee safe, you see."

"You were?" she said.

I nodded and smiled. "Aye, child, I was," I said, and couldn't help yawning again. "I'll be up no later than sundown. I am so very tired, I fear I may sleep the day through, you see. But will you still be here, when I am awake? I would like to speak to thee, still . . ."

She shrugged. "I have nowhere to go," she said quietly. "I'll have to be here."

"I am sorry for thee, child," I said. "But I am also glad that you will be here, still. But now I must rest, Elizabeth. Do not hesitate to make my home thine in the meantime; explore every drawer and shelf and pouch, if it will occupy thee."

"If you want me to," she murmured, and I smiled again and began to close the lid, but she began waving her arms all of a sudden.

"Uh—uh—" she said, and I stopped and gave her my full attention.

"I don't remember your name," she said.

"Mara."

"I'm hungry, Mara," she said.

Oh, Gods, I'd forgotten all about that! What was I to do now? Ahh, I remember now . . .

"Oh, yes," I said. "I am sorry, child. I'd forgotten thou must— Over there," I said. "In that black chest there. Open it, and look for a small leather sack. Yes, that one. Dost thou hear the coins? Take them out. Good, child. I give them to thee; take those coins and buy whatever food you can find in London."

"Money?" she said. "For . . . me?"

"Yes, Elizabeth. Take all of it, don't worry about my food, just buy whatever you need. Will you do this? Will you buy what you need, and return here?"

"Um . . . yes," she said. "Yes . . . um—thanks to thee, Mara."

I smiled and shook my head. "Please . . . only get what food you need, child. That will be thanks enough," I said, and closed the lid until nightfall.

Twenty-eight

"Do you understand what I am now, and why I must live as I do?"

Elizabeth and I sat side by side on her bedding. I had my arm around her and was doing my best to be as gentle, as trustworthy as I possibly could. She looked up at me expressionlessly and said nothing.

"No matter what others may say about me or my kind," I continued, "no matter what horrible tales you may hear of me, I wish for thee to understand that I would never, ever deliberately harm thee, for any reason. Do you believe me, Elizabeth?" And to my relief, she nodded. I smiled and rubbed her arm gently.

"I thank thee, child," I said. "It means much to me, that you would trust me so."

After a long pause, she asked suddenly: "Do you believe in God, Mara?"

"Uh . . ." I stammered, a little taken aback. "Wh— yes, I do, Elizabeth. I do believe that there is a god."

"But do you *believe* in Him?" she asked calmly.

"Um . . ." I said, shifting a little. "Um . . . no, child. I cannot—I am not allowed to worship Him."

"Not allowed?" she said.

"Well . . . it's more like— Well, let us only say that I don't think He likes me."

"Why do you say that?"

"Ohhh, simply—well, I have had not much fortune in trying to worship Him. That is all."

"Ohhh," she said, and we were silent for a time. Then: "Who do you worship, then?"

"Um—no one, really," I said. "I don't think I have any gods."

"My papa said, that if you don't worship God, then you worship the devil, instead. Do you do that?"

"No. I don't."

"Then who *do* you worship?"

"I have told thee, child, I worship nobody."

"But everyone has to worship somebody," she insisted. "And if you don't worship God, my papa said you burn forever."

"Many others besides thy father say that also," I said quietly.

"Then it must be true, if many say that. And priests say that, especially, and they talk directly to God."

"Do they," I said in a dead tone.

She nodded. "That's what everyone says," she said. I reached over with my other arm and lifted her onto my knee.

"They do say that, child," I murmured. "But do you believe them?"

She thought about it for a while and then said: "I guess I should, if I'm to go to heaven."

"I'll not try to lead thee from thy beliefs, Elizabeth," I whispered, and rocked her back and forth a little. "I only ask thee to judge others as you see them, not as others do. Do you understand?"

"I don't know . . ."

"Do you think I am from hell, child?" I whispered.

"No," she said. "But people would say you will go there, when you die."

"I make no predictions," I said, and held her close to me. "I make no claims to tell others what will happen

when they die. For some, they will enter a new world, perhaps a new life. And for others—for others their existence
may just *be* a hell . . ."

I shut my eyes as I held her, and we were silent for a
long time. I wanted to do something with her, play with
her, perhaps, but could think of no good games. Or maybe
not games . . .

"Would you like me to tell thee a story, Elizabeth?" I
asked.

She shrugged. "If you like," she said.

"May I ask you something?"

"What?"

"I was only wondering if perhaps your parents ever told
you stories."

"Um . . ." she said, shrugging again. "Sometimes.
When I was smaller, mostly."

"Oh," I said. "Do you have any favorite ones, then?"

"Um . . . I don't remember most of them," she said. "A
lot of them were about Mary and Jesus."

"Oh. Well . . . I fear I don't know any about them. But
I know some other ones. Perhaps you'll like them just as
well."

"Any story would be good, Mara . . ."

"All right, then; I'll try. Ummmm . . ." I had to hesitate
when I realized that I hadn't really prepared a story yet.
The Wagon Woman? The thought almost made me laugh;
I couldn't tell her *that* one. I might as well try and make
one up, then. Perhaps she wouldn't know the difference.

"I know one about a mother wolf and a . . . hunter," I
announced.

"A wolf?" she said. "But the hunter kills it, yes?"

"Well, I haven't even told the story yet, child!" I laughed.
"And as for the killing part, you will have to listen well . . ."

Making it up as I went along, I told her a story about
a mother wolf who had lost her mate to a hunter and had
to find her cub's food herself. She would go out into the

freezing snow and the bone-chilling wind and the rain and
fog and all sorts of dreadful weather to feed her cubs. Then
one day she and her cubs are discovered by the hunter,
who succeeds in wounding her with his arrow. She then
feigns death and waits until the hunter makes ready to
shoot her cubs. Then she leaps up suddenly and bites his
leg, making his shot go wild. She leads the angry hunter
away from her cubs, who then escape to their den. Both
the wolf and hunter limp after each other in the snow until
she can run no more, and she collapses by a tree. The
hunter is about to deliver the killing arrow shot, when he
is distracted by a great light, and he looks up to see an
angel (I thought I might as well keep Christian figures in,
just to please Elizabeth) hovering above the tree. She points
at him and chastises him for killing one of God's creatures
and then trying to kill its mate, thus leaving the young
ones orphans. He begs forgiveness but is told that forgiveness will be granted when he has redeemed himself, and
that means he is changed into a wolf himself and commanded to become the she-wolf's mate. It then falls on the
hunter to feed the cubs himself, and this wolf is distin-
guished from the others by a slight limp, where the she-
wolf had wounded him before.

Elizabeth didn't understand why this wolf was good,
when all the others were bad. I explained to her, best as I
could, that wolves were one of God's creatures, too, and
were not "bad" animals at all. Wolves were faithful to their
mates, and they didn't mistreat their cubs, which was more
than I could say for some human beings.

Elizabeth fell asleep soon afterward. She said she understood my story, since I'd explained to her about wolves,
and liked it very much.

I wasn't so poor that I could buy nothing for her. Still,
our money supply was tight. She had had to survive on

her own for a week or so before I discovered her, and she had become pretty scrappy and resourceful in the process. I didn't like having to sleep all day while she was out in the city, but at least she understood why I could never accompany her.

I did take her with me to my pub jobs. I always kept an eye on her while I waited on people, and she was usually quite well behaved and didn't bother my employer. Eventually I was able to talk him into giving her a few pennies a week to help clean dishes. She was very excited about having an actual job and especially loved the money. I wasn't paid much more myself, but I let her keep her pennies to spend them as she pleased, and always advised her to save as much as she could.

Every now and then, say once a month, I ventured out onto the moors and did some hunting. This was always during a full moon. I should not have left Elizabeth alone back in our cellar, but then, I much preferred that she not see me during full moons. I would summon some wolves and satisfy myself, and afterward, if lucky, I'd find a hare to bring back and cook for Elizabeth. I kept the pelts for future use. Naturally, I fed on the animal myself before preparing it for her, and found it was a much more palatable meal than a rat.

I did the best I could do for her with what I had. What hurt me the most was the few short hours we could spend together, but Elizabeth rarely gave me much of an indication that she was suffering for it. She seemed to have the attitude that any parent at all was better than no parent, but even with this attitude, I still felt extremely guilty for being able to do so little for her.

Eventually her sleep schedule began to shift to accommodate mine more readily. Simply because I did things with her only at night, she began to stay up later and later, and sleep later and later. But our schedules never actually matched, unfortunately. It seems that humans have a lot of trouble really adapting to night hours, especially when society has always been geared to the daytime. But that was fine with me. As long as we were getting more time to spend together.

We had few other opportunities to make money, but sometimes we had to make them ourselves—for instance, when poverty forced me to sell my ring. Not my wedding ring, of course, but the emerald one Gaar had given me later on. It had far more sentimental value to me than any amount of money paid for it. After many excursions into the wealthier parts of London, I was able to sell it to some nobleman for several coins and fine bits of clothing for Elizabeth. I accepted whatever was offered for it, in other words, which pleased me, since I now could help Elizabeth, but I felt empty for many days afterward.

One of the happiest memories I have is the time Elizabeth told me that, although people kept saying that vampires were bad, she felt safer with me than with any of those other people who said things like that. I started to cry and scooped her up into my arms and hugged and kissed her, and she thought I was being silly and laughed, but I didn't care.

Another time she slipped and addressed me as "Mama" in conversation.

"Elizabeth," I said, "did you hear?"

"Hear what?"

"You called me 'Mama,' " I said. She seemed embarrassed.

"Oh . . ." she said. "I'm sorry."

"No, no, I'd like . . . I mean, I would never want to replace thy true mother. She will always have a special place in thy heart, I'm certain. But I would be very proud to be called Mama, if you truly want that."

"Um . . . Um . . ." she said. Maybe I'd jumped to conclusions. But I wanted it so badly . . .

"Well . . ." she continued, "I guess you are my mama, now, I guess—"

She stopped and looked down, and I heard her sniffle a little.

"Elizabeth?" I said, "I hope I've not offended thee."

Then she burst into tears, and I knelt down and held her tight.

"What is it, child? What's wrong?" I said, but she wept awhile longer before answering.

"I miss them!" she cried. "I miss my Mama! Papa! They're dead, Mara! They're all gone!"

"Shh, yes, I know, cub . . . I know . . ." I whispered. "Yes, of course you miss them."

"They're all gone!"

"Yes, I know, cub . . . I'm sorry . . ." I whispered some more. "I know how it feels to lose a family. Believe me, I know . . ."

It was the first time in the two years I'd known her that she'd cried over her family. I hoped I personally hadn't brought it on, but I also knew that tears were good healers, and I kept holding her tight.

"Both of us . . ." I continued. "We're more alike than you might think, child. I, too, have lost people I've loved. And you know something?"

"What?" She sniffled.

"You never stop missing them," I said. "You'll always remember them. But you mustn't let your grief rule you; neither of us must. We owe it to them to keep going, and keep living. Do you understand, Elizabeth?"

"Uh-huh," she murmured. She raised her head, but did not look me in the eyes and wiped her nose with her sleeve and sniffled. I wiped away some tears with my thumb.

"So you keep crying, cub," I said. "Cry until no more tears will come. Tears can wash away many troubles."

"All right," she sniffled. "Thank you, Mama."

My heart leaped once in joy. This time, I knew the "mistake" was no mistake.

I had an interesting encounter one night. It was little more than an hour before sunrise, and I was on my way back home when I heard the sounds of a horse being ridden close by me. I paid little attention to it at first, even when I could tell the horse was being made to follow me from a certain distance. I decided to mind my own business and walk faster.

"You there! Woman!" a harsh voice called behind me, and it was only then that I stopped and turned.

I didn't recognize the man, but I did recognize that he was of the, shall we say, upper classes. It was also rather clear that he was very angry with me, but I did not know why yet.

"You walk the streets," he said, "barefoot. In rags. Half starved. How dare you allow this to happen to yourself?"

It took me a moment to get my bearings, to figure out exactly why he would be so angry that I was poor. It didn't take long once I'd gotten a good look at him, though.

"It displeases his lordship to see a poor woman such as I?" I replied eventually.

"I can see that you do not belong to the mortal world," he said. "You are as I am, yet you allow yourself to live amongst filth and rabble! This should not be!"

"Should anyone live amongst filth and rabble, m'lord?" I asked.

"There are those mortals who deserve such an existence," he said, "but I am not mortal. And neither are you. Yet you live as one, and a wretched one at that! Why do you do this, woman? Why do you scorn the power you have over others, the power that could bring men crawling to you, begging to obey your every whim? Why do you disgrace our kind?"

My answer to him would have taken far too much of both our time. Nor was I too sure he would even begin to understand, least of all appreciate it. I simply smiled a little and looked up into his eyes.

"If his lordship forgives me, I am tired and wish to return home," I said. "My child waits for me, and neither of us has much time before the sun appears."

He did not reply, but only glared for a while before turning his horse about and riding away. But I'm certain I heard him mutter, "Filth" before leaving earshot.

He was the first vampire I had met whom I had not been directly involved with, or responsible for, for that matter. I only pondered a short while on whence he might have come. I figured that Agyar might have converted others before he got to me. It would have suited him to involve himself with aristocrats, after all, or at least with those folks who were of wealthy families and who were destined to become aristocrats. Another thought, which I eventually chose to avoid, was that Agyar was still around and was "mingling" with the upper classes. This vampire did seem to have Agyar's attitude, though.

Either way, I never saw the nobleman again. I busied myself, as usual, in taking care of Elizabeth and doing what I could to get some money. The Plague was waning away. We were able to take more evening walks together without suffering the sights of plague-infested bodies and body carts everywhere.

We were preparing to return home one evening when Elizabeth began to slow down and kept looking behind her, and even though I hurried her along, she ignored me and eventually came to a stop.

"Elizabeth, why aren't you walking?" I asked. "It is cold and we should return home." I then took her hand and walked, but she offered too much resistance. This was getting frustrating.

"Dost thou want me to pick thee up and carry thee home, child?" I asked mockingly.

"No, Mama," she said, "I can walk."

"Good," I said, "because I want to return home, and you are not making things easy for me."

"I *am* home, Mama," she said.

"Huh?"

"My home is near here," she said slowly and quietly. "My old home. Before everyone died there. But I haven't been back here until now."

I said nothing to her for a long time, but only knelt down and stroked her head a little.

"Oh," I said at last, "I didn't know. Do you want to leave this place, child? Or—perhaps see it again?"

She bit her lip and looked off in another direction for a long time before answering.

"I think I'd like to see it again," she said, and I stood and took her by the hand and let her lead me through the streets.

She led me past several of the nicer homes, many of them even two stories, until we reached a faded old home, two story, all of wood and brick, in front of which Elizabeth stopped and stared. I was going to speak, when it became clear as to what she was staring at. There was some light visible within. I watched the windows for some time, hoping to spot some movement, but saw none.

"Somebody's there," Elizabeth murmured, and I bent over to whisper to her.

"It seems that way, child," I said. "But then, all is silent within. I see no movement. Perhaps it is only—"

I stopped only because there *was* sound and there *was* movement at that time. I brought Elizabeth closer to me, but no one emerged from the front door or appeared at any windows.

"I want to see who's in there," she announced. A slight chill crept up my spine.

"Are you certain you wish to do this, child?" I whispered. "I mean, it may simply be some other family who has— Elizabeth, come back here . . ."

My words were in vain, for she had slipped from my grasp and was now advancing determinedly up the steps to the door. At first I remained behind and called to her until she reached the door and knocked. I had little choice but to follow her up the stairs and take her hand as the door opened.

A middle-aged man appeared. He was of average height and build, better fed than most folks I'd seen, and dark-haired. He looked at me first, then at Elizabeth, who suddenly cried out in surprise.

"Uncle!" she cried, and rushed forward to grab his legs. But he was taken aback and immediately pried her away from him.

"Uncle Richard!" she cried again, and he bent onto one knee to get a better look at her.

"What? Unc— Who? I—" he stammered until his face lit up with recognition.

"Elizabeth?" he finally blurted out, his face flushed with joy. Mine may have been flushed also, but with growing dread, not joy.

"Uncle Richard" was all she said.

"It cannot be you, Elizabeth," he said. "your family has gone with God; we thought you were called with them!"

"No, I was not, Uncle!" she said, visibly bouncing with excitement. "I am here, and *she* took care of me!" she added, pointing to me. I shrank back a little, not expecting to be put under the spotlight like that. "Uncle" straightened up and scowled a bit as he gave me a quick going-over. I smiled weakly at him.

"And thy name, woman?" he said finally.

"Uhhhh . . . uhhhh . . ." I murmured.

"Her name is Mo— her name is Mara, Uncle Richard," Elizabeth finished for me.

"Let the woman answer for herself, child!" the uncle snapped, and then turned to me again.

"Took care of her, she says, woman," he continued. "Who are you? I do not know you. Art a distant cousin, perhaps? Didst thou speak with them ere they left us?"

"Um . . . no, Unc— umm, Master Richard; you see, I . . . I had not known her before her family . . . um . . . well, see, I found her in an alley and, um . . ."

"In an alley?" he said.

"Aye, master," I said. "She was alone there, and um . . . I . . . had no idea she had an uncle and . . . it was cold outside and all and I just . . . um—"

"Mara has taken care of me, Uncle Richard," Elizabeth broke in. "She has been good to me."

"Did you know the family at all, woman?" he pressed on, ignoring his niece. "Dost thou know what has happened to them?"

"I was told they died from the Black Death, Master Richard," I said. "But I did not know her family. You see, I found her in the streets, and um . . ."

"You took her from the streets?" he said.

"I thought she had no home, no family—"

"Did you not even try to find them?"

"Please, Uncle Richard, I was so frightened!" Elizabeth cried. "Mara found me and took me home with her, and I have been liv—"

"Be silent, girl!" the uncle cried, then to me: "Why did you not take her to the church, then?" We would have received word of my brother's passing on much sooner."

"Oh, please do not be angry with her, Un—" Elizabeth's voice sounded on the verge of tears, but her words were broken off by her uncle's icy stare. He turned to me again.

"Where have you been keeping her all this time, woman?" he asked.

"Um . . . only a few miles away, Master Richard," I said. "Master Richard," I continued. "We were only walking home, when Elizabeth wished to see her old home again, and we knew not that others would be living here again and um . . . I only did what I thought was best for her . . ."

We were all silent for an uncomfortably long time. The uncle let his gaze fall alternately on Elizabeth and me for some time, which made her nervous, as she moved closer to me and held on tightly to my robe. Then the uncle slowly smiled at me and placed his hands on my shoulders.

"Thou hast cared for the child all this time, and thou art neither cousin nor friend to her family?" he asked.

"Aye, master," I said.

"And have you a husband?" he said. "A family of thine own?"

"No, master," I said. "I am widowed. But Elizabeth is as a daughter to me, now."

"Perhaps I was harsh to judge thee, woman," he said after a time. "Thou hast done a good thing. A Christian thing, to care for this child during her great grief. And now God has delivered her back to us through thee."

"It would seem that way," I murmured.

"Aye, He has, woman! And we offer you our most gracious thanks!" he cried. He then bent down and took Elizabeth's hands gleefully.

"Welcome home, child!" he said. "God has returned thee to us!"

"Uncle," she said, and he let her hug him tightly. And after all the tearful reunions and greetings were through, Richard stood again, still holding Elizabeth's hands, and beamed at me.

"How shall we repay thee, good woman?" he said. "We shall keep thee in our prayers from now till we die, but what else ought we do?"

"Well, it—" I stammered. "I mean—you need not—"

"Thou must have something, good woman," he said. "Name it; if we are able to provide it, we will."

"Oh—well, that is most kind of thee," I said. "But—well, may I perhaps just warm myself by your fire for now? It is awfully cold here."

"Of course, good woman!" he said, and began guiding me to the door. "Come, child," he then said to Elizabeth, and we were inside.

The furnishings were humble, but they were far better than what I had become accustomed to. Actually, *any* furnishings would have been better than mine. Uncle Richard guided us to a small table before calling his wife from the bottom of the stairs.

"Heather!" he called. "Wife, come!" He was about to rejoin us when he added, "And wake our sons, also! A miracle has just happened!"

Meanwhile, I leaned over to whisper to Elizabeth, "I think your uncle and his family have moved in here, child," I said. "Was the house willed to him?"

"I don't know, Mara," she said. "I was hoping . . . it would be Mama and Papa here. I saw the light inside, and I thought it was them, come back . . ."

"I'm sorry, child," I said. "This house must be bringing back painful memories. Perhaps I should have taken thee to my home, instead."

"But Uncle Richard is here," she said. "Papa's brother. He can take care of us now. We won't have to live in an old room, and—" I shushed her as her aunt descended the stairs with three sleepy boys in tow. She seemed a number of years younger than her husband, and all three boys looked about Elizabeth's age, give or take a year or two. Richard explained excitedly what had happened, and I stood when he mentioned me, and I motioned for Elizabeth to follow.

Rather than great joy and relief, we were met with bewilderment. It seemed clear to me that Elizabeth and her

aunt had never met, but Heather extended her arms to
Elizabeth and beckoned her forward. I didn't realize how
tightly I had been holding Elizabeth's hand until she pulled
away from me to greet her aunt.

"You are Wayne's daughter? My niece?" she said.

Elizabeth nodded.

"I am your aunt, Heather. Hast thou heard of me?" she
asked. Elizabeth nodded again, and her aunt began stroking
her hair out of pity.

"You poor child," she said. "To have lost thy parents
and siblings through such a horrible sickness. But God had
mercy upon thee, and let thee live. But where were you all
this time?"

Richard told about my "adoption" before Elizabeth or I
could say anything. Heather then called me to her, and the
familiar questions continued: "You took care of her?" "Yes,
I did." "Oh, what a Christian"—and so on, until they offered to entertain us with food and more questioning. They
brought out bread and cheese, which Elizabeth feasted on
contentedly. I had some myself, if only to be polite, and
the questioning went on.

"Why did you leave the house, into the streets?" (Well,
she was terrified and confused, why else?)

"Why didn't you seek us out?" (How would a little girl
know where to start?)

"Why didn't you seek the clergy for help?" (Over half
the city was doing the same thing for the same problem.)

"Where have you been living?" ("But a few miles
away.")

"How have you been living?" (As well as possible, of
course.)

Nothing was said or asked about how she felt about
her experiences, and I was very pleased that Elizabeth
never once betrayed my nonhuman nature. Meanwhile,
they thanked me several more times for taking care of
her and offered various rewards. Food? Clothes? Money?

And, oh, how I wanted to shout out what I really wanted —Elizabeth!—but it was too late for that. I was losing her—slowly enough to be painful, and quickly enough to be a shock. Her aunt and uncle were discussing their role as Elizabeth's new guardians amongst themselves, and Elizabeth was chatting a little with her cousins. I felt like slipping away into the night and running home, but that was a coward's way. If I was to lose my child, I would do so with dignity.

I interrupted the aunt and uncle's animated dialogue, but found myself hesitating before I was able to speak.

"Master Richard. Mistress," I said. "I can see how excited we all are that Elizabeth has returned, but, um . . . I was wondering if there might be some place I can talk to her privately?" They looked at each other first, and then Richard furrowed his brow in thought.

"The study?" he said, and Heather nodded approval. She then rose and guided us to the stairs and up into the room. I waited for her to shut the door before sitting on the bed. Elizabeth waited for me to speak.

"Elizabeth, my child . . ." I said, taking her hands into my own. "They seem very pleased to see you. They even talk of making you their own."

"I heard some of that," she said. "Does that mean we'll be living with them now?"

"Umm, I—I am not so certain of that."

"What do you mean?" she said. "I know Uncle Richard will let us stay here, and you won't have to pay him anything!" She then rushing forward to hug me. "Oh, Mama! We are home now!"

Blast the child; she was making me cry. For all my "inhuman" might, I barely had the strength to pry her from me and hold back my tears. I tried keeping my composure by straightening out her robe.

"Now, Elizabeth," I said, "it is true; you are home now.

But this is *your* family, not mine. I have no say in what happens to thee next."

"Wh—what do you mean? Why can't you—"

"Hush. Let me finish. I—I—oh, Elizabeth, I am so afraid."

"Why, Mama?"

"Because—because of what shall happen next," I said. "I—I must leave you with your family now."

"What are you talking about? We can move out of that cellar now and—"

"Please let me explain, Elizabeth," I said, my voice choking. "It— I can only hope that you understand me. You see, this is your aunt and uncle."

"Uh-huh?"

"And—and that means, since your parents have died, they can be your new parents. Your guardians, that is."

"Uh-huh? But what's that—?"

"Shh, hear me, child," I urged. "This is . . . very diffi-cult because—well, because you may live here now, but I cannot. Do you understand?"

"But why not? We can both live here."

"Please, Elizabeth, you must—you must think of this," I said. "How could I possibly live here? Think of it. They would discover the truth about me."

"You mean, about you being a vam—" I covered her mouth quickly and nodded.

"Yes, child," I whispered. "And not so loudly, please. But—dost understand that?"

"Well, they don't have to find out. Not if they give you your own room."

"Uh—no, I fear it would not be so easy," I said. "Re-member, child: you discovered what I am within a day. How long could I keep it from them? And how long would they let me live once I was discovered?"

"But they wouldn't kill you," she said. "You're not a bad person. Why—"

"It doesn't matter how 'bad' or 'good' I am," I said. "I am a vampire. That alone is enough for them. Please believe me on this, I know whereof I speak."

"But—well, then I won't live here, either," she said. "I'll stay with you."

"That would never do," I said. "Now that they know of thee, you cannot expect them to let us go back to our cellar, and—and forget about thee. You are their niece—their family. They are not about to leave you with some woman who found you in the streets who—"

"Stop it!" she cried, tears bursting from her eyes. "I don't want you to leave me! I won't let you leave me!"

I leaned forward and hugged her long and hard.

"Shh," I said, when a knock came at the door. It was Heather out in the hall.

"Oh, please, mistress, another moment with her," I called, and she reluctantly agreed. I took both Elizabeth's hands into my own.

"Please do not think I am leaving thee, cub," I said softly. "I cannot actually live with thee now, but I will always visit thee."

"All the time?" She sniffled.

"Well . . . every night, anyway," I said. "Is that—will that please you? Every night I will visit thee, without fail."

"I want you to stay with me. I—I wish I'd never come back."

"Oh, Elizabeth, do not fault thyself," I said. "You were curious, nothing more. But meanwhile, you must be strong for me, for I know you are a brave girl, and I know you will obey your aunt and uncle as your own parents. Will you promise this?"

She opened her mouth to protest, but then a quick look from me made her close her mouth and nod, instead.

"Excellent," I said, and kissed her several times on the face and hugged her. "And you remember my own promise to visit you as much as I possibly can. For you remember how difficult things were for us; you know how hard we had to work to survive."

"Yes," she said. "But . . . I didn't mind. Sometimes it was fun."

I laughed and rubbed her head playfully.

"Yes, it was, wasn't it?" I said. "And you know, from the night I first saw you, I knew I would want you for my daughter. And you always will be my daughter."

"You'll always will be my Mama," she said, "even if Aunt . . . um . . ."

"Heather."

"Even if Aunt Heather is supposed to be now."

I kissed her again on the forehead and hefted her into my arms, where she wrapped her arms around my neck and let me carry her downstairs to rejoin her new family.

They thought something had happened to her until I explained that she was only tired, and that we'd simply been saying good-byes to each other. They informed us that Elizabeth would be adopted as soon as possible, but why were we saying good-bye? I explained that I had my own home which suited me, and the child was theirs now, but I asked their permission to visit her in the evenings. They gladly granted it and wondered if there was anything else I needed? I insisted on nothing, but I did not decline their insistent offer of some money.

Then it was time to say good-bye to Elizabeth one final time, and I bent down and called her to me. She was reluctant to approach, but I finally had her in my arms and hugged her long and tight. I did not look at her again, nor she at me, as I released her and stood to bid farewell to her aunt and uncle. They didn't seem very pleased at such a blatant display of affection, but I didn't care. I had left my frigid days behind me and wanted to keep them that way.

And then I had said all I had to say to all of them, and I was outside the house, and the door was closing. Then it was shut.

Twenty-nine

I kept my promise to Elizabeth, for the most part. That is, I visited her every night that I was able. Nights of the full moon were out, for instance. Her new guardians weren't very good with children's games or bedtime stories; childhood is really quite a new idea, historically speaking. Children were meant to behave as adults, or stay out of the way. But sometimes I talked her aunt into letting me see Elizabeth to bed so I could tell her a story.

Her relatives had a remarkable talent for making me feel frightfully uncomfortable. It was all the questions they kept asking: where I was from, where I lived, what I did, where is my family from, blah blah blah. I don't blame them, really; after all, I had come literally from nowhere to snatch up their little relative and take care of her for over two years. It's only natural that they'd wonder just what sort of person I was. But obviously, I just couldn't afford to answer all their questions, and I hate lying, even when it involves just holding back information. And they kept asking about my religious background, of which I had had none—but I couldn't let them know that.

She got alone well enough with her three cousins, which was fine, although I noticed that she did far more chores than they ever did whenever I visited. Because she was a girl, that is, not because she was an "outsider."

The years seemed to fly by before I knew what was happening. Soon, it seemed that every time I visited, Elizabeth had grown another foot taller. She was becoming a young woman before my eyes, and every time I looked at her, I would think of Kiri, and how she must have grown to be just as fair and pretty. Elizabeth was my reason to live then; truly my own pride and joy. She was bright, kind, polite, cheerful, and becoming prettier by the day. Her aunt and uncle were not quite so open with their feelings; in fact, they were often downright prudish, the uncle infinitely more so, but they weren't to be blamed, really. It was not exactly in fashion to "be free" with one's feelings then, and someone like me, who threw her arms around everybody she knew, made people like Uncle Richard uncomfortable.

The next thing I knew, Elizabeth was standing up to my shoulders, and she had all the marks of young womanhood about her. This was fine with Uncle Richard; he knew of a young man—from a good family, a wealthy family—in Cambridge who needed a wife. So a wedding was arranged. When I first learned of it, I almost cried, for that meant Elizabeth would have to leave London. The night before she was to leave for Cambridge, I asked her to walk with me. I held her hand as we walked and spoke.

"I will miss you, child," I said at one point.

"I know," she said. "And you know I will miss you, too, Mama."

"You'll be starting your own family now. Have your own children. I'm very happy for you."

"You don't sound it."

"Don't I? Ah, well, it matters not, cub," I said. "Fate has dealt its final hand, and we're to be parted for all time."

"Oh, Mama, you know I will visit London again," she said. "If I can, that is."

"I know," I said. "I know you will try your very best to return. But if you are unable to . . . well, you know you will always be in my heart."

"You will always be in mine."

"Yes . . ." I said, and then stopped walking.

"Is something wrong?"

"No, I—I just thought of— I would like to try something, Elizabeth."

"Try what?" she asked. I turned until we were face-to-face, and held her gently by the shoulders.

"Do not be afraid, child," I said, and concentrated. I had never charmed Elizabeth before, and thought I never would, but I felt that, this time, it was something I had to try. She was not expecting it, so it was easy for me to nudge aside her will and replace it with my own. I had never tried something like this; my plan was to place some of my thoughts, some of my feelings, hopes, and dreams into a small corner of her mind, and leave them there. Permanently. My plan was to leave her the most personal part of me—my thoughts—and let her carry them with her always. I wasn't sure exactly how to do it, or what the effects would be, but I would do it.

And I did. I don't know how long it took me to do it, but I waded through the ocean of her thoughts and found an island to plant my own thoughts on. They would stay there forever, always waiting for her to visit, if she so chose. I had given the essence of my being to her.

"Wake up, Elizabeth," I whispered, and she did. I didn't blame her for being disoriented at first; even *I* was a bit drained from the experience.

"Mama . . ." she whispered, "what . . . I feel so strange . . ."

I took her gently by the arm, and we continued our walk.

"Forgive me for the surprise," I said, "but I didn't know if it would work. I wanted to leave you one last gift from me, one very special gift. Elizabeth, remember this: no matter where you are, or where I am, from now on, you have only to think of me, and I'll be there."

"How could *that* be?"

"Oh, I don't mean *really* there, as I'm here now, but

here—" I said, pointing to her head. "My thoughts. My memories. Everything about me, cub. So if you're sad, or your husband treats you harshly, just think of me, and let the love I have for you comfort you. Will you do that?"

"Yes," she whispered. "Yes, it—it's wonderful, what you have given me. I can feel you even now. Your thoughts, and feelings. It's remarkable. Thank you, Mama-wolf."

She never did return to London, not that I know of. I am certain she must have tried, but was unable to. My life continued much as it had before: live everywhere and work any job I could get. The years—nay, centuries—were taking their toll on me. I had fallen into a rut of just existing, not living. I had acquaintances, not friends, and few of even those. I worked my jobs, went home, slept, worked again. Rarely spoke with anyone. I saw scores of people live, grow, age, and die, without ever having known them. Part of the distance I kept was intentional.

So there is the true curse of the vampire. Not the blood or the lack of sun, but the immortality. Agyar's "gift" to me. Those we love will only grow older and sicker and weaker, while we stay as "young" as we were when we died. Does the parent want to outlive her children? How about her grandchildren? Great-grandchildren? Friends? Spouses? Her own brother or sister?

I don't know what kept me going all those years, through all the wars, plagues, inquisitions, famines, droughts, revolutions, witch hunts, religious "reforms." And worst of all, the loneliness. Perhaps it's because, for all my existence as one of the undead, I was still afraid of dying. And still am. If I'm halfway there already, I don't want to complete the journey. I'd much rather turn around and go back the other way. Impossible, you say? Perhaps. I know of no vampire who has really, truly tried to regain his or her humanity. It's always been accepted as impossible. Perhaps.

I could go through a detailed history of little things that happened to me during the time I was in London, especially in the wake of great events such as (in no real order) the Renaissance, the Plague and Fire of 1666, the Inquisition, the Reformation, and every war fought up to World War I. But then, with some exceptions, all that really ever happened to me was that I remained poor, childless, friendless, unmarried, half starved, and often homeless. And, during most of the above-mentioned great events, things often became worse. I was unmarried, poor, uneducated, was limited to nighttime work only, and, worst of all, was female. Let's just say I became the world's longest-working waitress.

In the end, the waitress jobs proved to be a major liability. Read on, and see why. This was in the early eighteenth century.

I was finishing my shift at a crowded pub one night. In all of my jobs I always tried to avoid working during full moons, due to its effect on me, but every now and then I had no choice Tonight was such a night, and I had a hell of a time, wandering back and forth between all those men—old and dumpy and vulgar and ugly though they were—and still function normally. I wanted nothing more than to finish my job fast and get out of there, and find some safe place to "let off steam," as it were. But one particular gentleman (correction: he was hardly a gentleman) was constantly trying to get my attention, and whenever he succeeded, proceeded to make passes. Normally, I might have written him off easily and gone my merry way, but circumstances were different: the moon was at its height, and at last I could stand it no longer and promised to meet him after my shift.

This I did, he took me to some inn, procured a room, climbed into bed, and we proceeded to have sex. No love, no tenderness—just sex, nothing more. Not even good sex, for that matter. If the man was married, I doubt if he ever pleased his wife. Nonetheless, I hadn't been with a man for so long that it didn't matter how good he was, as long as he was a man. So to make a long story short, I lost control. I gave in to my urges and my hunger, and fed from him. Not converted him—just fed from him. And when I regained my senses, I cried out for what I had done and scrambled away from the bed. The man would not die, but he had been charmed into sleep and would be mighty weak and confused when he woke. But he would live, and that was most important.

Fortunately, no one seemed to have heard my cry, and the man was still asleep, and I cowered off into the corner, afraid, confused, uncertain what to do next. I hadn't taken blood from a person in so long I'd almost forgotten what it tasted like.

I would not leave without checking the man first, and it was then that I saw all of his clothes and accessories on the dresser. His money purse lay on top of the pile, but I looked away, trying to avoid that temptation, too. It didn't work. Before I could recover my senses, I had taken the shillings from the purse and run from the inn and into the streets. The moon's light glared at me, into my eyes and into my mind, but the hunger was gone. *I have fed, damn you, and stolen as well, is that enough for you?* I screamed at the moon, but in my mind only. I ran full speed and nonstop through the streets until I reached my basement home and locked myself tight inside for the night.

I had quit my job at the pub and found another one to work at. If that had been one of the poor fellow's haunts, I didn't want to be there to explain things to him. But, my luck being perpetually bad and all, this was not to be. Exactly one week later, somebody tapped me on the shoulder as I was setting down a platter of drinks, and lo, as I turned around, there he stood.

"Hallo, there, lass," he said. "Recognize me, don'tcha?"

"Uh . . . uh, no," I lied. "No, 'fraid I don't, suh," I added, and tried to continue another way, but he held my arm fast. I could easily have broken his grip but didn't want to make a scene.

"Aye, surely ye must, lass," he said. "We had quite a fine time together."

"Did we, suh," I said. "I ought to say that ye alone had a 'fine time,' 'cause—"

"That I did, lass," he said. "And I be lookin' forward to more fine times. If ye catch my meaning, eh?" he added, nudging me and winking.

"I'm afraid that would be impossible, suh," I said. "Y'see, I'm—I'm not who does such things. I-It was an accident, nothing more. In fact, I want to return your mon—"

"But all me friends know about ye now," he said. "They know how cheap ye are for such fine services."

"What?" was all I could gasp after a pause.

He smiled and nodded. "Ye could set yourself up for quite a bit of business, lass," he continued. "Bring some happiness to a lot of lonely lads. And they'd keep ye happy, too," he said, and then pulled out plenty of shillings and held them before me. My eyes widened, but I quickly regained my composure and made him put them away and grabbed a platter.

"Uh . . . uh . . . I have me work to do, suh," I flustered and hurried away.

But he wouldn't leave. All night long it seemed that everywhere I looked, he was there, drinking and staring at me. Sometimes I could almost feel him watching, and sometimes he would be talking to someone and pointing at me. I wanted to run from the pub and find somewhere quiet and private and just cry, but I had my job to do and couldn't afford to pull silly stunts like that. I would have to get away after my shift.

Well, the man (I believe Roger was his name, actually) and his pals cornered me outside and started questioning me and egging me on and pawing me and flashing money, until I could take it no longer, and told them I would do whatever they wished, as long as they would leave me alone afterward. And they decided amongst themselves, and then stuck me with a slimy old bastard with one eye and all his teeth either black or missing. But he had the most money among them and paid me well.

My boss was no fool, either. He knew what had been happening that night and promptly fired me when I walked in the next night. I had no choice but to turn around and go back home, but not before one of Roger's chums caught up with me and tried to strike up a conversation. I was in no mood for chitchat, however, and shoved him away and ran all the way home.

It didn't end there, though. I went into a slump and had a hard time finding another job. Expenses were chasing after me, as always, and I needed some way to get money— *any* way. The real jobs just weren't there, but I always knew what else I could do to get quick cash. And that's just what happened. I soon found myself haunting various pubs and taverns, at first dealing with Roger and his pals, and when they were short on money, other customers, as well.

I quickly learned how to be both discreet and efficient. I did find jobs at other pubs and taverns, and by this time, I could "do business" without any of my bosses finding out. I wasn't in it for the fun, I was in it for the money. It's a business, pure and simple, and almost any prostitute will tell you that.

I became much in demand rather quickly, and high-priced as well, a fact which irked my "competition" to no end. I had no pimp nor any brothel to operate from, but I was able to become successful enough just working the pubs. In fact, it got to the point where the poor folk often couldn't afford me. I considered heading for richer territory, namely, the as-yet unnamed "middle class." That meant working my way toward the wealthier parts of London. One might think finding customers would become harder as the clientele became richer, but I found little difference. For all their newly risen Victorian standards and Reason Worship, there were always plenty of depraved men about, no matter what social class they were in.

Thirty

"Evenin', suh. Out for your constitution?"

"Indeed, I am," he said.

"It's always nice to see people outdoors at night. 'Specially gentlemen like you. But—you're out alone, an' all. 'Ave you no lady of your own, suh?"

"No, I'm afraid not."

"Oh. Well, per'aps you wouldn't be mindin' a bit o' company, then, would ye?"

"I—I suppose not."

"Well, thank you, suh," I said, and slipped my arm into his as we continued walking. He stiffened a little, but I expected that. He'd loosen up soon, I knew that.

"Lovely night, innit, suh?"

"Uh, yes, uh—quite."

"Y'know, ye surprise me, suh," I said. "I mean, ye seem young an' 'ealthy an' 'andsome. And yet ye'ave no lady."

"Um . . . well . . ."

"Ever makes y'lonely, suh?" I asked. " 'Specially at night?"

"No, I—I try not to dwell on it," he said, pulling at his collar. "I have plenty of time, I'm sure."

"Oh, I'm sure y'do, too, suh," I said. "But still. I'm sure in the meantime ye'd like a little female companionship every now and then."

"Uh-huh . . . yes," he said, clearing his throat and stiffening more.

Wouldn't be long now. We walked some more in silence.

"You know . . ." he began finally, "I must say I . . . I never thought I'd ever actually speak with a woman of your sort. Least of all w-walk with one . . . That is . . ."

"An' 'ow do y'mean that, suh?"

"Oh . . . women of your sort, I mean. The sort who—who do what you do."

"Hmm, an' what's that that I do, suh?"

"I think . . . you know what I mean."

"No, you'll 'ave to tell me, suh. You'll 'ave to tell me right out what y'think I do."

"Well, I—I may be wrong, that is . . ."

"Come now, suh, y'can tell me. I'm a grown woman."

"Yes," he said, looking me nervously up and down. (I *was* taller than he, after all.) "Yes, you—certainly are."

"So what am I, suh?"

"Well, I think you—well, I think you want money from me."

"Do I?"

"Yes, you . . . want money for me, in exchange for— favors," he said, and pulled at his collar some more. I laughed a little, then smiled at him.

"Oh, you are funny, suh," I said. "I like that. Funny, an' 'andsome, too. But some'ow I think I'm only makin' things worse for ye. I meant no 'arm, suh, truly."

"Actually . . . I think you did."

"What?"

"Yes, you—oh, certainly not intentionally, but you do harm others, in your own way."

"Now, wait a minute, I never meant to insult ye, suh," I said, taking my arm out of his. "Can't blame a girl for tryin' to make a livin', so—"

"And just how *do* you make a living?"

"I'll just be leavin' ye now, I—I only wanted conversation—"

"Now just a minute, young lady," he said, grabbing my arm.

"I'm not so young as ye think an' take yer 'ands off me."

"I only want to ask you something."

"Well, what?"

"Only . . . only that, I wonder, Miss—er, I don't know what to call you."

"Call me Miss Smythe, then."

"Miss Smythe, thank you. I was simply wondering, if you could perhaps tell me . . . why?"

"Why what?"

"Why . . . why would a woman . . ." he started, then gestured with his hands. "Why do you . . . do what you do? Do you actually enjoy it?"

"Suppose'n I do," I said, shrugging. "Now if'n ye don't mind—"

"Oh, come now, that can't possibly be it. Women are— well, I don't claim to know the workings of the female mind, and this is one of the things I've never understood. That is, why women can be the most virtuous and chaste creatures on earth, and yet there are women who . . . who . . ."

I shrugged again.

"Guess some of us just can't reach such peaks 'o virtue, luv," I said. "Bloody shame, innit?"

"Now, listen, I'm trying to talk to you, not—"

"You wanna know why I do what I do, suh?" I snapped. He'd pushed me too far now. "Well, I'll *tell* ye. 'Cause there ain't nothin' else for us. There ain't enough 'usbands and fathers a-a-and brothers to 'take care o' us' like everyone say they's s'posed to, that's why! 'Cause *you* try bein' a lady, an' 'ave no school or 'usband or whatever, an' try to make a decent livin'!"

"Now wait a moment—"

"Nooooo, now ye've gone off an' blown me all out, so

now y'gotta listen! I used to 'ave a 'respectable' job, serving old bastards their food an' their ale, night after night. An' they wouldn't leave me be, that's what 'appened! Wouldn't let me do my job, kept pushin' an' pawin' an' grabbin' an' whatnot. How long y'think your 'virtuous women' can put up with that, eh?"

"Umm . . ."

"Yeah, they couldn't! I know I tried, suh; I tried to be one o' your 'virtuous women.' That's the way it works, suh. Always 'as. Makes me wonder 'ow I made it so long without this."

"It couldn't really be so bad," he said. "Could it?"

I laughed and turned to leave again. "You *are* funny, suh," I said. "But I better be off now. This was a nice talk but not very profitable, if'n ye follow me."

"Wait!" he said, and ran up to me.

I sighed and shut my eyes in frustration. "What now? I groaned.

"Only . . . Well only . . . it's just that, looking at you, I—"

"What?"

"It only seems that someone like you . . . someone like you isn't truly meant for something like this."

"Oh, Lord, none of us are, suh— "

"Well, what I meant was . . . What I meant was, that I have certainly seen others, like yourself, I mean, and— you're far different than they are. You're—you yourself said you tried to be a 'virtuous woman'—"

"And failed."

"But that's just it," he said. "You don't carry yourself, as someone who's failed at it. To look at you, one would think this . . . occupation of yours would be so far beneath you that the thought of it would fill you with repulsion. You're far too— Such a beautiful lady, but such an ugly way to live."

I lost track of how long I stared at him in silence. He

was an odd one, I gave him that. Yet I couldn't tell if his interest in me was forced, or if he truly cared. *Why is he doing this?* I thought. *What does he hope to gain?*

"I thank ye, suh," I said finally. "For the compliment. Many a bloke's told me I was beautiful, but not—not the way you 'ave. Not for your reasons. But don't put y'self out for me, suh; I'm too far into this now. Concern y'self with the other girls. Y'might 'elp them better. But I thank y'for tryin'. But I gotta go now."

"Um . . . well, I did try," he called after me. "But—could you tell me your name, at least?"

"Told ye: Miss Smythe."

"I meant your name."

"An' yours?"

"Hampshire," he said. "Edmund Hampshire."

"Pleasant talk with y'then, Mr. 'Ampshire," I said. "But if our paths should cross again, I'm Smythe. Mara Smythe."

I was not able to perform that evening. My concentration had been broken; doubts had been introduced. I tried and tried until no one but me was walking about at night, not even the blind-drunk pubgoers, so I went home. And once there, I thought—and thought—and thought of just about my entire life. Where I had begun, where I had gone, where I was now. And I cried for the first time in centuries. I didn't think I even could anymore. So this was the glory of immortality, was it? The great power we had over the beasts, and over men, which I used to get "customers." Glorious! How proud Gaar would have been of me. Even he might not have chased after me if he had just met me now.

I walked the next night, and the next, and so on, and all of them ended up the same way. Disastrously. I could barely even start conversations anymore, let alone talk men into an evening of fun and profit. The best whore in London had lost her touch. Finally, I could take it no more, and I ran all the way to the top of the building and screamed fit to burst my lungs. People opened their windows and hollered, and I hollered back, until I hollered one last time and dove from the roof, transforming as I fell.

As a bat, I flew faster and harder than I ever had before, and headed straight for the Thames. I landed on one of the banks and peered into the black river of rushing water. *Running* water. It kills our kind. Washes the skin right off our bones. It would certainly kill me. I only had to dive in. It might be painless, it might not. It might take several long, agonizing minutes to do its job. But it would do it, and I'd be free. I hoped . . .

Big Ben began to strike, then, and I kept staring at the water. Four o'clock. Dawn was but a few hours away. If I hadn't the courage to dive in just then, I could wait awhile. Maybe I should have just stayed out on the roof that night, so many centuries ago. Sent Lara away so I could have died.

My lips started quivering, and my throat tightened, and for the second time in many centuries, I cried, and I fell to my knees and crouched into a fetal position, and cried and cried. In my eyes, I was a coward, for I had not the courage or strength to finally end my existence after all that time. More than anything, I hated my precious immortality, yet my fear of death was still even stronger. Agyar was right; it *was* what I dreaded most.

I saw Edmund another night, and tried to avoid him when I did. He saw me, too, though.

"Uh, uh, excuse me," he kept saying, while trying to catch up to me. "Excuse me! Miss Smythe!" I slowed down enough for him to catch up, but didn't stop.

"Miss Smythe," he said. "It *is* you, isn't it?"

"Uh—why, yes, suh, it is," I said. "Must not 'ave 'eard ye."

"You seem to be in an awful hurry."

I slowed down to a normal pace now.

"Do I? Didn't mean to seem it," I said. "I'm just—walking."

"Oh," he said. "I see."

"Not for the reasons y'think, suh. This time I'm just walking."

"Oh? Has—have you been considering what I said?"

"Shouldn't be too quick to pat y'self on the back, suh," I said. "But, yeah, I been thinkin' 'bout things lately. Where I been, where I'm at. Don't much like what I saw, to be truthful. Seems I been messin' things up for meself right good these past few—years." (I was about to say "centuries.")

"Ah—well, but now that you've been thinking, you must realize that—that there are far better things for you, for a woman as—well, as refined as you. Yes, you are of the—er, working class, but you don't carry yourself that way. You are more—"

"I 'preciate what you're tryin' to do, suh, an' I thank ye for it, but right now I'm not much up to any conversations. Just thought I'd take a walk, that's all."

"I'm terribly sorry, Miss Smythe," he said. "I . . . never was much good at comforting people."

"I used to be that way," I said. "Takes time, but y'might learn. Meantime, I'll be 'eadin' back 'ome now."

"Yes, uh—well, perhaps you . . . might like some company, then?"

"But I just said that—"

"Silent company, I meant. We needn't talk."

I shrugged. "Suit y'self, suh."

And we did walk in silence, until we reached my building at last. Edmund hid it well, but I could feel his unease at being in a poor section of town.

"Well," he said cheerfully as he could, "so this is where you live?"

"Aye, suh," I said. " 'S all I can afford, I fear. But you— no doubt you got a fine place."

"Well, it's—comfortable," he said. "For me, that is. Perhaps—perhaps you could see it sometime."

"That an invitation, suh?"

"Uhhhhh, yes, I— Yes. An invitation, then. Perhaps you and I might be able to . . . have tea together some day. If . . . you don't mind?"

"Don't mind at all, suh," I said. "In fact, I'd be delighted to. Just give me an evenin' to go."

"Well, perhaps—tomorrow afternoon, then? I shall call on you, and—and walk you to my flat. And have tea?"

"Be delighted, suh. But tomorrow *night* it'll 'ave to be. Can't be with ye in the day."

"Very well. Tomorrow night, then."

"So when ye come, I'm in the basement flat there," I said, pointing to the grating window.

"Very well," he said. "I shall call on you, then. And—uh—" he said, reaching out awkwardly and taking up my hand. Then he kissed it.

"That is how the gentleman treats the lady," he said.

Not a bad place he had. Pretty much what I expected of Edmund, although its decor was not quite so Victorian as I'd expected. He did have quite a big library, I thought: a whole room devoted to his books. I couldn't read English well but, from what I gathered, a lot of them seemed to be about magic. Well, not real magic, certainly, but he had a number of intellectual-type treatises on witchcraft and other matters of the occult. I asked him about them, but he waved them off as relics of his youthful past, when he loved to read of the unusual and extraordinary. That's why those books were all off in a corner. And besides, he'd been well established in the Church of England for years. I accepted this and forgot about it. There was nothing "extraordinary" about the way he came across, and most importantly, nothing unusual in his aura, either. Normal human.

He poured a nice cup of tea, and we chatted for several hours before he confessed to weariness, but offered to walk me home, nonetheless. I didn't need an escort but accepted his offer. We parted with a kiss on the hand again and another promise to call on me.

I went back to work the pubs as before. As usual, the pay was barely enough to keep a roof over my head, but in the meantime, I still had a little bit of money left over from my old occupation. But I was determined I wasn't going to go back to that, no matter how poor I was.

An extraordinary advantage the Age of Machines brought about was the ease with which I could feed. Let me explain. Automation was all the rage now, and businesses were gong through major turnovers to get in step with the times. Huge factories were popping up everywhere, all automated, all made for mass production. Steel, textile, food products—and the slaughterhouses. Men could kill thousands of livestock per day as opposed to only dozens before mass production. I leave it to others to debate whether that's an advantage or not, but for me, it meant I never went hungry.

I didn't work at a slaughterhouse, but what they did— and I kid you not—was to open their doors before sunup and sell cups of blood to people who cared to buy any! Normal human beings were lining up at the slaughterhouses to drink their cup o' blood in the morning before going to their own assembly lines. Now, from what I hear, people who worked the slaughterhouses had been doing this for years, and modern workers probably still do it today, under the pretense that it's good for them, apparently. Either way, it was good for *me,* for now I had only to wait in a line and get my fill for a ha'penny, then get back home before dawn. Now, feeding on the rats was free, of course, but believe me, the improvement was worth the money.

Thirty-one

I continued to see Edmund. He was an odd fellow, very nervous and shy, but I knew he was quite fond of me. It took me longer, but I became rather fond of him, too. After all, he had shown an interest in me that went above my occupation at the time. To my eyes, that was a tremendous compliment.

He knew where I worked, and once even stopped in to visit. It was a middle-class pub, so he had no trouble fitting right in. He had a boring job as a bank clerk, but that boring job paid for his nice flat, too.

Usually we made plans to meet somewhere after my work and walk to his flat for more tea and scones. Otherwise, I went straight home. He had never actually been inside my flat, which was just as well, as it was quite a dump. Besides, it wasn't "proper" for a lady to invite a gentleman into her home, anyway. That was up to the men.

I always worked extra late at least one night of the week. On those nights, Edmund and I made no plans to meet. On this particular night it had been awfully hectic, and I was tired and dirty and wanted to get home quickly, so I ducked into an alley and transformed into a bat and flew up and away. Don't worry; London has bats all over the place, so my appearance would not have unduly startled the faint of heart, unless the transformation itself had been seen. But I was certain I had not been seen.

Edmund had invited me to a candlelight dinner, to take

place a week or so after the above-described night. When I arrived, I could see that he had gone to all sorts of lengths to impress me, from the lit candles on the table to the crystal wineglasses. And I was impressed.

"I'm so glad you could make it, my dear," he said, kissing me on the cheek. "For I have something very important to tell you tonight."

"Really now, Edmund," I said. "Looks like you're trying to outdo yurself tonight." (I was working on losing my cockney accent by this time.)

"Yes, well—I'm certain this shall be quite a surprise," he said, and he offered me his arm, which I took, and he led me to my seat. Edmund was not a bad cook; I don't eat, but I *can* eat, and his food never upset me. Normal food just goes straight through us, anyway; only blood gives us any nutritional value.

Nevertheless, dinner went quite well, although we did not talk as much as usual. I caught Edmund staring at me a few times, which concerned me and made me self-conscious, but I never called him to it. Then during dessert, he pulled out a piece of paper and appeared to be studying it intensely. He made a lot of faces at it and grunted sometimes.

"Edmund," I finally said. "Um . . . what's that there?"

"Hm? Oh, nothing really," he said, setting it down. "Sorry. It's simply a note I've received from my brother, only I can't make out a word of it."

"Your brother?" I said. "Oh, the one in India."

"Yes. But whatever it is he's written, it seems to be in some strange language. Can't figure it out. But no matter—"

"Well—perhaps if I looked at it . . ." I said.

"You?" he said. "But I thought you couldn't read."

"I beg your pardon, suh—sir, I actually can read, write, and speak a lot of languages a lot of people 'aven't—haven't—even heard of!"

"Is that so?" he said, apparently amused. "Why, I had no idea you knew such things."

"Well, I do," I said, reaching out for the paper. "Give me a look at it, would you?"

"Very well, my dear," he said, and handed it to me.

Well, I actually couldn't make heads or tails of the message. Not only could I not understand the message, but for some reason it was even difficult for me to *see* the message.

"Does it make any sense to you?" he said.

"Um . . . no . . ." I said, momentarily losing my thoughts. "No, I . . . can't translate for you. Sorry," I said, and tried to hand it back to him.

"Perhaps if you read it out loud," he said, pushing it back to me.

"Out loud?" I said.

"Yes," he said. "Perhaps it will make sense when listened to, rather than read. You can do that, can't you?"

"Oh . . . I s'pose I could, Edmund . . ." I said. "Let's give it a go . . ."

I shall not repeat the words here, for reasons of safety. You see, the words of the message became clear as I read them out loud, and then faded back into haziness as I continued on. And the more I read of the message, the harder it became for me to think. And when I tried to stop, Edmund's voice came in again, egging me on, pushing me to read and keep on reading, and my thoughts became hazier, and my will became as sturdy as mud.

When I reached the second to last word, my mind was so much slush. It must have taken an eternity for me to mouth it, and when it was finished, I could not go on. My eyes were open, but just barely, and I could not move a muscle.

"You have one more word to go, Mara," Edmund's voice went on. "Read it. Go on; I have confidence in you . . ."

Aaaaaaaaaashhhhhhhhtaaaaaaaaa . . ." I said at last, and

my eyes could stay open no longer. I could also not move, and there were several moments of uncomfortable silence, before I felt the paper taken from my hand, and then I felt Edmund's hand turning my head to face forward.

And I still could not move. I could not move! My thoughts, my mind, everything was crystal clear once I had read the last word, but now I could not move a single voluntary muscle even the slightest bit. I had been in frightening situations before, but nothing was so terrifying as this feeling of utter, total, absolute helplessness that now took hold of me.

Edmund took my hand and placed it in my lap, and then opened one of my eyelids, apparently to see if anything odd had happened to my eyes. Something *had* happened; I could not even follow his movements. Paralyzed, just like the rest of my body. Then he shut my eye again, and I heard him sit down and sigh.

"Well, well," he said. "It seems to have worked. Extraordinary. I have never, ever, until now, tested the effectiveness of any of the spells in any of my books, but this one has, indeed, been effective."

Release me! I shouted at him mentally, but his mind seemed not to have "heard" anything. Or he heard, but chose to ignore.

"And if this has been truly effective," he continued, and I heard him rising from his chair, "then you ought to be able to hear everything I am saying even now. But—you are completely unable to move. Correct?"

I'd "correct" you, suh, if'n ye'd but let me go, I would . . .

"How silly of me," he continued. "If you can't move or speak, then how on earth am I to expect you to be able to answer? So," he said, putting his hand on my shoulder, "I'll simply have to assume that you *can* hear me, and act accordingly."

He walked away from me, and his voice came from some

feet away but still in front of me. I heard him going through some drawers.

"I suppose I should explain myself to you, if you can hear me, that is," he said. "You see"—his voice was now moving toward me—"I know what you are. Oh, no, no, I don't refer to your once being a—a 'lady of the evening' and all. Or, come to think of it, I suppose one *could* refer to you that way, couldn't one?" He was just in front of me now.

"You, my dear, are a vampire," he said, "and the fact that this spell worked on you and no one else proves it. Oh, you probably wonder: 'How? How could he have known?' Quite simple, really. I saw you transform yourself into a bat—which certainly no human being could do—and fly away, less than a week ago. Now, naturally, I at first thought I'd been imagining things, but then, the more I pondered what I'd seen—or thought I'd seen—the more I realized how many things about you all seemed to fall into place. Your small appetite for normal food; blood is your diet, not human food. The fact that I have not ever seen you during the daytime; the sun really must burn you, then, doesn't it? But most importantly, the fact that this spell I've discovered—not to mention the heptagram you are seated directly in the center of—and it was most fortunate you had not seen it when you were seated!—has worked on you and you only. It is a spell that works only on vampires, you see."

I felt him place something against my chest.

"I—I think it only fair to tell you how sorry I am that it must end this way, Mara, because—well, to tell you the truth, I had planned to ask you to marry me this very evening, before I discovered this awful truth about you. But I don't see how we can now, for I have no choice but to destroy you, for you are a—well, a creature of darkness. But I hope you can hear me, and understand, Mara . . ."

"Oh, Jesus . . . Oh, God . . . He's going to do it. And

there's nothing I can do to stop him! Not one goddamned bloody thing!

Farewell, Gaar . . . Elizabeth . . . all of you. Perhaps we may meet in death. I pray so . . .

"Blast it, who could be coming by at this hour?" Edmund grumbled as the knocking interrupted his task.

Yes! Yes! Someone at the door! Answer it, Edmund! Answer it!

"Well, don't you even dare to make a sound," he whispered into my ear. "We'll simply have to wait for whoever it is to go away."

No! Answer it! See who it is! After all, it could be somebody terribly important, right, Edmund? Right?

"Shh," he said as the pounding continued. And then, too soon, it stopped, and I could hear slight footsteps moving away from the door and across the front of the flat.

No! No! Don't leave! Come back! Come—!

"Eddy!" a voice called from outside. "I say, Eddy! Are you at home! I see a light inside, but I wonder if you're home!"

Let him in! Let him in!

"If you're inside, Eddy, please let me in!" the voice continued. "It's Nigel and I'd like to see you for a bit! Are you there, Eddy!"

"Nigel?" Edmund whispered to himself.

Yes, it's Nigel, Edmund! Go see Nigel! You love Nigel! You want to see him again!

"I say, Eddy!"

Eddy still kept silent, and soon we heard Nigel turn to leave again, and a lump came to my throat.

"N-Nigel, wait!" called Edmund, and the footsteps stopped and came back to the window.

"Was that you, Eddy?" he said. Are you home?"

"Um . . . uh . . . yes!" Edmund called. "Yes, I am home, but, um . . . er . . . g-go to the door! Walk to the door, Nigel!"

"Well, that's more like it," Nigel said, and Edmund rushed back to put all of his things away and rushed past me to get the door.

One cannot see Edmund's dining room from the doorway, but I could hear everything clearly enough.

"Eddy!" Nigel called when the door opened. "How have you been! It's been years, hasn't it?"

"Er, uh—yes! It *has* been years! In fact, it's quite a surprise to see you again!"

"Yes, well, you're going to be seeing a lot more of me very soon now, as I'll be moving back to London! In the meantime, I won't be here after tonight, so I thought I'd—"

"Oh, it's very kind that you thought to visit me—"

"So what have you been—"

"—But this is really an awful time to stop by, Nigel, you see uh—"

"Quite all right; I only have time to say hello and then—"

"Hello. Now you must go—"

"What, pushing me out the door? What's all this, then?"

"I'm terribly sorry you can't stay, really I am, but—"

"What—what's going on, Eddy? Stop pushing me!"

"I am very busy right now!"

"What, at this hour of the night? I should think you'd be ready for bed by now."

"Yes, well, I will be soon, now if you'll just come by tomorrow—"

"I told you, I'll be leaving London tomorrow and won't be back for at least a month! Now I thought I'd be kind and visit an old friend before then, but it seems this old friend has forgotten common courtesy! Now I'd like to at least step over your threshold, unless that threatens your livelihood, for heaven's sake!"

"No, no, you mustn't go in there—!"

I could hear him entering the room, and even heard Edmund's desperate attempts to grab at Nigel's arms and pull him back.

"Now you stop all this . . . Oh! I'm sorry!" Nigel said, apparently at the sight of me. "Please forgive me, madam, I—"

"For godsakes, Nigel, get out of here!" Edmund screamed.

"What? Eddy, will you tell me what's the matter with you? I'm sorry, madam, I never meant to— Wait a minute . . ."

"You, sir, had no right to force your way into my house!" Edmund screamed right back. "Now you will remove yourself or I'll call the constables!"

"Call the constables?" Nigel said incredulously. "What in— Eddy! What is this! Unhand me!"

The sounds of a brief struggle then ensued, of which Nigel appeared to be the winner.

"Wait! Stop! Look! Eddy, look!" Nigel said, and then his next words were almost a roar. "For godsakes, Edmund, will you look there?" The struggling then stopped.

"Can't you see there's something wrong with your lady friend, here?"

"No! She's fine, I tell you—!"

"Oh, nonsense, just look at her!" Nigel was right in front of me now.

"Don't touch her! You mustn't touch her!"

"Well, can't you see she's fainted?" he said, and then right at me: "Hello? Can you hear me? Can you speak at all?"

"Don't touch her, I say! She—she mustn't be moved!" I felt a small breeze in my face, as though Nigel were fanning me with a napkin.

"I said get away from her!" Edmund's voice cried right in front of me. He and Nigel seemed to be struggling.

"Have you gone mad, Eddy? What's the reason for all this?"

"You must leave here, Nigel, or she'll kill you!" he croaked. "I was only trying to protect you!"

"Protect—? Kill—? You're not making a word of sense!"

"Please; just trust me, and believe what I say, and leave now and save yourself. This—this 'woman' you call her, is no woman at all! She's a creature of darkness, Nigel. This woman is a vampire!"

There was a moment of silence, and then I heard Nigel shove Edmund away from him. His voice had become a low growl.

"Oh, you've come up with some queer things before, Edmund, but this is too much," he said.

"Nonononono— No," said Edmund, rushing up beside me. "I'll prove it. Look there; see? A heptagram. Now the hepta—"

"Oh, come off it Eddy, you've gone daft!"

"No, no! Nigel—don't you see? The heptagram! I—It's what one uses to—to catch a vam—"

"Get away from her, Hampshire . . ."

"You must believe me!! I—I— One night, outside of a pub, I saw this woman right here, and she actually *transformed* herself—"

"I said—get—away." Nigel's voice boomed, and Edmund stopped babbling. Then I heard him move away as Nigel moved behind me.

"Oh, dear God in Heaven, she will kill us," I heard Edmund whimper.

Hands grasped the back of my chair, and I was tipped back slightly and pulled backward. I felt a tingling as Nigel pulled me though the barrier of the heptagram, and then out of it. My eyes shot open, and who should I see but Edmund, now plastered against the wall in terror. I could move. *I could move!*

"Oh," said Nigel, and I stood up from the chair and turned to face him. He was taller than I, with brown, wavy hair, blue eyes, a long, rough, but still gentle face, and a great big scarf wrapped about his neck. He was beautiful, and I wanted so much to just sink into his arms and thank him over and over again, and cry my eyes out. But I chose to maintain a calm demeanor, and only smiled very daintily.

"I see you've recovered, madam," he said. "We'd thought that you'd fainted."

"I . . . I must have."

"Oh, Nigel, she will kill you," Edmund whimpered from against the wall. "She will kill us both."

"I said that's enough out of you!" he called to Edmund, and then to me: "Pay him no mind, dear lady, it's simply a game we'd come up with."

"This is no game!!" Edmund cried, and dug through a drawer quickly and pulled out a big cross. He held it out and started moving forward slowly.

"Get away from her, Nigel, and watch this!" he said. I was afraid, then. Not of the cross, but of the fact that Edmund *did* seem like a lunatic. Wild-eyed. Covered with sweat. A crazed grin on his face. I'd never thought such a transformation was possible for him.

"Watch, and you will see," he said in a low, determined voice. "You'll see that I'm speaking the truth! That woman is no woman at all, but an inhuman creature of darkness! A wretched servant of the devil himself!"

Whew! I hadn't heard talk like this since the Middle Ages.

"Eddy, forgodsakes—"

"Just watch!" he said, and stood right in front of me, his cross practically touching my face. The crazed look on his face was slowly starting to fade the longer he held it before me.

"What on earth do you think you're doing?" Nigel cried.

"This cross can burn her skin at a touch!" Edmund said. "Just watch!" he said, and pressed it to my forehead. I reached up and took it from him gently, and he backed away in horror and fear when he saw that it was not hurting me.

"But—but—" he said.

"Are you quite through harassing this poor woman?" Nigel said.

I put the cross onto the dining table. "It's all right, good sir. No harm was done," I said in a very quiet voice.

"My faith . . ." Edmund was muttering. "It's not strong enough. It must be stronger than her power . . ."

"Eddy, you've gone stark-raving mad," Nigel said in quite a matter-of-fact voice. "I couldn't possibly know how it happened, but I wouldn't be surprised if all those witch books and things didn't have something to do with it. I thought you'd given up that silly interest years ago."

"Oh, I had," he said in a strange, singsongy way. "I had, truly. But when I found out about her, well, I had to look vampires up. I had to know how to destroy her. Yes."

"Madam, I think we'd better go," Nigel said. "Quickly."

"I think so, too."

He offered his arm to me, which I took, and keeping a wary eye on Edmund, Nigel escorted me from the flat.

"She will kill you, Nigel. She will kill you," we heard before shutting the door behind us. Nigel hesitated before this and said, "Of course, Eddy; I'll be careful of that."

And then we were outside, alone. Nigel took up my hands, and held them to his chest.

"I wish I knew what to say to you, madam," he said. "I wish there were some way for me to apologize for all this . . ."

"Say nothing, then," I whispered.

"What's that?"

"You have nothing to apologize for, sir," I said in my best accent. *"I should be the one apologizing to you."*

"To me? What on earth for?"

"Oh," I said, "I suppose . . . simply because of what you went through, to help me get away from there."

He shook his head sadly. "Eddy was once a good friend

of mine," he said. "I can't believe— He was always such a reasonable, stable fellow . . ."

"Do you truly believe he's mad?" I asked.

"Of course he's mad!" He said. "Why, you saw with your own eyes, heard with your own ears! The things he said! And to a lady, no less! If that was not madness, then what is?"

"I suppose . . . He did frighten me a little, with what he was saying . . ."

"It's those damned books and artifacts of his!" he continued. "Eddy's always been odd about looking into all that—supernatural, ghosts, witches, devil-worshipers and what not! I always wondered just what it was all for, but now—! I swear I'd think all those books had been giving him delusions! In fact, they have been, as you just now saw! A vampire, indeed! Oh, madam, I am truly sorry that *you* were the victim of his delusions. Where on earth would he come up with that notion?"

"What notion?"

"Why, that you are a vampire, of course!" he said. "But—right now it would be best if I saw you home safely."

"Oh, there's no need—"

"I insist. I don't trust Edmund anymore, not now. What if he should follow you?"

"I doubt it," I said, and started walking. I caught a glimpse of Edmund's front curtain moving as we passed by, but I kept my gaze straight ahead.

"Once you're home safely, I'd think it wise that I come back here, and see if he's calmed down." Then he sighed heavily. "Aye. Somehow I had the feeling I'd get no sleep tonight."

"You needn't lose sleep on my account, suh," I said.

"Oh, not on your account, no errrr—I meant—terribly sorry. I mean *some*one should look in on him again, and it certainly oughtn't to be you."

"I understand, suh," I said, and we walked on in some silence. Then: "By the way, suh, I don't believe we've introduced ourselves. I'm Mara. Mara Smythe."

"Ah. Nigel. Nigel Clarke." He extended his hand, and I shook it daintily.

"Pleased to make your acquaintance, Mr. Clarke," I said. "And . . . thank you."

"No thanks necessary," he said. "But . . . I must say you're taking all this quite well. To have tolerated such—such wild accusations and insults . . ."

"I've stood worse, to be honest, suh," I said. "I mean, worse things have been said, about me, I suppose . . ."

"Worse than that? I can think of little that's worse than all that."

"Oh, you know how people can be," I said. "How cruel they can be."

"Too true, sadly," he said. "Too true."

Finally we reached my flat, which Nigel was obviously not very impressed with. Apparently he'd thought I had "real" money, as he and Edmund had. I only had on a fancy dress that night because Edmund had bought it for me. Nevertheless, Nigel politely kept any comments to himself. So I thanked him and restrained myself from losing control and throwing myself into his arms and kissing him over and over for saving me from the worst experience of my unlife. Maybe later, I thought.

Before leaving, he took up my hand and kissed it, as Edmund had, only this time I almost fainted when Nigel did the kissing. It's easy to fall in love with someone if he's just saved your life. But, of course, it wouldn't have been "proper" to show such infatuation. Nigel became embarrassed, however.

"Oh, I'm sorry, Miss Smythe, I—that was awfully forward of me," he said after the kiss. I only giggled.

"Is something wrong?" he asked. I giggled again and shrugged.

"Uh—no, Nig— uhh, Mr. Clarke," I said. "You're not at all forward. Not at all. In fact, I—I'm quite honored."

"Oh," he said. "Well, that is nice. But I ought to be going now, then— "

"Uhh—might I be seeing you . . . sometime in the future, then? Mr. Clarke."

"Nigel."

"Nigel it is," I said. "And of course you must call me Mara now."

"Very well—Mara," he said, and his eyes twinkled some. "But I'll be away come tomorrow, but when I return in a month's time, I— perhaps if you'd like to meet with me then."

"I'd be honored, suh."

"The honor is all mine, dear lady," he said, and he stared at me for a moment until "But I must be getting to Eddy . . . poor, poor bastard. I wish I knew what in God's name drove him to this."

"I hope it wasn't me," I said, but he smiled and shook his head.

"You should try not to think about all this, Mara," he said. "Go to sleep. Get some rest, and hope no bad dreams come from this."

"I'll try, suh."

Eventually he parted from me, and turned slowly to start up the sidewalk again, back to Edmund's.

"Um—Nigel?" I called, and he stopped and turned back to me. I descended the steps to my building and walked up to face him.

"I was just wondering . . ." I said, "do *you* believe in vampires?"

"Me?" he said, as though I were addressing another. "Actually, no. No, of course not, no. They're simply creatures of old tales and myths. Now, you don't believe in them, do you?"

"Well . . ." I began, "let's just say I'm not—quite so certain of myself about such things as you are."

Thirty-two

It had been about a week since my brush with death. Three weeks until Nigel returned. I'd been counting the days, you see. Meanwhile, I had good cause to be concerned for myself; I hadn't heard from Edmund in that week, nor would Nigel be able to tell me what had happened until he returned. I wanted to go to Edmund again and talk to him, but I decided not to take the chance. He truly had looked like a wild man that night . . .

I awoke at sunset, as usual, dressed, cleaned up, and otherwise prepared myself before heading for the pubs. It wasn't until I'd reached the door that I saw that my lock had been broken. It couldn't have rusted, I was sure of that; the padlock looked like it had been forced to break. I opened the door and stepped into the hallway cautiously. No suspicious people about, so I inspected the lock further. It was then that the landlord's wife came bustling by.

"Oh! Miss Smythe! You're 'ere!" she cried. " 'Ave you 'eard about the ruckus?"

"Um—ruckus?" I asked. "I see tha' me door seems t' be broken . . ."

"Tha's jus' it, Miss Smythe!" she said. "Somebody tried to break into yer flat today! Some lunatic, 'e was!"

"A lunatic?" I repeated.

"Yyyeeeesss," she said slowly. "Some loony straight from the asylum, I'm sure 'e was! Tried to break your door down, an' that's when the Mister fetched the bobbies, an' then 'e started goin' off 'bout monsters bein' in there, an' ow' e' 'ad to kill 'em all!"

"What what what?" I asked. "When was all this?"

"Why, jus' t'day, Miss Smythe!" she said. "Past noon. An' ye know somethin', Miss Smythe? 'E looked an awful lot like that bloke ye've been seeing these past months. Ye wouldn't 'ave been 'aving rows with 'im lately, now, would ye?"

"Why . . . uh . . . are you *sure* this was the same man?"

"I dunno. You tell *me*, Miss Smythe," she said, "Wha' sort o'blokes're ye consortin' with, anyways?"

"Um— Well— No one at th' moment, Mrs. Thorpe," I said. "I 'aven't been with Edmund, if that's who the 'lunatic' was, for almost a week. Nor am I to ever be with 'im again."

"Well, 'oever that loony was, 'e kept goin' on 'bout there bein' monsters in your room, an' shoutin' an' 'ollerin' an' raisin' a ruckus I ain't seen the likes of since I lived near the asylum as a li'l girl!"

"Ehmm . . . that sounds awful," I said.

"Oh, it was, I tell ye that! Why, the bobbies 'ad to drag 'im out of 'ere! Probably took 'im to the asylum, I should 'ope."

"Um . . . I should 'ope so, too," I said.

"Meantime, I been keepin' an eye on yer place from time to time, 'til ye showed up. But I can't guarantee 'e didn't take nothin'. Better give yer place a look-see."

"I will," I said, "but I don't think he meant to steal anything 'ere. But thank ye, Mrs. Thorpe—for watchin' me things, that is. An' if the bobbies really took 'im to the asylum—well, I can only 'ope he's not able to bother us no more."

"Amen to that, miss."

* * *

Another brush with death. I hadn't even been aware of it. And it certainly answered my questions about Edmund. Lord, he'd seemed so stable, so reasonable, so . . . so normal. I blamed myself for what had happened to him, of course; if only he'd given me the chance to talk to him, instead of jumping off to conclusions about us "creatures of darkness." But everybody did that, so I could not blame him for going along with the crowd.

I fell into a slump soon after Edmund's arrest. He would have been sane, and a free man, if I hadn't been what I am, I was certain of it. What was the point of all this? I wondered. Was Agyar right? Was there no way out of this existence save death? Was there truly no way to return to humanity?

I knew one place to look, and that was in Edmund's books. Since I'd been welcome in his flat for some time, it was a simple matter to enter it and get his books. Now that he'd been put away, he had no use for them. Unfortunately, I couldn't read English all that well, but I knew enough to be able to teach myself better by actually reading the books.

In one of the books was that spell Edmund had used on me. That one was an honest-to-goodness book of magic, but I read only the ones that had to do with vampires, of which there were few. I wasn't interested in how to levitate tables, I wanted to *cure* myself. But in the end, all my searching proved fruitless. The books were written for human beings, and spells about us supernatural types were of the offensive or defensive kind. That meant How to Catch a Werewolf, How to Bind a Demon, and so on, but nothing on how to cure them without killing them. I counted about sixty ways one can destroy a vampire, and about forty ways to create one (barely any of which were true, by the way), but none on how to help one.

Nigel was good to his word. He called on me soon after returning to London, and invited me to tea. His flat was just as nice as Edmund's, only more disorderly, considering that he was still unpacking. We made casual but nice conversation, much of which was about his job as one of the shipping clerks for a textile factory. Of myself, I said little, except how I was only a waitress. He lamented some more about Edmund, as he'd heard about his friend's commitment to the asylum, but I kept quiet about it. The evening ended with him escorting me home, and kissing my hand again. This time I kissed him on the cheek, though, which embarrassed him. Ahhh, if only he'd known what naughty thoughts I really had . . .

Fortunately, Nigel was not as reserved as Edmund had been. I introduced him to long, deep kisses fairly soon in our relationship, but nothing much more than that. It was obvious to me that Nigel was the sort to wait for marriage for any more, and I certainly respected that, always remembering how I had once been.

For the six months that we were together, I felt young again. Young as when I'd first met Gaar, alive, happy . . . and human. But like any relationship with my kind, there were the inconveniences. Only seeing each other at night; holding back my true past to him; spur-of-the-moment excuses as to why we couldn't be together during full moons—and so on. But all of that we weathered quite well without much difficulty, although I wasn't sure when my luck would run out.

We'd been together six months, and I'd invited him over to my flat. I knew he didn't really like the place, but I insisted, and he begrudgingly accepted the invitation. He told me that he had a surprise for me that night, and was hoping maybe we could be someplace . . . appropriate for it, but since he wouldn't tell me the surprise, I didn't know what was "appropriate."

I'd managed to be up during the day (after covering the window good and tight) to prepare his favorite meal of split pea soup. I also had some tea, pudding, crumpets, and other goodies for him. It was evening when he arrived, and I kissed him a long time before letting him inside.

"I'm so very glad you came, Nigel," I said, leading him down the stairs. "Um . . . I know you'd rather be elsewhere than an old place like this, but—well, this is my home, you know."

"I know," he said softly. "I understand. In fact, I was just thinking that, perhaps this *is* the perfect place to say what I'd like to say."

"Oh? Well, then, have a seat there, and we'll—"

"No, no, I'd– like to stand for this," he whispered, and took up both my hands. We stood face-to-face.

"Mara, I– you know that I'm quite fond of you," he said.

I liked this beginning. "Yes," I said.

"And I realize we haven't known each other as—well, as long as we ought to have . . ."

"Mmm hmm?"

"Well, what—what my surprise was, was— Mara, I want you to marry me."

I didn't answer. I couldn't answer; there was so much joy in me, I could not move. He misinterpreted this, however.

"I—I hope I wasn't—wasn't too forward, then," he said. "I mean, I—I could certainly wait for another—"

I threw my arms around him and kissed him good and long to shut him up. Eventually his surprise left him, and he got the message and wrapped his arms around me, too. We spent the next few minutes this way.

"M-my . . ." he said when we parted. "M-my word."

I laughed and kissed him quickly again.

"This must mean that I *wasn't* too forward," he said.

"Not forward enough," I said.

"What?"

"Nothing. I meant— Yes! Yes, Nigel, I want nothing more than to marry you! Yes, yes, yes, YES!"

"You are an exceptional woman, Mara," he said. "You're not like so many women I—"

"Oh, stop giving me reasons, you silly man, and sit! Sit! Sit!" I said, and ushered him into his seat. I took my plate of snacks and held them out to him.

"Tonight I have fixed you your favorite meal, my love, and then you can tell me how beautiful and 'exceptional' I am. But look, here are scumpets, and pudding, and—"

"Scumpets?"

"No, trumpets," I said. "Tumpets or—oh, take them, I've lost my mind tonight!"

He laughed and took the plate. "Well, thank you, anyway, my dear," he said. "I shall enjoy your trumpets."

This was a perfect evening. I was in love, my man had now asked me to marry him, I would be his wife and cook and clean and do all those wifely things for him, and all would be beautiful.

I made him stay seated while I set our plates at the table. He said that the crumpets were good, the "trumpets," too, and now was the time for the main meal. I grabbed some old rags to hold on to the soup pot and took it and began carrying it to the table, when one of the rags slipped, and my thumb became exposed to the red-hot bottom of the pot.

I yelled and dropped it immediately, only the pot landed onto my foot, as well, and I genuinely screamed this time. Nigel came immediately to my side, and I was in so much pain then that it did not quite register yet just how my appearance had been changing. Fortunately, he had not yet looked me in the face.

"Mara!" he cried. "Are you all right? Here; let me see your hand . . . let's look at it . . ." he said, and I pulled out my hand, which had only suffered a second-degree burn, and let him look it over.

"Lord, the way you screamed," he mumbled to himself,

then: "Your hand doesn't seem seriously hurt. We only need to put some . . . uh . . ."

That was when he glanced up at me, and it occurred to me then that I had lost control of my appearance. My mouth was still open from all the screaming I had done, and I quickly let my tongue slide across my teeth. Sharp.

Time stopped. I knew what he was seeing. Red eyes, gaunt, drawn face, inhumanly long and sharp canine teeth. I made no effort to change them back; it was too late for that. And for all my great age and experience, I knew that I was the biggest fool on earth.

After an eternity, Nigel made a small noise, as though trying to clear his throat. My appearance was unchanged, and he shifted about uncomfortably and looked at the floor.

"Uh-heh—" he said, "you're uh—you've got some soup there . . . on the floor . . ."

Still in slow motion, I followed his finger to look at the hot, oozing mess I'd made of the evening, and mechanically took a rag and knelt down to sop up the soup.

"Would you . . . like some help?" he said.

"No," I said, never looking up. In the meantime, I worked on straightening out my appearance so the illusion would once again be that I was human. Nigel cleared his throat quietly and sat down.

"There's some soup left in here," I said. "Like any?"

"Umm—- No, no, I—it's all right," he murmured.

"That was . . . quite an accident," he said after a long pause.

"Yes," I whispered. "Quite."

"Mara," he said after another long pause.

"Yes."

"Stop that a minute," he said. "Stand up."

"Got to clean this up, suh," I said. "Got to clean the mess."

"Stand up," he said. "Come on, stop that."

He had to come over himself and take the rag from my

hand, and help me to my feet. Then he made me take a seat, but I still couldn't look at him.

"Look at me, Mara," he said.

"S'prised you want me to," I murmured.

"Now stop that," he said. "Come, look up now." I did so. I assume he expected to see that face again.

"Now what . . ." he began. "What *was* that, Mara? What is it that I saw?"

"You saw . . . you saw *me,* Nigel."

"Did I?" he said.

I nodded. "Edmund was not quite so mad as you thought, was he?" I said.

"I don't understand you."

"What 'e was sayin' to you before," I said. " 'Bout my bein' a vampire."

"Of course, but that was only a . . . a fantasy of his."

" 'E was wrong, when 'e said I as going to kill you," I said. "I never meant 'im no harm, Nigel. I loved 'im. I wouldn't think of 'urtin' 'im."

"You're very upset, Mara," he said. "I can tell you . . . your speech is changing—"

"I never meant you no 'arm, Nigel," I said. "I love you, even more than I loved Edmund. I—I wasn't lying, I *do* want to marry you, more than anything. I can be a good wife, just like all the others. Just let me show you."

"Well, of course, of course you'll be a good wife," he said. "I don't— Of course you can . . ."

"You don't even believe that yerself, Nigel," I said. "I can feel it in ye. You're just as scared as I am. And I don't blame ye. All this is my fault. I been tryin' to hide myself, keep you from knowin' the truth about me. Oh, it's always there, tryin' to force its way out, but—I didn't know how. I didn't know how to tell you without your goin' mad the way Edmund did."

"I'm—I'm not really sure what this 'truth' is, Mara."

I sighed. "Ye saw my face, love," I said. "I don't see

'ow you can be confused still. Unless you're so stuck in science an' reason an' all that you can't believe in magic, even if it's right in front of yer face!"

"That wasn't magic, it couldn't have—"

"I told ye, Edmund was right!" I said, grabbing both his hands. " 'E said I was a vampire, and 'e wasn't mad about it, either! But 'e was wrong, that I would 'urt 'im. Or you. All I want is to be human, Nigel. All I want is to . . . to walk out in the sun, an'—an' eat *real* food, not dogs an' rats an' whatever I can find! I want to . . . to hold my hand under a waterfall an' not 'ave the flesh come right off the bones. I want to . . . I want to age, Nigel! I don't want to be ageless anymore! I envy old people, did you know that? I envy them!"

"Yes, of course, Mara, you're—you're becoming quite excited," he said.

"Oh, God, now you think I'm mad."

"No, no, of course not, of course I don't think that—"

"I know I must sound it," I said, calming myself. "Forgive me, Nigel."

"Of course."

"But I know this is all my fault, for not telling you this before, but—it was so hard . . . I knew you wouldn't believe me, or if you did, you'd be afraid."

"I'm not afraid."

"You're terrified, love," I said. "I know. But I don't blame you. All I wanted was to . . . to show you that even monsters need love, too."

"But I thought that monsters *can't* love," he said.

"Can't they?" I said. "Aren't they the ones who need it the most?"

No answer.

"Aye," I said. "Being hated . . . feared. Not something I much care for, really. All them stories 'bout vampires killing people, makin' them slaves. Now they got that—

whatsit, Dracula? Well, I never met no one named Dracula, I tell you that. Don't think I'd want to."

"I'm sure you wouldn't."

Then we had the longest silence of all. Neither of us moved from our seats, nor did we even exchange glances. Then finally, Nigel broke the silence.

"Mara . . ." he murmured, almost inaudibly.

"Yes."

"I know that—well, I know that you've said 'yes' to my . . . question and all, but—um . . ."

I knew what he meant, but let him continue.

"Well, what I mean is, considering this new situation, I'd like to—well, perhaps take some time to . . . reconsider our situation. If it's all right with you . . ."

I said nothing first, but leaned forward enough to take his hand and bring it up to my lips and kiss it. I held it next to my cheek afterward.

"I understand," I whispered. "You may certainly reconsider. But of course, I may always hope that nothing will change, and we'll be married, still. But it must be for the same reasons. I won't let you marry me out of pity, and certainly not out of fear of my 'wrath,' should I be refused. And much as I'm tempted to, I will not beg."

"That would be beneath you," he said. "That much I know."

I forced a smile and shut my eyes.

"However you see it, love," I said. "But I will not beg."

I didn't beg. And the answer was what I'd expected. No. He gave all sorts of reasons, all of them very good and logical. Most of them had to do with the social impact of our marriage (or, what would the neighbors think?). I choose not to condemn him to Shallow Persons' Hell for that explanation. Then there was the sheer impracticality of such a union, and the different hours we'd have to keep, blah blah. In other words, he was afraid to. I took his answer best as I could and decided not to blame him, but deep, deep down inside me a knife had been stuck into my soul, and then twisted.

I thanked him quietly for telling me his answer, and thanked him for all the wonderful times we'd had, and then asked him to leave. Permanently. At first he hesitated, as though he wanted to say something, but then made his final good-byes and left my life forever. And as I shut the door, the numbness was returning. The numbness I'd felt when I first saw my home village in flames, destroyed; the numbness I'd felt when I first learned that Gaar had died; when I learned that Leta's attempt to kill me had failed, and on and on. Nothing but numbness in my life, and I was sick of it.

Two minutes after shutting the door, I threw my coat across the room, raced back up the stairs, burst out of the room, ran out the building, down the steps, down the street, running, running faster and faster until nothing alive could match my speed, and leaped into the air and transformed, and flew off into the night.

I flew to the moors and landed, and stood in the middle of nowhere and howled. Howled and howled, until I heard other howls join in—wolves—but I did not stop. Soon the wolves themselves came, and they gathered around me in a circle, and we howled the entire night through, only stopping because sunrise was near.

There isn't much else I can say of the rest of my time in England, other than that I never saw Nigel again, nor Edmund, and life continued on as usual: a job here and there, always moving, waiting in line at the slaughterhouses, and coping with the loneliness. Just coping, though. The years crept along interminably, but they finally reached the twentieth century. Alas, I could not say that things picked up immediately. It took the war to do that.

The first world war, that is. And there was my sign to pack it in and go. I was already tired, very tired, of London, of pretty much the whole world. But I loved London, too, and there were many tears even after I made the decision to leave and find a fresh life. I probably should have left right after breaking up with Nigel, but it took England being buffered about by Europe's squabbling to get my fanny in gear. It has to do with being old and set in my ways, I suppose, but I finally took my cue and made plans to see the Land of Opportunity, or America (whichever came first).

BOOK IV

Thirty-three

Getting to the States was an experience in itself. Since I couldn't really afford to use a passenger vessel—and think of the problems *that* would have caused—it was back to stowing away on the cargo ships. I got hold of a good, sturdy wooden box, threw my few things into it, plus myself, and nailed it shut from the inside. All this I did in the cargo area in the middle of the night; my crate looked just like all the others.

Fortunately for me, it worked; I was loaded on board with all the rest of the crates. I don't remember very much about the trip itself, as I slept most of the time, but once we reached the shores and began unloading, I was jostled awake innumerable times before I gave up even trying to sleep. I believe my box was put onto a cart of some kind. Later, my ride on the cart stopped, and crates on top of mine were being removed. My crate was ignored for a long time, but I could hear people moving about. Suddenly other crates were being piled up on top of mine. *Oh, bravo,* I thought.

I could tell by the sounds that it was still daylight, and therefore working hours, and since my crate was being ignored now, I was able to drift off into sleep again.

When I finally awoke, I was hungry and bruised all over. Careful listening revealed no sounds of labor, so I assumed it was nightfall and past working hours. But the question was, how to get out? I tried pushing the top open, but there were those damned boxes on top of mine. After some consideration, I took a deep breath, turned, and slugged the side of the box, thus showering the floor with splinters and wooden shards. Vampires are rather strong, you recall.

The box started cracking some more as I scrambled out of it. No sooner had I gotten clear of it then the box gave in to the weight on top of it, and the whole stack piled on top came crashing down in a mighty din. I must have jumped thirty feet back from fright. It seemed like an eternity before the horrible tumble ended and the dust finally began to clear.

Right on cue, I heard footsteps fast coming toward me. I didn't see who it was, neither did I want to, for I couldn't afford to be found in this warehouse in the middle of the night with no explanation. Fortunately, vampires can be absolutely silent, not to mention practically invisible in bad light. I heard voices converging on the accident site, but by this time I had made it halfway across the warehouse. Finally, I reached the main entrance, but the doors were securely locked; only I managed to spy a few open windows some twenty feet or so above. A backward glance revealed no pursuers, so I leapt up without a sound, climbed through, and plopped to the pavement below. Getting back onto my feet, I sniffed about for anything out of the ordinary, and scrambled away in whatever direction my legs would take me.

I stood on a dock overlooking the harbor and watched the flickering lights of New York. *So here I am,* I thought. *In the very nation that I had smirked at so long ago when it had declared war on the king.* Now here I was, seeking refuge in it from yet another war. *So how do I get to the city?* I wondered. I can easily fly across, but not with all the junk I'm carrying. Well—maybe I can. I've got the wingspan for it, I hope. I doubt if I'll get tired. Hmmm . . .

Taking a deep breath and gripping my sacks between my toes, I leapt up and forward and transformed. My sacks skimmed the water a good distance before I was able to gather enough speed to keep them and myself sufficiently aloft. It was not an easy trip, believe me. I could do no less than full exertion, sometimes more, it seemed, lest I and my precious sacks sink into the waters below. And it was cold—bitter, bitter cold that whipped and stung my face until I thought it was going to crack right off. Meanwhile, the island seemed no closer than before, and the pain of overworked muscles threatened to paralyze my efforts. But I shut my eyes and dared not slacken even a bit.

Here again, my so-called tirelessness was taxed to the limit, and by the time I slammed headfirst into the beach, I was ready to lie motionless for a thousand more years, and even that might not have been long enough. I lay flat on my belly, still in bat form, and tried to think of nothing, but I could not help babbling to myself. *Ahhh,* I thought. *So this is America . . . or America's sand. It's very good sand, actually . . . I may be the first immigrant to taste its sand. I wonder if others would like sand. I could set up a little shop and sell sand . . . or sandwiches. Ah, what a funny . . . Errrrrrrg . . .*

Pulling my face from the sand was no mean feat. It could not have been very late at night, for I could hear a bit of activity in the streets ahead of me. Hmm, no one seemed to be on the beach with me, but in the meantime, it might be a good idea to change back from a bat. After transforming, I picked up my sacks, dusted them off, and headed toward the wonderful city.

Things were the same as when I first entered London. I needed food and light-proof shelter. Some stray animals took care of the food, but where to sleep? I had little enough money as it was, and it wasn't even American, but a bank could help with that. That would have to be later, though. Soon after I found my food, I figured I might as well settle for some out-of-the-way place rather than go bothering people in the middle of the night. So while I had become used to dwelling in better places over the years, I decided that a night in the sewers wouldn't kill me.

I had slept in worse places. But I certainly had no intention of staying there permanently. Once sunset arrived, I was out on the streets again, looking for potential abodes and places of employment. And maybe it was because I could only deal with people at night, but I had a hell of a time finding even a closet to rent out. Too many landlords were asking for immigration cards, as well, and it wasn't until that time that it dawned on me that, by God, I was an illegal alien! No passports, no cards, no anything. I also couldn't get a decent job without any of those, either.

I understand now that my solution was rather stupid, but it did get the job done. It was actually very simple. The immigrant registration areas operated pretty well into the night on good days, so it was a simple matter to wait in line in one of those places, and once my turn came, to "charm" the fellow behind the counter and make him give me all the cards and paraphernalia I needed. Once he did, I told him to forget about me, and then I let him go. Life went on normally for him after that. So that was a lame way to handle it; well, I did it and there's little I can do about it now.

Eventually, I was able to find a small flat in Brooklyn. And soon after, I was able to find various odd jobs that all added up to give me a modest living. I started contemplating putting my money to work for me around that time, meaning investing it. I had learned a little about how stocks and bonds and investments worked from Nigel, and it seemed a good idea to give it a try. It wasn't very easy finding only night work, after all. So I acquainted myself with a nice broker chap and had him invest what money I had saved up for me.

Things went rather well that way for a while. The more money I was able to invest, the more I made, until I had almost all of my money in some relatively stable investments. I wasn't out to be rich, after all, just comfortable.

And then everyone suddenly lost all of their money all at once. Others might have, but I certainly hadn't foreseen the Crash of 1929. And into nothingness went all my investment money. I was so shocked, so much in utter disbelief that nearly all of my money was gone, just like that, that I tore up most of my flat and possessions in mad frustration. I also chopped off a goodly portion of my hair; since then, I've worn it short. I had not lost my temper like that in years.

Actually, the Depression wasn't quite the horrible experience many historians like to make it out to be. Folks seemed to stick together and were more inclined to help those in distress than during these present days. Or at least, it seems that way.

Like most everyone else, I couldn't find any sort of permanent job during this time nor well beyond, actually. Again, I was stuck in odd night jobs (the best of which was as a telephone operator), doing errands for people, and panhandling. I slept anywhere available, which meant that I could have very few possessions. I did, however, manage to obtain an original lobby card for *Dracula,* which I've kept with me. Not that I actually enjoyed the film very much, but it's just something to have.

Things didn't really perk up until around the time of World War II. This was when I decided I wanted to be a teacher. I made this decision after talking to an acquaintance who *was* a teacher and who absolutely loved her job and her students and everything about it, except for maybe the pay. It was something I had not yet done, and even though I had never spoken to any large group and was terrified at the thought of it, somehow the job really intrigued me.

I had to take night classes, of course. This made the process to get a credential much slower than it normally is, as night classes are never as varied or available as normal daytime classes. I also had a frightful time getting through those dreadful history textbooks; I didn't recall the real thing being so boring. But, after many years at community colleges, universities, and wherever else classes were offered, I obtained a teaching credential. In history, of course, but not beyond the high school level, which was fine with me. But I couldn't teach normal high school kids (*daytime,* remember?). I didn't want to, either. I figured I'd just continue what I'd been doing before, meaning night classes, only facing the class this time, not the teacher.

By the 1960's, I was getting a bit tired of New York. It was just becoming too frantic and hustle-bustle for me. I'm neurotic enough as it is. It was too much to have everyone else around me be neurotic, too. That, and perhaps the preposterous speed with which technology was advancing now was starting to get to me. Television had already reared its electronic head some years before, which I thought was simply incredible at first, even magical, but the magic wore off, especially when what was seen was getting more and more graphic. But television was hardly what made me leave New York for its evil twin, Los Angeles. Again, it was all sorts of things, none of which were any more important than the others. I was rather excited about leaving, actually, for now I could finally experience an honest-to-goodness airplane ride to get there.

I was very fortunate that it was possible to travel at

night, and not in the cargo hold, for once. Most of the time I kept to myself and just looked out the window; my seat companion slept most of the time, anyway. It was the first time I'd ever had coffee, too, and I've been hooked every since.

Thirty-four

I arrived in Los Angeles and immediately headed for a hotel or motel, set up camp there, slept by day, and in the meantime, looked for any nighttime teaching job I could find. I had enough money with me at the time to find a small flat in downtown Los Angeles, which in those days was just a tiny, tiny bit safer to live in than it is now.

Many waitress jobs later, I managed to get a hold of a nice teaching spot at a community college. This was the early seventies, mind you (when music wasn't yet disco, thank God). This was also when I met Jackie.

Now, my classes cater to "make-up" learners, meaning mostly those who want to finish up their high school education. And there are always plenty of those who have not. Jackie was apparently one of them.

I knew from first sight that she was also of the undead persuasion, and from the knowing glances she gave me, I knew she knew the same of me. It's in our auras, you know. What struck me about Jackie is that she seemed far too intelligent, too . . . professional, to not have finished high school. But later I learned that she had been converted at age seventeen—the age she appears to be, anyway—and that explained a lot. Being converted as a teenager is a lot like getting pregnant, then; one's chances of finishing high school drop significantly. Her education had to continue via the real world after she dropped out of school and left home, which was in 1955, I believe.

We became friends during class and after, once the session ended. Now she's my best friend. Jackie has unofficially named herself my social director, much as Leta had centuries before. This means it's her job to make certain I learn to "loosen up" and do "fun" (crazy?) things. The first party I ever went to with her was a Hallowe'en party. She tried to get me to go as a vampire, but I refused and went as a pirate, instead. The whole thing was a total disaster, because some jerks had spiked the punch, and I got stumbling-blind drunk from half a drink and almost attacked some poor fellows dressed as zombies. Jackie had to pull me away from them and drag me out the door. I woke up in her apartment, where she gave me some coffee and became my friend forever for it. To this day, I have never even tasted the punch at any party. Vampires can get dead drunk from one glass of beer; now you know why Dracula never drank "vine."

Another thing Jackie did was to introduce me to a group I hadn't really thought existed: the vampire population. That is, I hadn't thought there were as many in Los Angeles as there actually were. At the time we numbered in the tens (in Los Angeles, that is), but since then, we have certainly gone up. I'm not saying this to frighten you. I should think it'd be clear by now that—well, that vampires are people, too. Most of us had our status forced upon us, as Jackie and I had, only yes, there are some, but very few, of us who wanted our "gift" of immortality.

One of those who did want it was Theresa. She was converted about two hundred years ago at age twenty-five in Sicily, came here about a hundred years ago, used her power to become filthy rich, and basically lived the life of a spoiled playgirl. She was the sort who took full advantage of the "vamp" stereotype and wore long black, very revealing dresses, lived in a mansion, and got a big kick out of seducing men and feeding on them (but only sometimes converting). You've probably guessed I never took much of a liking to her, but unfortunately, she was also Jackie's friend, which caused me to have more run-ins with Theresa than I normally would have. Jackie tried to convince me that Theresa and I had much more in common than either of us cared to admit, and I did see that she reminded me too much of the worst parts of me. There was also something else about her that made my neck hairs bristle when she was too close to me, although I didn't learn why until later.

One more surprise for me was when I discovered that I was already something of a celebrity amongst the undead crowd. A lot of that was Theresa's doing. One of her hobbies was history, only her subject was vampire history. To my knowledge, she had every book ever written on vampires, and many of them were *by* vampires. Apparently I'd actually been listed in a number of those books as one of the "elder" vampires who "held great power" or some such nonsense. Theresa was always trying to get me to exploit my power to the fullest, but I saw no use anymore for flashy displays of brute strength and pyrotechnics. Apparently she'd rather I be out leveling mountains or something, which I've been told I could actually do if I wanted.

I managed in the mid-seventies to scrounge up enough money to buy a small two-bedroom house in Culver City. I'm still making payments on the damn thing some ten years later. Never ends, does it?

One night in 1985, I was in a department store to buy this sweater I had spotted some time before but hadn't had my checkbook with me to buy. As usual, I hadn't planned my night well and ended up arriving just before closing time, and of course I thought I still had an hour to shop. Well, I barely had time to throw the sweater on and bring it to the register. The assistant manager was there, but he'd already shut the door and was waiting for me to finish so he could let me out. His name was Jim (nametag said so). He escorted me to the door but also struck up a conversation with me along the way, and by the time he'd opened the door for me, he'd asked me out for coffee. Now normally, I'd have brushed him off for being so forward, but he just seemed a lot more . . . more honest and sincere than other men who used their usual pick-up lines on me. I accepted, but admittedly only because I had time to spare. And I love coffee.

Our "date" was uneventful, for the most part (so was the coffee); the usual chit-chat, where one doesn't learn really anything about the other. But meanwhile, I started getting the feeling, and Jim commented on this, too, that we had met somewhere before, and he wasn't referring to the department store. But we had no answers for each other as yet, and ended up exchanging phone numbers and calling it a night after I drove him home.

I went about my business as usual over the next few nights. Jim was still hanging about in my thoughts, but I couldn't bring myself to call him back. It's not that I didn't think it was "proper" for women to call men, it's simply that I've never been much good at making the "first move" in social situations. That was one of the things Jackie was trying to work on with me, too.

To my good fortune, Jim called me a few nights after our first date, and I agreed to another. Dinner at a dance club, it was. I'm not much good at dancing, myself, but Jim was quite a hit; it embarrassed me to be dancing with someone who had actual rhythm. He didn't seem to mind my lack thereof, fortunately. He drove me home this time, and walked me to my door, but rather than demanding a kiss as other men I'd dated almost assuredly did, he took up my hand and kissed it. I offered him coffee, but he politely declined, and then waited for me to be safely inside before departing.

Our third date was at his apartment. He'd insisted on cooking me a steak dinner. And when I arrived, he'd really gone all out: candles, quiet background music, a tablecloth. My heart skipped a beat. A romantic! I thought. Rarer than a two-headed snake: a thoughtful, romantic man! It wasn't just an act, either, that much I knew. It's not easy to lie to or deceive a vampire, unless one is a vampire oneself.

The steak was fine (would've been better if uncooked), but I ate little of his salad (makes bellyaches). Then after dinner, he took the dishes into his kitchen, and went over to change the music. Then I had something I hadn't had since I'd been human: a headache. A big headache. A worse, more splitting headache than any I'd ever imagined could be. I winced and rubbed my temples and tensed and relaxed and did all I could think of, but it wouldn't go away. Then I heard a voice say, "Are you all right?" and suddenly the headache stopped, and I looked up.

I screamed. My very worst nightmare came true. Agyar himself was standing right before me! But what—? How—? Where—? I didn't know what to do, what to think, I couldn't even start deciphering if this was real or not, and I looked about in complete panic until a hand was placed on my shoulder, and I looked up and made ready to scream, but—

"Mara?" Jim said, his hand on my shoulder. "What's wrong? I didn't scare you, did I? What made you yell?"

I looked about desperately, and stood up to look even better. Jim was rubbing my arm now, trying to calm me down.

"What—?" I said. "But— But—"

"Mara, what's wrong?" he asked. "Did you see something?"

"Yes, I—" I said, and looked at him now. "Jim, was— was that you? Just now?"

"Was *what* me?" he asked. "All I did was hold out my hand, and then you freaked out. What happened?"

"But I thought you were—I saw—" I stopped for a long time, trying desperately to sort out this mess. *Was all that real? It couldn't have been. He's dead. I killed him myself.*

"Mara?" Jim said.

"Uh uh uh—" I said, snapping myself back to reality. "Uh, yes. I'm sorry, Jim, I was just—please forget anything that happened. It was . . . I just had a headache, and I guess I was seeing things, or something. Forget it."

"Well, OK," he said with a sigh. "If you're OK now. Just don't go screaming at me again."

"Sorry."

He laughed softly and took my hand and led me to the middle of his room, where he started dancing. I was embarrassed, but he took both my hands now and started twisting me to the beat. I laughed and eventually let go of his hands and started dancing on my own. Soon the song ended, and a slow song followed it. We weren't dancing now, but stood facing each other. I'd never slow-danced before, and wasn't sure how, until Jim came toward me and held his arms out. I met him in a loose hug, and he began swaying back and forth, and I followed. Eventually he moved closer and hugged me tighter, and again, I followed. We swayed back and forth for a while before I rested my head on his shoulder, and I shut my eyes and thought of nothing. He put his head on my shoulder, too, and we stayed as we were, even after the song ended.

"Jim?" I said after a long time.

"Mmm hmm."

"I really like you," I said. "A lot." Then I turned my head a little and kissed him gently on the neck. I felt his hand against my ear, and he guided my head up until our gazes met. There was something very old about his eyes, very sad and hurt. But Jim was such a cheerful fellow; if he were in great pain, somehow I don't think he was ever aware of it. There was so much that drew me to him, I just wished I knew what it was.

I felt myself leaning forward, and he followed, until our lips met in a brief but warm kiss. Then we kissed again, and then again, and that fourth one lasted all through the next song. It made me forget the horrible thing that I'd seen only minutes before.

Thirty-five

That night I had a surprise waiting for me when I returned home. Well, first I had a message from Jackie, who asked me to call back, so I picked up the phone and dialed her number, when—

"Hi!!"

I started and dropped the phone. It was Jackie herself now, next to my dining-room table.

"Oh, Lord, Jackie, don't *do* that!" I said, catching my breath.

She snickered. "Sorry. Just thought I'd scare you," she said.

"Hu ha," I said. "But what was your message, then?"

She shrugged and smiled strangely. "Nuthin'. Just thought I'd call. Where were you?"

"Out."

"Out? Doing what?"

Now it was my turn to smile strangely. "Just . . . out," I said.

"Ahh, come on, you can tell *me* who he is, Mare," she said.

"Oh? Are you implying that I was out with a 'he'?"

"Just asking," she said. "You'll tell me who it is, eventually. But in the meantime, are you in for the night? Got anything else planned?"

I shrugged. "Nothing really important," I said. "Why?"

"Good. I wanna show you something," she said, and headed for my front door. "Come on," she said, gesturing.

I followed reluctantly. "Show me what?"

"Just look out there," she said, opening the front door. "Go outside and look."

"You bought a new car or something, dear?"

"I wish. Go on, look outside." I sighed and stepped past the door, and looked about. And then to my left were three women, who jumped up from the shadows. I started and looked them in the eyes: mistake. I remembered their eyes blazing red before my consciousness faded away to blackness.

I woke up in Jackie's car, surrounded by the three women. They were some of Jackie's friends: Lynnette, Tania, and Victoria, and I was confused.

"Welcome back, Mara," Jackie said from the front seat. "Come on, get out." The others climbed out of the car, and I followed, still in a daze, and saw that we were in a parking lot somewhere. Jackie came up to me and put her arm around my shoulder and led me away from the car.

"We're really sorry about making you sleep, Mare," she said. "But how else were we supposed to kidnap you?"

"What? Kidnap me? What is—"

She stopped me in the middle of the lot and gestured toward a neon sign atop a building. It said "Joy's," and under that was "Every Thursday Night is Ladies' Night!" Jackie and her friends had gathered into a foursome, meanwhile, and I heard Jackie start counting. The next thing I knew, they were singing "Happy Birthday"—to *me!* Afterward, they started whooping and hollering, and Jackie took me by the arm to lead me to the building.

"Happy birthday, Mare!" she said, and others shouted the same.

"What the hell are you talking about, Jackie?" I asked. "This is all a joke, right?"

"It's your birthday present, babe," she said. "And don't try to hide your birthdays on us anymore, either!"

"I didn't think I was trying," I said. "My birthday is March 23."

"Yeah!" she said. "Septem—! AAAAAAUGH!"

"March 23?" said one of the others.

Jackie slapped her hand onto her face. "Maaaaarch . . . Maaaaarch . . ." she kept saying. At the time I was too shocked to be angry *or* amused, although anger was gaining the lead.

Tania slapped Jackie on the shoulder. "You loser!" she said. "Did you fuck up again?"

"Now don't you call her a loser," I said, then to Jackie: "In fact, now that I think about it, you've *never* gotten my birthday right, have you, luv?"

"Like I said, a loser."

"AAAAAUGH!' '" Jackie said.

"So *now* whadda we do?" another said.

"Frankly, I haven't the faintest idea what it is you're doing," I said. "But if you're going to go through all this trouble to kidnap me and knock me out, what worse could you do to me?"

"Happy *un*birthday, Mara," Jackie groaned. "This'll be your *un*birthday present. Forgive?"

"Them I forgive. You I don't," I said. She knew I wouldn't mean that for long.

I learned the hard way what "Ladies' Night" really means. After the usual hassles getting past the bouncer (Jackie will always look seventeen, fake ID or not), we found a small table to one side of the dark, smoky, and very very loud room where—you guessed it—a male strip show was in progress. The dancer was already down to his undies when we were seated, and Jackie and her friends started whooping and hollering right along with the other lust-crazed women there. Another attempt at "loosening me up," I figured.

A waitress came by to take drink orders (all of us had virgin drinks) in between the acts. Then, to my dismay, Jackie spotted Theresa in the crowd, and she spotted us. She forced her way out and came to our table, and invited herself to a seat next to me.

"Hello, ladies," she said. "What brings you all to a place like this?"

"This is all for her," Tania said, pointing to me.

Oh, great, I thought. *Now she'll think—*

"Who, Mara?" Theresa asked. "You mean this was all *your* idea?"

"Well, actually—"

"Oh, it's all my fault," Jackie intervened. "See, I *fucked up* and thought it was Mare's birthday, and we were going to take her someplace fun."

"Whether I wanted to or not," I muttered.

"Anyway, it's her unbirthday present now."

"Oh," said Theresa. "So it's *not* your birthday."

"No. And again, this was *their* idea, not mine."

"Ah, well, don't worry. You'll still enjoy the show, anyway."

Oh, Jim, where are you when I need you? I thought. The next show was starting, which was somebody dressed as Geraldo Rivera. He played with the crowd, pretending to be hosting a show, and then the music started up, and the stripping began. Our waitress brought our drinks, so I sipped my diet drink quietly while the others yelled and carried on. Jackie kept slapping my arm to get me to watch, which I did, but it was just too ridiculous for me to deal with. It was all I could do to keep from laughing.

Then when I looked again at the show, I noticed that a fog was starting to creep onto the stage and out into the crowd. At first I thought it was dry ice, but "Geraldo" didn't seem to react as though it were expected, nor did any of the pit security. I looked at Theresa, who—as I expected—was deep in concentration. She was just playing,

I knew, but Theresa has a tendency to let things escalate into chaos, so I concentrated myself. I sent her a flash of pain and made the fog disappear immediately. Theresa knew who was the culprit, and glanced at me with a pained expression. Fortunately, she knew better than to match brute strength with me, as I didn't want any more of a confrontation than that.

Then a sharp pain hit *me,* almost exactly as it had before, and I winced and held my temples again to try to stop it. It didn't last as long as it had before, and when I looked up, things seemed just as normal as before. Theresa was staring at me, but I could tell she'd had nothing to do with that pain, nor with the earlier attack. She seemed genuinely concerned, but I said nothing to her, and for the rest of the night, acted as though nothing had happened, but I always kept my senses on extra alert.

Jackie's advice to me, upon learning of Jim, was to tell him about myself. I agreed with her, but not at the time. At that time, I wasn't sure just how serious things would become between Jim and me, and I didn't see much use in telling him until we were genuinely an "item." Yes, I had supposedly learned my lesson after Nigel, but I just wanted to make sure the time was right. And even if I did tell him, the hardest part would not be getting him to believe me, but getting him to believe that I wasn't out to bite his neck.

Jackie would just as soon prefer I not go with humans, anyway, because of the risks involved; she herself tries to stick with "our own kind." I can understand that, but to be honest, there's really not that many of us around, to begin with, relatively speaking, and even fewer compatible men. That, and I'm not a hopeless practical like Jackie, but I am a hopeless romantic. Let's put it this way: humans are alive, and I don't just mean physically. I mean emotionally and psychically, too. Most of us really do try to stick to other vampires, but even so, it's difficult to not be drawn to humans for their . . . well, for that "spark" they have that we lack. It may very well be the human soul; I couldn't say for certain. My attraction to humans is certainly not to make them "one of us," not like those in damned movies. I just honesty like the companionship of human males (romantically, that is) more than that of other vampires.

The full moon came, as it always does. I was afraid to go with Jim that night, but we had become so much closer by then; I couldn't stay away from him. The fact that we never saw each other except at night had not yet become an issue, and it was this night that I decided I would have to tell him before it did. At his apartment, that is. First, we had to go out.

We went to a dance club and hardly sat at our booths all night. I was leading *him* in most dances tonight; the moon had given me rhythm, for once. Jim, being human, lacked my energy and eventually insisted that we take a break. He ordered a beer, and I just sat and stared at him. *Tonight,* I thought. *Yes, the time is right. But at his place . . .*

"Whew!" he shouted over the music. "How do you do it, Mare? You're not even sweating!"

I shrugged and kept on smiling.

"Sure you don't want something to drink?" he asked. "Not even a Coke?"

"Mmm, not this time, no, thank you," I said, reaching out and playing with his fingers. "I think . . . I think maybe we should, maybe we could go back to your place? Could we?"

He took my hand and squeezed my fingers gently.

"Sure," he said. "Anything you like."

* * *

I remember he had a lot of trouble getting his keys to unlock his apartment. I waited patiently while he struggled, pounded, then started swearing at the door, at which point I gently nudged him aside and turned the keys for him. I went inside while he put his keys away.

"Nice touch," he said with a bit of jealousy there. "Remind me to get you next time I'm locked out."

"You invited me in," I murmured. "Nothing could keep me out now."

"Huh?"

I came to my senses then and faced him.

"Sorry; nothing. Just talking to myself."

"Ah. Well . . . So. Like anything, first? I mean, something to drink? Eat?" He started to walk past me, but I took hold of his tie and pulled him toward me gently.

"No, thank you," I said, and started kissing him. "I'm trying to cut down." *Later, I thought. After we're done, I'll tell him.*

We kept at it awhile, and Jim hit all the right spots to get me worked up (i.e., the neck), until I took his hand and made him follow me into his bedroom.

"Not quite so . . . shy as I thought," he murmured. "Are you?"

"Is that what you want me to be?"

"Mmm, maybe not tonight," he said as we sat on the bed and commenced lip-mashing. I must admit that I turned on the charm during that kiss, which can have the effect of flooring even the most hard-hearted of men.

"Ohhh, God," he said as we parted. "That was incredible."

"Like some more?"

"Oh, yeah," he said, so I gave it to him.

* * *

I knew I was going to tell him after we were done. That was always in the back of my mind. I had only once been with a man during a full moon before, and I could hold it back no longer; I had to have this one time with a man, especially a man who I was coming to love.

I had no idea I had lost control until it was almost too late. All I remember, for the most part, was how incredibly alive I felt for the first time in years, nay, centuries, how exhilarated, and, it turned out, how hungry. I looked up at the ceiling during my climax, then shut my eyes and let my thoughts soar. I opened my eyes again and locked gazes with Jim, who had become suddenly serene the moment my eyes met his. I could feel his thoughts, and they were all of me, and I decided then and there that I loved him with all my heart, and I brought my face close to his and kissed him anywhere and everywhere, working my way to his neck, and there was a hot, sweet rush of liquid flowing into me, renewing me, making me . . .

"Oh, God . . ." I whispered soon after I came to my senses and looked upon Jim's limp, seemingly peaceful form. "Oh, Jesus . . . What have I done? Oh, God, forgive me, I thought—I thought I could control myself!"

I scrambled off Jim in a panic and stood at the edge of the bed, stark naked, eyes threatening to cloud with tears. "Oh, God, oh, God," was the only coherent thought I could summon for many moments, before a scrap of reason found its way into my head, and I crept forward to reach for his wrist. A pulse; a strong one!

Holding back tears, I fumbled out of the bedroom to look for something to write on. I found some in the kitchen and scribbled a hasty message. I was terrified that he might be awake when I reentered the bedroom, but he still lay there, sleeping, but now a bit anemic. I put the note by his nightstand, gathered my clothes, and left as hurriedly as I could.

I was so distraught as I walked from his apartment toward the bus stop that I started running—a slow job at first, but getting faster and faster until I was running far faster than normal humans can, but I didn't stop there. I couldn't care less then if anyone saw; I transformed into a bat in midstep and flew away toward home.

"Call Jackie, call Jackie" was my one thought this time as I arrived home. She was my best friend, my one-and-only confidante, to whom I could tell anything and everything. If she couldn't give me advice, she would at least listen, I knew that.

Busy tone. I hung up and dialed again. Busy again and again and again, until my frustration built up into a rage, and I almost broke the phone slamming it down, so I broke the wall, instead. Slammed my fist straight into it. I was going to do so again, but common sense saved the night, and I, instead, let myself fall forward onto the kitchen counter, buried my head in my arms, and wept the night through.

Thirty-six

"I don't get it." That was Jim.

"What do you mean, you don't get it?" That was me.

It was the next night, in Jim's apartment. Jim looked as I expected he would: pale, drawn, circles around his eyes. He wasn't completely ghastly, though, just a little ill.

"Well, what do you mean, you're a vampire?" he asked. "You like to wear black and drink blood or something?"

"I don't wear black, where'd that come from?"

"Well, where are *you* coming from?"

"Look, I can see we're not getting very far here," I said. "I don't see where your confusion is coming from. Jim, I'm trying to tell you what I am, because—well, because I care about you, and—and to explain things to you."

"Oh, my God," he said suddenly.

"What?"

"You like dead things, don't you?" he said. "Oh, *please* tell me you're not into dead things!"

"I am *not* into dead things," I said. "Don't be morbid. Jim, what exactly do you think I mean when I say I'm a vampire?"

"I don't know," he said. "You like blood, I guess. What—"

"What—what is a vampire, Jim? This is important. I want to know what, to you, a vampire is. Real or imagined, I don't care."

"Uhh—well, as far as I know, they're guys who bite beautiful girls' necks and fly around."

"And that's it?"

"I guess; so what is this about, Mare? What I really want to know is why you left last night like that!"

"That's—that's part of what I want to say, love," I said. "But it's important that we get this first part settled."

"You don't bite beautiful girls' necks, do you?" he joked.

"Um—why don't we try this, then," I said, rising and moving in front of the couch. "You've already voiced the misconceptions about us that I thought you would. Now I don't blame you; really, I don't. I mean, you've been taught what everyone else was taught."

"What's this about, Mare?" he asked, a touch of fear in his voice.

"I just want to clarify some things," I said. "Above all, I want you to remember one thing: Dracula was an asshole. All right?"

"Yeah, I can agree with that," he said, smiling nervously.

"I have to prove to you that I'm telling the truth, or we'll go nowhere from here," I continued.

"Prove—? You're going to prove you're a vampire."

"Yes, Jim. And please don't be afraid. You won't be harmed in the slightest."

"Wait a minute, what—?"

His words stopped the moment I began concentrating, and then dropped to the ground. By the time my hands hit the floor, they'd become wolf paws. The transformation was complete.

The smell of fear was so strong it almost had *me* afraid. Jim's aura was going crazy—jumping and flickering and shifting all over the place to match his chaotic thoughts. I heard him make a noise as though he were about to scream, so I transformed back and held my arms out to try and calm him.

"Now—now please don't yell or scream, Jim, it's OK,

I won't hurt you," I said, and he cringed back on his couch, mouth agape.

"How the hell did you do that?" he asked in a hoarse whisper.

"It's all right, love," I said in my most soothing voice. "I'm . . . I'm not going to hurt you. I just wanted to prove I was telling the truth."

"Neat trick," he said, forcing a laugh. "How'd you do it?"

"It's no trick, Jim," I said. "That was real."

"Yeah," he said, his aura still crazy. "Yeah, sure."

"May I sit beside you?" I asked. "I won't hurt you, I came to talk to you, Jim. That's all I came for."

"Uh . . . uh, sure," he said. "Have a seat."

I sat beside him and took his hand. He looked at his hand, then at me, then looked down, apparently afraid to look at me anymore.

"Thank you," I said. "Look, I know it's hard for you to believe, but—"

"A werewolf," he murmured. "My girlfriend's a werewolf."

"A werewolf? No, no, Jim, that— I'm a vampire! That's what I was trying to show you!"

"Well, why didn't you change into a bat, then?"

"Do you want me to?" I asked, rising.

"NO! Uh, no. No. That's OK," he said, pulling me back down. "Really."

"Well, all right," I said. "But I am *not* a werewolf."

"Of course you aren't."

I sighed and fought for my next words. "So, then, Jim," I began, "I came here, not just to tell you this, but—but to apologize, also."

"Apologize?"

"Yes, I—you see, I was going to tell you this last night, but—well, it was the full moon and all and—"

"The full moon."

"Yes," I said. "Just like tonight. Well, not like tonight, because last night's was fuller so its effects were stronger and—"

"Hoa, hoa, hoa, hoa," he said. "Hold on. Full moon? You mean you *are* a werewolf."

"No, I am not a werewolf, Jim, please listen to me!"

"Fine; fine," he said. "You're not a werewolf."

"Oh, Lord, you still don't believe me," I groaned.

"No, I do," he said. "Really, I do. You're a vampire, and—and you turn into dogs. I mean wolves. Sorry."

"You don't believe me," I said. "I can feel it in you. I can feel your emotions, Jim, when they're strong enough, and right now—"

"Can you, now."

"Yes. And right now you're confused. Worried. Not sure whether to believe me or feel sorry for me. And I don't blame you. Really, I don't."

"You keep saying that."

"Sorry," I said. "But—look. Whether or not you do believe me, I came to apologize to you. Because I was supposed to tell you last night, but I lost control, Jim. I swear I didn't know what I was doing until it was almost too late. I almost— I almost converted you, Jim. And I only thank God that I didn't, because if I had, I—I don't know. I don't know what I would've done."

"You almost 'converted' me?"

"Yes, it's—it's our word for making people into vampires," I said quietly.

"You . . . almost made me a vampire?"

"Yes, Jim," I whispered. "And I'm so sorry. I thought I'd be able to control it, I—I'd never been with a person before on a full moon, and I guess I found out the hard way why."

I had barely finished speaking when Jim suddenly leaped up, bolted from the room, and ran into the bathroom. I followed him immediately and stood in the bathroom doorway. Jim was in front of the mirror, inspecting his neck. Inspecting what I'd done to it.

"Jesus . . ." he whispered.

"I—I'm sorry, Jim," I said. "Please let me explain—"

"Those are teeth marks!" he cried.

"Yes, but I didn't—"

"You *bit* me!" he yelled. "You actually *bit* me! Jesus Christ, I thought those were shaving cuts!"

"Jim, if you let me explain—"

"You!" he cried, facing me and backing away. "You get away."

"But—but—"

"Get away from me! Go suck somebody else, you hear? You're not getting any of *my* blood!"

"But—but I'm *not*—!"

"Get away!" he roared, suddenly lunging forward and shoving out of the bathroom and against the wall. Then he ran to the living room and looked about frantically while I came after him.

"Jim, please!" I cried. "I—I came to talk about that! I didn't mean—!"

"You stay away from me! Get! Get out!" he yelled, rushing into the kitchen.

"But Jim!"

He rummaged through a drawer and pulled out a butcher knife. A butcher knife! It didn't matter if it wouldn't harm me; he was ready to kill me! I backed away while he advanced slowly.

"Jim, you can't mean this!" I cried, my voice starting to choke. "You don't really think I ever meant to hurt you?"

"Stay away from me," he said, his own voice wavering. His eyes were watering. I'd never been more tempted to charm somebody as now, but I couldn't. Not him. I couldn't do that to him . . .

"Please . . ." I begged, tears falling now. "Please, Jim . . ."

"You're not getting my blood . . ." he said, tears watering his cheeks, too. "You're not making me like you!"

He'd backed me up to the door now. I stopped but he kept coming. Soon he was only two feet away, the knife pointed at my throat. Perhaps my own fear prevented me from taking it from him, or even charming him. Either way, I could take it no longer, and I reached behind me and turned the knob on the door and started opening it.

"Oh, God, Jim," I whispered. "I thought you wouldn't be afraid . . ."

"Please go," he said. "Please leave."

"I'll leave . . ." I sobbed. "I'll go. I'm sorry, Jim . . . Please forgive me . . ."

"Gooo!" he cried suddenly, and I panicked and flew through the door. In the hallway, the door suddenly slammed shut in my face, and bolts and chains were being done.

"JIM!" I cried, but no response. "Jim . . ." I then whispered, and walked away.

At Jackie's the next night, I had reached a stage of numbness. I spent most of my time there just sipping my coffee and staring at nothing. Jackie sat with me awhile, but then went into her darkroom. For now, she sells the admission tickets at a nightclub, but would rather make a living doing free-lance photography.

I wasn't really there for advice, anyway. I just needed to be around someone. Jackie understood that and knew she didn't have to sit there all night and pity me. I was doing a good enough job pitying myself.

A sudden wind blew into the apartment, and I didn't even turn to look, but soon there was a Whooosh sound, and a shadow appeared. I turned enough to see that Theresa had flown in through the window.

"Oh! Hello, Mara," she said cheerfully. "Where's Jackie?"

I pointed to the closed door.

"Oh," she said, and went over to knock on the door. "Jackie? It's me, Theresa. Will you be out soon?"

"Well, not for ten minutes at least!" was the muffled reply. "Something important?"

"No, just came by to visit," she said. "Do you want me to leave?"

"Not if you don't want to," was the reply. "Sit down, if you want. I'll be out."

"I'll be right here!" she said, and headed to the table where I was sitting. She sat in the chair in front of me and smiled.

"She's popular tonight," she said. "Are you just visiting, too?" I shrugged.

"Something wrong?" she said.

"I'm fine," I said. "Just came for some coffee."

"Ahh," she said. "You know, you are such an enigma, Mara." I cocked an eyebrow. "I've tried for years to figure out what makes you tick, but—nothing. You're not like any other vampire I've known."

"Is that good?"

"I don't know yet," she said. "For instance, how you were converted. I don't believe you've ever told anyone that story." I shrugged and sipped some more coffee.

"Long ago I was happily married, and then along came someone who didn't believe that I was," I said. "Beyond that, it's just details."

"Yes, yes, the details, woman," she said. "It's the details I *do* want."

"Why?"

"Because the only thing that's ever said of you is that

you're from England, and that you're thousands of years old. But you won't tell anyone any more. Not even Jackie."

"She's never asked," I said. "So you're saying, you're only interested in this for historical purposes, is that it?"

"Yyyyyes," she said as though she were forcing it out. "You know that our history is my hobby. For historical purposes, then. Perhaps you'd let me interview you."

"Ah hah," I said. "You know, I'm really not in the mood for any discussion right now, Theresa."

"Well, it can be later, then. Please? For instance, I'd love to know if it's true that you were converted by the *first* vampire! Is that true?"

"I'd rather not discuss this right now, Theresa. I get headaches thinking about him."

"So the First is a he," she said. "But that means you *were* converted by him. Or knew him, at the very least. Do you remember his name?"

I sighed in frustration and looked away.

"His name, Mara," she continued. "All I need is his name. Then from there I can——"

"Look, just leave me alone, all right?" I cried, flinging my arms about. "Stop asking me about the goddamned 'First,' all right? I told you I don't want to talk about it!"

There would have been silence afterward, except Jackie's apartment was shaking from the force of my anger. Books quivering; furniture shaking; pictures banging repeatedly against the walls. Soon after it started, Jackie bolted from her darkroom.

"Hooooe!" she said. "Terry, is that—? Mare, what's wrong? You're spilling my stuff!"

"Trying to calm down . . ." I growled, and worked at calming myself, and, therefore, the apartment, down. Eventually her walls stopped shaking, and nothing fell or broke, thank goodness. Theresa was trying to hide her fear, but I knew better. I stood and grabbed my purse.

"I'm sorry," I said to Jackie. "I'll—I'll go now."

"What happened? Do you wanna talk about it?" she asked. I forced a smile and shook my head.

"No, no, I'm fine now," I said. "I'm going home."

"I'm sorry," Theresa said almost inaudibly.

I ignored her and addressed Jackie again. "I'll call you," I said. "Or come by, or something. Is that OK?"

"Yeah, sure," she said quietly. "OK."

I had daymares for four straight days after Jim threw me out of his place. Most of them were like being trapped in a vampire movie: cobwebbed castles, graveyards, ghastly undead creatures, and even one vampire blood-drinking orgy. I was usually the observer of all of this, only in the worst dream I was the one being sacrificed in the orgy. That was the last one.

I woke up screaming and felt the sweat on my face. I didn't know how much longer I could take this; I missed Jim so much, and I knew my guilt was causing all those dreams. But he hated me; I had to force myself to stop thinking about him or go mad.

After getting dressed and grooming myself, I decided to take a walk to clear my thoughts. I had just shut the front door behind me when I saw a man in the shadows. I started to scream, when he stepped forward.

"Jim?" I said.

"Hi, Mara," he said. "Hope I didn't scare you or anything."

"I—no," I said. "I just didn't see you. Jim, what—what are you doing here?"

"I dunno," he said. "I guess, um . . . well, were you going somewhere?"

"Oh, just . . . just a little walk. Um . . . would you like to join me?"

"Uhhhh, no," he said. "I just thought I'd come by, see how you were doing . . ."

"Oh," I said. "Well . . . not too well, to be honest."

"Oh. Sorry to hear that. Anything serious?"

"Uh, well, actually," I said, then stopped and looked down, fidgeting. "Um, listen," I continued. "Would you like to come in?"

"I thought you were taking a walk."

"I changed my mind. Too cold, anyway. Maybe you could have some coffee?"

"Uh—sure," he said. "OK." I opened the door again and stepped inside. Jim followed slowly, stopping at the threshold to look around, and then stepping through. I waited for him in my living room.

"I—I don't have much to offer, actually," I said. "Just . . . coffee, and . . ."

"Coffee's fine," he said.

"Fine," I said. "Um . . . have a seat?" Wordlessly, he sat at the edge of one of my couches. I went into the kitchen.

"I was going to call you, you know," I said. "Just uh . . . just to see if you were still angry with me."

"Oh," he said. "No, that's OK. I mean, I'm not mad anymore. I don't think."

"Oh, good," I said. "Because . . . well, I was very upset that you wouldn't let me explain. In fact, um . . well, that was why things haven't been so good for me lately."

"Me, neither," he said. I always had coffee brewing in my house, so I had fresh cups for us right away. I carried both mugs from the kitchen and handed him one. Then I sat on my other couch across from Jim.

"I forgot to ask how you like it," I said. "Did you want sugar? Cream?"

"Nah, nah, I . . . I take it black," he said.

"Oh, all right," I said. There was a long silence while we drank. I broke the silence.

"I missed you, Jim," I said. "I'm really glad you're here, now."

"I couldn't sleep," he murmured. "I haven't been to work for two days now."

"You—you look much better than you did before, though," I said. "Your color's come back."

"And I feel like shit," he said. "Nightmares every night. It's like I've been stuck in all these old vampire movies every night. You know I even dreamed about an orgy? Only everyone was a vampire. Oh, God, it was disgusting."

"Uhhh . . . Believe me, I—I know what dreams like that are like," I said.

Jim sat staring at the ground for a minute, and then looked up at me suddenly. "How long's this gonna take, Mara?"

"H-how long is *what* going to take?"

"You know what I mean," he said. "How long is *this* gonna take?" he asked, gesturing to his face.

"I still don't know what you mean."

"How long will it be until I'm a vampire?" he cried. "How long until I'm like you?"

"Uh— But you're NOT going to become a vampire," I said. "I—I didn't take enough—enough blood."

"Then how come I'm not getting any better?" he asked. "How come I'm sleeping in later and later, and need sunglasses just to go outside? I *must* be turning into a vampire!"

"No, no, Jim, believe me, you're not," I said, rising to go over to him. I sat the edge of my coffee table and took both his hands. "You're not," I continued. "You'll get better, believe me you will. Right now it's—it's as though you had the flu or something. Eventually you'll heal, and—and get better. Do you believe me?"

"I dunno," he said. "I dunno what the hell's going on. What's happening to me, Mara? Am I becoming a vampire, or what? I don't know!"

I leaned forward to hug him, and held him tight while I spoke. "It's OK," I whispered. "I know how you feel, believe me I do. The same thing happened to me so very long ago. I was drained slowly, you see, and didn't know what was happening, and I became sicker, more miserable, more—"

"Gee, thanks," he said. "Thanks a lot."

"Oh, no, no, I —! I'm sorry, that was the wrong thing to say. No, you're not going to die slowly, or miserably; you won't die at all. What I took that night was— It was just carelessness. Stupid, irresponsible carelessness, and you can't imagine how very sorry I am for that. Will you forgive me? Please forgive me, Jim. I—I love you, Jim. The last thing on earth I'd want is for you to be like me, for you to become a vampire. I love you."

"I'm scared."

"So am I," I said. "I'm afraid for you, for me; afraid of fucking up again like that. You don't have to love me, too, right now, but—I'd like you to forgive me. Will you?"

"Sure," he whispered after a silence. "I forgive you."

And the rest of the night we spent making up, as they say.

Thirty-seven

After a month's time, I figured that Jim was used to me enough to handle our Hallowe'en party. No, we don't hold human sacrifices then; it's just that most of the folks there would be vampires, and I told Jim that. He actually seemed rather excited about it, then.

The party was at Michael's place, which was customary, although sometimes it was at Theresa's (which I'd never been to). They have big enough houses to hold big bashes like that, although anyone who doesn't help pay for the Hallowe'en party isn't allowed to go. We can bring guests, however. It's never officially a costume party, but a lot of people wear strange outfits, anyway. I always go as a vampire, meaning as myself.

Michael answered the door. I introduced Jim, and then he led us upstairs to where all the fun was. He had the biggest living room, and all the furniture moved against the walls made it look like a ballroom. He had a huge buffet table off to one side, plus a free bar. Well, mixed drinks were one dollar, but no vampire drinks those, anyway. Jim and I headed for the snacks, and soon Jackie came up behind me and covered my eyes. Then the little creep took my picture as soon as I turned around. I snatched for the camera, but she laughed, and kept it out of reach.

"I don't have enough pictures of you!" She laughed. I glared at her. "I promise I'll let you have one."

"No! I don't want one; you always take the worst pictures of me," I said.

"They're natural shots," she said. "But, anyway, when are you going to introduce me to him? I'll bet this is Jim."

"Hm? Oh, oh, yes, this is Jim," I said, putting an arm around him. He stuck his hand out. "Jim; my friend, Jackie; as you can see, she likes to sneak pictures of people."

"Nice to meet you," he said, and they shook hands.

"You know I'm going to avoid you all night if you don't put that away," I said.

"I promise, no more shots of you," she said. "I swear on the ancient blood of my ancestors, who fought in the Great War of the Ancient Enemy, who passed their tales through the ages to—"

"All right, all right, I believe you!" I said. Somehow I knew she and Jim were going to end up being great friends; they had the same bizarre sense of humor. Then Jim put his arm around me and smiled a food-filled smile.

"Well, just take one picture of us together," he said.

"Oh, you look so photogenic, too," I said. "Put that camera away, Jackie! Put that— !"

In another room, a little smaller than the living room, Michael had hired a DJ, complete with rotating light show. Jim wanted to dance, but I wasn't up to it quite yet, and wanted to take in the scenery first, so to speak. I knew early on that Theresa was at the party (of course), but she seemed to be ignoring me as much as I was ignoring her. Jim and I were together for most of the evening, but as it wore on, we started drifting away and "exploring" on our own. I was at the bar, getting some coffee, and was planning on rejoining him among some chitchatters, when I was tapped on the shoulder. It was Jim, and who was he with but Theresa!

"Mare?" he said. "Do you know Theresa? She asked if I'd dance with her for one song. OK with you?"

"Wh— Wh—"

"He won't be stolen for long, dear," Theresa said, slipping her arm into his. "I just wanted a partner, that's all."

Jim leaned forward and kissed my cheek. "I'll be right back, babe. Love ya," he whispered, and they walked away toward the dance room. I was completely speechless. That—that *hussy!* I could tolerate him dancing with someone, but *her*—! She knew perfectly well how I felt about her, and—and she was still doing things like this to me, always pushing me to the limit, trying to—

My thoughts were interrupted by yet another splitting headache, this one far worse than any of the others. I cried out and almost dropped my coffee, but managed to set it down before doubling over in pain, trying to keep my throbbing skull from splitting. *Why?* I thought. *Where are they coming from? Am I sick? Is someone actually doing this to me?* The pain was too great to tell what was causing it, or why, until—as all the others had—it stopped. Just like that. As though I'd never felt a thing. I groaned and rubbed my nose, and then looked up to see . . .

My mind wasn't even allowed to register who it was I saw, only I remembered that I knew him—in fact it was—!

I heard a loud noise, and I was in my car. The keys were in the ignition, but I was sill parked where I'd had the car earlier. What the hell? I thought.

"Jim?" I said, looking about. Not next to me. Not in the backseat, either. I looked out the window and saw Michael's place, where it had always been, and saw someone who might have been Jackie walking toward it. I got out of the car slowly and looked around some more. Seeing no one, I shut and locked the door and walked back to Michael's.

Again he answered the door, but didn't look very happy to see me.

"Oh, you," he cried. "Calmed down by now?"

"Calmed down—? Um—Michael, have you—have you seen Jim? I mean, the man I came in with. Is he still here?"

"I don't know. Haven't seen him since you stormed out of here," he said. "Maybe he took a taxi."

"Wh— what did I do?" I asked. "Er, uh—well, do you think I could look for him? I just had the . . . strangest experience."

"Umm—" Michael said. "I suppose if you go fetch him. But—I'm sorry, Mara; I really can't have big scenes like that anymore. I think you and your friend need to go somewhere and talk."

"Big scene?" I said, following him up the stairs. "Was I involved in something? I just had the strangest experience . . ."

"You said that," he said, and left me as soon as we arrived upstairs. I stood where I was and looked about the room. The party was going on as before, only I couldn't see Jim. Jackie sauntered up to me, though.

"So . . ." she said, sipping a soft drink. "Changed your mind, huh?"

"I don't know; what was my decision before?" I said. "Look, did something just happen, Jackie? I was in my car, but I don't know how I got there. Was that you I saw coming back here?"

"I guess, I don't know," she said. "So, uh —you're OK now, then? Not mad anymore?"

"Um—I guess not, no," I said. "But—really, I thought I would find Jim. He wasn't in the car with me. Oh, he didn't leave, did he?"

"The last thing I remember, he was . . . dancing with someone," I said. "Dancing with . . . Theresa! Jackie, he was dancing with Theresa!"

"Yeah?"

"Where is she? I don't see her, either!"

"Check the music room," Jackie said, and hit me on the arm. "Catch you late—" was the most I heard, because I immediately rushed for the dance room at her suggestion. I didn't mean to be rude, but my imagination was going crazy. Yes . . . I was remembering things. Theresa was dancing with him, and I was upset, and—and another headache . . . I had another, and then . . . and then what?

A scan of the room revealed no Jim or Theresa. And another, and another. Nowhere. Now I did have good cause to be worried. But where to look? Which room? Were they even here at all?

I hated doing what I decided to, but I could think of nothing else at the time. I took a deep breath, and concentrated on Jim. On his name. On his thoughts. On his soul . . .

I could feel him now. He was near, in the very building, in fact. Another room somewhere, but where? I felt him obeying the call, starting to come to me, when something stopped him. He was being held back—physically and mentally—so I concentrated harder. Someone was trying to "outcharm" me, and I had a damned good idea who it was. She didn't have a chance.

There was more resistance, so I concentrated harder, and was about to break Theresa's hold by giving her a good mind blast, when I felt a scream, and my mind was assaulted by horrible, frightening images. There was blood and death everywhere, a ghastly stench, shadowy things groping, pulling, tearing off body parts, clawing and biting, and all this was happening to *me* (I think?), and I yelped and broke off contact with Jim.

My God, what was that? I thought. What on earth was I doing, I was tearing his mind apart! I knew where Jim was now, but I was yet to figure out what I had just experienced, and where those images came from (him?).

I discovered them in a bedroom, on the bed. Theresa lay on top of Jim (fully clothed, thank goodness), her teeth closing in slowly on his throat. The next thing she knew, she'd been hefted to her feet by the scruff of her neck, and

I held her before me by the throat. Theresa dared not struggle, or get her neck snapped. Objects in the room were shaking, including the bed. I have seen what a vampire looks like when beyond rage; the eyes become pure black, the voice begins echoing, and the body begins to glow. Let's just say that I became the source of light for this room.

"M-Mara," Theresa said. "Y-you'd probably like an explanation."

"NO," I said, and slugged her full in the face. She flew fifteen feet across the room and slammed into the wall, crumpling to the floor into a formless heap. I went immediately to Jim, who was coming out of his trance, and helped him up, meanwhile doing everything I could to make my features go back to normal. He groaned, and I slung his arm around my shoulder and lifted him up.

"Hey," he said. "What—? Mare? What are you doing?"

"TAKING YOU HOME," I said.

"Whoa, what's with your voice?" he asked. "Hey, isn't that—?"

"DON'T LOOK AT HER, JIM," I said, opening the door now. "I'M TAKING YOU HOME."

"She looks hurt—!" he said, but we were out of the room now, and I helped Jim across the room toward the downstairs. It seemed as though all eyes were upon us—I still had a slight glow—but we made it to the stairs without incident. Jim kept trying to protest, but I wasn't rational enough to explain things to him, not without making small objects start exploding. He had to be patient with me once again.

Finally, we reached the car, where I unlocked the door first.

"Get in," I said.

"Will you at least tell me what the hell's going on first?" he demanded.

"I will, love," I said in my calmest voice. "I promise

you, the minute we get home I'll explain everything. But please, right now I'm—we just have to get out of here. But as soon as we're home . . ."

"You promise."

"I promise," I said. "As soon as I get you home."

He got in reluctantly, and I unlocked my side and climbed in. I shut the door, I had the keys, I stuck them in the ignition, started the car, looked up, and screamed.

Agyar! Just like at Jim's, just like . . . like at the party! He'd been at the party, and I remembered him looking me in the eyes, and then Jim and I got into a terrible fight for no reason, and I'd stormed away!

I threw the door open, rushed out onto the street, and . . . nothing. No one there. Not even a trace, not even residual magic, if he'd used that to disappear. Jim got out of the car, also, but had no idea what had happened.

"What is it?" he asked. "What did you see?"

"I—I—" I started. "Get in the car, Jim. Get back in the car. Now I *really* have to get you home."

"Mare, what—?"

"Please!" He obeyed, and I climbed in and started the car again, and sped away from the curb.

"Hey, easy on the jump-starts there," he said. "Come on, slow down."

"I—I have to get you home," I said.

"Well, come on, let me drive if you're gonna be like this. Watch it!"

I slammed on the brakes as a pedestrian ran across the crosswalk.

Jim gripped my right arm. "Calm down, Mare, what'd you see?" he asked. "Come on, what made you freak out back there?"

"I—I saw someone," I said. "Someone who's dead. Supposed to be dead. Was—I don't know, Jim. I have to get you home, fast. I don't want you hurt."

"You can go now," he said, so I moved on. "You saw

someone who's dead? Who? I didn't— Come on, slow down! Look, let me drive, OK?"

"I don't want to waste time changing places! God, I've been such a fool! All the signs, clues hitting me on the head—literally! And I ignore them, I—I don't even *think* about them!"

"Mara, for the love of God, please let me drive!" he said. "I don't know about you, but I know I can die in a car accident!" I didn't answer for a while, my mind too preoccupied with what I knew I had to do, and Jim hit my arm lightly.

"Huh?" I said.

"Please let me drive, Mara. You're gonna get us killed!"

"Um— Um—" I said, trying to sort everything out, "Yes. Yes, I'm sorry. You drive."

I was just about to pull over when my body suddenly became rigid and my mind was on fire and I felt an overwhelming urge to . . . to go. Go south. Head south. Then I could move again, and my body sat up and started working the car's controls again.

"Hey, I thought you were gonna pull over! Pull over!" Jim said, but his words meant nothing.

"I'm —being—called!" I said. "Help—me!"

Jim cried out and leaned over to wrestle me for steering control.

"Mara, why are you doing this? Do you want us both killed?"

"Help me!"

"Well, *let* me, then! Quit driving like a maniac! The cops'll be after us any second now!"

"Can't—stop!" I cried. "Help me! Put me out!"

"Oh, right, I'm supposed to bash you over the head?" he said. "Come on, you're scaring the shit out of me!" He managed to bring his foot over to my side, and started pushing on the brake while I was pressing the accelerator. The car started squeaking and lurching all over the road, and I was trying to work with him, but calling cannot be resisted. No matter how long ago it was last used, I found. I did manage to calm myself, not much, but at least it became a little easier for Jim to steer and brake.

Eventually it appeared that the car was being driven normally, even if it took two people to do so. The closer we got to our destination, the stronger the calling became, and the more frightened I became. Soon I was so terrified that I could function no longer, and Jim was forced to drive from the wrong side while I mumbled directions.

Finally, we reached the place: Theresa's house. But it wasn't Theresa who'd sent for me. Jim parked the car for me and turned it off and handed me the keys. I took them without looking at him.

"Is this the place?" he asked.

"Yes," I said, not turning to look at it. I did face Jim, however. "Jim," I said, "I want you to go home now. Leave me here and drive home; don't even look back."

"Huh?"

"Don't question, just drive away," I said. "I was trying to get you home, but he called me, and—and I couldn't stop. Go home, Jim.."

H stared at me a long time, and then smiled slightly. He reached out for the scuff of my neck and squeezed it—hard.

"You're gonna tell me what the hell is going on here, Mara," he said in a very low growl. "I am sick of this bullshit."

"Jim—"

"Tell me!" he said, and I reached back to take his hand from my neck.

"You know I could make you leave, Jim," I whispered.

"By hypnotizing me, right?" he said. "But you won't. I know you."

"Jim, please—"

"No, *you* listen," he said. "Whatever's going on here is scaring the crap out of you, and I'm—"

"I— I've already lost somebody to him, Jim . . ."

"Who? Who is this guy you're so afraid of?"

"An old enemy," I said. "Please; that's all I'll say. Now you have to get out of—"

"No."

"I don't want you hur—"

"No!"

"Jim, you're not being—"

"NO!" he roared. "Now, goddammit, Mare, we're going in there; all right?"

"Wait!" I cried. "Wait. All right, Jim. I won't stop you. But—please promise me this. It's a compromise."

"What—"

"I want you to stay in here and wait for me to go to the door, and—"

"No—"

"Please listen," I said. "I want you to wait for me to go to the door, and if nothing happens, if I'm not attacked, or . . . I don't know, if things seem OK, then you can follow me. But—if something *should* happen, then I want you to get home immediately! Do you promise?"

"Oh, right, if something happens, then I'll be coming in after you—!"

"Do you promise?" We stared at each other for a long time, and then Jim sighed loudly.

"Yeah, sure," he said. "I promise." I kissed him long and deep and then got out of the car. Theresa had a huge front yard, so I had a decent distance to go until her front door. I looked back once at Jim, who had his face pressed against the glass, and then continued.

Why can't I feel him? I thought. *Can he really hide his presence so well? I can't tell where he is, or even if he's here at all. But the calling led to here . . .*

I reached the front door, and knocked. I'd never been inside this house; I couldn't have broken in if I'd wanted to. *But Theresa's at the party, still, I think.*

A moment later, the door opened, and Theresa peered out.

"Mara," she said.

"Theresa," I responded. "Is—"

"Come to finish the job, eh?"

"No, I—look, I was *called* here," I said. "And only one person can call me. Where is he?" Here?"

"Why, I don't know who you mean."

"You know exactly who I mean," I said. "Your precious First, that's who. Now he called me here, and almost killed me and Jim in the process. Now you let me in there, and let me deal with him once and for all!"

"Not if you're going to take that tone with me," she said.

I took a step forward, but then remembered the barrier. Theresa was enjoying herself.

"All that great power of yours, and you're stopped by an old wives' tale, eh, Mara?" she said.

"Look, um—Theresa—you're not the one I want to see. It's him. He's inside your house right now, I know this, and—"

"Do you?"

"I was called—*here*," I said, losing patience. "Now where else would he be??"

"Behind you," a voice said, and I whirled around just in time to be shoved through the doorway. A flash of pain struck me as I passed through the barrier keeping me outside, and felt all of my strength leaving me. By the time I hit the floor in a crumpled heap, I was helpless. But I was on my back and was able to watch Agyar stepping over the threshold, Jim's unconscious form held up by the neck. He loomed over me and smiled.

"Hello, Mara. Did you leave something behind?" he asked, and tossed Jim to the ground next to me. I tried to reach out to him, to check his pulse, his breathing, but could not. At least his aura was still there, but weakened.

Agyar stepped all the way through and shut the door behind him, and then knelt down in between Jim and me. He took my chin in his hand and moved my face around.

"Hmm," he said. "Haven't changed much, have you? Same old wounded puppy-dog look. Same old hair. Same stupidity. Right, Mara?"

I couldn't answer. Then he stood and kicked me in the gut. I doubled over only from reflex and coughed.

"Right, Mara?" he roared, then knelt down again and held my head up by my hair. "You stupid bitch!" he hissed. "What did you think you could accomplish by coming here? Did you think you could kill me? Eh? And who is this . . . *thing* next to you? Your dinner? Your pet? Or perhaps your lover? Oh, wipe that look off your face, he's only asleep. Who knows, he might actually serve some purpose tonight."

He let go of my hair with a yank, making my head hit the floor quite painfully. Agyar stood up to full height again.

"You make me sick," he growled. I looked at Theresa, who stood beside him. She was looking at me, too, but her expression was blank.

"Let's go," Agyar said, and bent over me again and grabbed the back of my sweater. Theresa carried Jim in her arms, and Agyar started dragging me down the hall, Theresa following. Up and down the halls we went, Agyar dragging me all the way. Then there was a painful trip down some stairs, and, finally, I was dragged into what must have been Theresa's library. Bookshelves lined all four walls, and the furniture within had been pushed up against the wall. Agyar dragged me to the center of the room and left me there while he stepped back to one of the walls. Theresa laid Jim, who was still unconscious, onto a small couch. I could not look directly at anyone, but could hear them speaking.

"So, Theresa," Agyar said, "aren't you going to invite our guest in?"

"Hmm? Oh, yes, of course. Now, Mara; you know you are always welcome in my home." Instantly, my strength returned, and I did not hesitate to roll onto my feet and leap straight for the exit. Then Agyar clapped once, and I was thrown back into the center of the room. I stood up, wide-eyed, until I saw the glowing lines on the ground. I turned around slowly to see that I was in the middle of a huge heptagram. Ten feet in diameter, and its lines were glowing faintly. Agyar had activated it.

"You won't be going anywhere for a while," he said. "This is too important to let you get away."

"What is this," I growled. "Release me!"

"Oh, you've never seen one before? Why, this is—"

"I *know* what it is, Agyar," I said. "I said release me!"

"Not bloody likely."

"I concentrated on his mind, and looked deep into his eyes. ''I mustn't be here, Agyar . . . You must reLEEEEEEEEE!" My mind turned inside out, and I doubled back in pain and covered my eyes. Meanwhile, I could hear Agyar chuckling quietly.

"I thought you said you knew what this was," he said. "But obviously you didn't know you can't use your powers to escape."

"What the bloody hell do you want with me?" I roared. "So like you, isn't it; keep them helpless while you sit back and torment. Just like a coward, isn't it? Or don't tell me you're still trying to make me your wife?"

"Oh, God, no," he said. "Don't make me sick. No, I've come to my senses about that; you were hopeless then, and always will be."

"*I'm* hopeless. You kill my husband. Make me a widow, make my children orphans, and you thought I'd learn to love you after all that? You make *me* sick."

"You're going to die tonight, Mara!" he spat. "You, and

your—your *pet!* Both of you are going to die slowly, and miserably, but not before I've gotten what I need from you."

"You think I'm actually going to give you something?" I asked. "You are sick."

"Oh, you will," he said. "Believe me, you will. I did learn something about you after one hundred and fifty-three years, you know."

"I could say the same thing of you."

"Good," he said. "Then you know my methods."

"As cowardly as they are, yes, I do."

"Ohhhh," he said. "You hurt me."

"Theresa, is this what you expected from your First?" I asked. "Did you think he'd be some sort of god, who was wise and noble? Look at him, Theresa! Look at how he is!"

"She is looking," he said, putting an arm around her. "But it doesn't matter what she sees."

I looked more closely at her. She wasn't in a trance, I knew that, but—well, what was it, then? I looked at him, confused.

"A little something I should have done with you, when I converted you," he said. "But like a fool, I thought you'd make a better wife with your will completely intact. It's not charming, not quite. But during conversion, I placed a . . . well, sort of a mental block, in her mind. Now she can certainly go about her business, and live a perfectly normal life, but then, when I so wish it, her will completely shuts off—and she can hear, think, speak normally. But will do anything I say. *Anything.* Isn't that right, Theresa?" he said.

"Yes," she said. Then he left her side, but I couldn't help staring at her, still. Her eyes seemed to be almost begging me to help her. Or were they? A chill crept slowly down my spine.

"But enough fun and games," Agyar said. "Now to the favor you owe me."

"I owe you nothing," I murmured, my gaze still on Theresa.

"That's beside the point, actually," he said. "You're going to give me what I need."

"You should be dead," I said. "I killed you."

"Well, thank you," he said. "You should be dead, too. But, obviously, I didn't die, and you don't deserve to hear why not."

"If you converted Theresa . . ." I began, "why didn't she know your name?"

"She didn't know me as Agyar," he said. "I was Antonio back then. But it's so much more appropriate this way, *nicht?* You, me, her—a true family in blood—reunited at last. Say hello to your little sister."

"I hate you," I murmured, which only amused him. "I despise you more than anything else on this earth."

"Well, whatever makes you happy," he said, and pointed to Jim. "But, meanwhile, see your pet there? Cute, isn't he?"

"You even think of touching him, and I'll—"

"You speak as though you were actually in a bargaining position, Mara," he said. "Is that what you thought? If I did anything, do you really think you could stop me?"

I said nothing.

"Well?" he roared, but then laughed. "Ohhh, you are something," he said. "Oh, I know you; just threaten some wretched loved one of yours and you're on your knees, begging for mercy. I must thank you for bringing your pet along."

"He is not my pet!"

"Yes, I know," he said. "He's your boyfriend, no doubt. Humans as lovers. Have you no pride? And I suppose you've promised never to convert him."

"Have you learned nothing of compassion in three thousand years, Agyar?"

"Five thousand years," he corrected. "But yes; believe it or not, I *have* learned something of compassion. For instance—the human there. I've decided to let him go."

"Yes, right now!" I said. "Harm or change him in any way and *I won't* help you! That's a promise!"

"Picky, picky," he said. "I'll let him go, keep your airhead on your shoulders. But not until I've finished with him . . ."

"Don't you touch him!" I cried. "I told you I wouldn't help if you did!"

"Oh, but you will . . ." he said. "And he's the one who'll make certain you do."

"What?"

He didn't answer, but gestured toward Jim, who suddenly began to stand up; only his eyes were still closed. He reached his full height, and started walking toward me, until he passed over the lines and into the circle. I backed away and looked at Agyar. His eyes were shut and he seemed to be deep in concentration.

"What are you doing to him?" I asked. "Stop this, now!"

"Mara . . ." I heard Jim say, and I looked at him, and into his eyes. Into his . . . smoldering eyes . . . So lovely . . .

Jim, I thought. *I love you so much. I'd do anything for you . . .*

He smiled and took both my hands. I smiled back. I wanted to do something for him. Anything, if only he'd tell me . . .

"Thaaaat's a girl," he said. "Look right at me . . ."

"Yes . . ." I said, "Wait. You . . . you can't . . . hyp-hyp—"

"Of course I can," he said. "I always could."

"Yes . . ." I said, now remembering, "Yes, always . . ."

"Now I want you to do something for me, Mara," he said. "I want you to think back. Think back to the night you first took my blood."

"I . . . remember . . ."

"Gooood," he said. "You remember it well, don't you?"

"Yes . . ."

"You remember how it tasted," he said. "What it felt like."

"I . . . tried to forget," I said.

"No, no, no, you mustn't forget, darling," he said. "You must remember. You must remember what it was like. You must remember what it tasted like."

"Tasted . . ." I said, "no, I . . ."

"Tell me, Mara," he said. "Tell me how much you liked it."

"No, I . . . tried to forget . . ."

"But you can't forget good blood, can you? Noooo, of course not. Not when it tasted as good as mine . . ."

I started shaking, and tried to look away from him and at Agyar. Jim took my chin and made me look at him again.

"No, no," he said. "You have to look at me. Only at me."

"Yes . . . only at you . . ."

"You know it tasted good, Mara," he said. "You know you enjoyed the feeling it gave you to take it from me. Admit it!"

"I—! I can't—!"

"You *can* Mara!" he said, grabbing me. "Tell the truth, Mara! Tell me how much you loved it!"

"Stop! Please!"

"Not until you admit the truth, not just to me, but to yourself!" he cried. "Tell me how much you loved my blood!"

"I—! I loved it!" I cried, breaking down into tears now. Why was Jim trying to hurt me? I didn't understand; I loved him, why was he hurting me? But he held me just as tightly as before, and kept on relentlessly.

"What did it feel like to drink from me, Mara?" he said. "Did it make you feel good? Powerful?"

"Stop . . ."

"Look at me, Mara! Look!" I obeyed. "Do you love me?" he asked.

"Yes . . ."

"Do you want me to die?"

"No . . ."

"Do you want me to be yours forever?"

"Yes . . ."

"Then take me!" he cried. "Make me yours, Mara! Claim me for eternity! You know how to do this!"

"C-can't . . ." I whimpered. "P-promised . . ."

"Yes, a promise to *me!*" he said. "But I want you to break it now! You can't have me forever if I can't *live* forever."

"Not . . . fair . . ."

"Not fair? What isn't? That you want me forever, and I want you forever, yet you'll do nothing to bring this about? Is that fair?"

"Please . . ."

"Is it fair that I'll die of old age, and you'll stay forever young, forever strong and beautiful? Is *that* fair, Mara?"

"No, please . . . S-someone . . . someone make you . . . s-say this . . ."

"I say this for myself!" he cried. "I want to be immortal, Mara! And if you love me, you want me to be, too!"

"P-price to pay . . ."

"Price?" he said. "Insignificant, compared to what's gained!"

"S-sun burns . . . Blood . . ."

"Yeeeees, the blood," he said. "The best part of all, wouldn't you say? You remember, don't you, Mara? How hot . . . and thick . . . and sweet it was?"

"Stop . . ."

"Do you remember . . ." he continued. "Do you remember that—that rush of warmth, and power, that flows through you as you drink, that dizzying, intoxicating rush of hot, thick lifejuice as it—"

"Please—!"

"—As it flows past your throat, into your belly, warming every part of your being, filling you with such life as you'd never known before!"

I had no strength to stand anymore. Jim held me up completely. I couldn't even raise my head to look at him, and could only listen, and shake from fear.

"You'd do anything to get that feeling again, wouldn't you, Mara?" he asked. I felt my head nodding itself. "And here I am! You can have that feeling again, Mara! Take me! Take all of me! Make me immortal!"

"AAAAAAUGH!" I cried, and fell to my knees in a sobbing heap. Jim bent over and forced me to my feet again. He held me against his chest while I wept loudly.

"Thaaat's it . . ." he said, patting my back. "Let it all out . . . It's been in so long, hasn't it . . . So very long . . . It's time to accept yourself now, Mara. Time to embrace all that you are, and use that power. Enjoy it!"

He took my chin and raised my head to look at him again. I tried to look away, but couldn't. His eyes . . . He smiled and brought his thumb up to my mouth and stuck it in. He pressed it against a fang, then brought it out. There was a blood spot on it. He reached up and squeezed his thumb, and made the spot bigger. My eyes were riveted to that thumb. I groaned.

"Amazing, isn't it," he said, apparently admiring the spot. "Just one tiny little prick, yet it holds millions and millions of tiny little red blood cells. All for you, Mara. All for you . . ."

I could stand it no longer, and grabbed his thumb and shoved it into my mouth, and began sucking. I had never tried so hard to get blood in my life. One prick won't yield much blood, but that didn't faze me. I'd drain him dry through the one hole, if I had to.

The thumb was pulled from my mouth, and I snatched for it, but Jim held it away and then threw up a hand before my face. It was only a hand, but it had the power to hold even me back. I hovered before it, waiting for a signal— any signal—to begin.

Jim smiled and pulled his collar away from his neck, and I believe I drooled on myself then. Then—what I so wished for—he lowered his hand, and smiled. I howled and grabbed Jim's suddenly limp body and lowered it to the ground, where I'd best be able to feed. I hovered over his face for a moment, to savor it—oh, I loved him so much— and brought my teeth closer to his neck.

I saw myself suddenly, in the daylight, long hair— straight, *human!* I was smiling, and then . . .

Me again, same as above, only in my warrior's vest. But I was not smiling.

I felt a slug in the face, only I wasn't hurt. Then more images, one after the other, piled on, overlapping, repeating. Many of them were of me, some were of other people. People I'd never seen before, people I *had* seen before, but centuries ago. Leta. My children. Then blood, and death, and limbs tearing, and a last split-second image of Agyar's face, before my head snapped up. Jim was on the ground, in my arms, still asleep.

Jim, I thought. *So familiar . . . as though we'd known each other. No, I don't believe in it; I don't believe in it! But, then, I didn't in vampires, either. Thought they were old wives' tales . . .*

"Gaar . . ." I whispered, holding Jim and cradling him. "Gaar, forgive me . . . Please forgive me. I didn't know . . . I never dreamed . . . Oh, my love . . . My love . . ."

"No!" a voice roared, and I was blasted away from Jim

and hit the other side of the circle. Agyar was by Jim, grabbing his arm and pulling him from the circle. I cried out and scrambled across the floor, reaching for and missing his foot as it was pulled across the lines.

"No!" I screamed, pounding in vain against the barrier, "Let him go! You can't have him! I won't let you!"

Agyar stepped away and went back to the old ways: blackmail. He held Jim up by the neck, threatening to choke him, or perhaps snap his neck if I didn't calm down and comply. I calmed myself.

"Much better," Agyar said.

"You promised . . ." I whispered.

"I promised nothing," he said.

"Why did you do this?" I asked. "Why . . . humiliate me when you had me . . ."

"Revenge, of course," he said. "But now the games are over, Mara. Time to comply. Time to work the spell with me."

"The *what?*"

"The spell," he said. "A spell for all time. And all you have to do, and Theresa, too, is to stand there and look pretty while I do the casting."

"And for that you go through all this."

"Of course," he said. "I have to have fun, too, you know. But I might as well tell you how it works. I have found a spell that contains so much power that the one who receives it has to have plenty of power of his own. Such as me. Meanwhile, he needs channelers to help him receive all that power. Such as you, and Theresa. Even the channelers need to be strong enough to handle the energies, and—get this—they must be BOUND to the caster by blood. Isn't that perfect? Why, vampires are more bound by blood than even family members! This spell will make me a god, Mara! I can do anything now. *Anything!*"

"You haven't cast it yet."

"Pshaw!" he said. "You're as good as dead. But now . . ."

He took a step back and clapped his hands once. The heptagram's lines stopped glowing, so I immediately bolted for Jim so I could scoop him up, only I was yanked back by Agyar. He'd grabbed my hand as I passed, and I found myself unable to let go! I struggled to pull myself—and Agyar—over to Jim, only Agyar reached out to Theresa, who took his other hand.

"Get her other hand!" he said to her, then to me: "It's no use fighting, witch, you can't let go!"

I held out my free arm as far as it would go, almost . . . almost touching Jim, when Theresa reached in and grabbed it. There was a small flash of light where our hands touched, and I felt a brief tingle, and then found myself unable to let go of her, either. Together Agyar and Theresa dragged me to the center of the heptagram. I tried to break free, to transform, to do *something,* but nothing worked.

"Struggling isn't going to help you," he said calmly. "Not while that spell is on our hands."

"Release me!" I spat. "You'll get no help from me!"

"No choice now," was all he said, and then shut his eyes. I continued to struggle and try to peel my hands away from theirs, but still no use. I looked at Theresa, who had that same blank look, and then at Agyar

He had started to hum at this time, and it was increasing in pitch and volume. He had his head back and his eyes shut, and I saw that Theresa was now doing the same thing. She began to hum, too, and I became so fascinated by what was going on that it took me a while to notice that I was doing it, too! The spell! I thought. It's affecting *me!*

Fighting it wasn't doing me any good, for soon my head was dropping back, and my eyes were closing, just as theirs had. By now, Agyar's hum had become a number of tones, not very musical, but unearthly in their power. Theresa had joined in, and it took every bit of strength for me not to help. I helped, anyway.

Other sounds were mixing in with our tones. The sounds of wind, and of thunder, and of rumblings from nearby objects that were shaking and falling from their places. Then Agyar changed the sounds he was making, and formed them into what had to be words—only they weren't heard in my ears.

And there was the energy. Energy that whipped and rushed and flowed all in and out and through my body, sometimes lifting me up, sometimes down, and I fought to keep it away but had to shift my focus on just surviving all of it. For as the energy rushed in and out, it began to pick up any power that was nearby, and in my case, it was my life energy. The power was channeling through me just fine, not to mention taking my own power along with it, and I managed to open my eyes long enough to see that it was having the same effect on Theresa. She was already on her knees, her body drooping toward the floor, and only Agyar and I were keeping her up. I was down on one knee by now; only Agyar was standing tall and basking in the power that we were giving him.

I was dying; I knew that, we both were, but at least I expected something like this from Agyar. Theresa must have thought she was going to share some of that power with him. *At least I'm not the only fool in the room,* I thought. I lowered my head and prepared for the end. *I've failed,* I thought. *I've failed everyone; everything. Especially you, Jim. My beloved Jim . . . Gaar. I am nothing . . .*

Amongst the great howls of the wind that whipped all about us, I heard laughter—Agyar's laughter, of course, and it was booming and hollow, as though the power that filled his being was giving him the greatest pleasure anyone could experience, and it grew louder and louder, until it drowned out all other noise. By now, my thoughts were leaving as I felt the last bits of life I had left being ripped from me, and I began preparing myself for what came next, when a scream pounded against my ears, yet I still could not let go to cover them.

The scream went on for an eternity, and I would have screamed myself if I had the strength, and I was suddenly pummeled by waves and waves of even stronger energy, blasting in and out and up and down and all through my body. The screaming rose and reached its climax, just as the power rushing through me reached its peak, and I was suddenly thrown back and away from the circle.

"Yoldbt, kup," I heard through a haze. I had no strength to answer or see who it was yet, however.

"Kup, Mare, mongge up," went the voice again, and I felt something patting my cheek. I felt some strength coming back, so I tried to speak.

"Uh," was all I could muster. Oh, well. The patting continued.

"Doan dye me et, Mare." It was more familiar now. *"Mon, ya old bat."*

Jim! I thought.

"Ohhhhhh," was still all I could summon. *Give me time, love . . , Just keep patting me, love . . ,*

"You can't die on me now, not after all this," he said. With a supreme effort, I forced my eyes open into a slit.

"Hey, there ya go," he cooed, still patting me. "I knew you couldn't die. You're too tough."

"Nnnnnnnnn," I said.

"Nnnnnnnnn," Jim repeated. "Sounds like Frankenstein. But we all know a vampire could kick his ass any day, right?"

"Any . . . night," I corrected.

He laughed. "I knew not even this could get you, Mare," he said. "You wanna know something else?"

"Uh?"

"He's dead," he said. "That, uh, Mr. Supervampire is dead. Burned to a crisp. And it looks like Theresa is—"

"Dead?" I whispered. "Agyar? Dead?"

"Dead," he said. "Stuck a stake in him, and—he just exploded! I had to jump behind a desk just to get out of the way!"

"Dead?"

"If that isn't dead, I don't know what is," he said.

"Where?"

He pointed off to the side. "Over there," he said.

"Help me up," I said, and he brought me up to a sitting position. From there I could see a good portion of the room, if you could call it that now. It more resembled a construction yard. Tables were on top of shelves, shelves were on tables, books were everywhere but on the shelves, and plaster, wood, plastic, metal shrapnel, and God-knows-what-else covered the floor. There were also two bodies that lay perpendicular to me at opposite sides of the room. One was Theresa's, who lay almost upside down in a twisted heap, her head set in such a way as a normal head would not be. The other had to be the smoking corpse of Agyar.

"Nice place they have here," Jim mused. "Kinda reminds me of my room when I was a kid."

I ignored him and tried to stand. Jim stood before I did and gave me a steadying hand. I was wobbly, but vertical now.

"You sure you wanna stand up?" he asked. "Why don't you lie down while I get an ambulance—"

"No," I said quickly. "No ambulances. No hospitals."

"Mare, you're barely alive!"

"A hospital couldn't help me," I said. "They deal with humans, not me."

"But you're hu—"

"I want to look at him," I said. "Help me over to him." He did so.

I looked down at Agyar for a long time before either Jim or I spoke. His body had been charred, and part of his chest had been blown out. His mouth was frozen open into that last scream he had made before his death. I searched down into my soul, as deep as I could go, and found nothing of his presence. Absolutely nothing. Agyar was dead.

I could not help but look at the body, but Jim was not used to such sights and had to look away.

"What happened here?" Jim asked softly. "What was he doing to you, Mara? I woke up, and looked at you, and—you were barely standing. Like he was draining you."

I put my head on his shoulder and shut my eyes. "He was, my love," I whispered. "He was. All to get some 'power' of his. And I see that Theresa didn't survive it."

"Yeah," he said with a sigh. "But why her? What did she have to do with this? I guess he grabbed her, too, huh?"

"Mmm, sort of," I said. "I'll explain later. But—we're free now, Jim. Both of us. You may not realize it, but your soul is free."

"My soul?" he said, then his voice became soft suddenly. "I had a weird dream, while I was knocked out like that. I was—I wasn't me, but somebody else. It wasn't now, it was—in another time, another century. You were in the dream, too; in fact, we were married."

"How did the dream end?"

"It . . . it became a nightmare real quick," he said. "Like I was running from something, and then these . . . things grabbed me, and tore me apart. I mean, they tore me apart! Tore off arms, and—and drank the blood right in front of me! And I couldn't stop screaming . . ."

I leaned forward and held Jim close to me. He let his head rest on my chest, and I shut my eyes and rubbed his head.

"I know, Jim," I whispered. "I know what you saw. I saw it, too. In fact, that 'dream' that you had saved your life."

"Huh?"

"I'll explain to you later, my love," I said. "I'll explain everything to you. Everything about what's happened, about me, about you . . . about us."

"You're getting weird on me again."

"Quiet," I whispered. "Let me be a sentimental old fool. I love you, Jim; I've loved you for sixteen hundred years, and I may love you for sixteen hundred more."

"How long did you say?"

"All will be explained."

Epilogue

Jackie was told of what happened, of course, only it was difficult telling her about Theresa. She had to be told the entire story before she would understand exactly why Theresa had died. In simple terms, though, she was drained of energy. Never mind the broken neck; things like that don't kill us. The spell drained her life away, just as it almost did mine.

I helped Jackie with Theresa's funeral arrangements as best I could. Yes, she had been my enemy, but I don't think she was entirely evil. I don't think she understood exactly what Agyar was about. In that way, she was just ignorant, and if anyone is an expert on ignorance, it's me. But even ignorant people deserve funerals.

There were no "ashes to ashes" speeches there, only a few words each from friends, and she was buried in her own coffin—yes, she was one of *those* vampires. Somehow, listening to Theresa's friends, I got the impression that Jackie was really the only one who cared about her. For that, I grieved with her, but I'll be the first to admit that I wanted Theresa dead too many times to not be a hypocrite.

Officially, I do not believe in such things as reincarnation, and neither does Jim. But I saw what I saw in his soul; he had to be Gaar come back to me. I explained Jim's "dream" to him, but it took a fair amount of persuasion to convince him of its possibilities. Eventually he came to believe it on his own after I'd taught him how to look into his own mind. And after he believed it himself, he became practically a new man: happier, more energetic, and more "free" with the world. And I did, too, because I learned that love *can* conquer all; it just takes a while sometimes. A *while* while, in our case. But don't get the idea that we've become New Age junkies or something. We don't dwell on what we've learned; by now, we've been taking it for granted, and don't even discuss it much, not even amongst ourselves.

By the above, you've probably figured out that Jim and I are still together. I married him. As soon as we'd recovered from that night with Agyar, I asked him to marry me. Yes, I asked *him* to marry *me!* I could hardly believe it myself, once I had. Me, so liberated? Fortunately, Jim took me even more seriously than I did, because he said yes! So we'd only been together for three months; I knew we were right for each other. And, obviously, Jim did, too. Must have been that Gaar part of him telling him so, though he didn't believe in it yet.

I started planning the wedding with him right then and there. In fact, I got so carried away with things that Jim didn't get to bed until three A.M. I keep forgetting he has to keep human hours.

It's been about five years now since our wedding, and we've been quite happy, despite the obvious problems that came with such a union. But overcoming the challenges has brought us closer together in the long run, and isn't that how a marriage is supposed to work, anyway? And oh, yes, the wedding itself was an adventure, with all of Jim's close friends and relatives grumbling about a nighttime ceremony. Jackie was my maid of honor. No bridesmaids, and we had decided on double rings. We said our own vows at Jim's suggestion, as by his reasoning, it was going to be an unusual ceremony, anyway—to us, that is. To everyone else, it seemed entirely normal, except for the late hour. Considering how few people I know, my guest list versus Jim's was a show of lopsidedness. But that's all another story.

As for my present family life, I've decided to leave that as private as I can. We have managed to adopt two children, a boy and a girl, and I had no idea it would be such a long and arduous process. That, and keeping my vampirehood from the adoption agency was a feat in itself. But that's another story, too, one which I would prefer remain away from the media. I still teach, and Jim was promoted to full manager at his department store, though he's been looking around for something different.

As I mentioned before, I can only speak for myself when I say that I would like to "come out of the closet," but I know there are those humans who would prefer we maintain a low profile. For those of you who feel that way, my sincerest apologies. But I'm tired of hiding myself from people. There was only so long I could lie about myself, and obviously, I hit the breaking point.

I don't claim to be the best representative to speak for all vampirekind. I'm no role model; my faults are too great. But this book has helped me understand a lot about myself and others. I don't even care if anyone buys it, especially considering how bloody long it is. But I hope that those of you who have sludged through it have gained at least some insight into the feelings of one monster. I'd love to meet and talk to all of you in person if possible, but it's not very likely, of course. So I offer you my thanks, instead, and my love for letting me share this with you.

Dear Reader,

Pinnacle Books welcomes your comments about this book or any other Pinnacle horror book you have read recently. Please address your comments to:

Pinnacle Books, Dept. WM
850 Third Ave.
New York, NY 10016

Thank you for your interest.

Sincerely,
The Editorial Department
Pinnacle Books

ABOUT THE AUTHOR

Traci Briery is the author of five horror novels, including THE VAMPIRE JOURNALS, which is the sequel to THE VAMPIRE MEMOIRS. She lives in Massachusetts.

BOOK YOUR PLACE ON OUR WEBSITE AND MAKE THE READING CONNECTION!

We've created a customized website just for our very special readers, where you can get the inside scoop on everything that's going on with Zebra, Pinnacle and Kensington books.

When you come online, you'll have the exciting opportunity to:

- View covers of upcoming books
- Read sample chapters
- Learn about our future publishing schedule (listed by publication month *and author*)
- Find out when your favorite authors will be visiting a city near you
- Search for and order backlist books from our online catalog
- Check out author bios and background information
- Send e-mail to your favorite authors
- Meet the Kensington staff online
- Join us in weekly chats with authors, readers and other guests
- Get writing guidelines
- AND MUCH MORE!

**Visit our website at
http://www.pinnaclebooks.com**